PRAISE FOR
TEARS FOR CAMELLIA

Tears for Camellia is an excellent and gripping portrayal of a moving story about a female immigrant. I have read few novels as deep and eloquent as this one. It will not let you down.

Kelu Zheng
Writer, translator, literary critic
Professor at Shanghai Normal University

This novel has narrated a good story, and a good story will never be antiquated. The Chinese version of *Tears for Camellia* has been very popular, and its English version will be enjoyed by more readers.

Jinghong Xiao
The research professor with the Chinese Writers' Association

Reflection on immigration literature usually takes the form of reflecting spirit using a spiritual approach. *Tears for Camellia*, on the other hand, reflects spirit with flesh. To be more exact, it reflects the human soul of a woman selling her body. This reflection gives the reader a more thorough, transparent and incisive insight, but it is a very complicated insight, mixed with love, hatred, deep regret, pity, and all five flavors (sweet, sour, bitter, pungent and salty).

Tianguo Hong
Literary critic,
Ex-president of Chinese PEN Society of Canada

This work depicts a tragic female character up against social reality and serves as a warning to the world.

Da Lu

Senior news correspondent

The tortuous odyssey of a beautiful, ambitious Shanghainese woman. Part love story, part cautionary tale, *Tears for Camellia* takes you from Asia to North America, with a Canadian connection.

Elizabeth Warrener

Retired librarian from the Toronto Public Library

Tears for Camellia

A Social Butterfly's Spiritual Journey Overseas

Written by Bo Sun

Translated by Baimei Sun

PURPLE PEGASUS
INCORPORATED

Published by Purple Pegasus Publishing Inc.,
26632 Towne Centre Drive, Suite 300.,
Foothill Ranch, CA 92610
USA

For more information about Purple Pegasus Publishing visit purple-pegasus.com

First published in 2019

Library of Congress Catalog Card Number: 2019942734
ISBN: 978-0-9966405-5-8
Cover design & interior design by Lamplight Studio

CONTENT

Tears for Camellia

A Social Butterfly's Spiritual Journey Overseas

Written by Bo Sun

Translated by Baimei Sun

Chapter One

A Perplexing Case of an Anonymous Female Corpse

1. A Female Body on the Niagara River

Like an enormously wide crystal curtain, Niagara Falls dashes down from the sky, with full grandeur and momentum. While beating the rocks and splashing the water, the flying torrents roar with thunderous sounds, which can be heard clearly several miles away. The air is permeated with spattering water drops, like smoky rain or pale dew, and is mixed with howling north wind. The whole atmosphere seems especially chilly and harsh, adding a touch of desolation and melancholy.

The piercing wind and icy water drops, however, cannot deter tourists from coming to admire this famous scenic spot from all over the world. They come well prepared and are almost "armed to the teeth". Some are standing quietly in front of Niagara Falls, wearing long overcoats and fur hats, unwilling to leave such gorgeous scenery. Some are walking on the snow-covered sideways, wrapped in down-felt heavy coats, towards the Falls. Others, covered all over with heavy clothing, show their two eyes only. Viewed from afar, they resemble clumsy robots, creeping on the wet and slippery road.

At around 1 pm on Jan. 1st 2001, two American tourists going to Niagara Falls discovered simultaneously an anonymous female corpse floating on the Niagara River in Canada, about 800 meters down from the Falls. As soon as the local police got the information, they immediately dispatched five police cars to the scene and blockaded the Niagara Boulevard. Two ambulances, with sirens ringing, followed along the river. Not long afterwards, marine police arrived in a motorboat breaking the ice. A robust police chief was directing these policemen to retrieve the female body from the water, with a walkie-talkie in one hand and making gestures with the other hand…

In the editors' office of "Toronto Weekly", five editors on duty during the holiday were watching TV nervously – the live coverage of the scene from long shots to close shots. They were arguing endlessly with varied opinions: murder for money; manslaughter, murder to silence somebody, or killing related to love.

Right at this moment, Mr.Guo, the editor-in-chief, charged into the office, looking as if travel-worn and weary. As a rule, he should have been at home on holidays. Looking at his subordinates and wagging his fat head, he opened his mouth, "You are still here? Why not rush to the scene?"

Fan, Jianhong, the director in charge of interviews responded, "Chief Guo, Niagara Falls is 140 kilometers away from here. It will take at least an hour and a half to get there. When we get there, the police might have left." Obviously it was a mild way of refusing to obey the supervisor.

Guo's round face was suddenly pulled longer. He yelled impatiently with a frown, "Don't you ever have any sense of alert for news? Radio 680 has clearly identified the dead person as an Asian. It might be a Chinese. It would not be that easy to retrieve a body in such chilly weather. What do you think, guys?"

With the whole room in sudden silence, people gazed at each other in blank dismay. They all knew what the chief actually meant, but nobody intended to cause any trouble to himself, so they just kept mute.

Fan, Jianhong gazed at the stern face of the chief helplessly, thinking defiantly: who would like to travel such a long way in the world of ice and snow? Besides, the English media will cover the story in a big way and we can just translate the articles into Chinese. Our Weekly will be published on Saturday. It is only Monday. Who knows what other more spectacular events would happen these days? What's the fuss! Even if the dead person is a Chinese, we still have plenty of time to find more background material...

"What we need is first-hand news! It will take about an hour to get there, as it's not rush hour. Jia, Feng, as you are more experienced, you go at once with some other staff." Without thinking, Chief Guo raised his left wrist to look at his watch and ordered a tall man in a firm voice before he headed toward his own office, without looking back.

Li, Zhihao, a news photographer, carried all his apparatus and drove his Toyota cross-country car at the speed of 130 kilometers an hour on the westbound QEW Highway around Lake Ontario. Countless vehicles crushed the thin ice on the highway, with white broken ice cracking under the wheels. He was reticent while holding the steering wheel, with knitted eyebrows. Feeling as if burning with a sense of urgency, he did not pay any attention to Jia, Feng, and Wu, Xiaoxian in his car.

As it had snowed heavily a few days before, leftover white snow could still be seen along the highway. Some icicles were hanging from the trees. Part of the snow on the roof of a house had melted, revealing irregular patches of black. The whole ground looked like a huge abstract landscape painting: places without snow resembled dark ink while the road trampled under the wheels looked like gray color in the middle and the remaining snow seemed like intended blank space in the painting.

Sitting beside the driver, Jia, Feng, noticing the rising speedometer, was scared with cold sweat on his back and hands. Wu, Xiaoxian, sitting in the back, screamed with fear, begging the driver to slow down.

"My buddy, slow down! If you drive at such speed we'll go to hell before we get to the Falls!" Jia, Feng, unable to stand it any longer, yelled.

"How can we snatch any picture if we slow down? Maybe they have left already." Li replied, with perfect assurance.

Jia talked loudly to his ears, "Aren't you afraid the police will catch you?"

"It would be a speeding ticket at the worst. In Taipei, with a second's delay, you might lose a good shot." Li replied bluntly, like a piece of hard ice with sharp angles.

Wu screamed in a loud voice, "So you don't care about your life?! I don't want to die on the job – I haven't enjoyed my young life yet!"

Li shouted in a hoarse voice: "OK, no arguing. I'll keep at 130 kilometers an hour. Didn't you notice Chief Guo's terrible facial expression? Without good shots, how could we report to him afterwards? Last time he was dissatisfied because nobody was on the scene of the kidnap. How he flew into a rage because nobody showed up at the bank robbery a couple of days ago!"

"If the dead woman is really Chinese, we'll be busy for quite some time." Jia seemed to talk to himself.

Li said, shaking his head, "What a shame! So young and too soon to go to God. From the pictures on TV, she looked pretty."

"As the old saying goes: beautiful women were born under an unlucky star." said Xiaoxian while heaving a sigh.

"Beauty Wu is thinking of herself, right?" Li always liked to tease her.

"Darn, don't always talk of beauties. Lady Diana passed away at only 36. There are bad guys everywhere."

The mere mention of Lady Diana aroused fury from Jia's heart. He burst out, "Who takes no pity on beauties? But she should also blame herself -- she loved so much to be in the limelight."

"Simply flirtatious. What had become of her – dating her old flame behind the Prince's back?" Li interrupted at once.

Somewhat angry, Xiaoxian said, "I don't want to talk to you any more. No men are good. As the saying goes: magistrates are free to burn down houses, but the common people are even forbidden to light lamps."

The two men laughed heartily at the same time, with a touch of lewdness. As if infected by their strange laughter, Xiaoxian uttered an uncontrollable sneering laugh. The crisp laughter, mixed with the rolling sounds of flying wheels, composed into a wonderful and inspiring "melody of winter" in the chilly air and flowed like waves on the highway bound for Niagara Falls.

2. A Terrifying Face

The casual chat and laughter along the way did not affect the driving speed. Only a little over an hour later, the Toyota SUV driven by Li, Zhihao had already entered the City of Niagara Falls.

This city, with a population of around 80,000, located to the south west of Toronto, is world-renowned for its wonderful Niagara Falls. Over 20 million tourists from all over the world come to visit it. The recently established casino has attracted more local and American travelers and promoted other commercial development, so it has become a world-class travel and entertainment resort with a well-deserved reputation. To be more exactly, Niagara is situated between the City of Niagara in Canada and the City of Buffalo in the United States.

With the Falls drawing closer, Li, Zhihao, gazing far into the distance, drove directly to the place with crowds of people. As expected, he found several police vehicles parked along the Niagara River, with a helicopter circling in mid sky. Quite a number of TV reporters, standing on the high embankment, were broadcasting the news nervously.

Glancing in all four directions, Li, Zhihao suddenly talked quickly in a demanding tone and with gritted teeth, "No parking space. Beauty Wu, sit in the car. Hurry up or we'll have come in vain.

Hurry! Be quick!"

Wu, Xiaoxian was caught unawares when Li, Zhihao parked the car suddenly on a side road and threw the car keys to her. He quickly got out of the car, his workbag on his shoulder. Jia, Feng, jumped out of the car from the other side and swiftly followed Li towards the scene. Instantly, Li climbed up the highest embankment and raised his Nikon camera. Slowly, the helicopter was laying the hanging corpse beside the ambulance. Everybody was focused on the ambulance. Li, Zhihao was pressing the camera shutter constantly, just like a soldier at the front, shooting non-stop with a submachine gun.

From the camera zoom, Li, Zhihao could see very distinctly. The face of the female body was pale and swollen, with the sunken eyes like two dark holes. There were bloodstains below her conjunctiva. Her nostrils looked black as if they were carved with ice. Her lips were a little open, as if she wanted to utter some words. Her mouth was stained with blood. Her long wavy hair resembled a wig on her head, with some of the hair frozen. She wore a pair of glistening gold earrings. The whole face looked terrifying, like a female ghost's. She wore a blood-red down-felt coat, with a pair of tight black jeans. Her black leather boots seemed to be forced onto her feet. On the middle finger of her plumpish left hand was a diamond ring.

More and more on-lookers were gathering here, at least 70, in spite of the severe winter weather. Some covered their noses with their gloves; some were shaking their heads with regret; others were making gestures and still others were making comments among themselves.

A tall high-nosed and blond-haired man said to his girlfriend, "Look, from how she looks, the god of death hasn't taken away her original beauty."

"Yes, she still looks pretty. What a shame! She must be from Asia, maybe she is Chinese," said a blue-eyed, red-haired woman in astonishment, with her hands closely in the man's arm.

At that time, both of them calmed down and glanced at Jia, Feng, with a nondescript expression. The four abstruse eyes seemed to convey the message: the dead person is your compatriot. Embarrassed, Jia, Feng felt ill at ease. His face turned fiery red at once, as if he had been stabbed in the chest.

The helicopter was roaring up to the sky at an increasing speed. Jia, Feng managed to get close to the ambulance with great effort. At that time, Li, Zhihao had already jostled through the crowd and aimed his camera lens at the rear door of the ambulance.

Several policemen wrapped the corpse with a white sheet, so only the contour of a tall figure of the dead could be indistinctly seen. Four policemen, carrying the stretcher, pushed the dead body into the ambulance.

A throng of reporters surrounded the fat Police Chief Simon, asking various questions, all eagerly and at once. He did not answer anyone, just notified his policemen, using a walkie-talkie, to leave the scene. Then he talked to his supervisor with a cellular phone and glanced around himself.

"City TV" obtained the privilege to interview Chief Simon on the scene at once. Jia, Feng and Li, Zhihao were standing very close by, with Li's camera lens set on the chief.

"Chief, would you please brief us on the female corpse?" The lens was directly at the TV program host and the chief.

"First of all, I feel regret for the first murder case in our Niagara Region in 2001. This is also the first murder in Canada this year. Based on the current situation, the female body is Asian, with obvious strangling wounds on her neck and scratches on her hands. It's hard to decide if this is homicide or suicide. Detailed reports will be announced after an autopsy. There will be a press conference in the Police Bureau at 4 pm tomorrow." The police chief briefed precisely, showing his experience and capability.

Hardly had he finished talking when Chief Simon waved to the media and walked toward the police car. Several policemen followed closely behind his tall and sturdy figure, leaving no trace at all, like a terrible hurricane.

When Jia, Feng and Li, Zhihao returned to the gray Toyota, Wu, Xiaoxian was still angry with clenched teeth.

"I just came here for sightseeing; just to stay here to guard your car!" Her spearhead was directed against Li.

Li, holding the three rolls of film, boasted proudly, "Great achievement. I'd have shot nothing if I'd been a bit late."

"What kind of a reporter am I without going to the scene? I love my job just for its thrill!" She yelled with her lips turned up, looking as if she wanted to swallow him alive.

Li laughed contentedly, "That's wonderful. Next time when there is a murder case or a funeral, we'll invite you there for the thrill!"

"Damn you, what can we expect from a dog but a bark!"

"No other choices – we had to seize every second. If we had waited for a parking space, nothing would have been accomplished. OK, I'll treat you to something nice. Zhihao must be tired driving all the way." Jia, Feng tried to smooth things over.

"What is there except McDonald or Burger King? What about treating us to sea food back in Toronto?" said Wu, keeping a straight face.

"I have a new discovery – you are most beautiful when you are in a fit of temper. You are a cold-blooded beauty. What about shooting a set of photos for you as compensation?" Li grinned cheekily, looking at the rear mirror.

Straightening up, Wu grabbed Li's hair with all her strength.

"SOS! Cold-blooded beauty is going to commit murder!" Li shouted.

She uttered a sinister laugh, feeling avenged and mentally balanced. Women usually don't want to suffer any loss.

"Stop fooling around or there would be a traffic accident!" Jia screamed and ended the brawl.

The car, full of laughter again, headed towards a nearby McDonald's.

The magnificent sunset was burning like a fire on the grayish horizon. This charming scenery, rarely seen in cold winter, formed a striking contrast with thin-ice-covered Lake Ontario. Li drove the car steadily at a high speed on Highway QEW east bound toward Toronto's landmark – the CN Tower.

"A pretty person went to the other world, just like that. Anything could happen in this world!" Halfway, Wu, Xiaoxian in the back seat seemed to be talking in a dream.

"Nothing is predictable in the era of the internet. Just overnight, one could become a billionaire or a beggar. People's values are upside down and indecipherable." Li was in a pessimistic mood.

Jia said, smiling, "I believe in 'drink today while drink you may'. I have to be worthy of myself. I'd feel happy if reminiscing in the future I have no regrets."

"Drink today while drink you may? It's easier said than done. The stress of life in the new century has stifled us. It's so hard to live in an unrestrained way." Xiaoxian looked quite sentimental.

Jia tried to bring them around, "Murder cases do not happen every day. Don't give way to foolish fancies or have self-pity. Xiaoxian, why don't you drink a cup of wine every night and enjoy life as an immortal like me?"

"Life will be even better tomorrow!" Li cut in, with a weird laugh.

They returned to Toronto ten minutes later than expected. Entering into the brightly lit office of editors, most of the staff was off duty except Editor-in-Chief Guo, who was sitting there watching TV. As soon as he saw the three coming in, he stood up at once, narrowed his eyes into a smile, as if greeting honored friends from afar.

"As I expected, you got there just in time, right? I saw your brilliant image on TV." Guo looked very proud of himself with his protruding belly.

After a brief report of what happened on the scene, Jia, Feng added on purpose, "Luckily Xiao Li made a prompt decision and asked Xiaoxian to wait in the car. Otherwise we'd have shot nothing."

"Excellent! We should bring into full play our spirit of teamwork. You and Xiaoxian follow up this case and attend the press conference tomorrow. If the dead woman is Chinese, we'll have to make a big deal of it. News photographers should join the team in due time. As far as I remember, no Chinese has ever died in Niagara Falls. What adrenaline pumping news! Good news!"

Wu, Xiaoxian shrugged her shoulders while Li Zhihao stuck out his tongue stealthily toward Jia, Feng. As the saying goes: the media crave to see the world plunged into chaos. News stories are created from chaos. People are thrilled by chaos.

3. The Bewildering Case of the Female Body

The next afternoon Jia, Feng and Wu, Xiaoxian were on the QEW again following the westbound sun and braving the chilly cold wave. Like a couple of dating lovers on a spring outing, they drove to the Police Bureau of Niagara Region, laughing all the way.

At five minutes before 4pm, they arrived in time for the meeting. Everyone present looked Canadian except the two of them. Simon, the fat police chief, presided over the press conference. He was reading a report.

"Friends from the news media: the autopsy from the Forensic Science Center came out last night just in time and shows that the female body discovered on the Niagara River on Jan. 1st 2001 is Asian. She died three days before her body was discovered, that is, at 5am on Dec. 29, 2000. Her age was in the range of 25 to 30. Her height, 5 ft 6 inches and her weight, 110 pounds. The neck of the dead body shows signs of strangulation with a nylon rope. There is a huge blood clot in her left chest and a three-inch scar on her right arm. They are evidences that there was a struggle before her death. Her blood was Type O, but bloodstains of Type AB were found under her nail. Besides, semen of the same man was discovered on her briefs and the wall of her womb. According to the forensic doctors' preliminary judgment, the dead person entered the water 200 meters down from Niagara Falls. If it were not for the partly iced lake in this snowy weather, the body would have been washed into Lake Ontario by the torrential Niagara River. It is still hard to judge whether she jumped over Niagara Falls herself or was pushed by somebody with force."

Glancing at the people present around him, Simon continued with his report, "The Forensic Science Center will make a further examination and analysis of the Type AB blood on the dead body and the semen on the wall of her womb. As everyone knows, it is very complicated and time-consuming to collect DNA from a sample. The sample left in the female body could be a hair or a fingerprint. The next step will be collecting a certain amount of DNA and making a gene atlas by adopting the chemical procedure of chain poly-reaction. This procedure will create the secret codes of 9 key locations, with which experts can compare the codes of the same locations of other DNA samples. All this requires a lot of time…"

"Is it homicide or suicide?" asked a TV reporter in a loud voice, too eager to interrupt the Chief.

Chief Simon raised his head and answered, "Too soon to reach a conclusion. From what information we have on hand, I can only say: murder can't be ruled out. We have set up a 'Special investigation team for No.1 female corpse', with me in the lead. Don't hesitate to talk to me regarding this case."

"What was the dead wearing? Made in which country?" asked a blond lady reporter with a pair of wide-rimmed black glasses.

"She wore a blood-red down-felt coat of "Shangyu" brand, made in Shanghai, China. Her black jeans were Calvin Klein. Her leather boots were Bally. Her pink briefs were "Three Guns" made in Shanghai, with one side torn. The dead woman wore a sapphire necklace in a heart shape and a valuable diamond ring as well as an Omega watch." With the information in hand, Simon showed thorough familiarity with the subject.

A whiskered reporter went on to say, "Can we assume that the dead came from China, or rather, from Shanghai?"

"No comment. The Japanese or Canadians can also wear clothes made in Shanghai. We've found out that these two brands of Shanghai garments have been imported to Canada and are for sale in all the big stores. Without confirmed evidence we can only say that the dead woman is of Asian origin," another policeman interrupted.

Finally the police issued the computer-composite color picture of the dead person's face and urged the media to publish it in the newspapers so as to seek leads.

Chief Simon added, "Please let your readers know that we have opened a hot line. The public has great potential, as human beings have to live in a certain milieu."

After the meeting Wu, Xiaoxian was reluctant to leave and purposely let the others leave first. Feeling puzzled, Jia, Feng was going to ask her why when she rushed to the side of Chief Simon. Jia also followed at once.

"Chief Simon, we came all the way from Toronto," she said while offering her business card.

"Our editor-in-chief paid particular attention to this case and sent us especially to pursue its development. In my opinion, it's a ninety per cent certainty that this woman was from Shanghai." Wu showed her female instinct for public relations skill.

"How do you know?" As a courtesy, Chief Simon gave her his business card.

"As a rule, women prefer to wear local underwear. Canadian women like products made in USA or Canada, or European famous brands, with only one exception, something they brought from their native land. This is especially true of Chinese women who would pack a lot of underwear before going abroad. Besides, the dead person's coat was also made in Shanghai." Xiaoxian's English was very fluent, as it was said that she had learned it in a Christian school.

Chief Simon smiled with narrowed eyes. Showing his teeth, he told her, "You could be a nice detective, Miss Wu. Your analysis inspired me. It seems that the deceased might have been from Shanghai. Still, we police have to talk with facts."

Jia, Feng cut in, "We'd have to follow to the end if she were really Chinese. We hope you will provide us with more information."

"Sure. I'll give the latest news as the first thing. We might need your help as well." He shook their hands and left.

"Jia, Feng, I'm pretty sure she was from Shanghai like you."

When they were walking out of the Police Bureau toward the parking lot, Wu's words increased Jia's inner pressure. After all, he was also from the biggest city in China. This sort of "native land complex" is hard to describe. He felt a bit disgusted when somebody called Shanghai people sly or stingy, or a Shanghai man sissy.

Avoiding the subject, Jia said nonchalantly, "Enough to keep us busy. Chief Guo especially likes news regarding the Chinese."

"Ours is a Chinese journal. Of course we are concerned about the Chinese."

Jia looked serious, "Do you think it was suicide or homicide?"

"All signs point to a highly possible homicide. As the valuables are still on the deceased, it doesn't look like a murder for money. It's most likely a murder for love with such a beautiful woman. Probably two men were vying for her attention and the loser intended to kill. In a snowy night, the killer entered her bedroom, raped her after a struggle. He was afraid that she would call the police, so he strangled her with a nylon rope and dragged the body to a car before dumping her into Niagara Falls at midnight…" She made gestures with a vivid description.

Jia burst into a fit of laughter, "Just like a detective story. It would be nice if it were that simple. There might be another possibility: she struggled with him before she was raped. The thug escaped and she lost the courage to go on living. As a last resort, she committed suicide… Or she might have failed in her business and was deeply in debt, so she killed herself to end everything."

"In my opinion, suicide is not likely. How much courage one

has to summon to jump into such falls! Even stone-hearted women wouldn't be so brave. I can't imagine it, even if you were to lend me your courage. It's so high – I'd be scared to death!" Wu talked with gusto in the car.

Jia said seriously while tightly holding the steering wheel, "There is something in your analysis. When one is desperate, his psyche is distorted. Unimaginably, he would resort to anything and regard death as the best way to get rid of troubles and to get self-satisfaction. Of course, there are internal causes of the dead person and the external factors of the environment. This can't be explained in a few words…"

"Chief Guo will be excited about the development of the case. He'll ask us to stick closely to it." Xiaoxian murmured to herself.

Jia nodded with similar feeling. Both of them were quite sure that the dead person was most likely Chinese and that the case would exhaust them. They were also aware that only by keeping in close contact with Chief Simon could they obtain the first-hand and the latest information.

Chapter Two

The Dead Person Verified as a Prostitute from Shanghai

4. Puzzle Solved by the Old Security Guard Who Identified the Dead Person

Wu, Xiaoxian never expected that Police Chief Simon would take the initiative to offer information to her the very next day after the news conference, at 11am on Jan. 4th.

On the other end of the phone, Chief Simon laughed with a touch of humor, "Miss Wu, you should really take on another job and report to the Police Bureau tomorrow morning. Just as you inferred, the dead person has been identified as a woman from Shanghai."

"That's wonderful! Just as expected. Gorgeous! Gorgeous!"

As if she had won a lottery, she shrieked repeatedly in English in spite of herself. Obviously she was carried away by the unexpected good news, while her trembling hand held the phone.

Such a deafening shriek, lingering in the office for quite a long time, disturbed all her colleagues, who had to stop their work. Dozens of eyes fixed on her radiant, happy face and dozens of ears strained to hear what she was talking about. Even Editor-in-chief Guo was attracted by the shriek and dashed to see what had happened. Jia, Feng, sitting opposite Xiaoxian, understood tacitly after catching a few of her English words. He immediately felt a warm torrent all over his body, with his head buzzing.

After a few minutes' talk with Chief Simon, Xiaoxian hung up the phone, still radiant with joy. She rose at once, as if she were presiding over a news conference. She would feel she'd missed the flight if she reported on the case one second late. Glancing around her, she shouted to Chief Guo, "The dead woman was from Shanghai."

"Oh, that's wonderful!" Chief Guo made a sudden big stride toward Xiaoxian and requested the whole story from beginning to end, his fat face twitching.

Standing there, she reported briefly what Chief Simon had told her over the phone. It turned out that Bailey, the old security guard at 100 Lakeshore Building in Niagara, called the police hot line after watching the late night TV news. He told Simon that the dead woman looked like Miss Zhang, the Shanghai lady residing in Suite 414. He said repeatedly that he hadn't seen her for the whole of last week. The police asked him to identify her remains the next day. At around 10am this morning, Bailey arrived at the morgue next to the Police Bureau. After a brief glance at the female body, he insisted that it was Miss Zhang of Suite 414 and told them vividly that her English name was Camille. With tears in his eyes, Bailey chattered to the police that Miss Zhang was kind and warm-hearted. She would say hello to him whenever they met and she even presented him with a bag of Chinese candies at Christmas. Chief Simon made an appointment with the two reporters to go to the dead woman's apartment at 3pm that day.

"This time we'll have to exert ourselves to the utmost to publish a special edition which would be difficult even for a daily newspaper. Other articles can be postponed to next week and I'll consult with the typesetting division to postpone the deadline till 10am tomorrow. You'll have to put in some extra work after you return tonight. Just a reminder: try to take more pictures: if we don't have enough news articles, we can publish a few photos…" Chief Guo, in high spirits, gave instructions, unwilling to neglect any detail.

His joy was almost as great as Columbus' discovery of the New Continent. The radiant happiness of this man in his fifties, hardly displayed normally, indicated to his colleagues in the editors' division that his previous judgment was 100% accurate. Due to his excitement, the staff knew that this case would keep them busy and exhaust some of them.

At 3pm on Jan. 4th, Jia, Feng, Wu, Xiaoxian and Li, Zhihao arrived in time at 100 Lakeshore in Niagara after a swift drive. As they stopped the car, they found two police vehicles and a TV Station car parked nearby.

The three rushed to the entrance of this high-class condo and went up to the fourth floor after showing their ID. At the end of the corridor, they found Suite 414. Blocking the way, a young policeman did not allow them in, but whispered to another policeman inside. Through the door, which was ajar, they saw several policemen taking photos and heard the noise of people ransacking boxes and chests.

In the twinkling of an eye, Chief Simon swaggered out and waved to them while looking at his watch, "Just in time. You can come in. Hurry and take your photos."

Following Chief Simon, they entered. This was a two-bedroom suite with a southern exposure. With its cream yellow walls and pale gray carpet, the suite looked clean and simple. Four pots of white camellias took up a large part of the living room. Their light fragrance and beauty added elegance and a noble quality to the suite. It went without saying that the owner treasured the flowers as she did her own life. Perhaps a few thought-provoking stories were behind those pure Camellia flowers. Li, Zhihao, looking around himself, killed many a roll of film, without missing any valuable picture.

Slowly they entered the bedroom. On the wall was a huge half-length photo of the dead woman, with bright eyes, glistening teeth, aloofness in her eyes and a touch of charming flirtation in her smile. Her long black hair, worn down her bare shoulders and forming a striking contrast to her pale skin, displayed a sort of ancient Chinese sentiment. Jia, Feng couldn't help thinking to himself: She was a typical Shanghai beauty, somewhat like Zhang, Ailing's character Ge, Weilong, or Wang, Anyi's character Wang, Qiyao in their novels. This kind of temperament seems inherent in Shanghai women, like their patent, which is hard for women of any other cities to imitate. Just as the word "babe" can only refer to a Shanghai lady. If it were used for women of other cities, it would change its taste or shape, becoming neither fish nor fowl.

Li, Zhihao was gazing attentively and wide-eyed at the portrait, with his camera in front of him. He seemed lost, as if the woman reminded him of an old tale or a beautiful nightmare. As Jia, Feng pushed his arm on purpose, he looked as if woken from a dream and immediately started focusing his lens. He shot numerous pictures of this beauty with the flash on.

Several books were on the bed-side cabinet of the dead woman, with two English fashion magazines at the bottom, a Chinese book on EQ in the middle and a yellow hard-covered book on top, "Camille" by Alexandre Dumas (Jr.) in both English and Chinese versions. It was obviously the most treasured book, which she would not let out of her hand even before her death. Jia took a glance at the book, which was published by "Sanrenxing Press" in Taiwan in 1983. Many words were underlined with red pen and some English words were marked with the Chinese translation. When he read the front page carefully, he found her hasty handwriting: "Book purchased by Zhang, Yuanyuan at Eslite Bookstore, Taipei, Aug. 8th, 2000." Jia reminded Li to take a photo of the dead woman's handwriting.

Chief Simon walked over, waving a passport in his hand, "The dead person was Camille Zhang, born in Shanghai in 1971. This Canadian passport was issued in September 1997. I have phoned the Immigration Bureau and they will fax detailed information to our bureau. But, it won't come quickly. Would you please come to the Police Bureau tomorrow afternoon? Maybe you'll get more background information regarding the deceased. Probably we'll ask you to translate some Chinese material."

"Terrific! We are at your disposal." Wu, Xiaoxian responded promptly while Jia, Feng also nodded.

5. Clues to the Case Found in Photo Album

Just at that time, one of the policemen screamed loudly. It turned out that he had discovered a huge photo album in the built-in closet. Everybody went over to take a look.

The first few were the dead woman's personal photos, including pictures in front of Niagara Falls and at the base of the CN Tower in Toronto. The rest were photos with various men, both Asian and occidental, some with a touch of intimacy. Four of the photos were with the same Chinese man, one at the Yuanshan Restaurant Archway in Taipei. Jia, Feng looked at the date of the photo – Aug. 8th 2000, the same day she purchased the book "Camille" in Taipei. It seemed that Camille had an unusual relationship with this man. They looked like lovers, or at least ex-lovers, from the way they were hand-in-hand and shoulder-to- shoulder in the four photos.

Jia told Chief Simon about his discovery. Dark-skinned Bailey burst out after seeing the man in the photos, "Oh, don't make a fuss. I have seen this man, who came at least once a week. He even applied for overnight parking permits over several weekends. Let me think... oh, his name is Peter, perhaps a student. I haven't seen him for a long time, not even at Christmas. I guess they have separated."

"Very good. These are important clues. Your co-operation is very much appreciated." Simon asked a policeman to write down the details of their talk.

Chief Simon suddenly stopped leafing through the photo album and talked to himself, "Isn't that Arvid?"

"Who is Arvid?" asked Jia, pointing to the man with the dead woman in his arm,

Simon couldn't evade Jia's look, so he replied, stroking his beard, "He is an ex-City Councilor, forced to quit because of a sex scandal in April last year."

Still leafing through the photo album quickly, Simon pointed to the men hugging the woman, "This is David, son of the deputy chief of a casino, general manager of an American auto company in the opposite bank, a well-known playboy. This was the head of the motorcycle gang in Hamilton, who was killed last year. This bald man is Dominick, a famous lawyer, whose wife died last October…"

"It seems this Shanghai woman was quite complicated. Take all the photos to the Bureau." Simon ordered his subordinates.

Jia entered another small room with simple furniture. Besides a desk, there were only a closet and two chairs. His attention was focused on the computer on the desk. He was stopped at once when he walked toward the computer.

"Don't touch it, please. This computer will be taken to the Bureau as well, including all the discs. Maybe a lot of clues will be found." The policewoman, who introduced herself as JoAnna, talked very quickly.

She squeezed all the letters and photos into a huge cardboard box. A tall policeman stuffed a suitcase with the computer monitor and all the discs. Then they opened the built-in closet and took a few photos. Inside the closet were all kinds of dresses for all seasons and underwear of various colors.

Before leaving, the tall policeman put a long seal over the door. Chief Simon instructed Bailey not to permit anybody into the suite before the victim's family members' arrival in Canada for her possessions.

The three of them and two policemen followed Bailey to the underground parking lot. Pointing to a space marked with A414, Bailey told them, "This red BMW belonged to Miss Zhang."

One of the policemen wearing leather gloves inserted a leather strip from his handbag into the car window and opened the door, at a pace much quicker than a professional car thief. Then he obtained fingerprints from the car and took a few photos.

Standing in front of the car, Li, Zhihao pressed the shutter of his Nikon camera incessantly. Also in gloves, JoAnna put all the paper, maps, and an address booklet into a leather bag.

Before they took their leave, Bailey made another long-winded chat, "Please crack the case as soon as you can. Don't let the murderer escape. Damn him – to have killed such a nice lady! Beauties suffer miserable fates. Poor Camille, poor lady…"

JoAnna explained to Bailey patiently, "We won't let criminals remain at large. A good person won't be wronged and a bad guy won't escape justice. Thank you very much for your co-operation. We might trouble you again in the future."

Bailey, a little hunch-backed, stretched out his big hands to hold tightly Joanna's hand for a long time, as if he were the family begging for help. It seemed that only this police hand could catch the suspect. It was also obvious that the deceased showed respect to him and in exchange won the old man's trust.

Confronted with this scene, Jia and Li were filled with nondescript emotions. With clenched teeth, Wu exerted herself to hold back her tears.

6. The Deceased Confirmed as a Prostitute from Shanghai

With a cold wind howling and chilly clouds hanging low, it seemed a heavy snow would fall immediately. At noon on Jan. 5th, Jia, Feng and Wu, Xiaoxian were driving toward the Niagara Police Bureau on the QEW again. Both of them had swollen eyes and were in low spirits, because they had sat up late last night writing the news articles.

"That's terrific, we go to Niagara Falls as frequently as returning home." Yawning, Xiaoxian squeezed a few words between her teeth for fear that Jia might feel bored while driving.

With a dry cough, Jia told her, "I could hardly fall asleep after finishing the article late last night, with Zhang, Yuanyuan's image always lingering in my mind."

"Just because you are from the same city? Or because she was

21

pretty?" Xiaoxian made a grimace mischievously.

"What a shame. I am not boasting about beautiful women from Shanghai. I haven't seen any Chinese ladies in Canada as beautiful as she was. The expression in her eyes was so charming and her figure – a born model. Even Li, Zhihao, our aesthetic expert, was flabbergasted yesterday. Such a beauty is rare even in Shanghai."

Jia continued, "In my opinion, this case is not as simple as it looks. You see, those she dealt with were councilors, or well-known lawyers, big businessmen or gangsters. Maybe she got involved in smuggling or trafficking. It might not be a simple case of murder for love. Most likely it's homicide."

Wu looked pensive and talked slowly, "Judging from her high fashion dresses, such as Chanel, Jacob, Corbo Studio, Plaza Escada, Holt Renfrew etc, all the expensive underwear and coats, her Bocci shoes and the famous car, it is obvious that she earned a lot of money. We still don't know what her profession was, but from what old Bailey told us she often left home in the evening and returned home very late at night, or even early in the morning. She might be a social butterfly. As you know, her rent alone was $1,500. She wouldn't be a common laborer, with all her Cartier and Tiffany jewelry. She didn't have to occupy such a big apartment for herself alone."

"As a social butterfly, she might be a high-class one. Patronized by numerous men, she was just like the moon surrounded by a myriad of stars. Her beauty was used to her advantage," added Xiaoxian.

Jia sighed, "Beauty is also a women's source of disaster. Anyway, we haven't made the trips in vain – we've achieved a lot. Editor-in-Chief Guo is now reading the full-page proof of the magazine. He should be satisfied since we have more exclusive news than even the Canadian media. Circulation will jump tomorrow. Wait for Director Wang to treat us to wine."

"Drink wine? I am too exhausted to drink. What I wish for is a good sleep." Xiaoxian yawned again with her eyes narrowed to slits.

Without their notice, heavy snow like goose feathers fell fluttering from the sky, which was filled with dark clouds. The snowflakes, like butterflies flapping their wings on the car windows, bumped against the windowpane, then flew away to the other side. Such nasty weather inevitably brought great inconvenience to drivers. Jia was all attention while driving skillfully, with the four wheels rolling over thousands of snowflakes, leaving behind a string of screeching sounds.

By around 2pm, the ground was covered with silvery attire. Everything turned into a whitish mass. The unbridled snow was still falling wantonly, showing no sign of relenting.

Wearily Jia and Wu arrived at the Niagara Police Bureau when Chief Simon Just entered the meeting room. They had barely sat down or exchanged greetings before Simon handed each of them a document, a copy of archives which read:

File of Police Bureau of the City of Niagara
File Number: 20010101
File Category: Homicide (Suicide not excluded)
File Date: Jan. 5th 2001
Case Registration Date: Jan. 1st 2001
Individual Information: Name: Camille Zhang (Since Aug. 20th 1997 when she became a Canadian citizen. Her original name was Yuan Yuan Zhang, 章媛媛 in Chinese language)
Sex: Female
Date of Birth: June 2nd 1971
Place of Birth: Shanghai, People's Republic of China
Nationality: Canadian
Passport Number and Date of Issue: VE674654, Sept. 10th 1997
Height: 5 ft 6 inches
Weight: 110 pounds
Skin Color: Yellow
Eye Color: Brown
Hair Color: Black
Marital Status: Divorced (Married to Li, Tianci, an immigrant from Hong

Kong, on April 3rd 1994 and divorced on Aug. 25th 1997)

Occupation: Co-owner of a Chinese restaurant with Huang, Hong, a Chinese woman in Toronto; stripper in downtown Toronto after the closing of the restaurant; no regular occupation before death)

Address: Suite 414-100 Lakeshore Building in Niagara, starting Sept. 1st 1999

Telephone Number: 519-338-1818

Social Insurance Number (SIN): 532-848-732

Driver's License Number: Z9542-89007-10602

Date of Entry into Canada: Feb. 2nd 1994

Stay in other Countries and Time: Tokyo, Japan, from Mar. 8th 1992 to Feb. 2nd 1994

Emergency Contact: None

Criminal Record: No

Details of the Case Report: At 1:29 pm on the afternoon of Jan. 1st 2001, two American tourists discovered the female remains floating in the Niagara River in Canada, 800 meters down from Niagara Falls.

Chief Simon, waving the archives in his hand, said, "Now you see, we have this much information summed up from all sources. The deceased resided in different cities, even in another country. This will add more difficulties to solving the case, so we need ample time to do a varied investigation."

He drew out another copy from the archives and said with a wave of his hand, "This is a financial statement from the Royal Bank. At present, the deceased has a cash deposit of $110,000. She deposited $6,000 to $7,000 in cash every month. At the end of 1997, David, the general manager of 3P Auto Company in Buffalo presented her with a brand new red BMW 328i. He is the man in the photo with her... Based on our guess, she had engaged in prostitution for many years. The men she dealt with were various and quite complicated, so we need some time to crack this case. At present, we'll summon people concerned and continue to broadcast the dead woman's photo on

TV, hoping that the public will offer more clues to the case. We have also notified the Chinese Consulate General in Toronto, so that her family in Shanghai will come to Canada to confirm the identity of the deceased and make arrangements for a funeral."

After hearing this, Jia was dumb-founded, as if his head had been hit by a baseball bat. As the old saying goes: Townspeople would be in tears when they meet each other. Moreover, the dead woman had been confirmed as a prostitute. Initially he did not want this ominous title to be connected with his townswoman, due to a sort of "native place complex", but he had no way of avoiding it.

Chief Simon was talking to him, "Yesterday somebody mentioned that you are from Shanghai as well, aren't you? What a coincidence. You might be helpful in solving this case."

"Yes, I'm from Shanghai too and I'm of the same age as Camille Zhang." As Jia had no way for retreat, he would rather hold nothing back.

"That's wonderful! You'll be very helpful to us. To say the least, it would be easier for you to communicate with her family members." Chief Simon burst out laughing.

Jia felt a nondescript embarrassment when he was gazing at Simon's huge eyes. He fumbled for some words to break this awkward situation, "Chief Simon, Miss Wu guessed right: the deceased was really a prostitute."

Simon talked to Wu, smiling, "You are truly a detective!"

"I just relied on my instinct." Wu, Xiaoxian, smiling, responded with a touch of pride.

"Women's sixth sense is usually very accurate." Jia put on a cheeky grin.

After exchanging a few words, Simon suddenly reminded them seriously, "When you write articles, never mention anybody involved in this case to avoid alerting the suspects inadvertently. Just follow the news announced by our Police Bureau. I'll inform you of any new developments in time."

When they were about to shake hands and take leave, Simon looked at his watch and said with a smile, "It's getting late – I'm going to submit an application to our director for Miss Wu to work in this Bureau."

The three people's loud laughter broke the deadly silence in the meeting room, lingering for a long time in the police building, forming a striking contrast with the wind and snow outside. Undoubtedly, such pleasant laughter added gorgeous warmth to the white and chilly winter.

7. A Tragedy under the CN Tower

Everything seemed to be beyond people's expectations, but it was still reasonable and logical. "Toronto Weekly", published on Jan. 6th, was in such great demand that an additional 3,000 copies were insufficient. The cover of this issue was sensational: with Zhang, Yuanyuan's huge beautiful photo as the theme picture and especially the big black caption "Tragic Death of a Shanghai Beauty in Niagara Falls" and a female body hanging under a helicopter as a background picture.

Passing bookstores, newsstands or supermarkets, people easily found this eye-catching magazine. Some bought the magazine and started reading it, forgetting about shopping. In front of the "Dragon Source Cultural City" in the north of the city, at least 50 people lined up for the magazine. With copies in hand, they queued for the cashier and chattered in Mandarin, Cantonese or occasionally in Shanghai or other southern dialects.

A tall senior was reading the magazine and talked to himself, "Beauties were born under an unlucky star!"

"She was also from Shanghai. Who on earth would have killed her? What a sin! What a shame. Look, she was so beautiful! A typical Shanghai lady." A middle-aged woman, standing beside him, talked to him in Cantonese with a Shanghai tone.

"So pretty! What a pity! What a shame!" The man's hands were trembling as he held the magazine.

Several others standing in the front or back of the queue joined in their conversation. Some insisted that it was murder for love; others guessed it might be murder for money. Finally people shook their heads helplessly and sighed for the tragic passing of this beauty. Almost everybody's face displayed compassion or sympathy.

At around 12 pm, not an extra copy of "Toronto Weekly" could be found in any newsstands in the Greater Toronto Area – an unprecedented record in the magazine's history of ten years. Usually about 40% of the magazines would be circulated on the afternoon of the second day and 20% would be returned before the new issue was published the following Saturday. Director Wang regretted that too few additional copies had been printed the day before. He never expected that his unnoticeable magazine would be in the limelight when other Chinese media were so developed in Toronto. Hearing this good news, Chief Guo was so pleased that he immediately called Jia, Feng and Wu, Xiaoxian with many compliments.

For five whole days since the discovery of the female body on Jan. 1st, Jia had not enjoyed a good sleep for chasing the news, and writing articles. The special feature article of 50,000 words written by him and Xiaoxian, with Li, Zhihao's photos, was the focus of conversation in the city. As a news reporter, he felt mentally satisfied by this and the complimentary phone call from Chief Guo. Normally he should have had a good sleep that night.

It was late at night, however, and he had been in bed for two hours already, tossing and turning, counting to 1,000 and over, but he still could not fall asleep. His heart, like the cold moonlight, turned chilly. His mind was filled with a swirl of images of famous prostitutes such as Xue, Tao; Liu, Rushi; Guan, Panpan; Dong, Xiaowan; and Sai, Jinhua, as well as those in well-known western novels such as Katyusha, Ferdinand, and Marguerite. He figured that writers and poets and even thinkers, whether Asian or Western, of all eras, showed great compassion to prostitutes. As a news writer, he at least was sympathetic. Moreover, Zhang, Yuanyuan came from the same city and was of the same age as he was.

Since he failed to fall asleep, Jia got up from bed and gulped down some Chilean wine, hoping this dark red liquid would travel from his mouth to his throat and inner organs to warm him up and help him sleep.

With a wine cup in hand, he stood by the window and gazed far into the distance. The CN Tower stood upright with a black background and added manliness to the gentle city. The flashing microwave signals on top of the tower decorated the black and profound vault of heaven. Ever since he mounted this tower for the first time five years ago, he had had colorful dreams, but he had never shown so much concern for it or gazed at it for such a long time.

The magnificent CN Tower reminded him of the Oriental Pearl Tower back in his native home. The two towers, though unnoticed by many people, were both beautiful in different ways. Just like the CN Tower, the highest on earth, the Pearl Tower, the highest in Asia, added virility to the feminine Shanghai. It so happened that the people of the two cities held "a Conversation in the New Century between Shanghai and Toronto" on Dec. 29th, a week before, by international communications satellites on the two towers. The students of University of Toronto had communicated on the air with the students of Fudan University – his Alma Mater. Since then, the distance between the two cities had been shortened while their hearts were drawing closer.

At this moment, Jia was eagerly concerned about these two towers, because from the Pearl Tower, Zhang, Yuanyuan came here and under the CN Tower, a tragedy had occurred. He thought of Charles Dickens, the famous English writer, who wrote the popular novel "A Tale of Two Cities". Perhaps a profound novel "A Tale of Two Towers" would be written in the 21st century.

Pacing constantly in his room, Jia fixed his eyes again on the photo of Zhang, Yuanyuan in the current issue of the weekly on the computer table. His mind, like the splashing Niagara Falls, kept him even more awake. Raising his cup to the cold moon, he yelled to the sky, Zhang, Yuanyuan, Zhang, Yuanyuan, why did you engage in such an occupation?

To be a prostitute is the most degrading way of survival. What you sought was material enjoyment. Were you forced by circumstances, or did you indulge in sexual love as human nature, or did you have some undisclosed pain? All prostitutes may have a painful history of blood and tears, both in China and other countries, in the past or the present. You regarded camellia as your life and willingly connected your name to it. Who would have imagined that an Asian lady left her own country for chilly North America and played the part of poor Marguerite 150 years later?

Unable to control his thoughts, he let them run wild. It had been 20 years since China had "opened" its doors and millions of people had followed the trend of going abroad. Although "alternative females" like Zhang, Yuanyuan were in the minority, so far as he knew, there were still many of them. For mere survival, they had to use their body language to compose a few poignantly sensual love songs. It is a pity that nobody has written a book about "alternative females" in all their aspects, although it is an unavoidable and realistic problem.

Prostitution, a social phenomenon as ancient as human history itself, is too complicated. No wonder Alexandre Dumas (Jr.), a literary giant, once sighed with emotional amazement, "What on earth is prostitution? What is it? Is it promiscuous delirium in big cities or a permanent historical phenomenon? When will it end? Maybe it will perish after all mankind perishes? Who can answer my question?"

Poor Zhang, Yuanyuan, whoever killed you, your foe, your creditor, your rival in love, or you yourself…

In the chilly midnight, Jia, Feng decided to probe into Zhang, Yuanyuan's tragic fate, for intellectual reasons and as a mission for his job. He hoped that he would discover some useful clues for the police.

Chapter Three

Manhunt for a Curly-haired Chinese Man

8. Ex-Councilor's visit to the Police on his own Initiative

After Zhang, Yuanyuan's two color photos were broadcast on TV, the internal hot lines of the Niagara Police Office were ringing non-stop. Within 72 hours over a hundred related phone calls were received. Some said they had casual meetings; some had brief contacts with her while others admitted that they had been intimate with her. Even those who drank a cup of coffee with her or danced with her proclaimed that they had been her boyfriends. This kind of news exposure was really effective. The might of the news media could be seen from this case. No wonder the celebrities and politicians usually show respect to news reporters or try to evade them for fear of asking for trouble by saying something wrong.

At around 10 am on Jan. 8th Chief Simon was just swaggering into his office with a cup of coffee in hand when the telephone rang urgently. It turned out that Arvid, the ex-City-Councilor, had come to the lobby downstairs and requested to see him. Simon had not expected him to come without an invitation. "He is surely strong or he'd never have come along." Simon called his company a few days before and the human resources department said Arvid had left for Miami on Christmas Eve and would not be back until around Jan.

10th.

As was known to all in the City of Niagara, Arvid was a romantic and flirtatious politician, and womanizing was his greatest hobby. In April last year, he was compelled to resign because of an affair with his married secretary. At present he was a business consultant in a joint venture of the USA and Canada. With a master's degree of economics in the United States, he had been a financial analyst in a bank before he became a politician. His wife of French origin, his junior by ten years, still looked graceful. She must have been a great beauty when younger. Now she was a public relations manager in a company in Buffalo on the opposite bank. It seemed that she never minded her husband's affairs, which she even regarded as a kind of glory. She was no less flirtatious than her husband. It was rumored that she had an affair with her previous manager. At present she was involved with her family doctor, whom she visited once every week.

Simon had had some business talks with Arvid before, so they were old acquaintances. They now talked about the main subject without even exchanging greetings. To avoid misunderstanding, Arvid had to explain first that he and his wife had returned to the City of Niagara from Miami yesterday afternoon. He found out about the death of Zhang, Yuanyuan from her photos on TV at 10pm. He immediately called and talked for half an hour with his good friend, the Director of the Police Bureau, who asked him to talk to Chief Simon directly the next day.

Arvid, sitting with his back straight opposite to Simon, had a clear-outlined face, resembling Hollywood star Tom Cruise. His sun-tanned skin was in a striking contrast with the snow-covered white fields outside and showed his good health. He did not look like a man of over fifty, especially when he was talking with a radiant face. He looked like a man in his mid-forties, with a resounding voice and full of vitality. Like a magnet, he drew pretty women to offer their bodies to him.

Arvid drew out a cigar from the upper pocket of his suit, smelled it, put it between his lips and lit it with a lighter. He had to smoke several of these Cuban Montecristo brand cigars every day to brace himself, especially early in the morning. It was a habit of his for over ten years. His budget for cigars each month would be enough to feed an average family of four.

Exhaling a smoke ring and glancing at Simon, he started to talk candidly, "I had a good relationship with Miss Zhang, even very intimate for a period of time. I can say I know her pretty well. Not only was she beautiful and intelligent, she was also kind-hearted and understanding, which was rare for Western ladies…I never imagined that she would have died so tragically. It's not fair of God to do this."

Putting on a false smile, Simon said in a strange tone, with his somewhat bending right hand making a gesture in the mid-air, "My old friend, excuse me for asking but what kind of relationship did you have with her? …"

"Only as a general friend, of course. I treated her like a child – she was a bit older than my daughter. She told other friends that I was her godfather." Shrugging his shoulders, Arvid responded swiftly with clenched teeth.

"Really? Look at yourself, becoming younger and younger, and loved by everybody. Your intimate photos with Miss Zhang are still in my hand." Sipping coffee and smacking his lips, Simon spoke in the lecherous manner of a stout older man.

With a couple of strong puffs on his cigar, Arvid exhaled thick smoke and continued solemnly, "Just danced and had dinners with her. I swear to God that what I say is nothing but the truth."

"I was only kidding. Never mind, my old friend. My Mr. Godfather." Simon burst into a roar of laughter when he saw Arvid raising his right hand in all seriousness.

Then Arvid seemed to talk to himself, "Miss Zhang was not snobbish at all. She would respond to my phone calls both while I was a councilor and after my resignation. She was not like other women who tried to curry favor when I was a councilor, but refused to see me or answer my calls after I resigned. Simply absurd!"

Rising and turning to the file cabinet behind him, Simon drew a stack of photos from the files and showed them to Arvid, "Since you are so familiar with Miss Zhang, you must have known this guy."

"Sure! This is David, the general manager of 3P Auto Company on the opposite bank. This guy was Miss Zhang's boyfriend," Arvid blurted out.

Speaking of David, Arvid displayed a sort of deep-rooted hatred, with blue veins standing out on his temples. He claimed that he was the matchmaker for the two of them, but they fell out with each other after living together for just a few months. He didn't know the causes of their split. He heard Miss Zhang mention that David was overbearing and did not allow her to have any contact with other men. He did not make any more inquiry, as it was purely a private matter.

"Maybe it was my fault and I regret having introduced them. That guy was a notorious playboy, changing girlfriends frequently, one for several months only, and pretty girls at that…" Arvid's tone turned suddenly from indignant to admiring.

Simon responded to his comment calmly, "David has left for the Caribbean resort. We'll wait until he returns. Don't act rashly to alert him."

"Perhaps it's connected with him. Damn him, always dallying with good women." Arvid seemed to be talking in his sleep.

Chief Simon responded adamantly, "Well, we need conclusive evidence! Maybe we'll need your assistance."

Arvid nodded in silence and agreed wholeheartedly. While taking leave, he held Simon's hand and promised emphatically that he was willing to co-operate with the police 24/7 for solving the case. He would also recall in detail the whole period of time he had contact with Miss Zhang and provide any clues to this case. He frankly declared that he intended to repay Miss Zhang's genuine friendship with his practical words and deeds so as to offer solace to her soul in heaven.

Chief Simon became pensive after seeing Arvid off. From Arvid's tone he guessed that he and David might have had disputes with each other, maybe vying for the affections of the great beauty, Miss Zhang. As far as age and money were concerned, Arvid was no rival for David, so they eventually turned from friends to foes…

Probably because of his professional habit formed over thirty years as a policeman, Simon always tended to suspect everybody and everything in the world, especially in the process of cracking a case. He would not readily believe anybody involved in the case, be it the honorary premier or a grass-root citizen. At these thoughts, Simon sat down to take notes of the fragmentary ideas he had developed. Finally he drew sketches of Arvid and David and made a big question mark between them with a red pen.

9. Ordering the Arrest of a Curly-haired Chinese Man

Among the over one hundred calls from the public, the most interesting for the Niagara Police Bureau was the clue provided by the Guest Room Service of the "Holiday Inn". According to a security guard, a guest called the service desk at around 11pm on Dec. 28th 2000, reporting that a loud scream had been heard from the next room # 1212. When the guard rushed to the 12th floor, he heard somebody weeping feebly, so he knocked at once.

Answering the door was a curly-haired man, between 30 to 40 years of age, who looked to be Chinese. Through the door, which was ajar, the guard caught a glimpse of an Asian lady with shoulder-length hair sitting in a couch, her face covered with a facial tissue in her hand. The curly-haired man explained apologetically that he was having a quarrel with his girlfriend. When the guard asked the lady if she required any help, she shook her head and thanked him. Before leaving, the guard advised them not to disturb the other guests by making loud noises.

About half an hour later, the same security guard encountered the couple in #1212 again in the lobby on the ground floor. The man waved to him as a sort of greeting and the two left the Inn shoulder to shoulder. The security guard remembered clearly that the lady was wearing a blood red coat and a pair of black jeans while the man had on a long black overcoat. The man was about the same height as the woman.

The security guard of the "Holiday Inn" went to the police bureau to have his statement recorded, insisting that the dead lady Zhang, Yuanyuan was the one he saw in #1212 on the night of Dec. 28th. Then policewoman JoAnna showed him some slides, asking him to identify if the man in #1212 was in one of the pictures. The slides were made from the three photo albums of Zhang, Yuanyuan. It took the security guard around an hour to peruse them carefully. Finally he could not help shaking his head. He emphasized again, however, that the man had two distinct features – his curly-hair and short height.

After meeting with people concerned and summing up various opinions, "the Special investigation team for No.1 female corpse" held that the curly-haired Chinese man was the No. 1 suspect. As the autopsy report indicated, Zhang, Yuanyuan died at 5am early on the morning of Dec. 29th, -- which meant that 5 hours before her death, she was with that curly-haired man. Moreover, the blood red coat and black jeans also matched the clothes the dead woman was wearing when the body was retrieved from the water.

Another important clue was that Zhang, Yuanyuan often lingered in the casino at night according to what the workers in "Casino Niagara" reported. She preferred to talk with people, rather than gambling there. Occasionally she played the slot machines. According to the two waitresses in the bar of the casino, Zhang, Yuanyuan entered the bar with an Asian man at around 9pm on Dec. 28th and left an hour or so later after drinking a cocktail each. Due to the dim light in the bar, they did not see clearly if the man was curly-haired, but he was a short man wearing a long overcoat.

At a daily meeting of "the Special investigation team for No.1 female corpse" at 10am on Jan. 9th, all members were of the opinion that the short man drinking with Zhang, Yuanyuan in "Casino Niagara" was probably the same as the man in the "Holiday Inn". In other words, that curly-haired man was as close as body and shadow with Zhang, Yuanyuan the whole night. At least they were together after 9pm on Dec. 28th.

Chief Simon made a prompt decision, "We should order the arrest of this curly-haired Chinese man so the suspect will not escape justice. JoAnna, you take two policemen to the 'Holiday Inn' to look up the information and call me at once if you discover anything. Everyone else, stand by and do not leave the office within 24 hours."

Armed with guns, JoAnna and two other policemen hopped in a police car with sirens sounding all the way up to the skies, which echoed along the Niagara River for a long time, adding a touch of horror to the severe winter. In 20 minutes, the police car reached the "Holiday Inn".

Seeing some policemen arriving, the hotel owner was all smiles while greeting them, guessing that they had come because of the female body. The manager brought the three to their reception room and exchanged a few greetings. Then he ordered his staff to bring the guests' registration book. It was easy for the police to find that the man who stayed in #1212 on Dec. 28th was Lian, Haotien, residing at 443 University Avenue in Toronto. Having received JoAnna's call, Chief Simon immediately phoned the Toronto police to check the background of this man.

A few minutes later, the Toronto Police Bureau returned Simon's call, indicating that Lian, Haotien had registered a false address in the hotel. 443 University Avenue was actually the address of the Immigration Bureau. Upon hearing this, Simon's knitted brows became smoothed out, because he had likely discovered new information, which could further prove that the curly-haired man was a suspect.

Banging the table, Chief Simon called JoAnna at the hotel at once, "Lian, Haotien's address was false. 443 University Avenue was actually the address of the Immigration Bureau. We have to catch this guy, who may have premeditated this plot. Please co-operate with the hotel staff and make a comprehensive and careful check of all the information."

Upon request, the manager took them to the cashier's counter. After a 20 minute computer search, it was clear that Lian, Haotien checked in at 5pm on Dec. 27th and settled his account at 9:50 am on Dec. 29th , paying by Visa.

Using the credit card number, Chief Simon obtained Lian's personal information. Then he contacted the Federal Immigration Bureau and quickly gained access to his identification in details.

Name: Hao Tien Lian (連浩天in Chinese)

Sex: Male

Date of Birth: March 20th 1965

Place of Birth: Kaohsiung, Taiwan

Nationality: Canadian

Passport Number and date of Issue: VD365892, Oct. 5th, 1998

Height: 5 ft 7 inches

Weight: 130 pounds

Skin Color: Yellow

Hair Color: Black (with natural curls)

Marriage Status: Unmarried

Educational Background: Graduated from Statistics Department of University of Toronto in September 2000 with Ph.D.degree

Occupation: Statistics Data Analyst in CG Insurance Company (Toronto General Office) in Canada starting October 2000

Date of Entry to Canada: Aug. 7th 1995

Address: Suite 616 Royal Building, 1000 Yonge Street, Toronto

Telephone: 416-563-4626

Social Insurance Number (SIN): 569-458-641

Driver's License Number: L8346-95126-50320
Criminal Record: No

At around 3pm JoAnna called the CG Insurance Company and confirmed that Lian, Haotien was an employee of the company. He would come to work the next day as he was on vacation today. To avoid unexpected complications, Chief Simon reported this case to the Bureau Director and requested an arrest of the suspect Lian, Haotien that night in collaboration with the Toronto Police Bureau.

At 7pm Chief Simon, with four male policemen, all armed to the teeth, drove two police cars to the Toronto Police Bureau. The Deputy Director, a former classmate of Simon's in police school, stayed behind to greet him and offer help in the case.

The two were hugging and shaking hands when they met, as if they had not seen each other for years. The scene was a bit sickening. After exchanging greetings, the Deputy Director introduced Mr. Wu, a detective of Asian origin, to Simon before he took a hasty leave.

The five led by Simon, Detective Wu and four Toronto policemen made an immediate plan for arresting Lian, Haotien. At the end of the meeting, Detective Wu received a call from the security guard of Royal Building at 1000 Yonge Street to confirm that the parking lot for Suite 616 was still vacant. Based on the close-circuit surveillance camera, the owner's black Lexus had left the building at 3:10pm that afternoon.

Having heard Detective Wu's report, Chief Simon looked at his watch subconsciously – it was exactly 9:30pm. He glanced over everybody sitting there and said sternly, "Hey, we can't just sit here and wait. Let's act on Number 1 Plan."

The nine policemen in two cars flashed on Yonge Street in downtown Toronto. Six of them, armed with guns, drove two police cars with sirens sounding while the other three, in plain clothes, drove in a small civilian van. At 10 sharp, the three cars stopped in the outdoor parking lot of the Royal Building. Two security guards, already waiting for them, greeted and talked to Detective Wu, informing them that Lian, Haotien had not returned yet.

Two police cars were parked at both ends behind the building, with one policeman in each car. The four policemen, led by Simon, followed a security guard to enter the building. Simon and Detective Wu were in command in the office while two other policemen were patrolling in the stairways on the first and sixth floors. The other security guard jumped into the small van, leading three policemen in plain clothes to the indoor parking lot. The van was parked only 10 meters away from the parking spot for Suite 616, with one policeman inside the van and the other two patrolling with the security guard.

It was not until 11:30pm that the closed circuit TV showed the image of a Lexus entering the parking lot. Chief Simon, drowsy with sleepiness, was woken up by the security guard's shout. He rubbed his eyes with his hands and ordered everybody, by the walkie-talkie, to their assigned positions.

No sooner had Lian, Haotien stopped his car and come out of it than the security guard and a stranger suddenly appeared in front of him. He was so scared that he retreated and almost bumped the car next to him. With a guilty conscience, he felt his heart throbbing. The security guard took the initiative to greet him and introduced the tall man as a new guard he was showing around. Lian thus calmed down and left swiftly after muttering a few words.

Lian rushed to the elevator. When it came to the first floor, a sturdy middle-aged Canadian man entered and smiled at him. "Oh, I'm also going to the sixth floor." The man looked at the indicator lamp in the elevator and talked to himself, or rather talked to him on purpose.

From habit, Lian looked at his watch – it was 11:45pm. Usually he would not meet anybody at this late time. He wondered why he had met several tall, handsome and sturdy men tonight. It was simply absurd! When the elevator reached the sixth floor, he played a little trick and let the man get out first to see what he intended to do.

Lian followed that sturdy man in the direction of the stairway and turned toward his own apartment. After entering the room, he poured himself a cup of whiskey and sipped. He lay in a couch, took a deep breath and managed to calm himself down.

About 15 minutes later when Lian was going to the washroom, his doorbell rang suddenly. He tiptoed to the door and peeped through the magic eye and found, to his relief, only the security guard he had just met in the parking lot.

He opened the door ajar and the security guard told him in a low voice, "Sir, you forgot to lock your Lexus …"

"Oh, thanks a lot! I'll go right away." Now he recalled that he was so panicked he didn't lock the car.

Just at that moment, Chief Simon and Detective Wu dashed into the room. Caught unawares, Lian retreated a few steps.

"Mr. Lian, we suspect that you are connected with a murder case." Detective Wu gained the initiative by striking the first blow before Lian could react.

Waving a warrant for arrest in front of Lian, Chief Simon ordered, "Mr. Lian, please come to the Niagara Police Bureau with us."

Having seen two armed policemen with guns in hand entering the room, Lian nodded without uttering a word. From his facial expression, he must have known about the death of Zhang, Yuanyuan and been expecting a big disaster.

Detective Wu told him clearly and simply, "Bring a couple of things with you as you might come back in a few days."

Lian put on his clothes and took his briefcase, "I knew you would come for me. I can tell you, however, that I am absolutely not the murderer!"

"Mr. Lian, please rest assured that we will not wrong a good person. Everything will be done based on the law." Chief Simon said resolutely.

Without any attempt at resistance, Lian entered the elevator, escorted by four armed policemen and walked to and got in the police car obediently. Chief Simon shook hands and said goodbye to Detective Wu and the other policemen. As he sat in the car, he looked at his watch as usual – it was already 12:45am the next morning.

Two police cars, with red lights flashing and sirens sounding, flew to the Niagara Police Bureau on the highway via downtown Toronto...

10. A True Confession of Lian, Haotien

The interrogation of Lian, Haotien started at 10am on Jan.10th. Chief Simon was the principal judge, with Policewoman JoAnna of the special investigation team assisting and another policeman in charge of taking minutes and recording the session.

Chief Simon's eyes were blood-shot, apparently due to a severe lack of sleep. It went without saying that he had escorted Lian from Toronto at midnight and returned home at 4am. Lying in bed, he had been unable to fall asleep until early in the morning. With a cup of coffee in hand, he gulped it down in big mouthfuls. JoAnna was quite different. With her vigor and vitality plus her white complexion and tall and graceful figure, she looked sweet and charming.

Lian, Haotien's eyes were also fogged with sleep. With a dull look in his eyes, his nose seemed flatter and his mouth wider. His facial features seemed out of proportion. He was also holding a cup of coffee, as he needed caffeine to refresh himself. In his 36 years, this was the first time he had been in custody. It was hard to describe how he felt, -- he just stared at the ceiling the whole night.

Before Simon had a chance to ask a question, Lian eagerly announced, "I'll confess everything. But I can swear to Heaven that Zhang, Yuanyuan was not killed by me, absolutely not!"

"No hurry, Mr. Lian, take your time. Nobody claimed that you were the murderer. Please control your feelings and co-operate with us." JoAnna comforted him in a gentle tone characteristic of females.

Rubbing his beard as usual, Simon opened his mouth, "May I ask you, Mr. Lian, where were you on the night of Dec. 28 last year?"

"Zhang, Yuanyuan requested to meet me at 9pm in the bar of Casino Niagara. She got there ten minutes after I did."

"What's your relationship with each other? When did you get acquainted? The more detailed the better." JoAnna suddenly interrupted, so Simon glanced sideways at her a bit impatiently.

Sipping coffee, Lian started slowly, "It's a long story. I got to know her at the beginning of 1997. I was studying for a Ph.D. at the University of Toronto and she was a stripper at the MW Strip-Dance Club on Yonge Street. I had just been jilted, so I often patronized that club. We soon became good friends because she was the only Asian stripper there and she stopped me from worrying with her sweet talks. I visited her almost every week. She performed table dances for me and allowed me to fumble her breasts and bottom. Every time, I willingly tipped her over a hundred dollars, even three hundred dollars once. Time and again, I tried to go to bed with her, but she never consented, even though I offered to pay a thousand dollars. Maybe she didn't like my ugly looks. As you know, some other strippers will go to bed for a few hundred dollars…"

"Please focus on your relationship with Miss Zhang." Chief Simon interrupted him.

Nodding, he continued, "I know she had a boyfriend of European origin, who often came to pick her up after work. Other strippers told me that Zhang preferred to have contacts with local men. A Canadian in our computer department told me that he once went to bed with Zhang. In May of that year, my cousin, my uncle's son, came to Toronto for a tour from Waterloo. We went to the dance club and I introduced him to Zhang. They found each other congenial and talked a lot. She was even willing to let him fumble her body the first time they met. Usually, as you know, strippers will not let anybody touch them until they are familiar with the person. I waited for over a month before I was allowed to touch her, but not my cousin, perhaps because he is tall and handsome."

Licking his lips, Lian talked non-stop, "Over a year later, Zhang,

Yuanyuan suddenly quit dancing in the club. Nobody knew of her whereabouts although I made several inquiries. I felt as if I had been jilted again. Later I heard several rumors about her – she became the mistress of a millionaire, or she married a wealthy businessman, or she was still selling herself in Toronto."

"You've never met her again since then, right?"

"No, for sure. To tell you frankly, I once gave a stripper two hundred dollars for information about Miss Zhang. When I went to see this woman the next week, she had quit her job. Such women are not trustworthy."

Simon raised his voice, "When did you meet her again then?"

Finishing up his coffee, Lian continued, "During the summer vacation in August last year when I returned home to Taipei after my graduation, I had a chance meeting with Zhang, Yuanyuan in my uncle's home. Embarrassment followed our surprise. It turned out that my cousin had kept in contact with her without my knowledge. They were planning to get engaged in Taipei. I was scared out of my wits. Such a degraded woman can be flirted with, but should never become a wife. Moreover, our family clan is well known in Taipei and my uncle was vice-president of a famous university, a noted scholar and my aunt is from a distinguished family. For the family reputation, I couldn't help making a fuss about Zhang's true colors. My uncle flared up and attempted to drive them out at once. My aunt had a heart attack there and then and was rushed to the Emergency Department of a hospital. In a fit of anger, Zhang flew back to Canada alone. Their fond dream of engagement went up in bubbles. They regarded me as the culprit. My cousin got sick for some time and he hated me bitterly and didn't want to have anything to do with me…"

"What's your cousin's name and where is he now? His address and telephone number…" JoAnna asked just in time.

"He is Peter and his Chinese name is Lai, Wenxiong. He'll graduate this fall from the Department of Sociology in Waterloo University as a Ph.D. student. At present, he is still in Taipei to collect material for his thesis and to take care of his mother, who is hospitalized for a surgery. He is really a filial son! ..." Lian fished out an address booklet from his briefcase and wrote down Lai, Wenxiong's address and phone number on a piece of paper and handed it to Chief Simon.

11. Vain Attempt to Drug and Rape Zhang, Yuanyuan

Just as the police had expected, suspect Lian, Haotien knew a great deal about this case. After a brief recess, questioning resumed on the afternoon of Jan. 10th. Chief Simon was still the presiding officer with JoAnna and another policeman taking minutes and managing the recording system.

Chief Simon came straight to the point, "Let's return to the subject. What did you do after you met Zhang, Yuanyuan in the Casino at 9pm on Dec. 28th last year?"

Rubbing his chin, Lian answered, "We each ordered a cocktail in the bar. While she went to the washroom, I put some prepared potion into her cup. After drinking the cocktail, she felt like going to sleep, so I proposed to escort her home. We left the bar a little before 10pm. I drove directly to the Holiday Inn where I had booked a room. She went into a sound sleep as soon as she touched the pillow. I thought I could hold her beautiful body and enjoy the night, so that my dream of three years would finally come true. When I boldly took off all her clothes except her bra and briefs, she suddenly sat up with her eyes wide open. I was so startled that I jumped from bed as if I had encountered a ghost."

Glancing sideways at Simon, Lian found him looking enchanted by his story. He continued after catching a sight of JoAnna. "It turned out that she had taken precautions against me. She told me she had found out that I had put something in her glass, so she didn't drink it but swiftly poured it onto the carpet under cover of the dim light... She flew into a hot temper while dressing herself, and snatched the phone, intending to call the police. I knelt down at once, begging her to give me another chance, because I had just started my career two months ago. If I were indicted, my career would be finished. She was lenient with me and put down the phone as a sign she had forgiven me. I caressed her shoulders to comfort her as I often had when she danced for me. Since she didn't show resentment, I advanced further and attempted to caress her breasts. I asked to have sex with her and I was willing to pay anything, but she simply refused as usual. She would not allow me to caress her breasts as a little revenge for my tale-telling to my uncle and family back in Taipei."

He went on to say, "I was infatuated with that woman, heart throbbing and inner fire burning while smelling her fragrance. Unable to control my lust, I pounced on her and tore her underwear by force... Just at that instant, she claimed loudly that she suffered from AIDS. I was scared stiff like a log. This fatal disease is not to be trifled with. I put on my clothes at once because I was most afraid of death. She burst our crying while putting on her dress. Then the security guard of the hotel came knocking on the door, so she stopped crying. The guard asked a few questions and advised us not to make loud noises before he left.

"What happened after that?" JoAnna was eager to ask.

"She was weeping miserably because she really had contracted AIDS. She had got the bad news just a month before and now she took a passive attitude toward life. It was lucky that she hadn't got engaged to my cousin; otherwise he would have been ruined. From the expression in her eyes, I could discern her profound love for my cousin. I consoled her by holding her hand and escorted her home. It was almost midnight when we left the hotel."

"Where did you go after you escorted her home? At around what time? Did anybody see you? The more detailed the better." Simon said after drinking some water.

"She lived at 100 Lakeshore Building, which was ten minutes' drive from the hotel. I saw her entering the gate. Then I went to the casino. I returned to the hotel at around 3:15am."

Licking her lips, JoAnna asked, "Can you prove that you went to the casino alone after midnight? Can you prove that you returned to the hotel after 3am? You must tell the truth. It would be best if you had witnesses."

Lian shook his head, "I know you suspect that I'm the murderer. But I swear that I won't harm people, let alone kill them. You should also have evidence. I'll find a lawyer to secure my release on bail."

Lian added, "I wonder if there is a closed-circuit TV system in the casino. I entered the casino at 12:10 am and left at 3am."

Simon asked again, "I haven't asked why you came to Niagara Falls in such chilly weather and why you booked a hotel. Solely for visiting Zhang, Yuanyuan?"

"Actually two things coincided. My big uncle came to the United States for a trip form Kaohsiung, Taiwan. He didn't apply for a visa to Canada, so he came to Niagara to see me. It had been ten years since we had seen each other. I checked into the Holiday Inn at 5pm on Dec. 27th and called Zhang, Yuanyuan immediately, but she was not at home, so I left a message. Early the next morning she called me back. Half an hour after I checked into the hotel, I drove to Buffalo to have dinner with my uncle and sister. I returned to the hotel at midnight. If you don't believe me, you can check the customs' records at the US-Canada border."

"Why did you register a false address when you checked in?" Simon raised his head and asked sternly.

"I was afraid I might get into trouble after seeing Zhang, Yuanyuan. I know she was hard to deal with."

JoAnna asked with a long face, "Why did you prepare the sleeping potion purposely for Zhang?"

Lian whispered, lowering his head, "To tell you the truth: she was really beautiful. Like an Oriental Venus, she attracted every man. She had the most patrons in the MW Strip Dance Club. Clients queued up to see her. I was infatuated with her for several years, but she always refused to go to bed with me. I would not admit defeat although I failed to take advantage of her so many times. She was a mere prostitute. Why did she go to bed with other men, not me? Not even once! I can pay double. If I can't obtain something, I am even more eager to get it. That was why I thought of that damned plot. Unfortunately, she saw through my scheme. I went the extra mile to get her telephone number -- I got help from Lai, Wenxiong's sister."

"Do you know that it is a crime to put drugs in wine and attempt to rape someone?" Simon shrugged shoulders and announced loudly.

Lian nodded continually, "Damn me! Damn me! I should be punished for that. But I really didn't kill Zhang, Yuanyuan. It's the truth. You should absolutely not suspect me."

12. An Unmailed Love Letter

Just as she stepped into the office of "Toronto Weekly", Wu, Xiaoxian got a phone call from Chief Simon for help at around 11am on Jan. 11th. Panting, he told her that they didn't get anything valuable from Zhang, Yuanyuan's over 50 discs after a careful check by Chinese computer experts. The discs consisted of various kinds of material downloaded from the internet, such as Chinese literature, local conditions and customs and habits in Shanghai, make-up, and information on AIDS, but nothing written by Zhang. Just then, a computer engineer came to the police bureau and delivered happily to Simon a pile of printed Chinese material. This material had been retrieved from Zhang's monitor with the help of CBL Data Retrieval Science & Technology Firm. It consisted of a dozen or so articles in Chinese and English, which had been deleted within the last two months.

Normally the police bureau ought to find a professional translation firm to do the translation. However, it was hard to find any firm in Niagara, which could translate from Chinese into English and vice versa, and they were pressed for time. Chief Simon suddenly thought of the reporters for "Toronto Weekly". They had a good command of English and were familiar with this case, so Simon called Wu and invited her to help translate key parts of the manuscript, hoping to find some useful new clues. Of course, he made it clear that he would pay for the translation based on the rate set by the translation company.

Editor-in-Chief Guo, after hearing Wu's request, immediately asked Jia, Feng to his office and asked him to accompany Wu to the Niagara Police Bureau. He was concerned that Wu might not be able to handle all the translation by herself and thought that two people could do proofreading for each other to avoid errors. Moreover, he did not want a girl to drive such a long way alone. That fit in exactly with Jia's wish – to master more first-hand information.

With several dictionaries, such as the "New English-Chinese Dictionary", Jia and Wu rushed to the Niagara Police Bureau. At a little over 1pm, Chief Simon was all smiles seeing both of them coming, with his facial muscles inflating. He asked his secretary to prepare coffee and promised to pay both of them for the translation. His only wish was to see the material translated as soon as possible.

They followed Chief Simon to a small computer room, with two of the 4 or 5 computers turned on, apparently for them to type their translation. They glanced over the Chinese material handed to them by Simon. Among the over ten manuscripts, two were long letters in connection with this case, addressed to Lai, Wenxiong. One letter, written on Nov.15 th, described in detail how Zhang had contracted AIDS. It was hard to judge whether the letter was mailed to Taipei. The other one, written on Christmas Eve (Dec.24th), revealed the harassment of "the Thunder Motorcyclists Gang". It was not known either if this letter was mailed. Another ten essays, half of which expressed her nostalgic feelings for her family and friends, had nothing to do with this case.

Half an hour later, Jia and Wu reported the above to Chief Simon. He was very interested in the long letters and asked them to translate them word for word. After a consultation, it was decided that Wu would translate the first letter and Jia would translate the second. Simon granted Jia's request, as an exception, to smoke in the computer room. He even brought an ashtray from the next room for him.

Based on habit, Wu always liked to read the Chinese original first to understand its meaning fully before starting to translate it. Sipping coffee, she began to read Zhang, Yuanyuan's love letter.

"Wenxiong,

Maybe this is a letter that will never be mailed.

Because I really lack the courage to face the cruel reality: I am afraid my beloved one will float away from me after my terrible situation is made clear.

As you know, spiritual desertion is more horrible and frightening than physical and spatial separation. Since our relationship was upgraded from a business relationship between 'prostitute' and 'client' to that of 'lovers', you have been not only my physical support, but also my spiritual sustenance. Perhaps some people would jeer at me in a loud voice: What right does a prostitute have to babble about 'spiritual'? They are entirely wrong!

Prostitutes, whether in the past or present, at home or abroad, all have a bloodstained spiritual history. Whoever doesn't have a sophisticated mental world? For instances: Zhang, Yuliang, the child prostitute in Yangzhou, who succeeded as an artist in Shanghai, and Marguerite in Alexandre Dumas (Jr.)' novel.

Three months have elapsed since we parted at Chiang Kai-shek International Airport in Taipei on Aug. 15th. I feel as if I have been waiting for dozens of years. I have been counting every second during the 91 days. You could hardly imagine how I endured the hard time without you. I was like an animal without soul, only an outer form, or like a walking corpse in a deserted corner of a snow-covered country, taking a passive attitude toward life.

Wenxiong, please pardon me for lying to you again and again – I reminded you before that I am a woman who likes to lie. In this society permeated with dirty money and selfish desire, telling the truth makes you suffer losses while 'honesty' denotes 'vulnerability'. Every time you phoned me, I told you nothing but good news or made-up stories. In my opinion, it is unnecessary to let my beloved share my sufferings. You have already paid too high a price for me -- I couldn't repay you even in my next life.

I wonder if you and your family are still as incompatible as fire and water. I've told you time and again that there are sweet ladies everywhere on earth, but you have only one mother. Never sulk with your mother or argue with your father for my sake. It is not worthwhile to desert your family for a woman like me! Like an incense-burner used by dozens of men, I lost my female dignity a long time ago and have been deprived of my right to live a normal life.

What I feared most was eventually proven true yesterday – I have contracted AIDS, the fatal disease of this century.

I studied medical care, so I am only too aware of what it means to contract this deadly disease. At this moment, the following fits me most appropriately: 'There is no grief greater than the death of the mind.'

As you know, I suffered from a high fever and diarrhea from time to time after I returned to Canada from Taipei. At first I thought these symptoms were caused by stress. At the beginning of October, I had a high fever and vomited for ten consecutive days. Medication and injections were of no use. I felt so feeble and dizzy that I didn't have the strength to hold the steering wheel. I had to call a taxi to see my family doctor. I was sleepy all day long, but couldn't fall asleep at all, just staring at the ceiling, reminiscing the joyful days when we were together. In the recent two months, I have had no appetite at all – I vomit after drinking a little milk. I have depended on a small bowl of congee every day and have become thinner with each passing day. Every time you called, I tried to pluck up my strength to chat with you, so you wouldn't find out about my feeble physical condition...

Finally the family doctor requested a blood test – 6 CC of my blood for a HIV test. Two weeks later the report came out – it was positive, which means that I have contracted the AIDS virus. That was a preliminary 'sifting test'. Then they asked me to do several 'confirmation tests', which turned out positive again. The final 'immunization test' yesterday confirmed that I am a HIV carrier, an AIDS patient.

What a bolt from the blue! That destroyed the little hope I had and toppled me mentally. I know so much about AIDS that I can give you a few simple figures, hoping this will not scare you: about 40 million HIV carriers are struggling for life, with 10 to 12 years to survive. If there is any complication, they might die in a few months. At present around 20 million AIDS patients die of complications annually.

As the incubation period for AIDS can be as long as ten years, I don't know when I contracted it. Besides, it was most probable for a prostitute like me to contract this fatal disease. Even with condoms, it is still hard to avoid the contagion. Moreover, some evil guys refused to use condoms. Especially that Japanese womanizer Aokawa Kakuai who liked oral sex--, one of the easy ways to contract AIDS. He boasted of having sex with over a hundred women. What a nauseating guy!

Wenxiong, I really have conflicting thoughts in my heart. Normally I should have told you immediately because you were my only sex partner in the past year and several times you refused to wear condoms, as you often said you "don't like to wash your feet with socks on". So, it is possible that you may have contracted it (I mean from me, I hope you won't misunderstand it). You should have an HIV test at once to avoid more tragedy due to delays. I am also worried, however, that you'll break off any contact with me after you know the truth. Then my only little bubble of hope will burst in the twinkling of an eye. I don't want your family to know about this, otherwise they will sneer at you. Please excuse the selfishness of a weak woman! Behind the selfishness is all my love for you and my reliance on you.

The only thing for rejoicing is that our engagement was cancelled in Taipei in August. Otherwise it would be your lifelong burden. A lover can take no responsibilities, while a husband would be different, especially an honest man like you. Nowadays more and more people prefer to be common-law couples, so they can enjoy sex to their hearts' content without the responsibility of marriage. In another sense, it was very 'wise' of your parents to drive me out at that time. I don't bear any grudge against them. I am only grateful to you and respectful to your parents.

Wenxiong, whenever I come round, I will email this letter to you. If not, this will be a love letter never to be mailed. My God, whatever should I do?

Yuanyuan,

With eternal love for you,

November 15th, 2000
At Niagara"

13. Clues Revealed by the Tailing of the Gangsters

Jia, Feng finished translating this letter almost simultaneously with Wu, Xiaoxian after smoking at least 5 or 6 cigarettes, filling the ashtray on the desk. He knew Xiaoxian would complain if he continued chain-smoking. He stood up, stretched himself vigorously before he lit another cigarette and sat down again to proofread the manuscript at the computer. The original Chinese letter read as follows:

"Brother Wenxiong,

Please allow me to call you as such for the first time. In my heart, you resemble the cedar standing straight and proud, never bending, in the courtyard. I wish that your sturdy shoulders would forever be my reliable pillar and my tranquil bay to anchor at.

Again and again, I tried to entrust the flying snow to convey my sacred greetings to you: wishing you good health and a Ph.D. degree in the coming new year, and a speedy recovery for your Mother. Again and again, I shouted to you in my dreams: come back to me, my only lover!

It is now Christmas Eve. Niagara Falls looks colorful and romantic with the illumination of lights. Its magnificent grandeur is not covered up by the heavy snow or inhibited by the icicles. Compared with its imposing momentum and extraordinary wonder, I sense my humbleness and lowliness, for which I can't forgive myself, let alone beg God to forgive me.

Now that I am an AIDS patient, on the verge of death, I have no reason whatsoever to blame god or man, -- I myself committed the sin. Why didn't I have the ability to survive in a foreign country? Why didn't I follow my father's advice? Why did I indulge in material ease and comfort? Why did I seek vanity? The only thing that is worth pondering deeply is that many ignorant young men and women, after China's opening up to the outside world, followed the fad of going abroad, presuming that gold is everywhere overseas. A woman like me, however, weak-willed with a language barrier and no technical skills, would find it hard to adapt to the new environment. As the saying goes, immigration is a sort of spiritual remolding of oneself. Not everybody can stand such earth shaking "rebirth", which involves not only the language barrier and cultural differences, but also psychological adjustment.

I hope those parents who want their children to grow up to be useful, will think twice before letting them go abroad. They should take into consideration the kids' IQ (Intelligence Quotient) and EQ (Emotional Quotient) as well. Neither of these should be ignored. I am not exaggerating to scare you. There is Zhang, Yuanyuan in Tokyo, in New York, in Paris, in London...My name would be representative of "alternative Chinese women abroad", sooner or later, just like Li, Shishi; Chen, Yuanyuan; Liu, Rushi; Li, Xiangjun; Dong, Xiaowan; Sai, Jinhua... in Chinese history. Women of a kind have the same reputation, of which I am not scared. This is decided by history, from which nobody can escape, even with wings. Wenxiong, how I'd like to continue my autobiographic novel 'New Camille' as soon as possible so that the parents in the world will know what I think straight from my heart. My days are numbered – a little pneumonia would be enough to send me to Heaven. If I don't have enough time, would you please continue writing after you get your Ph.D. degree and donate the royalties to the "Canadian AIDS Foundation"? In my current circumstances, it's hard for me to think about writing, unless I am empowered by you after you return to me. By the way, your Mom would let you come back after the spring Festival. Find more time to be with her – a sick person likes family to be around. I share this feeling deeply.

Advised repeatedly by my family doctor, I started the "cocktail treatment" two weeks ago and at present I feel a little better. What's more important, I read on the Internet "the Death Diary", written by Lu, Youqing, also from Shanghai, prior to his death. I was encouraged by this book to battle AIDS. At 37 years old, he was fearless facing death and wrote the brilliant and touching last page at the end of his life. At 6:55 am, Dec. 11th he closed his eyes in happiness, leaving us his advice to "treat ourselves well". To me, death is not frightening, as everybody will experience birth, old age, sickness and death. The crux of the matter is how to live in the present. How should we treat ourselves well? I am considering doing something significant during my limited life. At least I can appeal to all of society to show concern for the "alternative women" and collect donations for AIDS organizations.

The "cocktail treatment" was initiated and researched successfully by a scientist of Chinese origin—He, Dayi. It uses a combination of medication for AIDS, only twice daily, two pills each time, very convenient, but very expensive. Luckily the annual 10,000 dollars' medical expense is covered by OHIP (Ontario Health Insurance Program). I am enjoying excellent benefits in Canada. This treatment, at the current stage, can only control the AIDS virus by reducing its spread within the body, but it can't kill all the viruses. The worst side effect of the treatment is that it can change the patient's appearance. That was why I refused to take it at first. However, considering that it can prolong my life, I brushed aside the problem with my appearance. I hope I will not turn into an ugly creature when I meet you at the end of next month. Looking through the window, I see busy traffic flowing endlessly. Joyous people are going to Christmas parties. Young men and women are enjoying the forbidden fruit. The annual Winter Festival of Lights attracts countless people from both the USA and Canada to Niagara Falls, which is permeated with a joyful atmosphere. Just as Dylan Thomas said: night is everything flowing. Faced with this grotesque and bizarre flowing, I suddenly came up with the sorrowful emotion: "The hustle and bustle belong to them, not to me".

Wenxiong, tonight, more than any night, I yearn for you, for your loving me wildly, every bit of me. I haven't got intimate with you for four and a half months. I will become a woman without a sexual drive, if I masturbate for long. Even at the end of my life, I have to enjoy ultimate sexual love. I will not regret it if I lie in your arms naked and die. That is how Adam and Eve created human beings. That is a right bestowed by God to every man and woman. Sexual love not only makes women more genteel, it also makes people healthier. Your vigorous sperm will enhance my immunity and may even help me resist the stubborn AIDS virus.

A few days ago I had a rosy dream. After we made love madly for several hours on the carpet, the whole room resounded with melodious screams like a butterfly's and the repeated music of "the Fifth Symphony" by Beethoven. You held me wearing a lavender gauze kerchief and lightly put me on the light blue bed spread, covering me all over from head to toe with white camellia flowers. Finally you covered my face as well, except my two eyes. You silently stood beside me, your tears dropping on the camellia flowers on my face. You watched me wordlessly until I closed my eyes... That is the way of passing I long for! What would be even better is that it could be telecast on the Internet to let the whole world know that an Asian AIDS patient "passed away happily". How magnificent and touching it would be!

Wenxiong, deep in my heart, I really don't want to leave you, not even for a day. I yearn for our short-lived love. That's why I didn't want to tell you about my illness. I tried to delay telling you until the last minute of my life. Of course, whenever we make love I always remind you to use condoms to avoid future trouble for you. We, the new generation, who were born in the 1970's, first and foremost live for ourselves. Even in death, we should maintain our "sacred self". Please pardon me again for my selfishness – absolute selfishness. However, my selfishness will never affect my fiery emotion and sincere love for you.

There is one incident I must tell you. One night at the end of last month I was so bored that I went to a nearby casino to kill time. Please don't misunderstand me: I was by no means soliciting. I just went for the slot machines to while the time away. Ever since you knelt down to propose to me, I have never touched another man. I swear to you that you are the only man worthy of my trust and I'll be faithful to you for my remaining time. Just as you said, my former self didn't belong to you. After I accepted your love, I belonged to you heart and soul. This fragrant incense-burner is solely yours. It was unexpected that a member of ' the Thunder Motorcyclists Gang' had been tailing me before I left the casino. I went out of the way to escape by the backdoor of the bar. I recalled what you had told me about this vicious gang. I had been involved unwittingly in their scheme to grab pretty girls for prostitution. I had been coerced to procure Chinese clients and my face was almost disfigured by another gang. To be far away from those gangsters, I moved to Niagara. All the above is recorded in detail in my novel 'New Camille'.

It seems that I should consult with you after you return as to how to deal with them, but they should absolutely not harm you. Anyway, I am an AIDS patient, what can they do to me? The worst is to perish together. I like Vancouver very much and I would be content to spend my last days in that scenic place. It depends on where you'll be working after your graduation next fall. I'll follow you wherever you go. I pretend to try to be away from you, but at the bottom of my heart, how

I want to marry you – this is a normal woman's aspiration. Women's words are usually contrary to what they mean. Thinking in one way, and acting in another – that's the women's way.

Wenxiong, a lonely heart is waiting for you to console it. A hollow soul is begging you for whole-hearted rescue.

Yuanyuan, your mischievous little sister

Christmas Eve, Dec. 24th, 2000"

After he finished the proofreading, Jia, Feng felt quite excited and sighed again and again, moved by Zhang, Yuanyuan's sincerity. He exchanged his translation with Wu, Xiaoxian to avoid the police's confusion in understanding the use of key words in the two letters.

At around 5pm Chief Simon, all smiles, took over the printed translation and began reading at once, without even greeting the two translators.

14. A Complicated Case

On the night after Jia and Wu finished translating the two love letters, Chief Simon held a meeting of "the Special investigation team for No. 1 female corpse" to discuss the case in detail. Ten days had passed since the discovery of the female body, but there seemed to be no substantial progress. Everybody was boiling hot with a sense of urgency.

First of all, Chief Simon informed them that there was not enough evidence to charge Lian, Haotien with murder based on the information they had at present. They had to keep him in custody, awaiting further information and DNA test results to see if there was any connection to the semen in Zhang, Yuanyuan's womb.

A policeman said eagerly, "In my opinion, Lian, Haotien's confession is not trustworthy. With a Ph.D. degree, it's easier for him to make up a whole story than to write a ten-page paper. It has been a long time since this case started, so he has had plenty of time to deliberate. There was enough time to prepare an academic thesis."

Raising his head and glancing at everybody, Simon said, "I think Lian, Haotien's confession is reliable to a certain extent. You see, he told us Miss Zhang had AIDS, and that has been proved in these two love letters. The timing of his trip to the casino with the dead woman matches the information the casino has provided. He also confessed that he tore the dead person's pink briefs in an attempt to rape her, which matches fully with what information we have..."

Policewoman JoAnna agreed with Simon's analysis to a certain extent. She pointed out seriously that the crux was: where on earth was Zhang, Yuanyuan from midnight to 5am on Dec. 29th ? Where was Lian, Haotien during that period of time? If he remained in the casino until 3am before he returned to the hotel as he said, then he could not be the murderer. If, on the other hand, he can't prove where he was, or find any witness or evidence, then he is still the biggest suspect.

The seven or eight people present mostly nodded in silent agreement with JoAnna's inference. Only Chief Simon shook his head in disagreement. He asked the secretary to distribute the copies of the English version of the two love letters and, clearing his throat, he began talking slowly,

"This case is not as simple as we thought; it is getting more and more complicated and difficult, like a snowball rolling. Read the two love letters in your hands, written by Zhang, Yuanyuan to Lai, Wenxiong. Please pay more attention to those parts I underlined with bold lines. These two letters at least provide us with the following important information: Number 1, the dead person had some connection with the Thunder Motorcyclists Gang. As you know, this is an organized criminal group with its headquarters in Quebec. Without any conscience, they commit all kinds of crimes and are especially powerful in Toronto and London, Ontario. Thus, Zhang, Yuanyuan might have been ruthlessly killed by gangs who murdered her to conceal a secret or for money, revenge, etc. Number 2, the dead person's connection with the Japanese Aokawa Kakuai was extraordinary. She hated him to the marrow of her bones. Where is this wolf? In Japan, in Canada, in the US or escaped to Europe? We may have to ask for help from the Japanese Embassy to obtain full information on Aokawa Kakuai. Number 3, the dead person wrote an autobiographic novel 'New Camille' with a lot of valuable information in it. If we could find the manuscript, the details of this case would be revealed…"

"It seems that Mr. Lai knows a lot of the truth. Probably the manuscript of 'New Camille' is in his hands; otherwise he can't possibly continue the writing. He has at least read the manuscript." JoAnna was anxious to interrupt while reading the love letters.

Stroking his beard as usual, Simon added, "That's the 4th point I want to mention. The dead person's relationship with her boyfriend is extraordinary and harmonious like water and milk. Their emotions had reached a spiritual stage, which also matches with Lian, Haotien's confession. Therefore, we must call Taipei and ask Lai, Wenxiong to return to Toronto right away. I'm sure he'll provide us with key clues."

A policeman wearing glasses suggested, "We should also contact the dead woman's family doctor who might provide more information."

Simon nodded in agreement. Just at that time, the Chinese Consulate General in Toronto called, informing them that Zhang, Yuanyuan's three family members had arrived in Toronto and would stay in the "Kailong Hotel" tonight. Simon promised to send people from the Police Bureau to Toronto to get her family and bring them to Niagara Falls to identify the corpse.

It was already 11pm, but the discussion on the case was still continuing, with the lights shining in the meeting room. This is a world of suspicion. Conjecture and suspicion resemble the two blades of a pair of scissors. Hopefully the ball of mystery would be cut open, the true nature of the matter revealed and the murderer caught and charged, so that the victim's name could be cleared.

Finally, decisions were reached by all present at the meeting that Lai, Wenxiong be called to return to Canada immediately; that the dead person's family doctor be contacted to get information on her disease (AIDS); that the ex-city councilor Arvid be further contacted for any possible details related to this case; and that General Manager David of 3P Auto Company in Buffalo, USA be summoned, as he was on intimate terms with Zhang, Yuanyuan for several months and even gave her a BMW car. They decided to postpone inquiring about Aokawa Kakuai until after Lia, Wenxiong returned to Canada.

Chapter Four

Corpse Identified by her Parents

With Revelation of a Girl's Inner Self

15. With Tears, the Parents Revealing a Girl's Heart

It was on the evening of Jan. 8th when Zhang, Yuanyuan's family received the terrible news. There were complications because she had left Shanghai directly for Japan and then she was transferred to Toronto. The result was that there was no information about Shanghai in the entry record for Canada. After the Chinese Consulate General in Toronto received the police notification on the afternoon of Jan.5th, they immediately contacted the departments concerned in China. Finally they found her family in three days with the help of the Entry and Departure Administration, Xuhuei Branch of the Shanghai Public Security Bureau. Thanks to the go-ahead given by the Security Bureau and the Canadian Consulate in Shanghai, the Zhang family completed all formalities for a visit to Canada within 48 hours. Air Canada also offered timely help in providing them with 3 half-priced tickets.

Although it was the first trip abroad for the dead person's mother and brother, they were not curious or interested at all. Her father had been on several business trips abroad-- during one trip he had got a contract worth millions of US dollars-- but he had never been so stressed as at this time. He hid and smoked in the washroom and did not eat or drink during the flight. When not smoking, he could scarcely breathe. The family of three never dreamed that they would come to this chilly country at the beginning of the new century for the funeral of their loved one – a tragedy for the white-haired to bury the black-haired.

Jia, feng and Wu, Xiaoxian, braving the heavy snow, came to the "Kailong Hotel" downtown where the Zhangs were staying, at around 10am on Jan.10th. They handed their business cards to the Zhangs and explained the purpose for their visit. The Zhangs kindly asked them to sit down. Jia talked to them in the Shanghai dialect, which made them feel more at home and warmed up the atmosphere bit by bit. Seeing that Wu had a long face with knitted eyebrows as if it were the end of the world, they changed to talking in Mandarin.

Old Zhang, thinly built, was obviously a chain-smoker. He was typical of the Chinese intellectuals with clear-cut features and a pair of black-brimmed glasses on a straight nose. He looked older than his age of over fifty, like a man over sixty, with countless wrinkles as a result of years' sufferings. He also showed the intelligence and capability characteristic of a man from Shanghai. He had graduated from Jiaotong University in Shanghai and was a senior engineer in an electricity company and a locally well-known electricity expert.

Mrs. Zhang, aged over fifty, still kept a graceful bearing, like a woman of forty, with a light complexion and fine features. From her dress and behavior, she seemed to be obsessed with cleanliness and she turned out to be a physician. Zhang, Yuanyuan looked exactly like her mother, -- like her twin in a younger version. To be exact, she was a copy of her mother, especially her clear eyes and her straight nose.

Zhang, Mingming, on the other hand, looked like his father, tall and slender, with a darker complexion as if his skin had been smoked. He was not typical of a man from Shanghai, but rather had rugged features, which attracted many a girl. He was a third-year student in the International Finance Department of Shanghai International

Studies University. It seemed that the old couple had deliberately planned while conceiving the two children – one resembling one parent, so each parent had his or her favorite. Eventually their wish was granted – the boy, handsome and stylish, looked like the father while the girl, beautiful and graceful, resembled the mother.

Faced with such a happy and harmonious family, Jia and Wu could hardly start their conversation. They looked at each other, with a tacit understanding, but did not dare to speak frankly. The whole atmosphere in the room, like the icicles under the eaves outside, seemed stone solid and repressive with bone-piercing chill.

It was Old Zhang who had to face the reality and break the ice to talk about the subject with gritted teeth, "Any clues to the case? Over ten days have passed since Yuanyuan's death."

"The police are summoning suspects. Please rest assured that the whole thing will come to light pretty soon." Xiaoxian stuttered in Mandarin with a strong Cantonese accent.

"Who would have expected the tragic death of Yuanyuan? …" Mrs. Zhang said only a few words in a husky voice before tears rolled down her cheeks continuously. Someone hearing her talk for the first time would assume that she had been born with a vocal cord problem or that she had undergone a surgery, which had weakened her.

Seeing his wife crying, Old Zhang started talking to himself, "It was really mysterious. At prime time on New Year's Day, Shanghai TV was showing the Air Talk in the new century between Shanghai and Toronto. Yuanyuan's brother, out of curiosity, phoned her, but nobody answered the call. For this reason, her brother was in low spirits for several days, as if they had telepathy."

"I assumed that my sister had gone south for a vacation; however, she had never mentioned it to me. I never imagined that it would be a phone call never to be answered. It's unfair of God! Who would kill my sister? She was such a nice person. I should have studied to be an international criminal policeman…" Zhang, Mingming talked with great grief, which showed his sincere love for his sister. The brother and sister had been on really good terms.

Jia, Feng raised his head and asked Old Zhang, "Did Yuanyuan phone Shanghai quite often? When was the last time she called?"

Nodding, Old Zhang replied, "About once or twice every month. She called on Christmas Eve, quite her usual self, laughing and talking, nothing abnormal. A few days before Christmas, she sent us 500 Canadian dollars for the New Year."

Mrs. Zhang added, "Ever since she left for Japan at the beginning of 1992, she sent us money every year around this time. She was such a dutiful daughter. Actually we have enough money in Shanghai. Every time she sent money, it was as if she wanted to tell us she was safe and doing well abroad, so we felt reassured. All her money, around 4,000 USD, has been deposited in the Bank of China for her."

Wu, Xiaoxian asked, "Did she return to Shanghai in recent years?"

"She returned at the beginning of 1995 when her Grandma was ill. She was in a hurry to leave after 3 weeks' stay because she was running a restaurant with a partner. She planned to come back to Shanghai in June this year for her Grandma's eightieth birthday. Now she is not in this world, but her Grandma has not been told…" She was suddenly choked with sobs.

Jia, Feng, in an attempt to divert her attention, asked, "Did she ever mention her boyfriend? Did she mail you any photos of her boyfriend?"

"Last August she told us she went to Taipei with a student from Taiwan. We guessed that was her boyfriend, but she refused to admit it when her Mom asked her over the phone. We didn't insist. When her Mom asked her about her personal life, she always said she'd like to make money first." Old Zhang replied slowly with a sigh.

With her lip turned up, Xiaoxian asked, "Did she mention her work in Niagara Falls?"

"Oh, at first she worked in a florist shop, then as a waitress in a casino restaurant." Mrs. Zhang blurted out.

Jia, Feng shook his head to hint at Wu not to continue asking questions. It was obvious that they did not know the truth about their daughter who had made up stories to fool her family. Like other "alternative women", she felt ashamed of what she had done and did not want to worry the family, so she kept her mouth shut. She was determined to taste the bitter liquor brewed by herself, and shoulder the responsibility by herself.

Facing Mrs. Zhang, Jia, Feng changed the subject on purpose, "Yuanyuan went to Japan in March 1992. What was her occupation in Shanghai before that? I am the same age as she was."

Sipping tea, she talked slowly, " I hope you won't laugh at us. We were not strict with Yuanyuan, although ours is a high-ranking intellectuals' family. Her Grandma doted on her and spoiled her. She scored average grades in her studies and even failed in physics and chemistry, but she wrote good articles. As a pretty girl, she loved singing and dancing, was a member of a singing group in the city's Children's Palace while in primary school and was a leading actress in her high school's cultural troupe. She was granted several awards. She also guest-starred in two TV series. She did not concentrate on her studies, but was fond of reading famous Chinese and foreign novels and dreamed of becoming an actress or a writer. In 1989 when she finished high school, she applied to art institutes, but failed in the entrance exams for a normal university by just short of ten points. She tried to apply the next year, but her father objected to her pursuing a career in the arts. He advised her to apply to a college to learn some trade and get a job. Finally with the help of my connections, she entered a health school unwillingly to study health care."

Taking a glance at her husband, Mrs. Zhang continued, "She managed to graduate from the health school after two years' study and became a nurse in a municipal hospital, also with the help of my connections. That hospital, with a good working environment, wasn't far from our home, which made both of us feel reassured. At that time we diverted our attention to her brother, hoping he could enter a key university. However, in just two months' time, earth-shaking changes occurred in Yuanyuan's mood, and she even attempted suicide."

Jia interrupted anxiously, "Why on earth did she do that? Could you please tell us in detail if possible?"

Old Zhang went on, "I figured it was at the end of October in 1991 that Yuanyuan suddenly disappeared. The whole family was scared to death and had to report to the police. She was found in 24 hours at the dock of Yan'An Road (East) along the Huangpu River. If the police had been a few minutes later, perhaps she would have jumped into the river. We asked her why and she just kept her mouth shut. Her mother knelt down in front of her before she revealed the truth. It turned out that in her second year at the health school, she dated, behind our backs, a young lecturer of a well-known university, surnamed Chen, from Hubei province. They had been dating for about one year when young Chen went to the US for a Ph.D. degree in computer science before Yuanyuan's graduation. He promised to sponsor her to come to the States in a few months, but he never contacted her. Later Yuanyuan learned by chance that Chen had sponsored his wife to the US. As if awakened from a nightmare, she realized that he had hidden his wife in Wuhan and flirted with her just for fun in Shanghai. She felt cheated and could not accept the reality. Besides, her classmates all thought that her boyfriend was in the States and that she would fly there soon. What a loss of face! That was why she attempted suicide."

Turning to glance at her son, Mrs. Zhang said, "At present I am not afraid of revealing our family disgrace: Yuanyuan once had an abortion because of that man Chen. I discovered this by chance, when I was sorting her clothes after she left for Japan. I found a notebook of hers, which recorded in detail her affair with Chen, including the abortion. I never mentioned this disgraceful event to her, so as not to hurt her. As this was her very first love, she was dealt a heavy blow.

Maybe we should be blamed because we reprimanded her and her father even smacked her for the first time after we found out that she was in love while in Grade Three of Senior High. After that, she kept it secret from us when she fell in love. It was only after that incident that we realized what was wrong."

"Did she still keep in touch with Chen? What's his full name? Where is he now?" asked Wu, Xiaoxian with great interest.

"It seems that he is called Chen, Zhiwei, like 'wisdom' and 'great' in Chinese characters. He must still be in the US, but we haven't his address. Never heard Yuanyuan mention any more contact with him. She hated him bitterly," replied Mrs. Zhang.

Jia talked to himself, "So Yuanyuan's first love was not smooth, -- it was full of tragedy. What a poor soul! Where is her notebook? Is it still in Shanghai?"

"I have brought it here. Maybe it would be of some use to the police." Mrs. Zhang said in a low voice.

Jia nodded continuously, just like Columbus discovering the New Continent. He told himself that he should try to get hold of the notebook as soon as possible.

Old Zhang stood up and poured more tea for them, "Ever since the suicide attempt, Yuanyuan was determined to go abroad to give vent to her anger. At first we rejected the idea of her going alone to Japan. Finally we agreed to let her change environment so as to recover from her terrible mood after the affair. To follow the fad of going to Japan at that time, we pooled enough money for her to apply to a language school and she obtained a visa in just a few months…"

16. The Consulate's Great Concern

"Dong, dong!"

Just as he was talking about pooling money for his daughter to study in Japan, Old Zhang suddenly heard rhythmic knocking on the door. The crisp knocking sounded like the result of good training.

It was no other than two police officers from the Niagara Police

Bureau. Policewoman JoAnna had been in contact with Jia, and Wu before, so they greeted each other by merely waving their hands. JoAnna, with bright and piercing eyes, in black uniform with a leather belt, displayed her slender figure and vigorous posture. Jia had talked in private with Li, Zhihao the photographer several times: why should such a beautiful woman work on the verge of death as a policewoman instead of doing other jobs? If Hollywood discovers her some day, she might be invited to star in a police movie.

The other policeman looked very young, perhaps just graduated from the police school recently. He had never met Wu and Jia, so there was the usual introduction. He was one head taller than JoAnna, like a high mountain or a bodyguard for her. At least he looked like her driver.

With an introduction by Jia, JoAnna exchanged greetings with the Zhang family. Jia was surprised that the Zhang couple spoke fluent English, although with some Shanghai accent. They could communicate quite well. It seems that more and more people from Shanghai speak good English with the reform and opening up policy. Or perhaps it is the glorious tradition left over by colonial Shanghai. Just as some foreigners joked: nobody would lose his way in Shanghai, as everybody on Huaihai Rd or Nanjing Rd can say a few English words.

When Old Zhang asked about the development of the case, JoAnna glanced at the two reporters as if she was afraid of making slips of the tongue to cause trouble before "the kings without crowns". Her facial expression, however, manifested some mystery. Finally she shrugged her shoulders, as if telling them, "No comment."

"Excuse me, is it true that the police haven't had a clue about suspects since my sister passed away over ten days ago?" Zhang, Mingming's fluent American English surprised everybody present. He was worthy of being a student of the well-known International Studies University.

"I am very sorry, but the details of the case can't yet be revealed so as not to alert the criminals. I can only say that it is not as simple as we imagined. It is very complicated and even involves other countries." JoAnna responded quickly.

"We, as family members, only hope that the murderers will soon be arrested and not at large, so they cannot harm other innocent people." Old Zhang seemed to be a bit impetuous.

JoAnna explained calmly, "We policemen fully understand what you think. But this case is really very complicated. Please allow more time and we'll severely punish the criminals and let the dead rest in peace in Heaven…"

Hearing these heart-warming words, the three members of the Zhang family began to calm down. The embarrassing and tense atmosphere eased a little.

As she tried to change the subject, JoAnna turned to Jia and said, "Our great reporter, you are so well-informed that you came before we did."

"As you know, it's no easy job to be a reporter. Just one slip and the good news story slips away." Jia responded swiftly in English.

"Ding-gua-gua, Ding-gua-gua!" JoAnna said in broken Cantonese, lifting her two thumbs.

Jia and Wu barely managed to control their laughter seeing her weird gesture. If it weren't for this tragic situation, they would have split their sides with laughter.

Soon the Education and Overseas Affairs Consuls of the Chinese Consulate General in Toronto arrived at the hotel. Both of them were capable and young, perhaps less than 40 years old. It seems a trend that the staff members sent to the consulate are younger and younger. They had made an extra effort in helping the Zhang family to get here smoothly. The day before, they had gone to the airport to receive them and had arranged for the hotel and dinner late at night.

JoAnna went to meet the consuls and held their hands, "We are grateful to you for your co-operation. Let me express thanks on behalf of the Niagara Police Bureau!"

"That's what we ought to do. Anything else we can do for you? Please call us and we'll do our best." The Overseas Affairs Consul blurted out while handing her his business card.

JoAnna opened her sexy mouth and said, "We'll certainly trouble you again. The case is not as simple as we imagined."

"Please ask Chief Simon to rest assured that we will try our best to co-operate," said the Education Consul.

Old Zhang talked in earnest, "These two consuls are so nice that we'll express our gratitude by writing a letter to the Ministry of Foreign Affairs. They are meticulous and considerate in every detail. They gave Mingming an overcoat for fear of his catching a cold. We got their phone call of condolence while we were in Shanghai…"

The Overseas consul tried to divert the subject, "Uncle Zhang, that's what we should do for Chinese people from overseas. We only hope that the case will be solved soon."

The tall policeman winked at JoAnna after looking at his watch, perhaps to remind her it was getting late.

Jia went up to JoAnna and saluted her mischievously, saying quietly, "Police Chief, can we pursue our news story?"

JoAnna replied humorously in front of Jia's naughty gesture, "If we had known, we wouldn't have braved the snow to come here. You could have given them a ride to Niagara. At most, Simon would treat you to pizza."

"That's different. Your visit shows great attention to this case." Xiaoxian also responded quickly, not to submit to anybody's superiority.

JoAnna lifted her thumb and smiled. Her body language indicated that she thought Asian women were great in flattering others.

The two consuls sent the three members of the Zhangs to the police car, shook hands with JoAnna courteously and were ready to take leave. Old Zhang, sitting in the car, waved again and again to the consuls to express his appreciation.

17. A Journalist's Sacred Mission

The snowflakes, like white lilies, were flirting and dancing wantonly in the sky before they unwillingly fell on the dirty highway, crushed under the huge wheels and turning into messy slush.

Jia, Feng, driving his black Toyota, followed the speeding police car closely to the city of Niagara Falls. Wu, Xiaoxian, sitting beside him, was in low spirits.

"Beauty Wu, why are you so upset at the beginning of the new century? Who made you unhappy?" Jia started a conversation on purpose when he found that she was in bad mood.

"Go to hell! It was Li, Zhihao who started this beauty business. I'll get even with him. Now you are satirical too. Well, why on earth are you so interested in this case? Even Guo, the editor-in-chief, didn't ask us to pursue this news story in heavy snow today. Do you really enjoy Niagara Falls in severe winter?" As expected, Xiaoxian bore some grudge in her heart.

Perplexed, Jia blurted out, "My lady, nobody ever forced you to come. It was you who called me last night. You came voluntarily."

"I was afraid that you would be lonely driving such a long distance. It would be disastrous if there were a traffic accident. I don't want to lose a handsome colleague in the New Year!" she retorted mischievously.

Smiling and grimacing, Jia joked, "So that's why. I have to thank you. Still, you won't find the word 'loneliness' in my dictionary of life."

"OK, I am not your match in talking glibly. You are interested in every detail of Zhang, Yuanyuan's case, as if you'd like to research her whole life, not merely write a news story. Just because she was from the same city and of the same age as you were?" Xiaoxian became serious now.

Jia cleared his throat and said, "So smart of you. I haven't had a chance to tell you that I intend to probe into Zhang, Yuanyuan's tragic life and continue writing her novel 'New Camille' if possible with the permission of her boyfriend Lai, Wenxiong. I'll exert my utmost to present the image of a new Camille at the end of the 20th century, although I can't rival Alexandre Dumas (Jr). As a news correspondent, I seem to have a sense of mission."

"So that's it. You should have told me before. I didn't expect you to be so ambitious. To become a great writer! You are worthy of having been an MA student of Columbia." Wu commended him with appreciation.

"That's nothing strange. Numerous well-known writers were reporters before. Hemingway was once a correspondent for the 'Toronto Star'. So was Xiao, Qian in China, who passed away at the beginning of 1999." Jia replied with perfect assurance as if he would be Hemingway the Second soon.

"No wonder you are so conscientious. Besides writing articles, you have ulterior motives. When you become a great writer, don't forget that I accompanied you." Xiaoxian spoke in a coquettish voice, rarely seen in people from Hong Kong.

"Of course I'll remember you. To tell you the truth, there are only a limited number of overseas Chinese writers, because many people have to make a living and don't have time to write novels. The writers in mainland China, however capable, find it hard to write about immigration. Some come here to survey the situation for a few months, like dragonflies skimming the surface of the water, so they cannot go into something deeply. I stayed in the United States for three years and have been on the forefront of the news world for five years in Canada. I have delved into life and accumulated a great deal of material. As the saying goes: Life is the spring of creativity." Jia became more enthusiastic.

"Not every reporter can become a writer. People like me can only write news stories. You are spectacular: every article of yours displays your literary talent, especially those big feature articles. Otherwise Editor-in-chief Guo would not think so highly of you. You'll surely succeed. Then don't forget to treat me to a great feast." Xiaoxian seemed to stick to "eating", which somewhat embodied the true colors of a person from Hong Kong.

Saluting her with his right hand, Jia replied like reciting acting lines, "I'll surely treat you to a sea food dinner. You just pick the best sea food restaurant in Toronto."

Xiaoxian smiled with lips closed, "Don't give me an empty promise. Unfortunately, Zhang, Yuanyuan's case is getting more and more complicated. If you write about it, the book might turn into a best-seller, popular in China, Hong Kong, and Taiwan."

Jia continued, "It's obvious that we can divide Zhang's life into three parts: her girlhood in Shanghai, her life in Tokyo and her career as a stripper in Canada. At present, we have some rough idea about the third part, but nothing on the first and second parts. My mission is to fill in the blanks with great effort. 'A waterside pavilion gets the moonlight first.' Now that her family members are here, we can get some information about her life in Shanghai. There must be some cause and effect in her turning to prostitution. She would not want to be a streetwalker; neither was she born a prostitute. This didn't happen in one day. Only by carefully examining every track in her life journey can we discern the true causes from all the physiological, environmental or social factors, which led her astray. Hopefully we'll find her enemy from the clues so as to provide the police with more information to crack the case. Frankly, that's the reason why I came especially to pursue the Zhang family in such heavy snow."

"Just now Yuanyuan's mother told us that she had a notebook in her possession. It would be best to get hold of it quickly." Xiaoxian interrupted.

"But they might not be willing to give it to us."

Xiaoxian said confidently, "Rest assured, I'll convince Chief Simon to let us read it first."

"Thank you in advance. We've learned a lot from the two hours' interview just now. At least two key points should be grasped: first, the loss of her first love was a heavy blow to her, which might be an important cause that led her astray; second, she attempted suicide 9 years ago in Shanghai. At present the police have not ruled out the possibility of suicide. Maybe we can study her sub-conscious to find clues to solve the case."

Xiaoxian admired him from the bottom of her heart, nodding continuously. But she insisted that Zhang, Yuanyuan was murdered, either for money, or for love, or by manslaughter. In her opinion, it would require extraordinary will power for a girl to jump into Niagara Falls on a chilly winter night when the temperature was below zero. She herself would not dare to jump even if other people "loaned her ten gallbladders" to add to her courage.

18. Cries of Anguish in the Morgue

The three members of the Zhang family, led by Chief Simon and Police- woman JoAnna, stepped into the Postmortem Center beside the Police Bureau. Jia, Feng and Wu, Xiaoxian followed them closely. They left their cameras in the car, obeying the order of the police not to take photos.

A staff in white was waiting for them at the door in a chilly wind. "The man in white" pulled a long face, perhaps due to his having dealt with the dead for a long time. As a result of this terrible "occupational disease", he had lost his ability to smile or exude even a trace of human warmth. He walked like a robot, without flexibility or facial expression.

They walked through a long, gloomy and winding corridor and passed one small room after another. On each white door was a card of the same format and same blue color, with black words, printed from a computer, of the name, date, and serial number. They knew it was the morgue.

Everybody held his breath and walked quietly, as if the building were a sealed glass ghost house with time bombs everywhere and they would explode if somebody uttered a word. The rhythmic echoes of the light steps, however, seemed even more frightening.

Around a corner, "the man in white" suddenly halted, pulled a key from his waistband and put it in the keyhole without even looking. The icy cold door opened all of a sudden and a nondescript weird smell entered everybody's nostrils – a bit moldy, mixed with a medicinal smell, as if from a freezer. What was even more irritating was the terribly low temperature, which was perhaps necessary to prevent the corpse from decomposing.

"The man in white" turned on the light, so the dark room finally lit up. The room was tiny – a single bed occupied more than half of the space. "The man in white" walked to the bed and skillfully removed the cloth covering the face, which hadn't changed much since the body had been discovered on January 1st. The face, not as swollen before, did not wear any make-up and kept its true colors so as to let her family identify it.

The face of the dead woman was as white as a sheet of paper, with the sunken eyes like two dark holes and the straight nose like an ice sculpture. Her nose seemed to have been broken and reset. Her lips were parted as if she had a lot to tell her family. The bloodstain at the corner of her mouth had disappeared. Her wavy hair was messy and the gold earrings were the only bright spots on her face. Old Zhang went up to have a look and nodded to Chief Simon closely behind him.

"Wa…" Just one glance at her daughter made Mrs. Zhang burst out crying bitterly at once. The resounding crying lingered in the whole building and filled the tiny morgue wave after wave.

She had the urge to lunge forward to hold her daughter's icy-cold hand and to listen to her heartbeats. She called her daughter again and again in her heart: my poor child, why did you go so early and so suddenly? Did you have anything to tell your Mom? Wake up, my dear daughter, don't you kid me! If God needs a life, then take mine instead, for compensation…

Her two hands, tightly grasped by "the man in white", could not move at all, as if by a pair of iron pincers.

"My sister…" Zhang, Mingming suddenly burst out crying and lunged toward the dead body from the other side.

Caught unawares, "the man in white" failed to keep Zhang, Mingming away. Just in the nick of time, Policewoman JoAnna leaped up in a big stride and grasped his hands tightly.

One problem followed another! The tiny morgue was filled with cries of anguish and the whole building seemed about to collapse.

It is with repeated persuasion by Chief Simon, JoAnna, "the man in white" and Jia that the three members of the Zhang family, still yelling desperately, left the room reluctantly.

"The man in white" turned off the light and shut the door quickly and asked Old Zhang to sign the identifying paper. His hand, holding the pen, became weak and feeble. After he signed, tears slipped down his cheeks uncontrollably.

Walking out of the Postmortem Center, Wu, Xiaoxian whispered into Chief Simon's ear for some time. Then she supported Mrs. Zhang with her arm. When they arrived at the meeting room of the Police Bureau, Simon obtained Zhang, Yuanyuan's notebook from her mother and asked the secretary to make a copy right away.

After a brief break, Chief Simon said to the Zhang family, "You must be tired today. You can take a rest in your daughter's former residence and I'll report to you on the details of the case after we bring you here at 10am tomorrow."

Wu thanked Simon again and again when she got the copy of the notebook. Then they followed the police car to Zhang, Yuanyuan's former residence – 100 Lakeshore Building.

Old Bailey, the security guard, was sobbing bitterly when he met the three members of the Zhang family, as if it were his fault that he didn't take good care of Zhang, Yuanyuan. Holding Old Zhang's hand, he stuttered, "Camille was a good girl. It's so tragic. This world is not fair!"

They followed Old Bailey upstairs to Suite 414. The fragrance of camellia still filled the room, but many flowers had withered away and the rest were drying up. Like the person gone, the flowers were fading away. Mrs. Zhang couldn't help crying again.

Policewoman JoAnna told Old Zhang, "For the time being, you can stay here. If you have any problems in the apartment, go to Old Bailey. This is my business card. You can contact me if anything happens. Tomorrow at 10 am I'll come to pick you up to the Police Bureau. As Chief Simon mentioned just now, he'll brief you on the case. Rest assured, we'll exert ourselves to crack the case so your daughter will not have died in vain."

Before leaving, JoAnna told Jia, Feng, "Continue your interview, my great reporter. Please take them sightseeing if you have time. There are several Chinese restaurants in the downtown area."

Mrs. Zhang, entering the bedroom and catching sight of the big life-like portrait of her daughter, she could not help crying her heart out after closing the door.

In an hour or so, everyone persuaded Mrs. Zhang that the living should go on living. She agreed to dine out. Jia, Feng was not familiar with the area and had no way to bypass Niagara Falls, so he just sped up. Probably the family didn't want to tour this world-famous wonderland in the rest of their life.

When Wu and Jia left Niagara Falls, it was already over 8pm. Wu, Xiaoxian was not too tired, but quite excited, holding the copy of Zhang, Yuanyuan's notebook in her hand.

"I am really grateful to you. Without you, we might not have obtained this notebook." Jia, Feng could not calm down either, driving the car swiftly.

Xiaoxian's face lit up and she told him, "Don't thank me; just treat me to a nice dinner when you publish the book."

"It's so pitiful that the Zhang family did not know that the daughter was a prostitute. What will happen when Simon has a showdown tomorrow?" Jia talked to himself.

"It's horrible. While identifying the body this afternoon, the morgue was so gloomy, with a sickening smell. Anyway, I don't want to talk about it. I'll be frightened at night. It's because of you that I'll have a nightmare." She complained and hit him playfully.

"A timely hit, or I'd be too tired to drive the car." Jia joked.

Wu, Xiaoxian became serious, "Is it possible that her former boyfriend Chen, Zhiwei came from the US to see her, but she refused to reconcile with him. After he raped her, the two had an argument and fight during which he killed her. Finally, he placed her body in the trunk of the car, drove to Niagara Falls, pushed her down, then escaped…"

"Excellent! What a good framework for a novel! In my opinion, it's not that simple. Still, we should report to Chief Simon and ask the American police to investigate Chen, Zhiwei."

"Where to find him? Like 'fishing for a needle in the ocean'. So many people have the same name Chen, Zhiwei." Xiaoxian sighed.

Jia responded, "I have confidence in the FBI which is really capable. Wait until I read Zhang, Yuanyuan's girlhood diary tonight."

Chapter Five

"Touching Diary of First Love"

19. Thought-provoking Diary of First Love

The glaring lights of the car, reflected by the snow and matching the stars high in the sky, added brightness to the chilly night and reduced some of the desolation and misery. Jia, Feng drove his black Toyota through the long night from Niagara Falls to the heart of the brightly lit Toronto.

It was already 11pm after he dropped Wu, Xiaoxian at her home and returned to his own residence. Without taking a rest while lying on a couch, he anxiously opened the copy of Zhang, Yuanyuan's notebook and started reading. Just as her mother had mentioned, it was her diary from September 1990 to January 1992, in the form of longer or shorter sketches, like an autobiographical novel, totaling around 40,000 words.

As a man of the same age as Zhang, Yuanyuan, Jia was only too familiar with the Chinese educational system of that era. Starting from elementary school, almost every pupil learned to keep a diary and handed it in to the teacher for correction as a sort of homework. The teacher would make serious comments on the diaries in class. At Senior High, because of the heavy pressure of mathematics, physics and chemistry, the homeroom or language teacher would compromise and ask students to hand in an article every week or every month at least, as "writing practice" or a kind of "ideological report". After graduation from high school, many people still keep the habit of writing in a diary. Some well-known writers admit candidly that they started writing from their diaries. Jia's writing career had started with his diary. His first published article in "Youth Daily" was "A trip to Changfeng Park" in diary form.

Obviously, Zhang's diary was weekly or monthly and written at random. Because she wrote it for her eyes only, it was bold and revealed a lot. All her consciousness or sub-consciousness was exposed vividly in her writing, truly reflecting the heart of a girl born in the 1970s. On Chief Simon's instruction, Jia underlined the key parts with red pen while reading. He might have to translate some key parts into English.

(*Respected readers: Chapter 5 is selected from Zhang, Yuanyuan's girlhood diary, with subtitles by this author. Of course, "I" is Zhang, Yuanyuan herself. The dates are the days when she wrote in her diary.*)

Early in the morning, Sept. 12th 1990

Some say first love is like poems of the Tang dynasty for people to chew and savor repeatedly. Others say first love is like the fresh olive for its delicious aftertaste. For me, first love is more like a thunderstorm in the summer: when it comes, it is non-stop and you can't escape from it even if you have wings.

The chance encounter between Chen, Zhiwei and me was irresistible, just like a shower without any premonition. For several days my mouth retains the taste of his tongue, a sort of manly flavor with a touch of smoky odor. How I covet the typical manly flavor! I have yearned for it for a long, long time.

Last Saturday evening, dragged by Lei, Yaping, I went to her R University to attend a dance sponsored by their young teachers. This is a key university in China, located in the suburbs of the city. Most students are from other places in China and they don't seem to have a good "reputation". To ridicule them, somebody concocted a bit of doggerel: "The male students are like wolves while all female students are very ugly". Maybe it was out of envy for the highly intelligent group.

It is not justifiable to say that Lei, Yaping is "ugly". Except for being exceptionally short, she has regular features and is almost pretty when she's not wearing her disgusting glasses. Upon graduation from high school, most students are around 160 centimeters tall, but she is not even 150 centimeters. After she took a lot of imported pills to increase her height, it was said, she reached 150 centimeters: her height increased by just 1 cm. She was my best friend in high school and helped me, especially in coaching me individually in mathematics.

This type of university ball is usually held in the students' dining room. A pretty girl like me seldom attends this kind of ball. I'd go to the dance hall of the Shanghai Ballet School or the Shanghai Beijing Opera Troupe. I am grateful to my parents who elaborately "made me", with a pretty face and full-grown breasts and hips. In the second year of Senior High, I was aware of my well-developed breasts and round buttocks, the pride of women. Besides, I am a really good dancer, trained at the Children's Palace while very young. I also attended a special crash course for ballroom dance in the Municipal Cultural Palace while studying at the health school and "enjoying life wildly" after school. I can dance skillfully. It's not that I think highly of myself. Shanghai is a place for cultivating new-trend beauties and it has nurtured a lot of big stars, such as Hu, Die; Ruan, Lingyu; Zhou, Xuan; Qin, Yi; Xie, Fang and Chen, Chong.

In the name of "A ball for welcoming the new students", it was in fact a forum for bachelor teachers to find girlfriends or for middle-aged teachers to find mistresses with whom to have illicit affairs. The dining–room-turned-into-dance-hall, although simple and crude, was quite spacious, with the capacity of holding over five hundred people, among them some handsome men and pretty girls from other schools, like me.

With a waltz on the sound system, people were dancing haphazardly under the dim lights. It was a simple slow three-step dance, but almost half of the couples were out of step. Some men were hugging their partners closely; some were simply kissing, while others were placing their hands on the women's buttocks, massaging them along with the music. I was reluctant to join in such a vulgar and crazy dance, so I chatted with Lei, Yaping and didn't go near the dance floor.

After a while, ear-pleasing tango music arose, but not a soul dared to dance. Perhaps they were scared by its complexity. The noisy dance hall suddenly quieted down. Just at that moment, a tall man wearing glasses dashed towards us, as if in a hurry to catch a plane. He greeted Lei, Yaping briefly in Mandarin and invited me to dance at once.

"He is the youngest lecturer in our department, named Chen, Zhiwei. He dances quite well." Seeing my reluctance, Lei, Yaping whispered to me quickly in her Shanghai dialect.

Her last sentence impelled me to stand up lazily. I wanted to see how well this "bumpkin" could dance. For many years, people in Shanghai have established the rule that all non-Shanghai-dialect speakers are called "bumpkins", be they from Beijing or Guangdong.

He looked serious and a bit nervous when he stepped onto the dance floor, as if he were shouldering the duty of participating in an international competition. Along with the rhythmic tune, his movements turned agile and his face beamed. I quickly followed him. The basic steps, the progressive side steps, and open promenade were all properly danced to the tune. He danced to his heart's content with me along an imagined circle. We dovetailed flawlessly while he was advancing and I was retreating. I enjoyed myself to the utmost with those more sophisticated steps such as the backward promenade, the sandwich, spirals and tapping. I felt as if I were floating on air, fully satisfied, following his sharp, precise and elegant steps.

Amid applause and whistles, he courteously escorted me back to my seat. I was just then aware of the fact that only the two of us remained dancing on the dance floor. Within a few minutes, I reversed my evaluation of this "bumpkin". Even a man born in Shanghai would not have danced the tango so expertly. This Chen, Zhiwei danced exceptionally well, -- he was comparable to professional dancers. He seemed to have received special training, because it is not easy to dance the tango well with a partner for the first time.

"You didn't come in vain, right? He danced so agilely and gracefully!" Lei, Yaping whispered in my ear.

Stealing a glance at the people sitting next to us, I shook my full-length pink skirt to hide my inner excitement and whispered to Lei, "It was worthy of my beautiful skirt."

It was a miracle to meet such a super dancer at a school ball. I regretted not having worn my prettiest skirt. Along with the non-stop music, Chen, Zhiwei invited me again and again to dance the rumba, cha cha, quick-step, etc. It was a pleasure to dance with him, thanks to his adept and elegant steps. I felt I was "dancing wearing feathers in rainbow colors and listening to celestial melodies everywhere".

What's more praiseworthy was that he always escorted me courteously back to my seat like a gentleman, unlike those who casually dropped their dancing partners anywhere they pleased. My vigilance against strangers was dissolved by his perfectly graceful dancing skills and his impression on me was growing more favorable. In order not to hurt Yaping's feelings, he invited her to dance two waltzes as a consolation.

He was strangely reticent, however, and said fewer than ten sentences to me during the two-hour dance, just answering my questions. Perhaps it was because he could not speak the Shanghai dialect and he was afraid that I would despise him for that. Perhaps he was pretending to be cool. I've seen a lot of hypocrites who do that.

When the ball was approaching the end, the lights on the dance floor suddenly dimmed and a huge candle burned at each corner. Although this was an imitation of other balls, it added a touch of romantic sentiment. Several hundred people caused a commotion on the dance floor, -- they dashed to invite their partners to dance. Anyone who was a bit slow couldn't find a pretty girl. The beautiful girls attracted more men. This was the high point of the ball, the finale of several hours of dance. Some people came to the dance just for this charming moment.

When the gentle music of slow four steps arose, the dancing partners hugged each other closely. They looked like passionate lovers, dancing face-to-face sentimentally. Under such intoxicating circumstances, I couldn't help falling into Chen, Zhiwei's embrace and letting his face touch mine.

"You are the most beautiful girl here tonight," he suddenly whispered into my ear.

"Do you have anything else to say?" I blurted out unkindly, sickened at such stereotyped flattery.

Just at this instant, he dragged me to the center of the dance floor. People around us were embracing. All of a sudden, he held me closely and kissed my lips madly. Before I had fully responded, his tongue was already twirling in my mouth.

My poor tongue, sometimes docile while licked, sometimes resistant, roused his beastly passion. We licked until our saliva spilled and then dried out.

If it weren't for the sudden halt of the music and the turning-on of the lights, we might still be kissing until we knelt down on the floor with weakened feet. Under the lights, I felt my face and body burning like a fire.

"All speech is superfluous." He escorted me to my seat and handed me his business card.

I never expected to start my first love with this baffling mad kiss. This tiny business card was my only matchmaker.

20. First Kiss – while still Wet behind the Ears
Late at night, September 25th 1990

To be precise, Chen, Zhiwei was not the first man who kissed me. My first kiss was given to my classmate Mao, Changyao in Grade Three of Senior High. I don't know why he was one year older than all of us and taller than the other male students. He was an outstanding student and is now studying at a well-known university in Beijing.

Probably because we were still wet behind the ears, my kiss with Mao, Changyao was only a light touch of our lips, like two petals, parting quickly. We did it stealthily and in a hurry for fear of being discovered. After that I even asked the silly question: "Would I get pregnant?" which made him split his sides with laughter.

He may have forgotten about me, but I will never forget him. In my not-too-heavy book of memory, his name will not be easily deleted. He was, after all, the first handsome boy I loved in secret in my girlhood. During the first semester in Senior Grade One, I began to like him after watching him play basketball skillfully.

To be fair, nobody was to blame for the end of our puppy love and it might be a lucky thing, at least for Mao, Changyao, who lived up to everybody's expectations and was accepted by a famous university.

It was those classmates who tried to curry favor with our homeroom teacher Mr. Ouyang and reported to him little things about us, plus some made-up stories. It was said that Mao and I went to see movies at the "Peace Cinema" hand in hand; that we went to the "Gujin Bra Store" together; that we ate French cake shoulder to shoulder at the "Laodachang Bakery" or that we kissed each other often.

That afternoon after school, Mr. Ouyang, looking serious, asked me to come to his office. Because he liked to be with girls and was sometimes a sissy, he was nicknamed "Sissy" behind his back by us girls. First he asked me to do homework in his office, then we returned to the classroom after it was cleaned up and he locked the door.

After sitting down, "Sissy" said candidly, "Zhang, Yuanyuan, you might have guessed why I asked you to stay behind."

I shook my head, pretending to be nonchalant.

Pulling a long face, he said, "Someone told me that you and Mao, Changyao are dating. Is that correct?"

Seeing me lowering my head, he continued, "Tell me, to what degree are you together?"

Growing impatient at my reticence, he stood up and talked to me with his face close to my eyes, "You even kissed secretly – in Xiangyang Park."

How did he know such details? My heart was beating fast. It was terrible that people might be shadowing us. It was worse than the Cultural Revolution. It seemed that I would not be able to get through the ordeal without saying anything, so I replied with my head lowered, "I swear to Heaven that it was our very first time – our lips just touched."

"Who took the initiative?" he sat down and asked as if he were interrogating a criminal.

"Both of us," I blurted out.

"Love in harmony and resonance," he said sarcastically.

He stood up again with his big mouth close to my ear and looked at my eyes lustily. "Did he touch you? The upper body or the lower body?"

I suddenly felt sick at his words. I recalled an article in a youth magazine, which stated that some people lived on prying into others' private lives. They feel happier if they know more details about lovemaking, about every step in a rape, etc. It seemed that "Sissy" belonged to this category.

"Did he put his hand under your dress?" He raised his hand while uttering a *lewd laugh before I replied.*

This kind of bastard was a peeper who would like to see me naked. I stood up, with knitted brows and gritted teeth, and yelled, "Nothing happened! That's the truth. What on earth do you want to do?"

He became subdued and returned to his seat when he saw me flying into a rage, his normally pale face turning a liverish color. He stammered, "Zhang, Yuanyuan, your teacher is doing this for your own good. Everybody knows that you are the prettiest girl in the school. I am afraid that somebody might take advantage of you... It's good that nobody touched you. It's good."

I thought this incident would blow over, but the sickening "Sissy" told my mother the whole story three days later. One evening at the dinner table my mother let it slip out that I was dating a boy. My stern father, frowning, immediately questioned her closely and my mother had to retell the story.

His face turning purple, my father flew into a fit of temper and scolded her for concealing such important information. I talked back, out of instinctive self-defense. He suddenly threw away his bowl and slapped my face. My Grandma stood up at once to fight with him. My younger brother, nine years my junior, was sitting there puzzled and dared not move at all. My mother also pulled a long face and started to engage in a battle of words with him. This was the only quarrel between my parents that I had ever witnessed. I have always been their favorite and my father never scolded me, let alone hit me, so I burst out crying, feeling wronged. Our whole home was in a mess...

With Mother's repeated persuasion, I promised to cut the knot and break off all contact with Mao, Changyao. After school that day, I found him and told him what my parents thought. He looked in pain and helpless. He stressed again and again that he liked me sincerely and dating would not have any negative impact on our studies... Later he didn't even say goodbye to me when he left Shanghai for Beijing. Maybe he still bore a grudge against me for my "wilfulness".

21. Distorted Senior High School Life
Afternoon, Oct.2nd, 1990

Mao, Changyao would never know that it was against my will to separate from him resolutely at that time. In the three years of Senior High school, he was the only "boy" in my spiritual life. In my numerous rosy dreams, he was my only Prince Charming. In my countless secret masturbations, it was his cool face and natural demeanor that appeared in my mind. After my father boxed my ears, my mother set the rule that I was not allowed to date during school years.

In retrospect, I realize that it was not only this early dating that caused me great misery. My senior high school years also made me unhappy. Although ours is an ordinary school, it has quite a long history and about ten of its graduates each year have the honor of entering well-known universities. That's why there is so much peer pressure among the students. Eventually twelve students, out of over five hundred graduates in my grade, were accepted by key universities all over China, which broke the record in the 40-year history of the school.

It is no exaggeration to say that the normal human nature of a girl was distorted by the heavy burden of study. The innocence and naivety during elementary and junior high schools totally vanish in senior high school. As early as in my elementary school, I was a choir member in the Municipal Children's Palace. I had several guest appearances on TV and entertained numerous foreign guests. It gave great pleasure to my family, especially my lovely Grandma, who would tell everybody that her granddaughter was an actress. Ever since then, I have cherished the dream of becoming an actress. At present, some of my old companions have become famous actors. They are lucky. But they might have forgotten me.

During my junior high school years, I was always the backbone of the art and cultural team. I wrote scripts, directed plays and guest-starred in TV serials. To enhance my literary level, I secretly read a great number of literary classics, both Chinese and foreign, whether I understood them or not. I read every issue of the major periodicals "Harvest", "Shanghai Literature" and "Bud". Since one of my poems was published in "Youth Newspaper" and I got RMB 10 Yuan for royalties, I have begun my dream of becoming a writer. I write something every week for practice.

Once I entered senior high school, however, I was besieged by the competitiveness for entering a university. All my dreams of becoming an actress or a writer were shattered. The competition among classmates was ruthless. What our parents instilled into our minds was that if another student got higher scores, it meant that you had one more opponent and your career would be threatened. Homework piled up and could not be completed until early dawn. My father persuaded me to stop guest appearances in TV serials. Such competition encouraged selfishness and individualism as opposed to collectivism. "Lei, Feng"(a selfless hero) turned into a mere historical name, mostly forgotten by us.

It was extraordinary that Lei, Yaping would take her precious time to coach me in mathematics amid such deadly competition. I was grateful to her and my mother often invited her to dinner at weekends as a sort of compensation. Lei, Yaping said that she liked to be with me for some inexplicable reason. She loved the kind of "intellectual scholarliness" in our home, maybe because she was born into an ordinary working class family and she yearned for a high-ranking intellectual family atmosphere. Usually children of poorer families mature sooner. Lei, Yaping was sensible and intelligent, so my mother predicted that she would grow up to be somebody important. It was reassuring to see me together with her.

Lei, Yaping hoped that I could enter an art university smoothly so my acting talent would not be wasted. Finally, however, because I was ten marks short, I failed my cultural exam and was not accepted even by the Music Department of a Normal College. Lei was as upset for me as if she herself had failed. I was so upset that I couldn't enjoy meals or fall asleep. I still bear a grudge against the kind of educational system in which one exam determines a person's life and I may hate it for life. Many talented young people cannot enter universities because they are a few marks short. Perhaps that is fairness for all. But if my parents were high-ranking officials, my fate might be entirely different. I might be sitting in a university classroom even with 20 marks short, let alone 10.

With my mother's meticulous arrangement, I entered a district health care school, against my will, to study health care after I graduated from senior high school. To tell the truth, I know only too well what a doctor is, as I've grown up in a doctor's family. In my mother's eye, nobody is hygienic, so we have to wash our hands all the time. When we got really sick or even ran a high fever, she acted as if nothing had happened and told us we'd recover after taking medication. I suspect that medicine is a sort of unemotional profession. Luckily my father seldom gets sick; otherwise their relationship might be affected.

The Health School is a middle-level special school for training nurses for district and area hospitals. My father insisted that, unwilling as I was, I should learn a trade so as to earn a living in this competitive city. The Health School is close to my home, so I can still live at home. Lei, Yaping has moved to her university dorm. She is a typical bookworm, -- Madame Curie is her idol. Besides, the only big room in her home has been occupied by her brother as the wedding chamber, so their home is very crowded. She seldom comes home and naturally we have very little opportunity to meet each other now.

22. Temptation from a Peasant's Son
Midnight, Nov. 5th, 1990

It's an irrefutable fact that more and more Shanghai men have become "sissies". They enjoy "shopping, washing and cooking", so they are nicknamed "Sister-in-Law Ma" (The pronunciation of this name is homonymous to "shopping, washing & cooking" in the Shanghai dialect – Translator's note). Sha, Yexin, a famous writer, published a play entitled "Looking for Manly Men" a long time ago. Regrettably, manly men are in short supply. No wonder Shanghai is a city where female culture has developed exceedingly, with women of different eras composing various tones with their screams.

In comparison, a peasant's son like Chen, Zhiwei posed an irresistible and greater temptation to me. A pretty girl from Shanghai like me prefers a dark and rugged man from other parts of China to a pale and intellectual man from Shanghai-- just like Mao, Changyao, whom I loved in secret in Senior High School, -- a tall dark-skinned man, maybe from Shangdong province.

My first chance encounter with Chen, Zhiwei was at the ball of R University at the beginning of September. His mad kiss on the dance floor aroused in me a romantic dream. At the over 200 balls I have attended, I have never met such a bold man. The others only teased me implicitly, or took advantage of me by hugging me closely, or invited me out for a cup of coffee or dim sum. In my health school, all 30 students are female, so I seldom meet boys. It's a normal physiological and psychological response for me to yearn for contact with a man. However, those I meet at other balls are mostly playboys, whom I look down upon, so I limit my dealings with them to dancing and drinking coffee. Chen, Zhiwei, on the other hand, is a man with cultural education. His little indecent behavior was quite refreshing to me.

After a mental struggle for over three weeks, I decided to unravel the mystery of this "cultural rascal". I took the initiative to phone him for dancing, but he gently rejected, saying that he was busy preparing for a TOEFL test at the end of October and then, he suavely asked for my home phone number. Only God knows whether his excuse about the test was true or if he was putting on airs purposely. These days more people are taking the TOEFL (Test of English as a Foreign Language) than those who are lining up at the vegetable markets. If not, the "Forward March Foreign Languages College" would not have done so much business and set up one branch after another. In Shanghai, there is a foreign language school on almost every street and all university students and some high school students are itching to take the test. It's known all over China and the world that people in Shanghai worship foreign things and toady to foreign powers. The great number of people taking the TOEFL test indicates that.

The more he put on airs, the more mysterious he seemed to me. Every day when I got home from school, I asked Grandma eagerly if somebody had called me, which made her a bit nervous. Just when I was disappointed waiting for his call, he phoned me yesterday, making me ecstatic. He invited me to a municipal ballroom dance competition – it's said the application fee alone was RMB 200 Yuan. I was as elated as if I had been the first Chinese to win a Nobel Prize for literature.

It so happened that I had no class that afternoon, so I went directly to the "Violet Hair Salon" for a special hairdo. I searched my wardrobe at home and found a fiery-red full-length dress low cut in the back with a golden hem. I looked like an elegant princess ready to be married, with a pair of high-heeled dancing shoes of similar color, my black and brilliant hair, and tall and graceful figure. At 3pm a taxi drove me directly to the location for the competition: "The Great World".

Unexpectedly, Chen, Zhiwei, was standing at the gate waiting for me in a swallow-tailed coat, just like an English gentleman. His glasses had disappeared, obviously replaced by contact lenses. He looked more handsome and flamboyant than on the night when I first saw him, only his skin was dark-- exactly the color I liked. We danced the waltz, tango and rumba according to the competition rules. In the final competition by personal choice, we danced the tango only, our forte. Eventually we won second place, with a cash reward of RMB 2,000 Yuan.

That night, the first three awards winners were invited to "The Red House" by the organizers for a typical German dinner.

After we left "the Red House", Chen, Zhiwei proposed to escort me home, which fit in exactly with my wishes. We slowly turned left from Shenxi Rd. (S) and sauntered on to Central Huaihai Rd. Our windbreakers made our shadows on the ground exceptionally long. This street, nicknamed "Oriental Champs Elysees", both prosperous and quiet, has been renovated in recent years to display its old charm. However, I concentrated on listening to his voice instead of enjoying the flashing neon lights or the superb variety of goods on display in shop windows. It seems that his eloquence is by no means inferior to his dancing skills. His standard Mandarin, with rhythm and cadence in tone, mixed occasionally with a few words in an awkward Shanghai dialect: this made me split my sides with laughter and I almost hit a passer-by.

It was this walk on an autumn night that gave me more information about him. He is nine years older than I, and both of us were born in June, -- what a coincidence! He was born into a peasants' family in Hubei Province. He did farm work and took care of his three younger siblings, who now work in commune-run enterprises. He was accepted into an ordinary university in Wuhan, studying mathematics. As he was the second university student in his village in the past 40 years, he had achieved glory for his clan. His parents were willing to spend their life-long savings for his university education. On the day he left home, all the villagers came to see him off, just as if they were welcoming government leaders for inspection. When he recalled the scene, he still relished this fond memory.

During the four years' study in Wuhan, he was awarded a first-class scholarship every year and worked after school as a teacher for children at their homes. Every month, he remitted money to his home in the countryside. What he could show off was that he had revised a theorem of a mathematic authority in Romania when he was in Grade 4: this caused quite a stir in the academic field. With his professors' recommendation, he easily entered the Computer Sciences Department of the well-known R University in Shanghai for a master's degree. After three years, he graduated with excellent marks and became a teacher at R University. Thanks to several of his theses' being published in world famous journals, an exception was made and he was promoted to lecturer in just half a year. At the age of 26, he was the youngest lecturer in his department and the second youngest in the whole university; thus, he became a man in the focus of the news media. Last month, his department submitted documents promoting him to be an associate professor to the Higher-ranking Academic Title Evaluation Committee of the university. But he was not interested in this title, -- he wanted to further his studies in the United States.

At first, he tried to get sent abroad by the government, but he found that he had to wait for a long time as a lot of teachers were lining up and most of them had already achieved the title of associate professor. He decided to try going abroad on his own, so he secretly took the TOEFL test and prepared for the GRE as well.

It was incredible to me, who yearned for university life, to listen to his story, which was like "The Arabian Nights". A son of three-generations of peasants, he studied while doing farm work, progressed from Wuhan to Shanghai and now planned to study in the United States at MIT (Massachusetts Institute of Technology). I worshiped him from the bottom of my heart before we got to my home. To tell the truth, my heart was absolutely captured by him. He was not a "cultural rascal", but a young man with high aspirations, a man worthy of my trust, a "Prince Charming" I had dreamed about… Whatever he wanted of me, I would willingly offer to him.

It was a pity that things went against my wishes. Normally it takes an hour to walk from "The Red House" to my home. I had him make a detour, so it took two solid hours. During the whole time, he kept his two hands in his pockets, with no intention to touch me. We just walked shoulder to shoulder and chatted, as if the mad kiss at the ball that night had never happened. Before our departure from each other, I gazed at him expectantly, begging him to kiss me again madly, from head to toe and from outside to inside.

He did not respond except to touch my shoulder slightly and whisper to me, "I'll call you after I complete my thesis. Tonight, all the lights on Huaihai Rd are lit especially for you."

With whole-hearted disappointment and perplexity in my mind, I didn't really understand his last sentence. Reluctantly, I watched him disappear quickly into the darkness…

Another sleepless night began for a poor Shanghai girl, without end, without orientation.

23. Going Crazy for you, my Darling, on Christmas Eve
Late at night, Dec. 26, 1990

All the roses in the world come into full bloom for me alone.

All the bottles of champagne on the globe are opened for me.

Although I'm still suffering from agonizing leftover pain and I'm clueless after my ecstasy, I would like to invite all my friends, old and new, to enjoy the pleasing melody "To Alice" played by me, with the charming roses in full bloom and the cups of champagne raised. I want to celebrate with you the coming-of-age of a pretty 19-year-old girl in Shanghai. She has become a woman overnight.

The Prince Charming who took my virginity was no other than Chen, Zhiwei, the young man I met at the ball at R University three months ago. It is incredible that a decent girl from Shanghai, the apple of her intellectual parents' eyes, a fair lady who grows up in a house with a garden, playing the piano and a high school campus belle would offer her precious virginity to a "bumpkin".

There are things in the world that can't be explained by logic or inference. In the realm of relationships between men and women, all theory seems pale and feeble and everything is destined. I have no regrets since I believe in fate. Just follow the course of nature and love will come in due course. The natural is the most beautiful and, beauty, as well as love, is embedded in nature.

Last night I had my third meeting with Chen, Zhiwei since I met him over three months ago. This was one and a half months after our second meeting. Although I couldn't fall asleep during the long nights for love-sickness, I was determined not to call him first because of my pride as a Shanghai lady and my anger for feeling wronged. My bottom line was that if he didn't phone me before Christmas, I would never want to see him again in this life. I was overjoyed to receive his call four days ago after I had been waiting impatiently for so long. He invited me to a dance at T University on Christmas Eve and I agreed more than eagerly.

T University is a well-known school, renowned for its beautiful campus, which is not far from R University. The ball is located next to the magnificent Building for Specialists, in a building, which is not huge, but exquisitely decorated, like a cute professional dance hall. Perhaps too many tickets had been sold, so the small dance hall was overcrowded with several hundred people, who were sitting shoulder to shoulder in a circle. Some people near the door were standing. The noise caused by the throng of people was deafening, but the lively atmosphere was permeated with Christmas festivity.

Chen, Zhiwei seemed very excited when he greeted me at the station, and rather light-hearted, as if treading on air, entirely different from the reserved man I had met previously. It was as if he had some good news to announce to the whole world. He praised me non-stop about my avant-garde and appropriate make-up and dressing – my red hair, my big earrings and leather jacket, I guess. He lauded me as the most beautiful lady in the whole city of Shanghai, as if he were a bit drunk. The "crazier" he got, the more airs I put on, looking standoffish, just to see what was up the sleeve of this "bumpkin".

After a round of waltz and disco, the atmosphere on the dance floor became lively. The tango music pushed the ball to the first climax. Like a proud princess, I followed him arrogantly to the dance floor and was responding to the touching melody, guided by his agile steps. This reminded me of balls at the end of the eighteenth century where Spanish lasses, decorated with roses, danced elegantly. It also brought to my memory the madness of our first encounter.

When the music stopped, he beamed with excitement and laughed constantly, as if his joy would jump out of his heart. I was perplexed by his non-stop praise of my dancing. I couldn't help but ask him what made him so happy; and if he need to consult a doctor for his "laughing disease". After my repeated inquiries, he finally revealed a piece of extraordinarily good news – he received the result of his TOEFL test yesterday: 630 marks.

No wonder he was so "crazy". It's no easy matter for people to get over 600 marks on the TOEFL – they belong to a group with a high IQ. Since he got such a high mark on his very first test, he was among the "cream of the elite". It seemed that it would be a possibility (and not just a dream) for him to enter a renowned university in the USA as he had also published several theses both at home and abroad. It proved, as well, that he hadn't lied to me – he really was preparing for TOEFL test. My suspicions totally vanished at that moment. What women hate most is to be cheated, and Shanghai women are not easily cheated.

At that time, the classic music "Rock Around the Clock" started. I dashed to the center of the dance floor with Chen, Zhiwei and we danced a crazy disco by swinging our four limbs strongly among the swaying crowd. Swing and sway with all our might, to seek the long lost balance. Revel to the feeling of the 1930s, to write a sequel to "Shanghai Foxtrot" by Mu, Shiying and a sequel to "Gossip" by Zhang, Ailing...

In the middle of the ball, Chen, Zhiwei suddenly grasped my hand and said, "Yuanyuan, I want to have a glass of wine."

"That's easy. Let's find a bar somewhere. My treat, to celebrate 630 marks." I looked at my watch, and it was 9 sharp.

"How about going to my University? The bachelors are having a dinner party tonight in the teachers' dorm."

"No problem. Let's go. I have to return home early so my father won't lose his temper."

It was the first time I had gone to the bachelor teachers' dorm in R University. Although he warned me about the building on the way, I was still sickened and ill at ease by the mixed smells of smoking and running shoes when I stepped into that 4-storeyed building. The corridor was pitch black with no lights on the landing. The whole environment was much worse than I had imagined.

Following him, I groped in the dark and we came to a room at the end of the third floor. As soon as I entered the room, a gentle fragrance greeted me. The room was spic and span, with two beds, two desks, two big bookcases and a guitar on the wall. I guess all the messy stuff had been hidden in the closet. There was a world of difference between this room and the outside surroundings, which shocked me.

Just when I felt puzzled, he explained with a smile, "It was not me, but my roommate, who keeps the room clean. He's also from Shanghai, a bit sissy and obsessed with cleanliness."

"Where is he now?" I'd like to meet this man from Shanghai, who "emerges unstained from the filth, like a lotus flower."

"He's gone home to Shanghai, with his family for the festivals, of course." He took off his coat while talking and hinted for me to do the same.

"Didn't you tell me that there is a dinner party?"

"Yes, just the two of us." He quickly got a bottle of wine from under the desk

and placed a bouquet of fiery red roses on the table. He filled two glasses from the bookshelf with red wine.

"Where are the dishes?"

"An attractive lady is a feast to the eye! Beauty and wine are quite enough."

After drinking some wine, he lit a candle, turned on the stereo and turned off the lights. I didn't know that the "bumpkin" was so romantic.

"It seems that you planned everything beforehand..."

Before I finished the sentence, his tongue was already in my mouth. I stretched my tongue unflinchingly and started a "life and death" battle with his tongue—I went forward, he retreated; he charged forward, I defended. When I felt hot all over, he skillfully undressed me and laid me on the bed. Then he raised the cup and poured wine slowly all over my body, like an old gardener watering the flowers, not missing any petal or leaf. Next, he knelt down at the bed, naked, and sucked the wine on my body, from my neck to my chest, from my belly to my legs and feet, not missing an inch. Then his sensitive tongue lingered meticulously for a long time on my breasts and the "bushy area", as if he were drunk or spellbound. I lay motionless, like a trained sleeping beauty, letting him massage my body up and down, at will.

When I felt a bit itchy with his lickings and each of my cells caught fire, the waltz from the stereo halted and familiar rock and roll music sounded. With the swift and strong rhythm, his supple body climbed quickly onto mine. I felt as if there were a warm comforter all over me, quite relaxed, but a bit out of breath. I couldn't help moaning lightly, with my body vacant and open, waiting to be filled. Suddenly I shivered all over and screamed myself hoarse after his powerful thrusts. Despite the great pain, I allowed him to push in and expand until he did it with skill and ease to fill my void. After a soul-stirring moment, he led me in dancing a swinging disco along with the rock and roll music. The dance steps seemed to be the extension of those steps on the dance floor previously, but more formidable, even reaching a peak... Only a single bed with a width of over a meter and the remaining candle witnessed the skillful dance.

After a long time on cloud nine, we landed finally. I lay in his soft arms feebly, my heart still pounding. He sat up, lit a cigarette of the "Red Pagoda Mount" brand and smoked. I snatched his cigarette and smoked with all my might before

I calmed down.

"I didn't expect that it was your very first time." He talked coolly to himself while massaging my shoulder.

"Aren't you lucky? I'm the last virgin in Shanghai!" I replied wittily.

"Then a bumpkin like me just came here to conquer the last virgin. It's worth the trip." He was perfectly content.

He hugged me again and whispered to me, "Rest assured – I'll be responsible for you."

I was so grateful to him for his simple and honest announcement that tears came to my eyes. He tried to console me as if I were a three-year-old child while holding my shoulders with his hands. Then he licked dry my tears with his tongue.

He was still perspiring on my chest, so I said jokingly, "How come you are still sweating? We're not dancing."

"A peasant always sweats even when at rest." He became unexpectedly humorous.

24. Request for Abortion with a Solemn Pledge of Love
Afternoon, May 15th, 1991

Ever since that overwhelmingly joyous "first night" over Christmas, Chen, Zhiwei and I stepped into a crazy "love season". As a girl who just started to be moistened by male dew, I could hardly stop it.

I am always yearning to meet him and dance, with our bodies, to the heart's content, to fill each void in our minds and bodies as well. In the fiery flames, we shout again and again: carnal desire is not a sin; it's the gift of Adam and Eve and the sincere worship of life.

While alone, I resemble a joyous bird, bouncing when walking and singing popular songs non-stop, as if I were the only woman possessing a man and all others are pitiably lonely people. In the Health School, my classmates and I are pretty crazy and we often crack sexy jokes among good friends. In the recent months I have become more aggravated and my buddies say I have become more beautiful and flirtatious. My self-satisfaction has brought me to cloud nine and I felt as if I were really "Miss Shanghai".

I could be unrestrained in the outside world, but at home I have to control myself and listen to my parents' instructions. I should strictly abide by the "family rules" as a filial daughter, so my father would not fly into a rage. Last time just because I dyed my hair red, my father said that I was being unreasonable, looking neither like a human nor a ghost. He argued with my mother several times for this, and the "war flame" was finally put out by Grandma's repeated intervention. My parents don't understand that I have grown up into an adult. In their eye, I might forever be a little girl. They don't know that their daughter is a "woman" in its real sense. They might be caught unawares when they are upgraded to be grandparents.

Since I became a sensible child, I have had the impression that my father was living in the last century. Although he has made investigation in several foreign countries, he is still a conservative engineer, like an antique, studying science and technology, dealing with icy-cold machines every day and becoming a man of icy-cold character. In my mother's opinion, my father was warm inside but cold outside. But I don't think so. Of course, my mother knows best. Relatively speaking, my mother, an experienced and knowledgeable doctor, is much more open-minded. She is familiar with the new terms in Shanghai, even some hot slangy expressions. As she was born into a well-to-do intellectual family and her parents were trend-followers in Suzhou, she naturally loves to follow the fashion as their only daughter. I have inherited my mother's gene in this respect. As the saying goes, "the pupil surpasses the master", I am more avant-garde and open-minded than my mother.

Every Sunday I become excited as if I were a newlywed woman returning home. After I get up early in the morning, I rush to "Harbin Food Store" to buy Chen, Zhiwei's favorites: cream cake, hot dog, dried beef, etc. and jump onto Streetcar #26, then transfer to other two buses for the teacher's dorm in R University. Sometimes, just for the sake of meeting my man a bit earlier, I would spend dozens of dollars by calling a taxi. That room, crude looking outside and clean inside, has become our "wedding chamber". Strange to say, I am no longer sickened by the smells of this building. I even feel that the stink smell is a special manly smell. Without it for three days, I can't eat or sleep well. According to the unique interpretation of Chen, Zhiwei, it is sort of "love me, love my dog." To tell the truth, as I am his woman, I am brave enough to sleep with him even if he stayed in a tomb with bones of the dead.

We spend the whole Sunday, for about ten hours, on the single bed with a width of over a meter. His roommate stays at home from Saturday evening to Monday morning, so we enjoy our full freedom during this period of time. As we don't meet each other every day, we always try to make up the lost time for our sexual enjoyment, with one like a sadist and the other a masochist. As the saying goes: A newlywed couple enjoys more after a brief separation. We have the same experience. Lovemaking is the only long homework we can do. As if he were marking university students' complicated papers, he leaves all kinds of signs on my body, from head to toe, some lighter and some heavier, sometimes slowly and sometimes quickly, with exclamation marks or big stamps on sexually sensitive parts.

When exhausted, we shut our eyes and rest for some time. After we wake up, we continue the game, until I am too weak to talk and almost dehydrated, and until this peasant has no sweat left and he surrenders. Then we lazily get up, have a casual dinner in a restaurant and then he sends me to the station. Sometimes he would call a taxi, handing the driver dozens of dollars and kissing me good-bye reluctantly…

However, as unpredictable as the weather, I got pregnant after three months' wanton revelry. As a student in the health care department, I have been very cautious and always asked him to wear a condom. The only exception was at a secret meeting in Hongkou Park. That night we lay on the soft lawn, inhaling the fresh air of early spring, gazing at the star-studded sky and envisioning the future American dream. He had received confirmed acceptance from three renowned American universities, only the amount of scholarship was not ascertained. He promised to sponsor me to the USA after he goes there to lay a foundation first… Unknowingly, he inserted his hand under my dress and skillfully brought it to the peaks. Suddenly I felt feeble and itchy all over, with a strong desire to be trampled upon. But I didn't have a condom with me. I thought I would be "safe" as it was three days after my period. So we did it without a condom in a dark and quiet corner, enjoying indescribable ecstasy, like carrying on a clandestine love affair. It was our first love making in the open air of Mother Nature and we enjoyed it fully. Who would have expected that the seed had been sowed at that time? It proves that "safe period is not safe".

When I showed him the test result, he was trembling with fear, with cold sweat dripping from his nose. After he pulled himself together, he hugged me tightly and kissed me slowly, sitting on bed, and dried my tears from my face. Then he patiently comforted me for a long time.

Finally he pledged his promise, "Rest assured, I'll be responsible for you for life. I have been determined to do so ever since you gave me your first night. However, you cannot get married as a student and your parents would not agree. Better get an abortion. I'll have to study diligently when I first get to the States, as competition would be a lot more fierce than at home. If I don't obtain scholarship, how can I continue with my studies? All those are top-notch universities with highest tuition. Even when you go abroad to accompany me, you would not have the energy to take care of a baby. You are still young, you can give birth to many kids in the future..."

Seeing not much response from me, he even knelt down before me. He raised his head and gazed at the sky, then talked to himself with his right fist raised and eyes shut, "Almighty God, be my witness, please. A peasant's son will not tell a lie: I swear that I'll marry Zhang, Yuanyuan. If I tell a lie, I'd be struck by thunder and lightning and come to a horrible death..."

I couldn't bear to see his pitiable yet pious expression, so I exerted my utmost to place him onto the bed.

"It's not manly to act like that. I've come here to consult with you. I don't request of you anything, nor would I go to your department to make a fuss, which may impact your career. This is a matter between you and me. I only want you to be nice to me. That's all. I'll be content." He was moved to tears by my simple words and stared at my eyes.

Faced with his begging expression in his eyes, finally I agreed to have an abortion as soon as possible. No sooner had I finished these words than he burst out crying like a baby. As the saying goes: a true man seldom cries. He is such an unyielding man at that. His tears made me trust him again for his sincerity.

In a month, that was the day before yesterday, I went to a district hospital for the abortion, accompanied by Chen, Zhiwei. It was through "the back door" by his old friend who studied in a medical school that they didn't check any marriage *certificate. In Shanghai, everything is done through "the back door", from visiting somebody who gives birth to a baby to cremation arrangement in a funeral home, from kids going to a famous kindergarten to children going to key high schools or universities. Countless people are crowded at "the back door" in all walks of life. Hospitals are places that connect closely with people's livelihood – giving birth, growing old, getting sick, or dying, so "the back door" is a must. That's why doctors are especially popular. For this, I have personal experience. My mother took home lots of gifts, which, she told me, were given to her by her colleagues. Actually her patients gave her the gifts. In recent years, they give cash instead of presents. Usually they place cash in envelopes and secretly insert into doctor's hands while talking, seeing nobody is looking around. At first we attempted to give an envelope with money to the doctor doing abortion, but his friend said it was not necessary, as he and the doctor are on very good terms. However, we owe his friend a debt of gratitude.*

Abortion is a very simple surgery and takes only a little over ten minutes. I studied about it in my textbook. However, I was still very nervous and shivering a lot while I was on the surgery bed, my heart filled with an unbearable sense of guilt. Who would have expected that a pretty girl in Shanghai bore a tiny life in her womb so early and departed with it so soon …

The words of the doctor with a huge mask before the surgery made me chew for a long time, "Have you made up your mind? You can still change mind. It's so important for a woman to give birth to the first baby and you are such a pretty girl at that."

25. The City with Recovered Carnal Desire
Late at night, June 10th, 1991

After the abortion I feel feeble, but I don't dare show any trace of my weakness at home. It is hard for me, a carefree person, to restrain myself. Chen, Zhiwei phones me every afternoon to show concern for me, but he lives too far from me – distant water won't put out a fire close at hand, so to speak. The only remedy that can temporarily relieve the pain in my heart is piano playing. Every afternoon after school, I play the piano for several hours until my parents return home from work. Luckily, my shape hasn't been altered; otherwise, any change would not escape my mother's sharp eye.

It was strange that my good friend Song, Lei eventually discerned the delicate change in my body's internal system and in my mind. She was the first friend I met when I entered the Health School. She is about my height, not very pretty, but modern-looking with meticulous make-up and sexy clothes. She is fond of drinking and smoking, showing an avant-garde trend. I learned dancing from her and she taught me smoking. I mentioned my relationship with Chen, Zhiwei quietly to her. On our way home after school this afternoon, she suddenly grasped my hand and dragged me to the "Hokkaido Bar" across the street after turning two corners. I thought something extraordinary had happened and she might need my help.

She waved to the waiters and flirted with them. Obviously she often patronizes that bar. A man in a formal suit walked over after we were seated. He gently patted her on the shoulder and lit a salon menthol cigarette for her while making eyes at her.

She blew a puff of smoke at him and pointed at me, "I haven't introduced her to you: this is my good classmate Yuanyuan."

The man stretched his hand to me, smiling, "a nice name, a nice name. Yuanyuan and Fangfang are popular names nowadays. Last time Leilei brought a friend named Fangfang, right?"

His words made everybody laugh heartily and enlivened the atmosphere. He at once lit a salon menthol cigarette for me. Apparently he was a shrewd businessman. It turned out that he's the boss of this bar. Song, Lei called him "Old K," a man who made a lot of money after working in Japan for some time.

Old K's eyes were fixed on me, with lewd looks, as if he were attempting to recall lost memory from my face or to find a way to make more money.

"Isn't Yuanyuan pretty? Your eyes look like those of a dead fish." Song, Lei sneered at him.

"She is the prettiest guest ever since I opened the business a year ago. O.K. Everything is free for the beauty today. Please order anything you like." Old K looked bold and generous, as if Li, Jiacheng, a millionaire, were his father.

"Not only is she pretty, she is also a virgin. You are interested, aren't you? Females from 3 to 80 years old are all to your liking!" Song, Lei became more exhilarated.

Old K also burst out laughing and said slowly, "Leilei, I can hardly bear what you said… O.K. If you beauties often patronize my bar, my business will be more prosperous. Enjoy your drink. I have other guests to attend to."

When fragrant coffee came, Song, Lei asked me bluntly, "You look gloomy recently. Didn't that bumpkin, that poor lecturer, take advantage of you?"

"No, we are still on the same terms, not too hot, not too cold." I replied perfunctorily.

"Yuanyuan, you can't hide the truth from me. You must have been in bed with him, just look at your pink face and raised hips, so sexy a few months ago, as if semen would spill out while walking. You might have had surgery…"

Hearing her words, I was on tenterhooks, so I kept my mouth shut and lowered my head. Then I took a deep breath to cover up my uneasiness. Perhaps, she thought I acquiesced.

She smoked and puffed out some black smoke, and then she started talking in a low voice, "It's normal to sleep with a man. Semen is the most nutritious stuff in the world. To tell you the truth, I lost my virginity when I was studying in Grade Two, Senior High. He was 13 years older than I, engaged in foreign trade. Last year he immigrated to Argentina and we separated. I had two abortions for him, at a cost of RMB 10,000 yuan each time. Not a single man is good. I had to extort money from him. Don't let chances slip away."

No wonder people say Shanghai women are "piggy banks". Song, Lei, a "shrewd and sharp woman", is just such a case in point. Relative to her, I seem a bit foolish. In the past half a year while dating Chen, Zhiwei, I spent more money than he did. He spent his money on preparing for going abroad. What attracted me in my heart was not his money, but something loftier than money, including my American dream. While I was pondering on those things, Song, Lei started to blabber again.

"At present I am involved with an American 'devil', whom I got to know at 'the English Speaking Corner' in the People's Park. He speaks fluent Chinese. He came to Shanghai to further his studies in Chinese acupuncture."

"So you have a connection with the world already. I really admire you, Leilei."

"What are you talking about? Don't be like a bookworm. The present Shanghai and the old Shanghai of the thirties are worlds apart, as the older folks

tell me." She raised her sexy lips to show that she was not convinced.

We can only read in novels or see movies about the old Shanghai, without knowing whether it is real or not. Our generation has nothing to compare it with. I don't want to live in the past. I would rather pay more attention to the present and look forward to the future. That's mainly why I selected the "bumpkin". At present, Chen, Zhiwei is a poor teacher, almost penniless, but his future is bright and hard to estimate. The United States is full of opportunities everywhere, especially for a man who knows how to study and enjoy life.

Song, Lei interrupted my train of thought by talking seriously, "Yuanyuan, actually I admire you, such a charming beauty. How many foreigners could you attract? Maybe they'd line up along the whole Huaihai Road. To be more objective, foreigners come to Shanghai to do business in the first place, but they also come for the Shanghai ladies. Shanghai women have to seize the opportunity, either by going abroad to be played with or by staying in Shanghai to play with foreigners. It makes my mouth water to talk about foreign men. They are tall and strong and well proportioned."

Talking about the body structure of men, she was much more serious than she is in class. Like an authoritative expert, she talked about how big and strong a foreign devil's body was and how comfortable she was with it. She also enjoyed new varieties of sex, such as oral and anal sex. She said she liked to ride on a man to have control and let him insert the deepest and enjoy the freedom. She also tried having sex in water to seek a stimulus of floating and sinking alternatively…She talked while making gestures vividly, like an old lewd woman, without any sense of shame.

Song, Lei has always been avant-garde, but I never imagined that she is so experienced in sex and is capable of compiling "Song's Sex Records". I admire her from the bottom of my heart. My secret and a little romantic affair is nothing compared with hers.

26. A Unique Departure
Evening, July 15th, 1991

I was sitting in the classroom absent-minded this afternoon, looking at my wristwatch constantly. My whole body and mind were trembling along with the second hand of the watch. I failed to answer the teacher's questions twice. At 10:30 am I held my breath subconsciously and raised my head to glance out of the window. A sense of loss arose by itself.

Just at that instant, my beloved Chen, Zhiwei was boarding an American North West Airlines flight and flying into the sky for his continuing education in the USA. He was not simply going abroad to study like many others from Shanghai. He was spectacular in that he would be entering MIT for a Ph.D. degree in computer engineering with a full scholarship. This has rarely happened in the history of over half a century at R University. That was why the university and department leaders paid special attention and gave him a special send-off. Although they knew people of extraordinary ability would not come back to the university, they still had to put on a show.

Originally I planned to see him off at the Hongqiao Airport, but he was worried that I might embarrass him by showing too much feeling for him in front of his superiors and professors. I agreed reluctantly. My send-off for him was moved up to yesterday. According to our arrangement a few weeks before, his last day in Shanghai would be spent with me quietly in our "wedding chamber" and we wouldn't even go out for dinner. He said he wanted to seize every second to enjoy fully the warmth and tenderness of a Shanghai lady.

For over half a year, I have realized more and more that sex is as essential, or sometimes more important, as eating and sleeping. For instance, once I suffered from a headache and felt uncomfortable all over, as if doomsday were approaching. This condition continued for two days and my mother's medication didn't help either. I had to go to "my man" and "dance" in bed to our hearts' content. I perspired profusely, all the acupuncture points were wide open, and all my pain was gone. With a good appetite, I ate a lot. He jokingly called this treatment the "magic cure". The same thing happened twice and the "magic cure" was really effective. That is what western doctors call "the imbalance of endocrine" or what Chinese doctors call "the imbalance of yin and yang", I guess. No wonder people say that a healthy sex life is conducive to longevity and beneficial to the female voice.

For women, sex is particularly important, because it is closely connected with feelings. It is not merely carnal enjoyment – women's carnal desire is, to a great extent, controlled by their feelings, while their feelings are tainted by carnal desire. If a woman does not accept a man in her heart and does not like him, she will absolutely not go to bed with him, unless she is a whore or a spy or has some ulterior motive.

Early yesterday morning, I went to school meticulously made-up. After one class, I stealthily left school. At the street corner, I hailed a taxi to take me to the teachers' dorm at R University and arrived at 11 am. I hurried to the third floor and knocked on the door. No response. Why wasn't he there? It was he who had decided on the time. Utterly puzzled, I pushed hard on the door. It suddenly opened with three fiery red roses dropping from it. I screamed with fright while he appeared from behind the door, put his arms around my waist and inserted his tongue quickly into my mouth. Then he took me to his bed, tore off my clothes rudely, like a wolf, and thrust into my body like a fierce beast. I adjusted all my nerve systems to catch up with his tempo and enjoyed the overwhelming "ecstasy".

After making mad love for some time, I felt as if I were awakening from a dream. Opening my eyes, I discovered a table of delicious dishes, all the favorite foods I love in the summer, such as chicken wings with distiller's grains, liquored crabs, cold cucumber, jellyfish, deep-fried shrimps, duck gizzard and two bottles of red wine from France. It turned out that he had ordered takeout from a nearby restaurant and just returned home ten minutes before my arrival. It was the first time I discovered that he was so meticulous and considerate. I was naturally grateful to him.

"We'll make it 'bottoms up' today," he said while opening the bottle.

"I'll follow suit until I get drunk." I held my fists together like an ancient Chinese.

"Do what you say." He handed me a cup of wine.

Two of us, naked, raised our cups, which clinked with a crisp sound.

"Wishing you a safe trip!"

"Wishing us an early reunion!"

He swallowed the whole cup of wine, and I finished half a cup to be on a par with him. He was holding me while I lay on his lap, feeding him while tasting the food myself, so he could do more important and interesting things with his hands. He was busy massaging me, sometimes in straight lines, sometimes going zigzag, or stopping to express his occasional amazement. Sometimes he lowered his head and used his agile tongue to lick, suck and absorb until I threw away my chopsticks, screaming flirtatiously. Then he climbed onto my body.

As usual, after love making, I lay in his arms and compared my skin color to his. My complexion is pale, that goes without saying, while his skin is close to bronze-colored, if not black. He is like my father. I like dark-skinned men, perhaps due to my family heredity. My mother's skin is pale and tender, like a juicy peach, although she is over forty. She is obviously a well-bred girl from the southern part of China. My father, in contrast, has black skin, as if filtered by smoke. He was born in Yinchuan, came with his parents to Shanghai, which he doesn't like very much but has never left. Although he is a veteran Shanghai man, he is typically manly thanks to his upbringing in the northwest. My paternal grandma told me that my mother married him because his dark skin was to her liking. But my maternal grandparents thought otherwise. I once secretly asked my mother why she married such a dark-skinned man. My mother attempted to avoid answering me. But she finally revealed to me: your father is healthy with the dark skin, exceptionally healthy. I searched my memory and recalled my father only suffered from a cold once. This proved what my mother said.

I secretly guessed that there must be something behind what she said as mother knew the human body so well, being a doctor. Now I have realized my mother's choice when she was young – just look at dark-skinned Chen, Zhiwei, who has inexhaustible energy and has performed so well. There is a striking contrast between a black man and a white girl, which arouses more excitement. Moreover, some foreign psychologists' research studies point out that black people's sexual desire is stronger than that of the white or yellow races. Is there any internal connection between the skin colors within the yellow race and sexual desire?

In three hours, the two bottles of red wine had been consumed and the two of us, holding each other, got drunk and fell fast asleep.

It was after 10pm when I opened my sleepy eyes, so I woke him up. He seemed to be still in a dream, with his eyes wide open. He touched my lower body and talked as in sleep, "My wife, I'd like you to wear a chastity lock."

"Go to the US and rest assured. You are my only man."

He suddenly burst into tears, "Yuanyuan, I'll get you to the US as soon as I arrive there."

"No hurry. You should concentrate on your studies first. When you have time to spare, write me more letters."

I handed him a cute photo album and an envelope with three hundred US dollars in it, which I had exchanged from all my savings at a black money market in front of the Overseas Chinese Store.

"I'll take the photo album, but not the money. How can I use your money? Am I a man?"

"What's the difference? Didn't you say I am your wife? I know you have only around two hundred US dollars. Just in case nobody comes to greet you at the airport. You have to carry some cash."

With my repeated persuasion, he finally accepted the three hundred US dollars. He was so touched and grateful that he burst out crying and tears rolled down my cheeks as well. In an instant, the two of us hugged each other, crying bitterly. This was crying for our departure since we don't know when we'll meet again. We tried to console each other, like "Ah Q", that departure was the beginning of another meeting.

("Ah Q" is the main character in Lu Xun's "the True Story of Ah Q". He is a victim of social injustice who seeks consolation in interpreting his defeats as moral victories. – Translator's note)

He held three roses with one hand and held mine in the other and sent me to the gate of the university. He called a taxi in the street and we kissed goodbye. I reluctantly got into the taxi and he handed me the three roses. The driver impatiently stepped on the accelerator and the car flew away.

"Why three roses?" I yelled while lowering the taxi window and waving the flowers.

"I—love—you!" He raised his hand high and stretched three fingers. His resounding voice pierced the night sky.

27. Rejection of the Mother River
Late at night, November 6th, 1991

The Huangpu River is the Mother River of the metropolitan City of Shanghai, and the river in the heart of every son and daughter of Shanghai. As I have grown up drinking the water of the Huangpu River, I have a special sentiment for her. The Huangpu River also takes good care of each of her children, based on mutual deep feeling, unless the child commits an unforgivable crime or can't redress a wrong.

A week ago, I wandered along the Huangpu River on the Bund for a solid 24 hours, in a mood of sorrows like that of young Werther in Goethe's writing. My dream of going to the United States to accompany Chen in his study was completely crushed overnight by a shameless lie. How would my good friend in high school Lei, Yaping, my good sister Song, Lei and other friends look upon me? They all knew that I had a boyfriend who had gone to study in the US and that I would soon leave for that place which is full of opportunities. I could discern the disdainful looks, which would turn into piercing arrows aiming at my body, now a mass of bruises. What broke my heart and gave me the most pain was that Chen, Zhiwei had taken advantage of an innocent girl's sincere feeling. A Shanghai woman, considering herself smart, was dallied with by a "bumpkin", and landed herself in a pitiable and miserable condition. It seemed better to shut one's eyes and jump boldly into the Huangpu River to end all trouble and misery.

The wind on the waterfront late at night was chilly. I walked along the river embankment, from the Waterfront Bridge to Yan'An Rd (S.) in the South, back and forth again and again the distance of about five kilometers between the two places. I sat on the ground when I felt too tired, then started wandering again. The sound of waves against the embankment mixed with the sirens of ships and added to my depression and disturbance. The scores of stretching international buildings, which used to look like crystal palaces, resembled black holes at present. The Gothic pinnacles looked like the tongues of wild monsters, while the Baroque pillars resembled vipers, springing on me with threatening gestures and deafening sneers. The sneers seemed to remind me: you are so young and pretty, your young life has just started, is it worthwhile to die for a "bumpkin"? Young woman, raise your head bravely. Tomorrow will be better.

Facing the river, I was torn with the conflicting ideas of jumping into the river or not. I spent almost a day and a night in this painful contemplation. I flipped a coin. If the side of the national emblem was up, I would not jump. I gambled several times and the side of the emblem was always up. Maybe it was my destiny not to jump. Just at that time, two local patrolling cops suddenly stopped me at the docks of Yan'An Rd (E.). They told me they had followed me the whole night after they had received a phone call from a passerby. After their interrogation, they found that I was the very person the police were looking for. Apparently my family had reported me to the police as a missing person.

As soon as my parents met me, they held me in their arms and cried bitterly as if we had been separated from each other for years. With my father's patient advice and my mother's request while kneeling down, I eventually revealed the despicable behavior of Chen, Zhiwei. However, I didn't tell them about the abortion, a secret I would keep for myself alone.

I waited for his letter every day after Chen left Shanghai on July 15th. No letters in two weeks, three weeks, then a month. Was he sick or had something bad happened to him? I was in a terrible plight, unable to savor food or fall asleep and depended on sleeping pills. He promised me, on the night before his departure, that he would write to me on the day he arrived in Boston. I made several inquiries at the post office and was told that it took only ten days for a letter to come by air, or three weeks at most.

At the beginning of September, I became a nurse in a high-class ward in a nearby municipal hospital, with my mother's help through the "back door". The job was not tiring, but I couldn't concentrate on it. I felt dizzy every day, with the image of Chen, Zhiwei in my mind all the time. Within the two weeks, the old head nurse flared up at me three times. Luckily she knew that the Deputy Principal was my mother's classmate; otherwise, she would have fired me for sure.

I could not stand it any longer when there was still no news at the end of September. I went to Lei, Yapping in R University for some information. She knew something about our close relationship, but never suspected that we were so intimate. As a typical bookworm, she was preparing for the TOEFL test, attempting to go to the United States before graduation to avoid future trouble, such as paying a training fee, etc.

Lei, Yaping was also puzzled by the fact that I hadn't received a letter from Chen. She thought I should have received one long ago. After our consultation, we had a good idea — to ask his instructor in the department when he was studying for his Ph.D. We heard that he was on good terms with his "boss". I still don't *know today why those post-graduates like to call their instructor "boss". Maybe they learned this from westerners.*

In three days, Lei, Yaping learned that Chen's instructor was the well-known Prof. Cai. Unfortunately, he had gone to an international seminar and would not return to Shanghai until the end of October. Hearing this news, I cried my eyes out, as it was the last straw. Lei contacted two of his classmates and they hadn't received letters from him either. It seemed that I had to wait for Prof. Cai's return.

On the third day after Prof. Cai's return, one of Chen's classmates secretly told Lei, Yaping that Chen's wife had arrived in Boston from Wuhan a week before to accompany him in his study. Prof. Cai had a phone call in Vancouver from Chen's wife. When Lei told me these words, I insisted that his classmate was too old and had a bad memory – he must have made a mistake.

The next day, Lei, Yaping accompanied me to visit Prof. Cai, who unwittingly confirmed what the classmate had said after I made my intention clear. It turned out that Chen, Zhiwei's wife was the daughter of his professor at university. It was this professor who had recommended that he apply for the renowned university in Shanghai. Prof. Cai even doubted that his good student would cheat girls…

It was not enough to describe my feeling as "extremely heart-broken". Why had I been so foolish? He didn't allow me to see him off at the airport; never let me meet his boss; returned to his hometown alone; never dined with me in restaurants close to his university; never introduced me to his friends… All these were carefully planned, foreshadowing his later deception.

I, a Shanghai woman, considering myself smart, was cheated and dallied with at his will. After he went abroad, I remained true to him. What a silly woman with a low IQ! Not a second one could be found in this huge city. No wonder philosophers say that women in love are the most stupid of all.

28. Far away from the Heart-breaking City
Late at night, Jan. 15th, 1992

After two months' struggle of hovering between life and death, I decided to leave this heart-breaking city as soon as I can. Although this is the place where I was born and brought up, I can't give vent to my anger if I don't go abroad. It would be best if I could go to the United States to settle accounts with that bastard

Chen, Zhiwei, cut off his private part and hang it in his wife's room as a specimen for her to worship. If I had money, I would hire a professional killer to cut him to pieces, not just shoot him.

Until now, I didn't realize why he had exerted himself to learn dancing: he did it to conquer the women in Shanghai. He said that he could only dance the simplest three slow steps when he first came to Shanghai. At a ball sponsored by the students' union, he invited five girls to dance and none accepted his invitation because of his "bumpkin" appearance. The sixth girl danced with him, but he accidentally stepped on her foot while turning. She pulled a long face, flung up her hand and verbally abused him in a loud voice, "You bumpkin, don't come if you can't dance!" She left at once, leaving him behind, embarrassed. Stripped of manly dignity, he just attempted to hide himself in a hole. Since then, he had made up his mind to learn dancing and to keep up appearances meticulously in order to conquer the arrogant and beautiful women of Shanghai... I never expected that I had become his plaything and a victim for his revenge on other Shanghai women.

During this period of time, Song, Lei offered a lot of consolation to me. We often went to the "Hokkaido Bar" and got familiar with Old K. Although I knew that Song, Lei was wild and even smoked marijuana, I needed her kind of craziness and abnormal stimulus at that time. Only by being around her could I forget temporarily Chen, Zhiwei, that heartless man. Only by airing my grievances could I keep my internal balance.

When Song, Lei and I were leaving the "Hokkaido Bar" late one night, suddenly two middle-aged strangers came in. They seemed familiar with Old K and talked with him merrily. The fatter one of them even said hello to Song, Lei, who told me in a whisper that these two businessmen from Taiwan were very rich. She decided to stay there and fleece them. With curiosity, I waited to see what would happen.

Just as she had expected, the two businessmen came over to talk to us – that seemed to be their motive. After they were seated, the fat one held Song, Lei's shoulder intimately and asked her to order anything she liked, on him. The thinner one sat seriously beside me and talked in non-standard Shanghai dialect about Shanghai dishes with me. We could not eat much, so we ordered a cocktail each. They ordered the house special Japanese Combo and talked with us while eating awkwardly. Song, Lei followed the fat man, after he put down his chopsticks, to a room upstairs where people had secret affairs under dim lights.

Song, Lei once mentioned to me that there was a comfortable "washroom" on the second floor, with a big couch for people to enjoy themselves. Old K charged RMB 200 Yuan for an hour per couple as a fee for the space. I saw that Song, Lei had gone upstairs so flirtatiously. I assumed that she must have gone to that "washroom". While I was thinking, the businessman beside me suddenly praised me for my beauty again and again. I asked bluntly what he wanted and he frankly stretched out his palm. I didn't understand what he meant, so he explained that he would give me RMB 500 Yuan for an hour, just to touch and massage me. I shook my head and he stretched out two palms. I still shook my head.

"How much do you want? You bid. A higher price if you go to a hotel." He looked a bit angry.

Old K came to intervene, "Boss Chen, this girl is a virgin. Don't be angry. Be patient."

"A virgin? Are there any virgins left in Shanghai? Let's bet. If she were a virgin, I'll pay her 100,000 Yuan…" He turned aggressive.

After Chen, Zhiwei deserted me, I became very sensitive to the word "virgin". Whoever mentioned this in front of me would anger me. With a girl's innocence I had offered my precious "first night", but I had been cheated by a "bumpkin" and had landed myself in a sorry situation… Boss Chen, you are out of luck if you happen to make me angry.

I stood up and yelled myself hoarse, "Go to hell! It's none of your business who I am! Go to your mother if you want a woman!"

I swaggered off at once before Old K and Boss Chen responded…

A few days later, Huang, Hong, one of my classmates in high school returned home from Shenzhen to Shanghai and invited me to the Longbai Hotel in the west suburbs. She had followed her brother to Shenzhen after her graduation from high school and it's said she is doing quite well.

I was surprised to see her fashionable and sexy dress, while her blond hair and the huge earrings made her pretty sophisticated. With a cigarette between her lips, she looked worlds away from her old simpler self.

I asked how she was faring in Shenzhen and she told me frankly that she worked as a secretary in a Hong Kong enterprise and as a mistress as well. The boss, aged over forty, paid for her accommodation and living expenses. Every month he came from Hong Kong to Shenzhen and spent two nights with her. Apart from monthly salary, the boss gave her 5,000 Hong Kong dollars as pocket money.

She puffed and said, "A lot of us in Shenzhen are called 'the second wife'. I am pretty lucky, as I spend only two nights with him. Some other women have to be with the men the whole week, without any freedom."

"Please pardon me, but what's the difference between you and a prostitute?" I was perplexed.

"It's the same in essence. But each man has his own rules. Some don't allow their second wife to have any contact with other men, and for that they have to pay a higher price. My boss doesn't permit me to bring any man to my residence. Apart from that, there aren't many other restrictions."

"So Shenzhen is like that?!" I couldn't help commenting.

"My great beauty, Shanghai is too conservative. There is nothing to be ashamed of. We get paid for our capability. Youth is our very capital… A wealthy businessman would choose you for your beauty. Just in a few days, people would come to see you. Maybe a young millionaire would marry you." She tried patiently to convince me.

She lit another cigarette and continued, "I followed my boss to Shanghai for a meeting for ordering goods. He has gone to the meeting. I'll try to make more money, then I'll go abroad to do business."

Finally she tried to persuade me to pursue success together in Shenzhen with her. I was a bit shocked. For me to be a "second wife"? I am not that degraded! But I didn't refuse her either, just to reserve a route of retreat, a way to escape.

After I returned home, I attempted to fish for my family members' opinions. When my father heard that I had a liking for Shenzhen, he immediately told me that no city in China would suit a person from Shanghai, except a foreign country. Shenzhen could hardly rid itself of the image of a small fishing village in terms of culture. He said that once Shanghai is developed, it will recover its old brilliance and will be on a par with New York, London and Paris, because it has a strong industrial foundation, flourishing culture and a favorable geographic location…I had to give up the idea of going to Shenzhen, faced with so many reasons.

After my mother found out that I smoked, she couldn't bear to see me getting more dispirited day by day. To help me get out of the shadow of being jilted and to start a new life, and for fear of my going to Shenzhen, she eventually agreed for me to apply to study in Japan. Actually I'll just register for a language school and then try to make money by working. My father didn't like the idea at first, because Japan reminded him of "the Nanking Massacre", which had left him psychologically traumatized. Finally he acquiesced to my mother's earnest and patient persuasion and grandma's repeated requests. Mother immediately pooled money and asked a former neighbor to register me in a language school.

Chen, Zhiwei, you heartless man, I'll eventually find you and kill you! I don't have your ability, so I'll just go abroad first. Someday, I'll find you in the US. Just wait and see!

Chapter Six

An American Playboy Summoned by the Police

29. An American Playboy Summoned

According to the decision made on the evening of Jan. 11th by "the Special investigation group for No.1 female corpse", David, the general manager of 3P Auto Company in Buffalo in the US was summoned. Originally, he was supposed to come at 11 am on the 13th, but unexpectedly he swaggered in at 10 am, saying that he had to attend a board meeting across the river that afternoon. Who knows what was up his sleeve? Just then, the three members of the Zhang family arrived as well. The plan was that Chief Simon would inform them of the detailed development of the case. Now he was caught unprepared and had to ask two other group members to read the documents to the Zhangs.

Chief Simon was surprised to find this Mr. David, nicknamed "playboy," was very courteous, even a bit obsequious and very co-operative. It was not their first meeting, -- they had contacted him for some other cases. Like his millionaire father, he was tall, had a straight nose and looked arrogant, as if he were the general manager of the whole world and everything revolved around him. This time, however, he did not put on any airs of importance, which astonished Simon. Simon realized that at least he was paying special attention to this case or he was on pretty good terms with the dead woman. Besides, he must have realized that the police had some information about his relationship with the victim. It was important for him to prove his innocence, to avoid being regarded as a suspect.

Sitting down, David took the initiative to tell Simon, "I learned about Camille's death yesterday afternoon, from Arvid, your ex-City Councilor. What a shame! Such an Oriental Venus just fell from the sky like that! How tragic… I came back to Buffalo from my Caribbean vacation in the afternoon the day before yesterday."

"When did you start your vacation?" Simon asked casually.

"Oh, let me think. It was at noon on December 27th, a Wednesday." David replied calmly.

Simon nodded. Out of professional habit, he first judged the possibility of committing the crime based on the time frame. Zhang, Yuanyuan passed away at 5am on the early morning of the 29th, while David had left Canada two days before. It seemed that he could not possibly be the murderer, unless he had hired somebody to kill her.

To cover up his rashness in asking the question, Simon said smiling, "Of course not. You were sunbathing on a beach at that time. Which lady went with you this time?"

"A French lady, from Quebec, a secretary at the American lawyers' office across the street. If you want her address, I'll give it to you now."

"Are you worried that I might entice your beautiful French lady? When I was at police school, I was nicknamed 'the wolf', you know…" Simon burst out laughing.

"You are so humorous, Chief! Nobody can compete with you in all Canada. At present, I am not in the mood to talk about women." David turned serious.

JoAnna, the policewoman, took advantage of the opportunity to suggest with a smile, "Would you please tell us in as much detail as possible how you got acquainted with Zhang, Yuanyuan."

David cleared his voice and talked in a kind and informal manner, "It was around the beginning of October 1999 -- I don't remember the exact date-- that I encountered her at the Niagara Casino. That night I was playing 21 in the VIP room on the third floor and lost over $9,000 in about one hour. I was worried: there was cold sweat all over me. I raised my head to look at the gambling banker, getting ready to push myself to struggle again. Just then, I saw a beautiful Asian lady sitting across from me, in a low-cut black dress, her long wavy hair properly hanging over her shoulders and her eyes sparkling. She looked both innocent and sexy. To tell you the truth, I grew up among pretty women and I'm called a playboy, but I have never met such a charming Asian lady. I cast a sidelong glance at her and she smiled with closed lips, and then walked toward me lightly, like a warm spring breeze. We nodded to each other. Strange to say, once she stood beside me, my gambling luck turned for the better and I won around $7,000 within an hour. She was still standing beside me, without saying a word, but always smiling. I won again and again, totaling $15,000 when I left the table at 3am."

David sipped coffee and went on, "She was simply a goddess of luck to me. Naturally I had to express my gratitude to her and invited her for a drink. When we were entering the bar, City Councilor Arvid happened to be leaving. I am an old friend of the wolf, so I greeted him. I didn't know that Camille and Arvid were old acquaintances, even on intimate terms. We three sat down for drinks and Arvid took the chance to introduce her to me, saying that she was not only shockingly pretty, but also smart, kind-hearted and broad-minded, meticulous in everything she did. He mentioned that she possessed every quality a good woman should have, as if he was eagerly promoting a new product for a company. Of course, he also lauded me to the skies, revealed my identity and told her that my father was a big share-holder in the casino. Arvid took leave after drinking a Manhattan. I drank another Manhattan and Camille had a Bloody Mary. Before leaving, I gave her $1,000 as a reward for bringing me good luck and handed her my business card. She gave me her cell phone number."

"Then you became good friends, didn't you?" Simon interrupted eagerly.

David nodded and went on, "Yes. About a week later, I dated her in the casino. She played "Baccarat" with me and I won over $7,000. That night, I invited her to dinner at the Hilton where I stayed, and she readily agreed. Then she followed me upstairs. That night I was thoroughly intoxicated. I never imagined that the Chinese lady was so charming, with exceptionally silky skin, so genteel and considerate. To tell you the truth, her tender affection was no less than that of a western lady... Soon I fell desperately in love with her."

Simon cut in, "That was when you presented her with a 328iBMW car, right?"

"Yes. At around the end of October. She used to drive a very old Nissan that had engine problems and needed repair. I asked her to throw it away. I took her to a car dealer and she chose the red BMW at the first glance. In fact, there were a lot of famous cars, but she didn't choose the most expensive car. She chose the least expensive one, unlike my previous girlfriends. From this I realized that she didn't want to extort money form me. Besides, she never asked me for cash, but I willingly gave her $2,000 to $3,000 for pocket money. She was out of a job at that time, perhaps attending an English class in a community college. I have a residence across the river. Usually I came on the weekends to relax in the casino here. I used to stay in Camille's suite in the Lakeshore Building. We were semi-cohabitants. The strange thing was that, although I am a womanizer, I fell deeply in love with her. If I didn't see her for three days, I was driven to distraction. Sometimes I would drive all the way at midnight to see her. I had never had this kind of feeling before, maybe because she was Asian, and she was somebody fresh to me, entirely different from my previous Western women. I was intoxicated and stupefied by her, especially her smooth and tender skin. I realized for the first time why some millionaires liked to have Asian women as wives. They possess unique virtues lacking in Western women, who wouldn't have them even if they were taught."

"Do your family members know about this? For example, does your arrogant father know?" asked JoAnna.

"I took her to my father's sixtieth birthday party at the end of November. That night I discovered that those who greeted her intimately were all in high social positions, including members of parliament, entrepreneurs, renowned lawyers and doctors, etc. From their eye contact, I discerned some extraordinary relationships. Some of them flirted with her in front of me, as if challenging me openly. Some cast strange glances at me, as if sneering at me. That night I felt for the first time that this Chinese woman was complex, somewhat like Marguerite in Dumas (Jr.)'s novel. She must be a high-class social butterfly, maybe backed up by an old and wealthy count, or somebody else's concubine…"

Chief Simon asked, "What was your father's opinion?"

David paused a while, then continued, "A couple of days later, my father had a special talk with me, advising me not to have much contact with such a woman. Probably some rumors regarding Camille had reached his ears. He is a very shrewd businessman, even in everyday life. He must have had evidence to reprimand me so seriously. He had never interfered with me although I had had around 30 girlfriends before. My father was a traditional descendant of the British, with relatively conservative values. He emphasized again and again that he didn't want to see me become a late twentieth century Armand."

30. Encountering a Chinese Woman's Fierceness

Chief Simon looked a bit impatient before he asked, "Then what happened to your relationship?"

Sipping some coffee, David continued, "I was deeply in love with Camille and wanted to spend every night with her. One late night, I swore I'd marry her, but she was nonchalant and said smiling that time would prove everything. The more I loved her in my heart, the more I hoped that she would cut her ties to other men, but she always gently refused to respond. One weekend I was in bed with her when a Chinese man phoned her. She went so far as to give me the cold shoulder and chatted with him, looking elated. After she hung up 15 minutes later, I flew into a rage, giving vent to my resentment at her dealings with other men. She was furious while putting on her clothes, saying that I had no right to prevent her from contacting other men. Just to scare her, I dropped a little vase. Unexpectedly she tried to smash a dictionary on my head. Luckily I ducked. Then she screamed, "Chinese women are not to be bullied." She even hysterically shouted, "Get out of here!" With indignation, I strutted to the door and walked out. It was the first time I had seen her in such a hot temper since we had met over two months before. She was as fierce as Western women. I encountered the other side of Asian women."

"So you two separated just like that?" Policewoman JoAnna asked anxiously while taking notes.

David shook his head, "No. I apologized to her over the phone and she said she was sorry to me. According to what she told me later, it was her uncle who had called overseas from Hong Kong. It had been a very long time since he called. After we reconciled, we got merrier and crazier. It seemed that we became more intimate after the fight. I bought a lot of gifts for her, such as Tiffany and Cartier jewels and Chanel, Jacobs, and Holt Renfrew dresses. I also took her to Miami for an intimate vacation. After we returned, she gave me the keys to her suite. This proved that she had started to trust me. Her oral English was quite fluent, so we decided after consultation that I would take her to my company for a visit. If she liked it, I would let her do some simple secretarial work. Of course, I tried to persuade her to move to the States, leaving her admirers behind, naturally. I wanted to possess her one hundred percent, all by myself. Love and carnal desire are always exclusive. As for my family members, I kept them in the dark for the time being. Some day they would accept her. Besides, I am independent financially and made all my money myself. Of course my father had offered me a lot of financial help when I started. To split from my family would be the worst…"

With knitted brows, he glanced at the three policemen present and went on, "However, what happened two days before Christmas, like a bolt from the blue, smashed all my dreams. As if driven by a ghost or God, I suddenly returned to her residence for a contract I had left there the night before. I failed to open the door, which had been locked from inside. I figured that something had happened, so I rang the bell at once. She came to the door in a couple of minutes and seeing me, her facial expression changed. I entered and found an Asian man sitting on the couch. He stood up to greet me. His name was Peter, a tall and handsome man. You can well imagine what a man and a woman were doing with the door locked. Moreover, she was wearing pajamas. People call me 'playboy' but I care about pure feeling. In love affairs, I can't bear to have an ounce of sand in my eyes. I expected her to be whole-hearted in loving me, as I genuinely loved her. I could not stand any carnal relations between her and other men… That very night, I phoned her from Buffalo to separate from her peacefully. She sounded calmer and more poised than I was. She said there was no need to explain. The end of an affair comes sooner or later. That Christmas was the saddest I had ever had. I drank a lot of wine, got drunk and slept, and woke up to drink again…"

As was his habit, Simon stroked his beard and cut in, "Did you two have any contact after Christmas of 1999?"

"We never met each other after our split. For her birthday in June last year, I asked a flower shop to send her a bouquet of white camellias, which was one of her favorite flowers besides roses. The next day I received a "thank you" call as a courtesy. It was obvious to me that she was leading a happy life. However, before last Christmas, she phoned me in low spirits. She wanted to invite me to dinner, but my schedule was too tight. There was a labor-management negotiation I was attending because of a workers' strike in our company. I told her to wait until January. It's a shame that we never met again."

With gestures, policewoman JoAnna asked, "Do you know the men she contacted frequently at that time? Do you know their names?"

David touched his head and answered, "So far as I know, her contacts include Dominic, a renowned lawyer; Reagan, the president of the Supremacy Computer Company; Harris, a famous surgeon across the river; and Mr. Wong, a senior engineer at Nortel, possibly from Hong Kong. Of course, there was that Asian man, Peter. I might have some of their business cards in my office and I can fax them to you. I'll try my best to recall and provide you with information so as to help find her murderer as soon as possible."

He immediately added, "I think that ex-Councilor Arvid is not good. The relationship between that wolf and Camille was extraordinary. He should have more information. Late one night, his wife called me on my cell, asking me if I drank with Arvid. She suspected that Arvid was involved with a Chinese girl. I guessed the girl was Camille. At the time, Camille was lying in my arms naked, so I consoled Arvid's wife half-heartedly and perfunctorily. No pretty girl could escape from that old wolf. Camille was a woman of such extraordinary beauty that any man would covet her. She revealed to me in our talks that their relationship had been quite intimate for a period of time and that they had often danced over the weekends and spent nights together in the States. I'm not sure if they went to bed together, though."

Chief Simon thought that neither David nor Arvid was good. They seemed to be a couple of clowns, who were still attacking each other. Let's see who would laugh last! They were both wolves, who dally with women, then desert them, without taking any responsibility.

Before taking leave, David repeatedly reminded Simon, "Don't forget to tell me the date of Camille's funeral. No matter how busy I am, I'll attend. After all, we had three months' love and at least I truly loved her. She was a lovely Oriental Angel. What a pity!"

Simon patted him on the shoulder and nodded when he saw tears in David's eyes. JoAnna watched Simon silently leave the office, perhaps touched by David's devotion.

31. The Zhang Family's Reluctant Acceptance of the Facts

As David's words were being recorded, the three members of the Zhang family were sitting in the conference room of the Police Bureau, listening attentively to the development of the investigation by two members of the special group. To avoid the language barrier, the Bureau had invited an interpreter from Toronto, although Yuanyuan's brother knew sufficient English and the old Zhang couple understood English.

When they learned that their own flesh and blood had been engaged in the oldest profession, they were all dumbfounded. The unexpected shocking news was worse than an earthquake or a hurricane. Their brains were hit hard by the devastating news – they just stood there, staring at each other, without uttering a word.

Mr. Zhang exerted himself to control his feelings and clenched both fists, with cold sweat all over him. As a father who had cherished his daughter as dearly as his own life, as a high-class intellectual of China, and as a famous electric expert, he could hardly accept such disgrace. He was a typical man who looked cold externally but was warm internally. Although his daughter had been just so-so in her studies, her natural beauty was the pride of the whole family. He had been strict with her ostensibly because he did not want her to be cheated. He loved her from the bottom of his heart. My daughter, my poor Yuanyuan, why did you choose this blind alley?...

On hearing the news, Mrs. Zhang suffered more than when she had heard about her daughter's death. She shivered all over, her face turning paler and paler, with her heart seemingly broken. Instantly she yelled, "impossible, impossible" and all of a sudden dropped onto the floor and fainted. Luckily the Police Bureau was prepared, so two medical personnel rushed from the next room, placed her flat on a couch, sprayed some medicine into her mouth and sprinkled a little water on her forehead. In five minutes, she came around and everybody present was relieved.

For Zhang, Mingming, on the other hand, everything seemed like stories in European or American novels he had read before. One image after another of prostitutes swirled in his mind, but he never imagined that such a tragic fate would befall his dear sister. Ever since his childhood, his sister had always been the epitome of beauty and purity. Everybody who saw her praised her beauty, but he would always add that she had a heart of gold.

Although none of the Zhang family believed that Zhang, Yuanyuan would have fallen into prostitution, they had to accept the fact reluctantly in face of all the material evidence provided by the police. God was blamed for his mercilessness toward such a feeble girl. Maybe it was due to sins committed by their ancestors, for which Yuanyuan had to endure disastrous consequences.

After the policemen sent them back to the Lakeshore Building, the whole family sat in the living room, stunned. They absolutely collapsed mentally. Mrs. Zhang grasped things left behind by her daughter, placed them on her face, smelled them, and slowly burst into tears, like one suffering from Alzheimer's disease. Old Zhang stood at the window, smoking vehemently, and staring at the lake without any facial expression. Zhang, Mingming gazed at the withering camellia, as if in a trance, with the images of Marguerite and his sister alternating constantly.

With the smoke lingering and the frightening quiet, the atmosphere was suffocating in the room. The three people were like vampires, motionless in different positions.

"Can you stop smoking? We are suffocating." Mrs. Zhang complained in a low voice because she could hardly breathe.

Old Zhang made a strong puff and said, "It's better to be dead. It was because of you that we let her go abroad. Now what has happened? Do you still want Mingming to go abroad?"

"That was because Chen, Zhiwei went to the US and deserted Yuanyuan, and she attempted suicide. I just tried to change her environment. Besides, you consented."

"Before I got the news, you had already mailed money to Japan. You acted first and asked afterwards. I had to consent even if I didn't like it."

Zhang, Mingming stood up and screamed hysterically, "That does it! Why are you arguing over this? She is dead. My poor sister!"

The couple were stupefied by their son's screams and shut up at once. It was the very first time that their son had flown into such a rage.

"We'd better consider how to hold a decent funeral for Yuanyuan. No matter how she was and whatever disgrace she brought to the family, she will always be my good sister. Forever! Money is no problem. There is still over $10,000 in her account. I will never use her hard-earned money. I'll try to get a scholarship for going abroad. Or perhaps I don't have to go away. At present there are plenty of opportunities in Shanghai, with a lot of foreign companies as well. Why do I have to go abroad?" Zhang, Mingming talked to the ceiling, as if he was spellbound, reciting some theatrical lines prepared for a long time, with rhythm and force.

In an instant, the couple felt almost simultaneously that their son had grown up. Perhaps the miserable suffering of his sister had urged him to maturity. This at least brought a little warmth to their broken hearts, a small consolation to them.

Just then, somebody rang the bell. It turned out to be Old Bailey, the black man, who pushed a little cart with ten pots of fragrant white camellias.

"These are my gift to Camille. Please accept them. She loved white camellias and often bought them," he said sincerely, his body bent.

"Thank you very much, but how can we let you spend the money?" Old Zhang said while getting $100 out of his pocket.

Old Bailey replied, "No, no. Don't belittle me. Your daughter was a nice girl. Really. Such a pity!"

Zhang, Mingming came to help with the flowers and explained in detail and in fluent English why Bailey should accept the money, but to no avail.

Bailey shook his head and said, "My friend owns a flower nursery and he let me have them for half price. I can afford it however poor I am. Why are the police so incompetent? They haven't caught the murderer yet. If it were the FBI in the US, they might have cracked the case long ago."

Mrs. Zhang replied, "The police have tried their best and discovered a lot of clues. But it seems the case is quite complicated and requires more time."

Old Bailey nodded, wiped the tears at the corners of his eyes and pushed the cart away.

At Zhang, Mingming's suggestion, the three of them started to set up a mourning hall in the living room. The huge portrait of Zhang, Yuanyuan was mounted with a black cloth and hung on the central wall over the table. On the table, covered with a black cloth, the pots of white camellia were placed. Old Zhang wrote four black characters in Wei style, "Rest in peace, Yuanyuan", and placed them below the portrait. The decoration was simple, but solemn and majestic.

The three of them stood in a row and bowed in silence to show their condolences, wishing Yuanyuan peace and hoping that her killer would be apprehended as soon as possible.

32. Bail for Lian, Haotien

The test results of Lian, Haotien by the forensic science center showed that his blood type was A, which did not match the O type of the deceased or the AB type of the blood stains under her nails. The DNA report showed that Lian's chromosomes did not match that of the semen on the wall of Zhang, Yuanyuan's womb. It was concluded that Lian's statement under examination was, to a certain extent, reliable and that he did not have sex with Zhang, Yuanyuan on the night of December 28th. At this point, there was not enough evidence to indicate that he was a suspect.

Lian, Haotien, however, could not provide any evidence to prove that he was in the Niagara Casino from 12:10 am to 3 am on December 29th. His image had not appeared on the closed circuit TV of the casino. The deceased had passed away at 5am, so the police had to make further investigations as to where Lian was during this critical period of time: it was still a mystery.

On the evening of the 13th, after Lian, Haotien had been in custody for three days and three nights, he was released on bail of $5,000, under the personal guarantee of the deputy general manager of the CG Insurance Company. The police requested that he do not leave the country for two months and wait for summons at any time. He agreed to all requests.

The three days in custody were like three miserable years to Lian, Haotien, who looked pale and old like a man of fifty, with an unshaven beard. He could not fall asleep for two nights, Zhang, Yuanyuan's full breasts and well-developed hips always lingering in his mind. As for himself, if he could not find any evidence to prove that he was in the casino from 12:10 am to 3 am on the day of December 29th, he would still be the prime suspect. He could not clear his name even if he jumped into the Yellow River.

Before leaving, he repeatedly told a policeman of "the Special investigation group for No. 1 female body", "I am absolutely not the murderer. I am a coward, not ruthless at all."

The policeman said, "Mr. Lian, we just follow Canadian law and we will not wrong any innocent person. Of course, we won't let off any criminal."

"I believe you. I really do. I am willing to co-operate with the police and come here when summoned. Once the culprit is caught,

I'll be at ease," Lian, Haotien mumbled with lowered head and then staggered away.

At 8pm that day, "the Special investigation group" held an emergency meeting. Some people blamed Chief Simon for releasing Lian, Haotien so quickly.

Chief Simon shrugged his shoulders and said, "What else could I do? We don't have sufficient evidence to keep him in custody, so I had to release him."

Policewoman JoAnna continued with the subject, "Now, we have no chief suspect. Please don't misunderstand me, -- I mean Lian, Haotien is not the prime suspect, but he remains a suspect. Just as Chief Simon has expected, this case is more complicated than we thought."

Simon cleared his voice and said, "At present, it's clear that a man with blood type AB raped Zhang, Yuanyuan between 12:10 am and 3am on the day of December 29th. Then, they argued and he killed her and threw her body into the Niagara River."

JoAnna added, "Based on the examination of information provided by Jia, Feng, the correspondent for the 'Toronto Weekly', Chen, Zhiwei, the first lover of Zhang, Yuanyuan, left MIT a long time ago. He worked in California for two years. It is not known where he works now. We asked Canadian Customs to check and they had no record of his entering Canada or leaving the United States, unless he changed his name. From her diary of first love, Yuanyuan said she bore deep hatred toward him and tried her best to take revenge on him by all means. The first lover a girl has is very precious. As the saying goes, so much love can turn into so much hatred. That's why I suggest that we ask the FBI in the United States to assist in locating Chen, Zhiwei. We may find another clue to break the case."

"In my opinion, we don't have to trouble the FBI for the time being. This afternoon, the Bureau Chief showed concern and asked if we needed more people or to ask the FBI for help, but I politely declined. Let's wait for Zhang, Yuanyuan's boyfriend, Lai, Wenxiong, to return to Canada from Taiwan. I firmly believe that he can provide us with important clues," said Chief Simon hurriedly.

A tall policeman said, "It's been thirteen days since we started the investigation, but we haven't had any substantial developments and today the chief suspect was released. This case is at a standstill, something we didn't expect at the beginning."

Simon snapped, "We have to admit that this case involves a lot of people and is complex. Besides, the statements of David and Arvid might be false. At this time, they are still fighting each other like dogs."

After around two hours' discussion, there was still no prospect of a solution. They returned to the former key questions: Whose semen was in Zhang, Yuanyuan's body and on her briefs? Who left the nylon rope mark on her neck, the bloodstain on her left breast, and the 3-inch scar on her right arm? Who was with her in the five hours before her death? Who raped her? ...

Chapter Seven

Old Flame of Love Re-ignited while Meeting again in Casino

33. Taipei Shocked by Terrible News

It was exactly 12 noon, Taipei time, on January 12th when Lai, Wenxiong received the phone call from the Niagara Police Bureau. The sunshine through the windows seemed feeble, even somewhat gloomy.

On hearing the terrible news about Zhang, Yuanyuan from Chief Simon, Lai lay flat on the couch in the living room like a drunkard, motionless with his eyes half shut, as at the last radiance of the setting sun or the momentary recovery of consciousness just before death. The coffee cup dropped onto the floor without his knowing it, and the pale gray carpet was stained with a dark brown coffee color, like a Chinese splash-ink landscape painting, with a black swirl in the middle and water drops or tears around it. The "water drops" and the "tears" were extending gradually like ink stains dissolving on the paper. Lai's mind was totally blank and he felt breathless, almost stifled, while tears rolled down his face involuntarily.

Just then, his sister Wenhui came downstairs. Seeing coffee all over the floor and her brother crying bitterly, she couldn't help screaming, "My God! What happened?"

Getting no response, she went over to shake his shoulders and asked again, "Brother, whatever happened? Don't scare me."

"She—is—dead." It took Lai, Wenxiong great effort to say these three words, as strenuously as if he had undergone surgery.

"Who?" Wenhui did not understand.

"Zhang—Yuan—Yuan. Are you satisfied?" He exerted himself to open his eyes wide to stare at his sister, as if he had just recovered from death.

Obviously the last words irritated Wenhui, so she replied sharply, "I wondered who died. Just a stripper."

"What about a stripper? She deserved to die? She was also a human being. Is anyone as abnormal as you are?"

"It's you who are abnormal to like such a woman." Wenhui, who never admitted defeat, retorted at once.

"Such a beautiful woman would not be found in the whole of Taipei." He talked to himself loudly like a madman.

"What's the use of beauty? What was the difference between her and a prostitute? Haotien told me everything…" Wenhui continued, her voice getting louder.

"Lian, Haotien, I want to kill you! Lian, Haotien, I must kill you! …" Wenxiong yelled hysterically, becoming totally irrational.

Hearing the noise, his father rushed out of his study and said angrily, frowning with displeasure, "Prostitute and killing! This house has turned into a gangsters' den. What nonsense! Your mother was just out of hospital yesterday. Can't you let her rest?"

Old Lai was dazed when he saw coffee on the carpet, and asked quickly, "What on earth happened?"

Wenhui replied indignantly, "That Beauty Zhang is dead."

"Wenxiong, is it true?" Old Lai approached his son, looking incredulous.

"Yes, Zhang, Yuanyuan is dead. Just now, the police bureau in Canada phoned." Wenxiong replied weakly.

"Well, beautiful women suffer an unhappy fate. How did she die? Was it homicide or due to other causes?" Old Lai sighed.

Just then, his mother upstairs, aware that something big had happened on the first floor, uttered a weak yell. Wenhui went upstairs and told her the news perfunctorily. After hearing this, the mother struggled to sit up and asked Wenxiong to come upstairs. About a month before, she had been diagnosed with intermediate stage stomach cancer. After a joint examination by many doctors, she had been admitted to the Taiwan University Hospital. That was why Lai, Wenxiong had delayed returning to Canada and failed to spend Christmas with Zhang, Yuanyuan as he had planned originally. He was scheduled to return to Canada after the Spring Festival. Four days before, Mrs. Lai had a successful surgery during which three quarters of her stomach had been removed. She was still feeble and pale.

Old Lai entered the bedroom on the second floor following Wenxiong. Mrs. Lai, sitting on the bed, felt a twinge of grief when she saw her son's pale face with tears on his cheeks. She gestured for him to sit at her bedside.

"Wenxiong, how did Miss Zhang die?" His mother held her son's hand, shivering.

"According to the police, her body was discovered in the Niagara River on New Year's Day. There are not enough clues in the investigation yet. They don't know how she died, so they asked me to return to Canada and help solve this case." He replied slowly with his head lowered. Wenhui took the opportunity to put a dress over her mother's shoulders.

"I should apologize to you. I am not telling a lie; I meant to talk about Miss Zhang with you when I recovered a little in a few days. Since this surgery, I have made some changes in my attitude towards life. The past has no significance for us, while the future is so unpredictable. It is most important to live in the present. I decided that, since you like Miss Zhang so much, we might as well turn a blind eye to your relationship. The important thing is your happiness. Now it's too late. If I hadn't been in the hospital, the tragedy might not have happened...Hey! It's my fault."

"Mom, don't say that. I'm not in the least blaming you..." Lai, Wenxiong couldn't help shedding tears again.

Old Lai shook his head helplessly while seeing this. Then he said to his son, "Do you want your big brother to accompany you back to Canada?"

"No need. He's very busy. Please rest assured that I'm able to cope."

Mrs. Lai told her daughter, "Wenhui, you try to book an air ticket for your brother, the earlier the better."

Wenhui nodded and went downstairs. Wenxiong was at a loss as to what to do, seeing his mother in tears. Old Lai came to the bed and helped her lie down.

Lai, Wenxiong tried his best to console his mother, "Mom, rest quietly and recover. I'll come back to see you after attending her funeral."

"Mom only feels sorry for you. Who would have imagined that Miss Zhang would pass away when she was so young? Heaven is really unfair." Mrs. Lai uttered the words with effort.

Old Lai confessed with regret, "Now I recall that we were cold to Miss Zhang when she left in August...O.K. I'll stop talking about it now that she's gone. Wenxiong, take some money to Canada to help her family hold a grand funeral. Anyway, you two truly loved each other."

"When she was alive, she didn't like to spend my money, so it's not necessary. If she knew in Heaven, she would not be happy."

Mrs. Lai turned over and spoke in a low voice, "Wenxiong, just listen to your Dad. We don't know her family's financial circumstances. In case they lack money, you can pay the bills. Take 10,000 US dollars with you."

"If it's not sufficient, just phone me." Old Lai was never so generous in money matters like this.

Lai, Wenxiong was moved to tears with gratitude and responded by nodding, "OK. Thank you very much, Mom and Dad."

The old couple looked at their deeply grieving son from different directions and shook their heads silently and helplessly. Lai, Wenxiong dried his tears and glanced at the sunshine in the room subconsciously. Gazing at his mother's pale face and at his father, he suddenly realized that his parents had understanding hearts. They stretched out their helping hands without any hesitation when he was on the verge of mental collapse. This filled his heart with gratitude. For the first time he understood the real meaning of "how pathetic the parents on earth are"…

34. Meeting the Beauty again in the Casino

Lai, Wenxiong, dazed and with leaden steps, boards a North-West Airlines plane at Chiang Kai-shek International Airport in Taoyuan, for a direct flight to Detroit.

In the two days and nights after he had received Chief Simon's phone call, he felt as if a knife were piercing his heart. He was so grieved that he felt numb, not different from a lunatic. He would not have prevailed without his family's consolation. Even taking sleeping pills, he could only get a few hours' sleep. He contemplated that it was his fault and that he had mentally killed Zhang, Yuanyuan, although he didn't kill her in person. He should not have let her return to Canada alone. He should have followed her to the Country of the Maple Leaf. He bore some responsibility for her death, at least in his conscience.

If it hadn't been for his mother's surgery; if he didn't have to collect material for his thesis; if he had been at her side in Canada… the tragedy might not have occurred. Of course, he hates his damned cousin Lian, Haotien the most. If Lian had minded his own business, Zhang, Yuanyuan would have been living in Taipei, ready for the Spring Festival, as his fiancée.

Lai, Wenxiong requests a whisky from the stewardess so as to have a good sleep and enough energy to answer the countless questions by the police. But after half a cup, he still can't fall asleep, while past events, like turbulent Niagara Falls, were revived in his mind.

In late autumn 1999, Ma, Yongping, his university classmate, came from Taipei to Canada for a vacation. As a rule, Lai, Wenxiong took visitors to see Niagara Falls, one of the wonders of the world. In spite of the chilly weather, the locals always entertained their friends from afar at this worthwhile scenic spot.

That evening, the falls, like an unfolded painting, colored with pale pink and green, bold and uninhibited, looked exquisite and magnificent. Ma, Yongping, nicknamed "poet" while he was a student, had published several of his poems, one of which was awarded a prize. In the face of such gorgeous scenery, he started reciting a poem while nodding his head:

"The sun shining on the Incense-burner Peak
Issueth Purple smoke to wreathe round,
Seen afar the cataract seemeth hung from the cliff top
To the water front of the Mount.
The flying torrent for three thousand feet
Ceaselessly dashing down headlong.
Is taken to be the Silvery Stream falling from
The ninth heaven to the ground."

(A poem by Li, Bai of Tang Dynasty and translated into English by Sun, Dayu. p. 235, An Anthology of Ancient Chinese Poetry and Prose, Shanghai Foreign Language Education Press -- Translator's Note)

Lai, Wenxiong felt refreshed and full of curiosity, as he hadn't seen Ma's old scholarly style for a long time. He asked smiling, "Got some poetic inspiration? That was fast."

"Wonderful, wonderful! If Li, Bai had come here for a visit, he would have written an even more powerful masterpiece." Ma, Yongping was still wrapped up in the poetic charm.

Ma, Yongping seemed to be enchanted by the wonderful falls and walked back and forth in front of them, without feeling the cold autumn wind. He asked ceaselessly about the mystery of the falls. Luckily Lai, Wenxiong knew only too well the relevant information after having entertained so many people there. He jokingly declared that he would, sooner or later, become an "expert on the falls".

Lai, Wenxiong made the introduction slowly, "The water of the four big lakes over the borders of the USA and Canada flows into the Niagara Region and turns into the falls due to the extremely slanting cliffs. Look-- the falls water flows into Lake Ontario from this canyon-like Niagara River, via the St. Laurence River, and goes to the Atlantic Ocean. The falls, formed by the pre-historic glacier lashed by the limestone, via Goat Island at the cliff verge of Lake Erie, parted into two routes and formed two falls with the same name."

Pointing at the faraway falls, Lai continued, "You see, the other falls, located in the US, looks like an enormous crystal curtain, with a width of over 300 meters and a depth of over 50 meters. This one in Canada, on the other hand, looks like a huge whitish curtain in a horseshoe shape with a width of almost 800 meters and a depth of nearly 50 meters."

Ma, Yongping nodded while making gestures, "That is to say, the falls, viewed from the Canadian side, is just in front of us. The scenery is most attractive here-- that's why many Americans come over here to view it."

Nodding, Lai, Wenxiong continued, "When there is the reflection of the sunset, matching rings appear and the scenery looks dreamy and illusory, with the seven-colored rainbow which can often be seen in spring and autumn. The water level of Lake Erie's upper reaches is 99 meters while the water level of the falls flowing into Lake Ontario is only 75 meters, so the falls flows over the whole year with such a difference in water levels. That's why it attracts visitors like you from afar every day of the year."

"To tell you the truth, I just aimed to see the falls during my visit to Canada. It's really worth the visit." Ma, Yongping looked enraptured, revealing his true colors as a poet.

"Have you got some inspiration? You can write on my back." Lai, Wenxiong pointed to his back and Ma, Yongping almost laughed his head off.

"What poems have I got? No more poems after Li, Bai. Wenxiong, it's a shame that I haven't written any for years. Taipei is such a crowded place that it's turning people into madmen. Is there any room for poets to survive there?" Ma, Yongping's words implied a complaint.

Lai, Wenxiong went on with the subject, "There is only half a step between a madman and a poet. It's not bad to become a madman if not a poet."

"Wenxiong, you have a better sense of humor than before. Has Canada's fengshui molded your temperament?"

Lai, Wenxiong continued in spite of the comment, "It's good to be muddle-headed occasionally... To tell you the truth, poetry is a kind of luxury for contemporary people."

"A superfluous luxury." Ma hit the nail right on the head.

Afterwards Lai, accompanied by Ma, stepped into the nearby casino unwittingly. It was the first time Lai, Wenxiong had ever come here since its establishment several years before. Maybe it was a childhood habit to stay away from "gambling".

Casino Niagara, built at a cost of 160 million Canadian dollars, faces the Rainbow Bridge between the US and Canada. This building, a combination of cement, glass and stones, stands among a colorful garden. The casino boasts a magnificent design, with classic elegance and an air of modernity. Patrons can view the gorgeous falls through the glass hall at a height of 80 feet. With the imposing falls, the casino has a unique grandeur, although it is not as awe-inspiring as the casino in Atlantic City, USA.

Surrounded by the sounds of betting chips and winning bells, nobody could have a quiet moment. Ma, Yongping soon got itchy hands for games of 21 points. Lai, Wenxiong did not like gambling and could not make head or tail of the game, so he went to the slot machines to kill time.

Glancing over, he found crowds of people in front of the rows of slot machines. The gamblers were concentrated on betting, pulling the rods and waiting anxiously for the angels of good luck, almost like the assembly line of a cotton mill. When he approached the machines, not a single one was vacant. Lai, Wenxiong had to stand there waiting dully.

Just then, a tall Asian girl walked towards him, like a fairy from the clouds in the sky, mysterious and beautiful. When she got closer, he felt a sense of familiarity, as if they had met before. As she opened her mouth to greet him, he recalled that she had to be Camille, the stripper he had met in Toronto over two years before.

"If I am not mistaken, you are Camille. We met in Toronto, over two years ago." He couldn't help starting a conversation.

With widely open eyes and quiet resolution, she said at ease, "You've got a shocking memory. I'm sorry that I don't remember your name as I've met so many people."

"You must remember my cousin Lian, Haotien, from Taiwan, a short man and a Ph.D. student at the University of Toronto."

"Oh, we are old friends. We met at least once a week then. Oh, now I remember. You study sociology at the University of Waterloo. I still remember your joke that cups are like breasts last time we met. I remember now. We talked merrily and congenially. You gave me a big tip that day. You also advised me not to engage in this and to go to school…" she said frivolously as if the lock on her memory had been flung open.

"Your memory is not bad either." He held her soft hands, felt the warmth and was unwilling to let them go for a long time.

35. Old flame Re-ignited Quietly

Lai, Wenxiong followed Zhang, Yuanyuan, hand in hand, to "Marilyn Hall" on the fourth floor of the casino, like a pair of lovers, or like a brother and a sister who had not met for a long time. The hall was named after the late movie star Marilyn Monroe, who starred in the film "Niagara Falls" when she was 26 years old. This hall was not very big, but it was exquisite, with elegant decoration and a tasteful environment that was very suitable for chatting.

No sooner had they sat down than Zhang, Yuanyuan skillfully lit a cigarette and put it between her lips. Lai, Wenxiong, who did not like it when other people smoked, was charmed by her way of smoking. He thought: a beauty is truly a beauty, with every movement so irresistibly charming.

She blew out a ring of smoke and said seriously, "I remember it well now. My leaving Toronto had something to do with your advice. You spent a lot of time persuading me to quit dancing and go to school during our last meeting."

Sipping his coffee, Lai, Wenxiong responded, "I just felt you are so lovely that it's a waste of your wisdom and talent to be engaged in that."

"Perhaps you didn't mean it when you said that, but I took it very seriously. I thought about it a lot when I got home that day. In the strip bar, nobody really cared about me except you. Later I took your advice into consideration when I decided to come here…"

"When did you come here?" Lai, Wenxiong asked with great concern, like a big brother.

"In August," she replied while sipping her coffee.

He asked with a little puzzlement, "Is there a strip bar nearby?"

"Of course. Which city in Canada does not have one? I have left it, however." With lowered head, she swallowed whatever she meant to say.

Gazing at her, he asked again with concern, "What profession are you now engaged in?"

"Wandering around, no regular job." She smoked and blew out rings of smoke to distract attention. Then she nodded gently, thought for a while and attempted to say something, but stopped short.

He raised his head in doubt, "No kidding. Do you work in the casino? It's nothing to be ashamed of."

She placed her cigarette on the ashtray, drank some coffee and answered in a low voice, "Don't be panicky after you hear the following. When I left Toronto, I thoroughly 'went to sea'. Do you know what that means? I come here almost every day to 'catch big fish', to pick up those wolves who win at the game. I just live near here."

"Oh, is that so? Women do not take this step unless they are driven to the wall. You must have been at an impasse and found it hard to tell," he showed some sympathy.

"This is all an incapable woman can do." She took up her cigarette again.

He nodded gently and said, "As the saying goes: people laugh at the poor not the prostitutes. I don't look down upon you but admire your resolution and courage. I admire two kinds of people in this world: one like you who dared to strip dance in front of men, which requires so much psychological strength; the other is men who rob a bank with wisdom, -- they must have very high IQs. Actually, with your appearance, it would not be hard to find a job in the hospitality sector and your oral English is pretty good."

"Well, how much could I earn by carrying dishes and mixing cocktails? I would make less money by working hard from morning till night than what I currently earn per hour! Besides, I don't have to pay any income tax -- everything is in cash. To tell you the truth, I have gone wild, like a kite with broken strings, flying aimlessly high in the sky, with no intention to get back to earth. It's impossible for me to do manual labor and accumulate one penny after another. I am not qualified to be a white-collar worker. Do you know that I need money, a lot of money at that! Life without money is simply terrible." She pulled a long face to make a terrifying gesture.

Lai, Wenxiong grasped her hand and said, "But you have to consider your future. You can't be like this for your whole life."

"Future? Do people like us have any future? The end of our

youth means our first death. When we are young and pretty, we have to make a lot of money. Nobody wants us after we are 30. We'll have to depend on ourselves then." She said this without any facial expression, as if she were reciting a prayer.

"Don't give yourself up as hopeless. You are really pretty and young. It is never too late to find a good man and start all over." He looked excited with his head raised high.

With widely open eyes, she retorted, "Who would want to marry people like us! We are a group deserted by society. Very few men are good. After exchanging a few words, they just want to take advantage of us in bed. To tell you the truth, your cousin Lian, Haotien is a big wolf. The first time we met, he wanted to go to bed with me. He should have looked in the mirror to see his own features. I have become afraid of meeting him and have tried to avoid him. Never tell him that I am here. Otherwise, he will pester me in a sickening way again. We are a group of weird people who either offer ourselves at once or never pay any attention to somebody. It all depends on our instincts."

"Rest assured, I rarely see Lian, Haotien. He is miserable enough – his girlfriend, instead of marrying him, eloped with an American guy. OK, let's change the subject."

"It seems that luck has brought us together. Are you interested in having a dialogue with my body? If you'd like to come, satisfaction is guaranteed." She gently massaged his hand, starting her favorite trick.

"Of course I would. Last time I had a taste of your devilish body and smooth skin in Toronto and I thought about this again and again. I even dreamed of you several times. Don't laugh at me… However, I can't today. My university classmate is still gambling downstairs. I don't want him to know anything about us. If this news were to reach Taipei, then I would be damned. My dad would kill me."

Somewhat disappointed, she knitted her brows, "You are such a grown-up, but still afraid of your father. It doesn't matter. I'll give you my cell number and you can call me any time. Maybe it's fate that has brought us together. I'm not willing to do this with just any man. For some bastards, I am never willing to, no matter how much money they offer me. I'd like to try with you, a man of virtue. Your witty and humorous remarks made a strong impression on me the first time we met. Moreover, at first you didn't dare touch me and made no improper requests. Remember, never give my phone number to Lian, Haotien, the wolf."

Before parting, he gave her his phone number and promised to get in touch.

36. Overwhelming Body Dialogue

Three days later, as soon as Lai, Wenxiong saw Ma, Yongping off to Pearson International Airport, he drove anxiously to Niagara Falls for a tryst with Zhang, Yuanyuan.

After they met at the front gate of the casino, they went straight to the Hilton Hotel nearby. Entering the room, she was at the helm. Every movement of hers attained the acme of perfection and every step was professional. He was like a pupil, obeying her instructions.

"You must be tired after driving for such a long time. Go take a warm bath and I'll rub your back." So saying, she helped him take off his coat.

He lay in the bathtub, naked, while she, wearing a robe, massaged his back with her fingers slowly and rhythmically. She rubbed his whole body with soap and closed the door lightly to let him rinse himself.

After his bath, she offered him a cup of brandy and said in a coquettish voice, "Drink first and lie down for a while. I'll go take a shower."

He drank a little and lay across the bed. Hearing the noise of water mixed with her singing, he felt a surge of commotion in his heart and waited eagerly for her return.

She flew to the bedside like a spring breeze. The transparent sleeping robe could hardly cover up the two wild throbbing rabbits on her chest.

"Are you anxious? Excellent performance is to follow." She said while taking off her robe, as if she were putting on a show purposely.

Now she had on only transparent silk briefs. It was more tempting than being totally naked. Suddenly Kundera's well-known words came to Lai, Wenxiong's mind, "Flirtation is an unrealized sexual promise." If baring her body in the strip bar was a kind of spreading the culture and a battle of wits, then her flirtation with him alone was a sort of enticement and an attempt as well. She started dancing to the music, and her two breasts looked like a pair of flying doves, firm and strong. Youth, youth was her capital. While gazing at her, he could not resist her temptation, with the flame of desire raging in his body, like the torrents of Niagara Falls outside the windows.

"Come over here, my young beauty." He issued a sincere invitation.

She seemed unaware of his calling and continued twisting her graceful curving body. How could he resist her enticement? He charged forward, held her onto the bed, and pressed her under his body with great force. Men try to conquer the world by means of women, while women try to conquer men with their bodies.

After a long, long "thunderstorm", he felt comfortable all over his body and her face turned pink. She was still lying in his arms, with one hand on his shoulder. His two hands were still holding the pair of white doves for fear of their flying away, so to speak.

"How refreshed I am! I've never enjoyed this so much in my over thirty years of life. You are an Asian angel, a devil." He felt absolutely contented.

She said coquettishly, "I told you that satisfaction is guaranteed. To tell you the truth, it was diamond cutting diamond. Who said that Chinese men are impotent? I have the biggest right to speak. Chinese men like you are not weaker than foreigners. They have more stamina. Those women, who boast that foreigners are stronger, have never touched true Chinese men. Or they have never aroused the interest of Chinese men because they are too ugly, so they have to resort to foreigners."

He was overjoyed to hear this and full of self-confidence. He held her close to him and slowly kissed her all over her body.

She said with great assurance, "You haven't touched women for a long time."

He nodded, "To tell you the truth, I haven't done this for over a year. I had a girlfriend who was a student from Taiwan, but she broke up with me at around this time last year, saying that she had no more feelings for me. Actually, she was seduced by a professor from Hong Kong…"

"That's all. Let's stop talking about unpleasant stuff."

After emotional lovemaking and cuddling for several hours, it was already night time with myriads of stars. The moon seemed brighter and the stars appeared to sparkle more than usual. The moon hung high for the two of them and the stars glistened for them too.

He drove his Volvo and they arrived at the "Good Wish Chinese Restaurant". They looked like a newlywed couple, talking while eating.

"Why did you come here alone? You were doing quite well in Toronto, weren't you? Other people would prefer to go to big cities."

She put down her chopsticks and whispered at his ear, "It's a long story. My misery could be made into a novel, 'New Camille', but I lack the talent to do it. You are a Ph.D. student, engaged in social studies. If you are interested, I'll tell you my story bit by bit. Maybe you'll become a best selling novelist. Of course, the time is not ripe yet."

He commented seriously, "It's a good subject matter and the title will be hot. Probably many publishers would vie with one another to publish it. After I complete my Ph.D. thesis, I'll start collecting material. Perhaps I can write a popular novel. I won an award for essay writing at university when I studied in Taipei."

"Don't forget to share your royalties with me." She said with pursed lips.

"For sure. We'll go halves." He suddenly put down his chopsticks and saluted her.

She opened her mouth and laughed foolishly, almost spitting out her food. She did not expect a man from Taiwan to be like that.

Then she started to talk to herself, as if in a dream, "It's true. My miserable traces have been left in every metropolis in the world: Shanghai, Tokyo, Toronto, and Niagara Falls. Plenty of source material for you to write about!"

"We'll co-operate with each other, or we can put both our names down as authors. You write the first manuscript and I'll make changes and touch it up. We'll write it in Chinese first and translate it into English later. We may have more royalties than we expect." He was getting thrilled.

"You might even get a Nobel Prize for Literature without knowing it. Right?" She was talking like a lunatic.

"I don't cherish such a wild ambition. It would be good enough to write a best seller. It's a shame that no writer from China has won this award. All Chinese writers have to exert themselves…"

"Bottoms up. Let's drink tea instead of wine." So saying, she raised the teacup in her hand.

Both of them raised their cups, feeling elated, as if they had signed a contract for a big business or they would soon win the Nobel Prize for Literature.

"I forgot to ask you: why do you like the name Camille? Influenced by Dumas Jr. 's novel?"

She explained slowly, "Since my childhood I have always had a love for camellias, especially the white ones. After I read Dumas Jr.' s novel 'Camille', I loved the camellia even more. When I was a stripper in Toronto, I called myself 'Camille', which was easier to remember for others. I even consulted some Chinese and English material in the library. This name is very popular in Britain, France and Italy. In Ancient Roman mythology, Camille is said to be a maid of the goddess Diana who is as light as a swallow and can walk on the surface of water, like a Chinese heroine. Unfortunately she dies in a battle."

"Is that so? You know so many stories." Lai, Wenxiong nodded with satisfaction.

It was already after 10pm when he took her back to the casino parking lot to get her car. It was a bit cold.

Before she left his car, he held her close to him, unwilling to part from her. She gave him a long kiss. He inserted, in passing, 4 hundred-dollar bills into her hand.

"That's too much. Two or three hundred are quite enough." She pushed the money away.

"Is it too little? It's my gift for our first meeting. Now go back home to rest. You must be tired."

"It's so kind of you. Thanks a lot. Call me. Bye." She jumped out of the car.

Looking at her slender and graceful figure, Lai, Wenxiong felt a twinge of tender compassion for her. He got into his car and started the engine. Suddenly he saw her, in his rear mirror, walking towards the gate of the casino, perhaps hunting for another target. He shook his head helplessly, sighed deeply and stepped forcefully on the accelerator.

Chapter Eight

Proposal for Marriage Accepted on Valentine's Day

37. Genuine Feeling Revealed with Meticulous Care

The plane flies continuously through the sea of clouds, with white cotton-like clouds floating outside the portholes. Lai, Wenxiong's train of thoughts resembles the white clouds in the blue sky, one after another, or an on-going TV series, one episode following another.

Ever since he and Zhang, Yuanyuan had their first intimate encounter on that day in 1999 when the maple leaves turned red everywhere; he had always remembered her shockingly pretty face and her full breasts and hips. No matter whether he was searching for material in libraries, or processing data in the computer room, or having meals in his residence, the image of Zhang, Yuanyuan would come to his mind unexpectedly. Late at night, his dreams would be filled with her.

Generally speaking, this kind of puppy love occurs at first love or first sexual intercourse. He thought that as Zhang, Yuanyuan was the third woman among the few who had gone to bed with him; he should not have been so excited by her. Only by comparison can one distinguish, perhaps. She stood head and shoulders above the other women for her natural beauty and wonderful temperament. With a "pure heart", she was gentle and knowledgeable, played the piano and danced well and appreciated painting and poetry. It was evident that she came from a metropolitan city. Compared with other dazzling beauties from Shanghai, she was even more elegant and graceful. After he questioned her, he learned that she had inherited her mother's features and her mother came from Suzhou. This was the answer to the riddle regarding her beauty. As everyone knows, Suzhou boasts picturesque scenery and pretty jade-like women, who speak gently and smoothly and have delicate and charming dispositions. Just take a few well-known examples: exceedingly pretty Xishi, gorgeous Lin, Daiyu and beautiful and intelligent Huang, Rong in Peach Island were all from Suzhou.

Without his knowing it, Lai, Wenxiong had introduced more worry and care into his life. The kind of yearning he felt day and night could only occur between lovers. When it was quiet at night, he could not help calling her and the two would chat and gossip for a long time. Sometimes Yuanyuan was not at home and he would keep phoning until 3am. Waterloo was not too far from Niagara Falls; about 100 kilometers away and over an hour's drive. The problem was he did not have time to go visit her with his tight study schedule.

When he was sober, he warned himself again and again: it was OK to have fun with her occasionally. It was perfectly justified to pay for sex. Physiologically speaking, it was better than long-term depression. Moreover, they both were willing, so they did not owe each other anything. He should not, however, cherish true feelings towards her. As the saying goes: actors have no real love and she was only a prostitute at that. Countless stories at home and abroad, in history or at present, proved that tragedy would happen some day.

Things are hard to predict in this world and many desired things do not run their course, especially in relationships between men and women, which can hardly be gauged by reason. Often people are inadvertently pulled in deeper and deeper until it is too difficult to get out. At noon, two days before that Christmas of 1999, Lai, Wenxiong had an unexpected phone call from Zhang, Yuanyuan asking for help. She complained about a terrible headache, as if her head would explode and said that she felt like attempting suicide. Without another word, he asked her address and drove quickly to #100 Lakeshore Building in Niagara.

She was moved to tears, seeing him arrive so fast. Opening the door, she threw herself into his arms. "How nice of you to come so fast! You must have been speeding in spite of the police patrols. Those bastards, who kept on saying that they loved me, told me they were busy when I called for help. Some of them gave the same excuses. They want me only when I am healthy…"

"Let's get in first." He helped her into the room.

She shut the door and locked it as a habit. Ever since there had been a break-in in the suite next door by a black man several months before, she was in the habit of locking her door for fear of intruders.

"How is your headache? You seem to be running a fever. Shall we go to the hospital?" He touched her forehead and asked with great concern, like a father, or a big brother.

With her face scarlet red, she said feebly, "I called my family doctor half an hour ago and he instructed me to take two Tylenol. Now I feel a little better. He told me to go to the hospital if nothing changes in two hours."

"You'd better lie down and drink a lot of water." He helped her to the bedroom while he sat at her bedside.

"I am so sorry to have interrupted your study." Her voice was hardly audible, as if she were talking to herself, and her eyes looked dull.

He comforted her, "It doesn't matter. I have no classes this afternoon. You just take a good rest. If you have a high fever, I'll drive you to a hospital. Rest assured. I'll go home later."

After a few chats, she shut her eyes, -- apparently she was exhausted, or maybe the Tylenol had taken effect and had lowered her temperature. He tiptoed to the living room after closing the bedroom door. He discovered several pots of white camellias on the floor, their delicate fragrance greeting him. It proved, as she told him last time, that she valued the camellia as much as her life.

He sat on the sofa, cross-legged, and started to read the local English newspapers. Thus, he began to purposely learn about Niagara City, just as he was beginning to understand the mysterious Zhang, Yuanyuan.

He was taken aback when he suddenly heard somebody open the door with a key. Then he heard the doorbell, which woke her up. She came out to open the door and in came a tall foreign man.

"Nothing has happened. I left a contract here last night." The foreign man went straight to her bedroom and searched for the document everywhere.

"I'm sick and have a high fever. I called you for a couple of hours, but your cell phone was not in service." She talked in very fluent English.

The foreign man turned a cold shoulder to her, as if he did not hear what she had said. With the file folder in his hand, he came from the bedroom to the living room and suddenly found an Asian man sitting on the sofa. Dazed, he pulled a long face.

"This is my boyfriend David and this is Peter, who came to see me from Waterloo." Zhang, Yuanyuan introduced them so as to rid them of embarrassment.

The two men said "Hi" to each other. Under such circumstances, with a young beauty in a sleeping robe in front of them, the two men inevitably felt embarrassed. It was better to have a tacit understanding between them. The embarrassment soon escalated into a psychological war of hostility. The psychological wars between two men are unpredictable. They could come or start at any time. Noticing David's disdain, Lai, Wenxiong did not bother to stand up and continued reading the papers, without glancing up.

David prepared to leave at once after he found the file folder. Before departing, he talked perfunctorily with Zhang, Yuanyuan, saying he had to rush to sign the contract. He looked displeased.

Lai, Wenxiong said nothing, but fixed his eyes on the two and kept everything in his heart, although he held the newspaper in his hands. He was thinking: David has the key to her apartment, so their relationship is extraordinary. Either they are lovers, or old flames at least, or she is "kept" by this rich man, like "the second wives" kept by those wealthy businessmen from Taiwan.

"Well! Only paying lip service, saying that he loves me, but he's nowhere to be found at the critical moment. Can I rely on such a man? He just regards me as a plaything. Wait and see: he'll phone to call it quits tonight. I'm not afraid," she couldn't help mumbling.

As if coaxing a child, he placed her in bed and covered her with a comforter, "Well, don't think too much. Better have a good rest. You are still running a fever. You haven't had any food, have you? I'll cook some congee for you."

"A Ph.D. Student can cook congee?" She gazed at him with surprise, with two eyes as big as light bulbs, but still dull.

"Where is the rice?"

"I finished it a couple of days ago and didn't have time to buy any more," she said, a little ill at ease.

He asked again, "Do you have preserved eggs?"

She shook her head, seemingly knowing nothing. Her naive expression disclosed her child-like innocence and loveliness. In Lai, Wenxiong's eyes, worldly-wise women without naivety were less feminine. The more mature men are, the more they prefer simple and pure women. A prostitute like her still has some invaluable innocence. This proved that she was not beyond redemption.

He said frowning, "Nothing? How do you live your life? Just go to bed. I'll go to a supermarket. Any Chinese stores nearby?"

"Yes, next to the 'Good Wish Restaurant' where we had dinner last time, there is a store run by a Vietnamese Chinese. Actually it's too troublesome to go there. Why not eat some bread instead? I'll go buy groceries in a couple of days."

"Oh, I have time to kill. I'll be back soon. O.K.?" It was like humoring a child.

"Take the key on the table with you and open the door by yourself. I'm still very sleepy."

He stared at her and said, "Aren't you afraid of my stealing things?"

She smiled gently, "Nothing valuable here. Besides, you are not that type of person. I've got sharp eyes and I can distinguish who is what kind of person with just one look."

"Then what type am I?" He raised his head, looking like a bookworm.

"You are kind-hearted, loving and caring, but chicken-hearted," she answered without thinking.

Perhaps she had hit the nail on the head: his face turned red and he sensed a burning sensation in his neck. He didn't utter another word. Deep in his heart, he couldn't help admiring this little woman's competence.

38. Daring to Say "No" to the Wealthy Businessman

Night, like an enormous beast, opens its mouth slowly, and lowers its head to kiss the vast land. Lights, in a myriad of houses, with a posture to rebuff the darkness, seem to engage in a life-and-death struggle with night. Niagara Falls outside the windows rolls on nonstop, produces deafening sounds and covers up all other sounds, including that of the cars on the road. No matter how night and lights fight each other, Niagara Falls sets its unique inherent rhythm, its own melody and its own score.

Lai, Wenxiong and Zhang, Yuanyuan, sitting face to face at the table having dinner, were like a newlywed couple. On the table were two big bowls of congee with preserved eggs and lean pork, steaming hot, as well as bread, fermented tofu and hot pickled mustard tuber. In her eyes, this kind of heart-warming family dinner was much better than those in magnificent restaurants. For so many years after she came overseas, what she lacked yet yearned for was just this "homey" feeling. On second thought, though, a person like her was not supposed to entertain such high hopes. "Home", to her, was a big question mark, or to speak more exactly, an unattainable dream.

She talked excitedly while eating, "I didn't expect a Ph.D. student like you could cook such delicious and smooth congee, comparable to that in the best Chinese restaurants in Toronto. The Chinese restaurants here can only fool foreigners. Neither fish, flesh, nor fowl."

Constantly flattered by her, he suddenly turned light-headed, as if he were a master chef. Wagging his head continuously, he intoned on the subject of congee, "In my opinion, congee can be counted as the quintessence of Chinese culture. The number of kinds of congee or porridge is intimidating. Both at home and abroad, in history or at present, many scholars have an irrevocable bond with it. Lu, You, a poet in the Song Dynasty, wrote a 'poem on eating congee':

'Everybody wants to live a long life,
Without knowing that longevity starts at present;
I master the easy method of Wanqiu,
Eat congee in order to be like an immortal.'

I think the reason Lu, You lived to the old age of 86 was because of his love of congee. Su, Dongpo; Fan, Zhongyan; Zheng, Banqiao and others wrote many poems in praise of congee. Cao, Xueqin was an expert on congee. In many chapters of 'The Dream of Red Mansion,' there are detailed descriptions of various kinds of congee or porridge."

Zhang, Yuanyuan cut in, "That's right. I read a short essay, which explained why contemporary writing is not as good as 'The Dream of Red Mansion'-- because the writers did not eat congee or they ate different kinds of congee."

"Of course they were not comparable. Cao, Yin, Cao, Xueqing's grandfather, had researched congee and compiled a book 'On congee'. Cao, Xueqin had naturally tasted many varieties of congee, or cooked congee, so he could write about it in such a detailed way." Lai really looked like a pedant.

She pursed her lips and said, "You've reminded me. Many scholars in mainland China treasure congee as they do their lives, such as Wang, Meng, the ex-Minister of Culture and the old writer Sun, Li, who loved cornmeal porridge. Female writer Chen, Rong, the author of 'At middle-age', liked cornmeal porridge as well…"

He handed her a slice of bread and said tenderly, "Don't just talk without eating. This coconut bread is quite good and very fresh. Eat more and you'll get stronger."

"The fermented tofu is delicious. Why did I never discover that these Chinese foods are available in this blasted place? I used to go to Toronto for them. It reminds me of rice in water." She said meaningfully.

He asked her, "Is it the previous night's rice in water that you Shanghai people like? That's not nutritious at all."

"That's true. But it is easy to cook in a few minutes. Since being abroad, whenever I am not feeling well, I cook a bowl of rice in water, plus some pickled veggie or hot pickled mustard tuber. It's so delicious, like a big dinner. I feel comfortable all over after eating hot rice in water and perspire a lot. Its effect is the same as that of congee to cleanse the bowels…" she continued eloquently.

He commented with a smile, "I'd rather say that eating rice in water is like going back to your hometown to relieve homesickness."

"That's it. Every time I have rice in water, I naturally think of Shanghai. My sentimental attachment to Shanghai cannot be broken."

"I read in some articles that many people from Shanghai were brought up with rice in water, so they have a special attachment to it."

"That was in previous generations. Nowadays, children are fed milk or soybean milk. The only son or daughter is the sun of the family, enjoying special protection. Times have changed and the kids are spoiled…"

Just then, David phoned from the United States. Only a few words made it clear to Lai, Wenxiong that it was the piece of cruel "bad news" that she had predicted.

Lai did not expect that Zhang, Yuanyuan would look so calm and unruffled, as if she had been prepared for this for years. Probably, she understood long ago that, being engaged in this oldest profession, she would be deserted sooner or later if she failed to satisfy men's vanity, or offended them unwittingly or failed to arouse their interest. She did not attempt to make any excuses, as separation was inevitable. It was only a matter of time. Finally, she sternly requested that he mail her keys to her by express mail and said that she did not want to see him again.

After she hung up, Lai, Wenxiong said with a bit of embarrassment, "Should I tell Mr. David that I am only a casual friend of yours? He is a wealthy businessman. Don't lose a patron for such a trifle."

"Not necessary. Should I be at his beck and call just because he is rich? Absolutely not! I told him a long time ago that he should follow three rules to be my boyfriend: No.1, he should trust me. No. 2, he should not interfere with my private affairs. No. 3, he should listen to me. There are so many rich people in this world, and quite a few are within my reach. To say nothing of the general manager of an auto company." she said seriously, with a long face, as if the words were also directed to his ears.

Faced with her ferocity, Lai, Wenxiong believed the meaning of her name Camille, the maid of a goddess, who was imbued with unique skill like a Chinese female warrior. She was a little Chinese woman with moral integrity to say "no" bravely to a big foreign businessman.

A little while later, she changed the subject nonchalantly, "I feel so comfortable after eating the congee. You really are smart. I used to think that you were only a bookworm."

"It's nothing. When there's a chance, I'll cook some dishes for you to taste, not much different from those in restaurants." He said proudly.

She was puzzled, "Did you ever work in a restaurant?"

"No, I learned merely from watching our maid cook at home when I was young. She could cook Shanghai dishes..." He was recalling old-time stories.

She was in a trance listening to his stories about his childhood in Taipei and about his family. From time to time, she asked a couple of questions. Later she ate another half bowl of congee.

He said smiling at her improved appetite, "You look much better and stronger. If you feel unwell, just cook some congee, which is a good medication for your stomach. It's called 'the No. 1 nutritious food in the world'. It seems to me that you eat too many meals at McDonald's, drink too much liquor and smoke too many cigarettes."

"People like us have to numb ourselves. No soul, only an empty shell—a spiritual void." She put down her chopsticks and sat on the sofa.

"I told you not to give up on yourself." He massaged her beautiful hair.

She buried her head in his chest and said, "Apart from my parents, nobody has shown so much concern for me or cooked for me. How would you like me to reward you?"

"Not everybody in the world wants a reward. Since fate brought us together, we are friends. It is nothing for me to do some little things for you. I am four years your senior and could be your big brother. Phone me whenever you have difficulties."

What he said made him sound like a big brother.

"Are you really so nice?" She was a bit skeptical.

He said smiling, "As the people from mainland China often say: wait and see."

Lai, Wenxiong held Yuanyuan and added, "If you really want to reward me, quit smoking soon."

She lay in his arms and replied coquettishly, "Give me some time. Ever since you advised me in our last few calls, I have not touched marijuana. I gave the last bit to the drug addict in the casino. Actually I took marijuana just out of curiosity, for occasional stimulus."

"As you have studied medical care, you know more than I do that smoking has no benefit, especially for women. All it does is increase wrinkles."

She touched his neck and said, "Give me some time and I will quit smoking."

He continued, "You should also cut all contacts with that Russian prostitute in Toronto. I've told you several times in my phone calls that you should not make such friends."

"I can't make up my mind. She gave me a lot of help when I was in great difficulty in Toronto. As a friend, I shouldn't fail to rescue somebody who is dying," said she helplessly.

"Didn't you promise me you'd turn over a new leaf? I've told you that you should have no contact with people like that. You lend her $100 today, and she'll want to borrow $200 tomorrow and $1,000 next month. Where did you get so much money? You are not a mint for printing bills. You could get involved in some disasters. You must bravely say 'goodbye' to those people!"

Nodding, she was moved to tears. It was really the first time she had met a man like Lai, Wenxiong, who advised her again and again to break with the dark side of society and start afresh. If somebody else had tried to control her, she would have flown into a rage. But she liked to listen to him and tried every means to change herself. She thought that perhaps this was the chance of a lifetime.

Before parting, she held his hand, unable to tear herself away from him, "Sorry to have troubled you. When I feel better, I'll help you feel more comfortable."

"I'll pay as well," he whispered while kissing her goodbye.

She replied humorously, "At least 50% off, or totally free."

Neither of them could stop laughing. The lewd laughter, like a sharp sword, pierced the serenity of night, drowning out the sound of Niagara Falls.

39. Proposal for Marriage by Kneeling down Accepted

Lai, Wenxiong did not expect that he would further intensify his concern for Zhang, Yuanyuan after he showed such meticulous care for her. Was it out of sympathy or pity, or carnal desire, or love? He could hardly determine the nature, -- maybe a little of all, or nothing of any. He felt a bit dazed.

For several nights, he tossed and turned in bed, gazing at the moonlight, and failed to fall asleep. With his eyes shut, Zhang, Yuanyuan's beautiful image and swirling figure would emerge in his mind. He could hardly control himself, and had to get up and drive for over an hour to see her. Only by indulging in her bodily fragrance could he fall asleep soundly.

He couldn't understand how she could have attracted his whole body and mind with her tender affection. He had just parted from her before he yearned to meet her again, like a youth in puppy love, always in a state of extreme excitement. This also reminded him of the good place south of the Yangtze River, which abounded with famous prostitutes: Dong, Xiaowan in Nanjing was delicate and charming; Sai, Jinhua in Shanghai was extremely overwhelming; Zhang, Yuliang in Yangzhou once painted an elegant "naked woman". At present, there is the touching story of Zhang, Yuanyuan, the contemporary "Camille", with the hero of the love story none other than himself, a Ph.D. student in sociology.

Soon they celebrated the first Valentine's Day after they had met. This is a day decorated with roses and chocolate. Every family and each pair of lovers are blessed with the great love of God. On that sunny afternoon, Lai, Wenxiong put on a brand new gray leather jacket, with a crimson turtleneck sweater, and looked radiantly vigorous, like a star athlete. Under the bright sunshine, he drove to Zhang, Yuanyuan's residence, humming a happy tune.

It went without saying that Zhang, Yuanyuan paid meticulous attention to her dress and make-up. After getting up early in the morning, she searched her wardrobe to compare one pretty dress with another and waited until noon before she decided that she would wear her simplest dress. In her judgment of beauty, natural simplicity was quite important. She had the self-confidence that she was born with shocking beauty and her dress was secondary. People praised her beauty even if she wore blue jeans. The V-necked crimson wool dress properly served as a foil to both her plump but curvaceous figure and her fair complexion. Her black shining shoulder-length hair had been treated with cream, so it looked especially charming. With light make-up, her black eye brows and almond-shaped eyes were gleaming and penetrating. She looked more graceful and affectionate.

The two hugged heartily at the door. Then Lai, Wenxiong took out a dozen pink roses hidden behind him and offered them to Zhang, Yuanyuan courteously. She held his hands and thanked him again and again. He felt a twinge of jealousy when he saw four or five bouquets of roses already on the table. He controlled his feelings, however, and pretended to be calm and magnanimous.

She seemed to sense his displeasure, so she smiled charmingly at once. "Among so many flowers, I like the pink roses the most."

"Is that so?" He smiled and held her in his arms.

"Guess what I've brought for you?" He quickly opened his bag.

"Underwear," she replied without thinking or looking.

"You guessed half right."

He first took out a set of black silk underwear, then an exquisite red box. He opened the box quietly and dug out, with his fingers, a sapphire necklace in the shape of a heart. Slowly he took it and fastened it on her white and tender neck.

"Are you crazy to buy such an expensive gift!" she said flirtatiously.

"How did you know?"

"I have received at least 20. This is the best, with the heart shape and all. You can't buy this for less than 3,000 to 4,000 dollars. Sorry to let you spend so much…"

With a thumping sound, he knelt down on his knees, interrupting her words.

"Yunayuan, please accept my love! Today, I'm specially asking for your love. Really. Give up whatever is past and start afresh. Let me share your suffering." As if reciting stage lines, he said this distinctly and forcefully.

"Get up, get up quickly. Don't act on an impulse." She tried to pull him up, but he held his ground.

"If you don't accept my proposal, I'll never stand up." He was firm like an ice cube.

"Don't be silly. I am grateful for your concern for me, but don't forget that I am a prostitute. There wouldn't be any future with me. Let's maintain the status quo. Isn't that good enough?" She attempted patiently to persuade him.

"No, I truly love you and can't leave you for a moment. I have known for a long time that I am genuinely in love with you, and am not acting on impulse. These words are from the bottom of my heart." He was still kneeling motionless on the floor, like a wooden man nailed to it.

She tried again to pull him up, but to no avail. How could she have such strength? Three Zhang, Yuanyuans wouldn't have succeeded. Moreover, he really meant what he said.

"Get up first and let's talk about it gradually." She stroked his head, as if humoring a three-year-old child.

"If you don't consent, I'll kneel here till dawn." He was as firm as a block.

For over 20 minutes, neither was willing to budge from this position, so the atmosphere was tense. Watching his expression, she could not control her tears, which rolled down his head, face and body.

"How could I not yearn for love? I am a kind of incense burner, though, used by dozens of men. It's no easy job to break with my past..." Tears welled in her eyes.

"I considered this and struggled. I don't mind about your past, but I care for your future." He was also in tears.

Tearfully, she helped him up. Along with her gesture, he stood up, elated.

The two of them, holding each other, cried their hearts out. For Yuanyuan, it was as if she wanted to cry out all her bitterness and empty it into the Niagara River. Lai cried his eyes out, as if he wanted to make a wreath of love with his tears. Their tears mingled together, spread outside the windows and mixed with the torrential falls, forming a wonderful and miraculous melody. It did not sound like a cry, but rather their laughter, a declaration of love at the end of the twentieth century.

The sunshine through the blinds, reflected on the two crying lovers, was glistening and crystal clear.

40. A Toast to a New Start in Life

Neither Lai, Wenxiong nor Zhang, Yuanyuan would have expected that their first Valentine's Day would be filled with tears. It was already dusk when they cried their tears dry, and rosy clouds were slowly moving to the west in the sky.

"Where shall we go for dinner? Would you like to go dancing in Toronto?" Lai, Wenxiong suggested.

Shaking her head, she said, "After crying like this, I don't want to go anywhere. Let's stay at home and have a Valentine's Day just for the two of us."

"We've got to have a decent dinner." He did not understand.

"That's easy. We'll order takeout. A French restaurant nearby is pretty good. With a phone call, they'll deliver within an hour. I've got nothing but liquor. I can mix any kind of cocktail you prefer."

He nodded and said, "Whatever the hostess says. I like liquor."

Zhang, Yuanyuan was adept at creating a milieu. Six long candles were lit on the table in the living room and the pink roses were put in the vase, while the other five bouquets of flowers were thrown onto the kitchen floor – a sort of demonstration for Lai, Wenxiong to see that she had drawn a line of demarcation between him and the other men.

She opened the liquor cupboard for whisky, rum etc. and opened the refrigerator for ice-cubes before she got busy mixing the drinks.

"I'll make a Manhattan for you, which will be as good as in a restaurant. Satisfaction guaranteed."

So saying, she handed a Manhattan with a red cherry to Lai, Wenxiong. For herself, she made a "blue Hawaii" with rum and blue orange wine plus lemonade, a typical tropical cocktail with the pale blue resembling the South Pacific Ocean and the ice-cubes like white waves.

The two of them sat opposite each other. Five or six dishes were quite enough for them. From the CD player came the sweet country music of Shania Twain.

They both raised their glasses and attempted to say something, but both stopped short.

She hesitated for a moment, and then asked wittily, "To what?"

"To the start of a new life." He raised his head to gaze at her, having found the appropriate words.

"Good. A toast to the start of a new life." She was smiling from ear to ear.

They sipped the liquor and gazed at each other without talking. This meant the significant beginning of their love. Nobody knew whether this would end in happiness or misery.

"You are really adept at mixing cocktails. A Manhattan should have this pungent taste. Although it's easy to mix, many bars can't make it properly. I don't know why," Lai, Wenxiong said to himself.

"Don't underestimate it. If you drink too much, you might get drunk."

"Of course, in old American English Manhattan means 'drunkard'. I forgot to ask you where you learned this skill?"

"In the strip bar. Just by watching the bartender, I acquired the skill. I can mix about 30 different cocktails, if not more. Just order it and I can make it."

Lai, Wenxiong nodded with pleasure and asked for another

Manhattan. After two cocktails, he started to recite a poem written to certain tunes:

Hills upon hills in light or dim aura glow;
Her cloudy hair sweeps o'er her cheeks like snow.
Painting her brows, she feels listless;
Combing, washing, all tardiness.
She mirrors herself to and fro;
Her face, a rose? She blurs the two.
She strokes 'broidered coat with a sign,
Where a pair of partridges fly.

(Translated by Prof. Zhao, Yanchun of Sichuan Foreign languages Institute – Translator's note.)

She was all smiles and asked, "Who wrote this poem? It is so beautiful!"

He was a bit drunk and replied, "It's a poem written to a certain tune with strict tonal patterns and rhyme schemes, in a fixed number of lines and words, by Wen, Tingyun, a poet of the Tang Dynasty. This is the most popular one of 14 "Pusa Man" poems, magnificent and elegant, and it gives much food for thought. The fourteen poems are a part of monumental work in Chinese poetic history with a far-reaching impact on the future. Do you know that many Chinese scholars in history have written patterned poems in praise of prostitutes? Some even say that it's not an overstatement to call the patterned poems of the Song Dynasty the literature of prostitution…"

Zhang, Yuanyuan, unwilling to lag behind, said wittily, "I only know that Mr. Lin, Yutang commented: 'Without prostitutes, music might have vanished in China.' I know as well that singing prostitutes are a part of Chinese culture."

His face lit up, "They are not merely related, but can't be separated. Just look at Chinese cultural history: in which dynasty did prostitutes fail to make a contribution? …"

She said coquettishly, "I didn't expect you to know so much about Chinese culture."

"That's nothing. Later, I can recite to you long, long paragraphs of poems from the Tang dynasty and patterned poems from the Song Dynasty. The latter are my favorites and I learned many by heart. Would you recite one? You were a cultural youth too, weren't you?"

She was a bit flighty, "I've forgotten all the ancient poems I learned by heart. Please let me go."

"OK, we'll make up later. Miss, another glass please, whisky plus ice-cubes will do..." He was getting happier, obviously a bit drunk.

Soon, the telephone was ringing again and again-- men wishing Zhang, Yuanyuan a happy Valentine's Day. She responded perfunctorily. Then she shut off all phones and her cell phone, to avoid interference with their mood.

The indistinct candles flickered in the room, where the two of them toasted again and again, telling each other distant stories. This was an unusual Valentine's evening, with flowers and liquor, with tears and love, with poems and emotion. No wonder they got drunk.

Chapter Nine

Twisting Route of their Love's Ups and Downs

41. Genuinely Falling in Love

Lai, Wenxiong is eating a Japanese snack perfunctorily on the plane. The food seems tasteless, perhaps due to bad cooking or to his poor appetite-- more to the latter. The past events, sweet or bitter, are interwoven and swirling before his eyes non-stop.

On Valentine's evening in 2000, Lai, Wenxiong and Zhang, Yuanyuan got dead drunk. The next day when Zhang opened her eyes, it was already 2pm. She found herself naked, and Lai, also naked, with one arm holding her, was still sound asleep. She shook him awake at once. Opening his sleepy eyes, Lai stretched out his arms to hold her and showed no intention of getting up. Every corner of the room was permeated with their carnal fragrance and every molecule of the room was filled with the element of love.

Urged again and again by Zhang, Yuanyuan, Lai lazily sat up. He collected himself and found an embarrassing mess of pink lingerie, black bras, men's white underwear and tissues littering the bed. He said thoughtfully, "It's a severe test of love!"

Zhang asked coquettishly, "Would you like to write a poem to eulogize it?"

He straightened himself up, sat on the bed foolishly, gazed at the ceiling and held his hands to pray piously, "My lord, we are grateful to you for your gifts to the two free hearts which got linked on romantic Valentine's Day..."

"Damn! A condom was not used. I might get pregnant." Zhang, Yuanyuan suddenly yelled with shock and seemed to burst out crying, her two eyes wide open.

Lai held her by waist and comforted her, "Don't scare me. Just once and you'll get pregnant?"

"Haven't you ever heard people say that more women get pregnant on Valentine's Day?"

He tried to humor her, "Don't kid me. I only know that more people lose their virginity on Valentine's Day."

"I'm not kidding. A few days ago I watched news about this, maybe on American TV."

He sat up and massaged her smooth shoulder, "What's wrong with that? I'll fall in love with a little Yuanyuan again."

"A wolf. You are a big wolf. What can you expect from a dog but a bark! I don't want to be an unmarried mother. I would like to enjoy the last phase of my youth."

He said expectantly, "Your daughter will be a great beauty."

She was probably not aware that after a man has had sex with a woman and begins to love her genuinely, he subconsciously tries to get to know her past, including her childhood, her family, her first kiss and first night with a man. Some men love their partners more after knowing the above; some alienate themselves from their partners, while others break up with them immediately. If you want to see how a woman grew up, it's best to let her give birth to a girl and witness her daughter's growth. Maybe that's an important reason why fathers love their daughters. They want to know personally their wives' past. Of course, this is also a sort of love, or more exactly, a transfer of love.

Talking about children, the two of them were yearning in high spirits. They both talked as if they would become parents the next day.

With clear and crisp laughter under the sunshine, the lovers longed for a future, magnificent and sacred, like the gorgeous sunshine. While they talked joyously, their burning bodies were also doing their jobs. Only by hearty lovemaking and forceful dancing could the lovers be worthy of Adam and Eve, who created them.

Starting on Valentine's Day, Lai, Wenxiong and Zhang, Yuanyuan fell in love, an unexpected turn of events for both of them. It seemed inconceivable that a modern-day Camille and a Ph.D. student in sociology could become so deeply attached. Some things in life cannot be judged by reason.

Lai pondered that it was not uncommon for some scholars to fall in love with prostitutes in ancient China and to leave their romantic stories to history. "The dream of Yangzhou in ten years" by Du, Mu won him the reputation of master of whoremongers. Liu, Yong, a great poet, lived a poor life involving and enjoying wine and whores. After his death, nothing was left for his burial. Many prostitutes contributed money for his grave and attended the funeral procession, all in mourning apparel. The scene reduced many people to tears. Zhu, Zhishan and Tang, Bohu, famous scholars in South China, both whoremongers, wrote many romantic poems. Would those ancient scholars have won immortal fame if they had not had any genuine feeling for the prostitutes? Lai, Wenxiong finally realized that no reason was required for love between a man and a woman, nor were there any rules to be found. Relationships must be pre-destined.

Zhang, Yuanyuan was determined to start afresh, so she cut off all contacts with other men and devoted her love to one man. Grateful to Wenxiong's respect and concern for her, she was obedient to him. Following his suggestion, she re-entered an English class and planned to study nursing, her old profession, in a community college in a year or so. He gave her a computer as a gift for her study. She learned, under his careful instruction, how to type in Chinese on the computer. Since she was on the Internet, it was not hard to kill time. Once surfing the net, half a day passed quickly. On the net, she could read the "Xinmin Evening News", the "Wenhui Daily" and the "Jiefang Daily" published in her hometown and learned details of what was going on in Shanghai. She paid special attention to "Shanghai, Huangpu River, Huaihai Road, Nanjing Road," etc. in the news, which alleviated her homesickness, although she missed her hometown even more.

As a literary youth who treasured books as her life, she soon discovered "Dragonsource International Books on the Net", especially its qikan.com with journals, which she liked so much that she browsed it almost every day. She subscribed to several electronic literary monthly journals, including "Great Masters" of Yunnan, "People's Literature" & "Chinese Writers" of Beijing, etc. She also loved novels written by Chi, Li, a female novelist in Wuhan; essays by Zhang, Xiaoxian, a female writer in Hong Kong; and novels by Liao, Huiying, a female writer in Taiwan. She felt closely attached to and searched for work by her peers, such as Wei, Hui and Mian Mian. In her eyes, the value of "Shanghai Babe" was not the bold description of sex or the worship of the six-inch penis of Mark, a German, but the existence of a new younger generation with drastically different material and spiritual yearnings from those of its forefathers.

The most interesting thing for her was to talk online with Lai, Wenxiong. It saved her long distance phone bills and was a new adventure. Sometimes she wrote love letters of two to three thousand characters. He could not help praising her literary talent. Once he said seriously to her that she might become a writer if she practiced enough. In two weeks, she received the magazines "United Literature" and "Crown" published in Taiwan.

Puzzled, she called him, "Since I can read the magazines online, why did you subscribe to the paper format?"

He explained slowly, "It hurts your eyes to be online too much. You would feel uncomfortable reading a whole book. In a couple of days, other magazine 'novels' will be mailed to you. It is very convenient to order online."

Moved to tears, Yuanyuan said quivering, "Wenxiong, it's so nice and considerate of you to do that. I don't know how to reward you in this life."

"What a fool! Not everything in the world is done for reward. Still, I'm a bit selfish. I don't want to see you wearing glasses. I hate it when women wear glasses." He convinced her skillfully.

"How glib you are. I'll read these magazines and I might submit some articles."

"That's wonderful! These three journals reflect the literary circle of Taiwan from different angles. 'United Literature' is an old magazine of high quality, representing the level of Taiwan literature at its highest standard. I used to read every issue of this magazine. 'Crown' and 'Novels', targeting the younger readers, aim at popularity, with special fashion designs in each issue. If you want to contribute, you can try the latter two magazines first. 'United Literature' prefers contributions by well-known writers..." His introduction of the literary circle in Taiwan showed his thorough familiarity with it.

With his hearty encouragement, she avidly read works by famous writers, both at home and abroad, such as Jia, Pingwa; Mo, Yan; Yu, Hua; Kafka and Faulkner. Her "dream of becoming a star" in her girlhood had been shattered; however, the "dream of becoming a writer" might be realized in the future. She had never been so self-confident. It was a tribute to the magic of love.

On the other hand, after falling in love with her, Lai, Wenxiong found that his reading efficiency increased and his research developed more smoothly than expected. In his own words, the balance of yin and yang had promoted the development of his thinking. On weekdays, he talked with her on the phone at night or chatted online with her. After two seminars on Friday afternoons, he drove eagerly to meet his lover. A brief week's parting seemed like a long, long separation. They usually were intimate for several hours.

In her body, he experienced real beauty. With her fragrance, he obtained inspiration. With her burning desire, he made numerous solemn declarations of man. Such an extraordinary beauty was the best gift bestowed on him by God. Who says that she is not the Oriental Venus? Who says that modern prostitutes are not as good as the ancient ones? He willingly bowed to her and would sacrifice everything for her. The flames of love had long ago burned her past shame to ashes. No wonder Dumas (Jr.) said, "Any woman who shows genuine feeling will raise a man to sublimation."

For several Sunday evenings, he racked his brains to find excuses not to leave the warm nest. She pretended to be unaware of his tricks and let him stay another night, to expand, burn and raise himself to sublimation in her body.

42. Making the Distinction between Right and Wrong

Spring with butterflies dancing among the flowers is lovely, but a leisurely weekend is even better. Flowers bloom for lovers, and wine gets drunk by lovers.

One Saturday evening with flowers and wine, the two of them were overwhelmed with joy when Lai, Wenxiong noticed a sorrowful look on Zhang, Yuanyuan's face. This kind of sadness can only be discerned with the sixth sense. Somebody who is not deeply in love, or a careless lover, would not have seen it. It was discerned by reticent observation and experience. Maybe it was because Lai studied social sciences and paid more attention to feelings. No minute changes could escape his sharp eyes.

Lai, Wenxiong lightly draped a sleeping gown on Yuanyuan's shoulders and held her closely in his arms. He asked her if she was a bit under the weather and she shook her head. He asked if he was too rough in bed and she said she preferred the excitement when he behaved like a rogue. He asked if her family members in Shanghai were OK. She nodded... Finally Lai became suspicious.

He asked again patiently, "Is that Russian woman making trouble again?"

Zhang didn't say a word, her head lowered. He asked with a

frown, "Yuanyuan, you promised that you would hide nothing from me. How can I help you if you don't tell me?"

She remained silent with a long face, like a marble statue. He couldn't stop himself and yelled with impatience, "I've told you so many times that I really love you, not just your body. Tell me about the Russian woman. Is her name Katyusha?"

Zhang, lying in his arms, nodded eventually and talked slowly, "It might be fate. One night Katyusha and I were seeking clients in front of a high-class hotel in Toronto when a skinny man came up to me. He attempted to grope my breasts while talking to me. As I retreated, Katyusha boxed his ears. That man was going to strike her with his fists when a tall man dashed from behind her and struck him to the ground with his fists. When police cars came speeding along, I followed Katyusha to escape… At that point, we became friends. She showed concern for me and sometimes introduced me to her clients. We lived together for awhile, not like lesbians: we just rented an apartment with separate rooms."

She went on, "Later she told me that the tall man was her boyfriend, nicknamed 'Hawk', also a Russian. Hawk seldom stayed in Toronto, but lived mostly in Vancouver, under the control of a drug-trafficking group. I wonder if you know that the anti-drug division of the RCMP, in co-operation with the American Drug Control Bureau, cracked a heroin smuggling case at the beginning of last year, confiscating as many as 20 kilos with a market value of 8 million Canadian dollars. It was said to be the biggest heroin smuggling case in Canadian history."

"I think I saw it on TV. The culprit was killed by the underworld, wasn't he?" Lai had some blurry impression in his mind.

Zhang continued with a nod, "Right. The dead person was Hawk. At around 3am early one morning, Katyusha and I were going to bed when someone knocked 4 times on the door. Katyusha told me that it was her secret signal with Hawk. When the door was opened, it really was Hawk, who looked flustered with a traveling bag in his hand. He said that he had flown to Toronto from Vancouver the night before and had stayed in a hotel near Chinatown. He had just fetched the bag of heroin from a truck that delivers seafood to Chinatown. When he walked to the hotel to get his car, he suddenly discovered two people watching him from a café across the street. He thought they were detectives in plain clothes, so he called a taxi at once and came directly to our place. He figured that the police were waiting for him at the hotel, so he knew he had to return to deal with them. He begged Katyusha to deliver the bag to a hotel in Windsor, where an American from Detroit would pick it up. Seeing that Katyusha was hesitant, he explained that it had been no easy job shipping it from Vancouver and drew out a huge roll of greenbacks. However, a reward of ten thousand US dollars failed to convince Katyusha. Finally he begged, promising to stop smuggling after this and to marry her, go away with her and have children. Katyusha, moved to tears, agreed to help him one last time. She took a handful of US dollars, stuffed the money into her handbag and gave me a handful too. Then she put the stuff from the traveling bag into another leather one and filled the traveling bag with clothes and handed it back to Hawk. He kissed her forehead and turned to leave."

"What happened then? Did you go to Windsor with her?" Lai, Wenxiong asked anxiously.

"Yes. I was afraid for her safety, so I volunteered to accompany her. I drove the car when we went there and she drove on the way back. Everything went smoothly and it was pretty simple. With the secret signal given by Hawk, Katyusha got in touch with the American man, who got into our car and took the leather bag. It was agreed beforehand that the buyer would pay the Russian in New York... Who would have expected that the American man would be arrested a few hours later? It turned out that he had long been tailed by the RCMP. While crossing the border to the US, he was caught red-handed by the American police. He admitted his crime and the police issued a nationwide warrant for Hawk and others. What was more tragic was that a body floating on Lake Ontario was discovered by the Toronto police three days later. It was none other than Hawk. The police suspected that he had been murdered to prevent him from disclosing the secret... After this misfortune, Katyusha collapsed completely. She lay in bed all day, like an idiot. Later she moved up North, and perhaps she found a job as a stripper. After that, we had no contact, not even by phone."

Zhang then sat up and continued while leaning on the bed, "Just three days before I left Toronto, I met her by chance at the cosmetics department in the Eaton Center. She said she had been looking for me. She became a stripper at a famous strip bar after she moved back to Toronto. I had made up my mind not to trust anybody, so I told her I was going to study in Hamilton, instead of telling her my real whereabouts. Before parting, she insisted on getting my cell phone number. After I came to Niagara Falls, I changed my number; however, the area code 905 is the same as in Hamilton, so she believes that I live there."

"It means that, up till now, she still thinks that you are in Hamilton and doesn't know for sure that you live here, right?" Lai said each word distinctly.

Zhang nodded and Lai smiled mysteriously. She failed to understand the real meaning of his smile.

She went on, "A few months ago, Katyusha was sick for a long time and could not dance. I made a special trip to Toronto to visit her. Seeing her misery, I gave her 200 dollars. She refused at first and finally accepted the money as a loan."

Lai held one of her hands and asked, "Why does she call you these days?"

Zhang grasped his other hand and said with her eyes wide open, "Wenxiong, I declare that I absolutely do not do evil things with her. I listened to your advice. She called to invite me to go to Hong Kong and Thailand with her, as she was not familiar with Asia. She wants to ship heroin to South America via Vancouver. She says that she'll pay all my traveling expenses and give me fifty thousand US dollars …"

"She is instigating you to traffic in drugs! My god! It's terrible! That Katyusha is audacious! Doesn't she know the risks? Canada has laws to send these people to jail… What are you going to do?"

"I am trying to think of a proper reason to refuse. If I give her a flat refusal, she will be displeased. A cornered beast will do something desperate, you know. What I fear most is that she will tell the police that I accompanied her to Windsor to deliver heroin. At present, this is an unsolved case after Hawk's death, as are many other cases in Canada…"

Lai talked with clenched teeth, "I'm not blaming you, but you should have told me about such an important thing long ago. Luckily I found it out before it's too late. Yuanyuan, I hope this will never happen again!"

Seeing his long face, like a hungry tiger, she acted like a spoiled child, kissed his neck, lay in his arms and talked in a low voice, "I didn't want such trifles to interfere with your study."

He lowered his head to kiss her face and said, "My lady, this is no trifle, but a big thing. Let me ask you solemnly: is there anything else you have hidden from me? Do you have any other contact with gangsters? You've got to tell me the truth."

She shook her head and reassured him. He asked again and she replied "No" once more. Gazing at her transparent eyes, he finally believed her. He was confident of his judgment, perhaps because he believed the old saying: the eyes are the windows to the soul.

Her sleeping robe disappeared without notice and her carnal aroma infiltrated his nostrils. As a habit, Lai touched her smooth shoulders, as if massaging her, and comforted her, "Don't you worry. I'll figure out a well-conceived plan for you to cut contact with Katyusha. It's better to keep far away from these types to avoid future trouble. We have to watch our steps carefully, so as not to have any further contact."

Zhang nodded obediently, like a little lamb. She turned suddenly and rubbed her two firm breasts against his chest and said coquettishly, "When have I disobeyed you, especially in bed…"

"You Shanghai babe, deserve to be spanked!"

Before he finished talking, her coiling body was around him like a snake. He also stretched his strong limbs to dance with the snake to their hearts' content. The resounding noise of Niagara Falls outside the windows was drowned by the growing symphony.

43. Breaking with the Gangsters

On Saturday evening the next week, Lai, Wenxiong, driving a dark blue Volvo, arrived in Toronto with Zhang, Yuanyuan. This was a carefully planned "scheme" aimed at safely "taking leave" of Katyusha, the Russian prostitute.

At 8pm sharp, they arrived at Le Papillon, a French restaurant on Church Street. Its entrance was not wide, but it was spacious inside, giving people the impression of a small mouth with a big belly. The large hall was lined with big green trees, and the white tables were covered with blue-and-white checkered tablecloths, simple but elegant. The burning candles with their little flames on each table endowed the restaurant with a romantic atmosphere. Lai, Wenxiong discovered this Quebec-styled French restaurant on the Internet. It said that the restaurant had been named the most popular French restaurant by the "Toronto Sun" for six consecutive years.

People usually wear formal attire to have dinner in this restaurant. Lai, Wenxiong was a bit casual, with a dark blue suit, sky blue shirt and a red-and-blue tie, looking simple but full of vigor and vitality. Zhang, Yuanyuan looked a bit mature in a low-cut light yellow dress, with a shining heart-shaped sapphire necklace, Lai's Valentine gift, hanging properly between her breasts.

They were seated opposite each other and sipping ice water when Zhang waved to a lady who entered. Lai looked in that direction and found, just as she had been described, a tall, statuesque and sexy beauty. She was in summer attire, wearing a flimsy black slip dress, carrying a small black leather bag and a black leather jacket. She came fluttering lightly, bringing a touch of spring to the restaurant. Zhang stood up to hug her intimately, sickening Lai a bit.

"This is Peter, my fiancé, whom I talked about over the phone." Her hand touched his shoulder to display their intimacy.

Katyusha introduced herself and politely shook hands with him. She spoke English with a strong Russian accent, so Lai talked in fluent Russian to her, "You deserve the reputation of the most beautiful woman in Toronto."

"You can speak Russian? That's wonderful," Katyusha replied in well-versed Russian.

Zhang was surprised because she did not know that Lai could speak Russian. After they talked in Russian for a while and realized that Zhang was a bit displeased, they reverted at once to speaking in English. Lai explained that he had learned Russian from a Russian lady at whose home he stayed when he came to Canada.

Katyusha said sarcastically, "So you cohabited with a Russian lady long ago."

Lai explained anxiously, "Not in that sense. The lady was over seventy and her hubby had passed away long ago. She was lonely with a big house and her children seldom visited her, so she rented out two rooms to students from abroad at a low rent. She loved to talk with us and made Russian meals for us on the weekends..."

Zhang continued with the subject, "It seems that this old lady knows how to enjoy life, spending her days happily by talking to younger people."

"Unfortunately she died in a traffic accident over a year ago. I got the news more than three months after the event. I was sorry to have missed her funeral." Lai said sadly.

"Good people die early in this world." Katyusha made the comment after pondering.

While waiting for the waiter, Katyusha whispered to Zhang,

quickly, using their jargon, "Where did you find such a handsome 'cigar'? A man who speaks Russian should be mine. Could you let me have him tonight? Then I can review my Russian and have a taste of the Chinese 'cigar'."

"Sorry, my beauty, this Chinese man can't satisfy you." Zhang refused to be eclipsed and answered while pinching her thigh.

Katyusha talked in high spirits, "I like something fresh! You promised that we could share good men."

"Sorry, I don't want to share this one." Zhang pinched her thigh again.

Katyusha's big mouth was close to her ear, "Can you tell me how he behaves in bed?"

Zhang raised two thumbs, which made Katyusha laugh out loud. She almost fell off the chair. The waves of lewd laughter from the two women drew supercilious looks from people at nearby tables. Some even cast disdainful glances at them. One man shook his head and trembled with anger, his head wagging uncontrollably after Katyusha raised her small finger to him.

Sitting opposite them, Lai, Wenxiong could hear indistinctly what they were talking about, but he pretended to be cool and collected, taking this opportunity to observe Katyusha carefully. She had distinct features with a high nose and bright, piercing eyes: she was alluring and charming. Her big mouth would be too large for most women, but it looked very sexy and was a special feature for her. Her dress scarcely covered her enormous and firm breasts, about one third of which were exposed to attract men's attention.

There was no doubt that the two ladies in front of him were both beauties. But if he were to make an objective judgment, the beauty of Katyusha had an enticing and promiscuous touch. All biologically normal men would have the impulse to touch her, or even better, to spend a night with her to experience her tenderness and licentiousness. The beauty of Zhang, Yuanyuan, on the other hand, had a graceful and elegant touch. She would not share her bed with average men. To say it more clearly, the former was a prostitute, whose body could be enjoyed by any man with money, but the latter was a high-class social butterfly, who was choosy.

They were talking heartily while savoring the steaks. After talking to her for a short time, Lai decided that Katyusha had been well educated and had gotten into some bad habits afterwards. According to Zhang, Yuanyuan, Katyusha had attended Normal College in the former Soviet Union and was determined to be a "people's teacher". Unfortunately, she met a man who belonged to the underworld and was swindled and forced into prostitution in Canada. Lai couldn't help but think of the words: Fortunate women are similar, but unfortunate women have their unique misfortunes.

Halfway through dinner, Zhang touched her belly apologetically and said to Katyusha, "We're getting married next week in Taipei and will go directly to California after our honeymoon…"

"I have a teaching job in Los Angeles." Lai interrupted.

"So you invited me here to say goodbye! Why didn't you tell me earlier? I haven't got a present for you." Katyusha complained.

"I didn't tell you over the phone for fear you'd spend money." Zhang took her hand.

Katyusha touched Zhang's belly and said mysteriously, "Are you in the family way?"

Zhang nodded and told her she would have the baby and work hard to bring it up. Recalling her own past, Katyusha said with moist eyes, "Congratulations to you both! You have a family at long last."

Then, Lai, Wenxiong took an envelope from his suit pocket and handed it to Katyusha. "Here is a little money for you, a token of appreciation for your concern for Camille. Without you, there would be no Camille today."

"Not really. We cared for each other and commiserated with each other. You just got a job and still bear a heavy financial burden. Keep the money for your kid." Katyusha unexpectedly spoke these touching words.

Zhang put the envelope into her hand and said, "Please accept this little token. You were sick for some time and it was hard for you to earn money."

Katyusha replied politely, "It was not too bad. Although we were not allowed to dance on men's legs, we still played tricks, such as letting them touch us to their hearts' content in the box seats. Their wallets would be emptied when they left. Recently, a gang of Russians often patronized the bar and two wealthy men would tip me over a hundred dollars…"

Lai talked smoothly, "Katyusha, please accept it. Otherwise Camille will give me a hard time…"

Seeing their sincerity, Katyusha accepted the cash. She asked them repeatedly to call her after they arrived in the US. They agreed and advised her to take good care of herself and to abstain from drugs.

Zhang talked to Katyusha sentimentally, "Who knows when we'll meet again?"

"It's easy to go to Los Angeles. After you give birth to the baby, I'll fly there to congratulate you." Her words enlivened the atmosphere immediately.

Later Katyusha looked at her watch and jumped up, "It's late. I've got to go to the police."

"Why?" Zhang was shocked.

Katyusha replied with a smile, "Rest assured, I have not committed any crimes. A group of off-duty policemen is waiting for me to strip."

Lai was puzzled, "Can you do it in the police bureau?"

Katyusha inhaled a puff and replied slowly, "This is Canada. Why not? They are off duty. I was told that one policeman would be celebrating his 40th birthday and his wife came to our bar for me. One hour for three hundred dollars plus tip. Pretty good."

"No wonder your dress is so sexy. To feed the big fish." Zhang said naughtily.

Katyusha glanced at Zhang and said, "You Chinese often

say: As a wanderer from place to place, I have to do it in spite of myself. Besides, I will take the opportunity to get familiar with those policemen. Some of them patrol in our area, so they might be useful to me in the future…"

Before parting, Katyusha whispered to Zhang while hugging her, "You've got to call me when you arrive in the US. Let me know if you need my help."

Zhang held her hands closely, her eyes moist with tears. Katyusha held Lai's hand and talked in Russian, "Don't you dare bully Camille; otherwise, I won't let you go."

Lai drove his Volvo quickly on Highway QEW, heading for Niagara in the west.

Feeling Zhang's sense of loss, he talked casually, "Katyusha is really a beauty. She is more elegant than I expected."

"She's not bad and is loyal to her friends. But she gets involved with gangsters. I guess the recent Russian clients want her to get involved in trafficking in Asia. I'm really worried for her. I know she needs the money. Did you notice that she stretched out her hand when you gave her the envelope, although she pretended to refuse?"

"I was afraid that she might refuse. In order to break with such people, you have to give $500, or even $5,000. It is called 'losing money to avoid disasters'. We repaid her kindness by offering her a little money to settle the accounts. We shouldn't be involved with such people. You never know: one day you might get killed if you stick with her."

Zhang said with a touch of sentiment, "Well, she was pretty good to me."

Lai nodded and looked at the clock in his car: it was exactly 10 o'clock. He said happily, "From now on, your cell phone number will be changed. That means that you have broken completely from the gangsters. Please keep the new number secret from everyone. I didn't list the new number with Bell Canada. Katyusha will not bother you. You don't have to be so cautious…"

Zhang said emotionally, her left hand touching his right leg, "Wenxiong, I'm really grateful to you. You are so considerate. Without your plan, I don't know how I would have refused Katyusha. Maybe I'd have followed the same old road to ruin and gotten involved in drug trafficking, because money is enticing and I can't resist my friends…"

"Say no more. Let bygones be bygones. Look, the moon is particularly bright tonight." Lai said meaningfully.

Zhang, with hot tears in her eyes, struggled with the few words, "Yes, it'll be a sunny day tomorrow."

44. Twists and Turns in their Emotions

Who would have expected that a major crisis would occur between Zhang, Yuanyuan and Lai, Wenxiong? They had been deeply in love with each other. Then, without warning, more than two months after Valentine's Day, there was a soul stirring "blow up".

As a rule, he spent every weekend at her place. This time, however, she tactfully refused, saying that a relative of hers was coming to Toronto for business from San Francisco and would stay at her place for two days to visit Niagara Falls.

His instinct told him that it was a made-up story. He had two reasons: first, he had never heard her mention any relatives in the United States; second, even if she did have relatives there, they would have informed her of a business trip one or two weeks beforehand, not at the last minute.

Out of respect for her, he decided not to expose her trick. On Saturday night, however, he was at a loss as to what to do. He opened a book, but could not read. He turned on the TV and failed to take in anything he was watching. Lying on a couch, he began to give in to foolish fantasies. Perhaps she was involved with another man behind his back and had to meet him secretly over the weekend. Probably David, general manager of the auto company, came to spend the night with her – the old flame was re-ignited. Or maybe there was some hidden secret to be resolved over the weekend… The more he thought, the more nervous he became and the more furious he was.

After 8 pm, he couldn't keep from phoning her, but nobody answered. He tried her cell phone, but it was turned off. He failed to get in touch with her after 9pm. Concerned about her safety and fearful that another man was involved, he had to drive to her place to see what had happened.

It was already 11pm when he arrived at the 100 Lakeshore Building. He rang the bell, but nobody answered the door. He called and nobody answered the phone. He went down to the underground parking lot and found her BMW there. This proved that somebody had picked her up for a date. He was furious.

He parked his car on a side street beside the entrance of the building and sat in the car, waiting to see what she was up to. Several other cars came in and went out, with no trace of her. He tried her cell phone non-stop, but it was still off.

After midnight, no more cars arrived. At 1am in the morning, a white Lincoln passed him. Lai, Wenxiong discovered the lady getting out of the car to be none other than Zhang, Yuanyuan, who was kissing a foreign man goodbye. Lai was beyond himself with rage.

The moment the Lincoln left, Lai, Wenxiong dashed out of his car and yelled, "Zhang, Yuanyuan!"

She was shocked to hear the familiar voice. Turning around, she made sure it was Lai, Wenxiong, and then walked toward him.

"So it's you. Have you been waiting long?" She spoke first when they met.

"You remembered to come back?" He spoke in a loud voice.

"Don't behave like that. Park the car and I'll tell you where I was when we go upstairs." She took his hand and walked to the car.

Lai had to force himself to swallow his anger.

After they entered the apartment, both sat face to face on the sofa, without any expression. Neither wanted to break the ice. The silence continued for ten minutes.

Finally Lai broke the silence, "Your relative has gone?"

"There was no relative. I told you a lie," she said frankly with her head lowered.

"Why did you lie? You don't trust me." He raised his head and shouted himself hoarse.

"Let me ask you: why did you wait at the gate at midnight? To check my room?" She also raised her head.

"I am not qualified to check your room. I failed to contact you by cell and was worried that something might have happened to you."

"Rest assured, I didn't jump into Niagara Falls."

"I wouldn't have worried if I had known that you had gone out in a Lincoln. I have never had the fortune to enjoy such luxury," he said sarcastically.

"Don't mutter and mumble. Say it directly. I'm not afraid because I haven't done anything wrong. I forgot to take my cell phone with me. I called you at around 10pm when I went out, but nobody answered."

"You remembered to call me, then. Well, that was another big fish, eh? Not everybody can afford to drive a Lincoln." He wagged his head, as if in a commanding position.

"What did you mean? God damn it!" She screamed and cursed in English.

He said slowly on purpose, "Don't get agitated. Have I hit your sore spot? Just tell me why you said that some relative was visiting while you secretly met a wealthy man. If you don't want to see me, let's have it out. I, Lai, Wenxiong, will not keep pestering you. A one-sided relationship won't do even if I like you."

"Make yourself clear. What do you mean by 'secret meeting with a rich man'? I told you before that you would have to meet three requirements if you wanted to be my boyfriend. You consented. I don't want to have to explain. Everything was open and above-board, caused by coincidence." She looked impatient.

He could hardly control himself, "Coincidence? Coincidence? It's easier to change mountains and rivers than a person's nature…"

"Get out! You get out of here!" She stood up and yelled angrily.

Her deafening screams and cries brought him to his senses. Still, it was too late to cry over spilt milk. His words had touched a sensitive spot; it was like rubbing salt in her wounds. She attempted to push him out, but he refused to get up.

"I'll call the police if you don't leave."

"Yuanyuan, I'm sorry I said that." He got up to keep her from taking action.

"Don't touch me. We are finished. I knew that you'd say something like this some day." She looked as if she was about to make a call.

He had to leave reluctantly.

She shut the door and burst out crying. She knew that men were dissatisfied once they got what they wanted, and that they tried to find out their lovers' past and get control of their present and future life. The more familiar they get with women, the more they try to control them. Men always want their lovers to be virgins, while they play around. Since she was a prostitute, would he ever feel at ease? Perhaps he would never rid himself of the psychological hindrance.

After thinking about it carefully, Zhang, Yuanyuan felt that it was she who was to blame. Wasn't it best to maintain the original relationship between a "prostitute" and a "client"? The Chinese character "嫖" means that the client has to pay money and the woman provides him with sexual services in return. Both sides are willing and owe the other side nothing. A woman like her was not qualified to fall in love...

45. Fallen Deeper in Love after Reconciliation

Lai, Wenxiong felt as if his heart had been broken when he realized that he had caused trouble by his loose tongue. After all, he was deeply in love with her. He should have listened to her explanation no matter what had happened. Maybe he really had wronged her. For three consecutive days he phoned her, but she refused to respond.

Early on the fourth morning, he had to go to her place to

apologize. He had thought about it for three days and decided that it was because of his love for her that he was so concerned and jealous of her contacts with any other man. He would attempt to explain everything and to reconcile with her.

At 10 am she heard the bell and, through the magic eye on the door, she found none other than Lai with a bouquet of yellow roses. Her fury had not abated, so she didn't want to see him. She returned to her bedroom to sleep. Having thought about it for three days, she had come to the conclusion that it would not bear any fruit to be in love with him. He merely sympathized with her and any love based on mercy would not last long. At present, she was young and served as a tool for his libido. Even if they made up after their first quarrel, there would be another. It was ridiculous for a prostitute to fall in love with a man: most situations like this would end in tragedy. It's not the era of the Song Dynasty when prostitutes helped scholars create a brilliant poetic culture. It's better to simply cut off emotional contact with Lai, sooner rather than later, in order to suffer less.

He went down to the parking lot and found her car there. He went back up to her door and heard the toilet flush. This was evidence that she was at home and still angry with him. He decided to employ "the ruse of self-injury" to move her. If she did not open the door, he would not leave.

It was 3pm when she woke up from a nap. Forced by her subconsciousness, she tiptoed to the magic eye on the door and found him still standing at the door. He heard a noise and rang the bell at once. She turned a deaf ear. Every ten minutes he rang the bell. She pondered and struggled with every bell. Is he thirsty or hungry? Where does he go to the washroom? Does he really love me? … At 8 pm when she heard the bell again, her heart softened. Through the magic eye, she found him pale-faced and in low spirits. She couldn't bear to resist. Her stone of heart yielded to his infatuation. It was better to let him in and tell him the truth. Maybe they would be reunited. She walked back and forth in the room and decided to wait another two hours. She'd let him in after he had waited for 12 hours.

He still rang the bell every ten minutes. After the twelfth bell, she finally opened the door.

Like comrades-in-arms through a life and death struggle, the two held each other closely and cried their eyes out.

"Yuanyuan, pardon me." He suddenly knelt down.

The moment he bent his knees, he collapsed on the floor like a loosened frame.

"Water, water..." He squeezed out a couple of words.

She quickly went to the refrigerator to get orange juice. He felt a little better after a large glass of juice.

"I almost fainted." He tried to stand up, but was still weak.

She helped him to the couch and started weeping, "It's your fault that you fell for a woman like me. Is it worth the trouble to love a prostitute?"

"Don't mention that word. I'm disgusted. I won't ask any questions or pay attention to anything. I only love you, genuinely love you." So saying, tears burst from his eyes and rolled down his face continuously.

"Don't cry. I hate to see men crying."

"Men don't cry over trifles. Yuanyuan, don't leave me, don't!"

"Do you regret what you said?"

He nodded forcefully. "Love requires forbearance and understanding. I'll follow the three points: trust you, obey you and not interfere with your privacy."

"You'll have to keep your promise! OK, I'll make some noodles for you. I haven't eaten either."

Soon she came out with two bowls of aromatic noodles with pork chops. The two ate like hungry wolves. In the twinkling of an eye, the two bowls were emptied.

"That was really delicious. It's the first time I've found noodles so yummy." He became lively again.

"Of course, even dog shit would be yummy if you haven't eaten for a whole day." So saying, she burst out laughing.

46. Her Secret Abortion Revealed

Right away, Zhang, Yuanyuan mixed a large glass of a white cocktail and placed it in the bedroom. Seeing Lai, Wenxiong's puzzlement, she said, "This is called 'Qiqi', a mixture of vodka and coconut milk. It's a pity I don't have any pineapple juice. This cocktail is symbolic of reconciliation. Hopefully, our misunderstanding will melt like the ice-cubes in the glass." The two of them drank it, with two straws, in one gulp.

Standing by the window, Lai gazed at the sky with his raised head and said emotionally, "Yuanyuan, how beautiful the moon is tonight! Look, the crescent moon is hanging there especially for us."

She nodded and said "the crescent moon" as if to herself. Then she couldn't help but sing in a loud voice,

"A cloud is floating over the mountain with a galloping horse,
A crescent moon is shining in the Town of Kangding.
I love you, first of all, for your good looks,
Secondly, for your ability to care for the home."

To Lai, Wenxiong, she sang much better than many singers at karaoke, and even better than those "stars", who sometimes make mistakes in the tune and words, although Zhang's voice was not comparable to those "golden throats". At least, it was an enjoyment of beauty to listen to her voice. She was singing with such feeling that Lai simply followed her, singing,

I can love any woman in the world,
You can court any man in the world,
Under the crescent moon,
You can court any man in the world."

The night was tranquil and graceful. In the room, it was dim and intoxicating. The "Love Song at Kangding", a song they never got tired of hearing, lingered in the room for a long, long time, joined by the sound of the falls outside in the dark.

The two of them were talking in whispers while sitting on the bed.

She felt extremely safe in his arms. He felt warm all over with desire. The sense of regaining somebody precious was expanding in both of them. He attempted to open her sleeping robe to indulge in her bodily aroma, but she warded him off with her hands.

"Wenxiong, I've got to tell you something important. But don't fly into a rage. You promised to think calmly about everything."

"Yes, Madam." He sat up straight and saluted. Both laughed loudly.

"Last Monday, I went for an abortion without your knowing it."

"Really? Don't scare me."

"I'm not kidding. Look, here is the doctor's certificate." She fetched a couple of papers from under her pillow.

"Remember we got drunk on Valentine's Day? The seed was sown that night."

"Just as you guessed."

"Yes. Your sperm is so active. I knew I was pregnant when I didn't get my period for over a month and then I started vomiting. I knew because I studied medical care. It was confirmed by a urine test."

"When did you decide to have an abortion?" He was holding her even more tightly.

"After constant consideration and struggling for several weeks, I finally made up my mind to have the abortion. I'm still young and don't want a baby so early. Moreover, how can I continue my studies with a kid? I know you are sincere, but you should not be distracted from studying for your degree."

"It's not that I'm blaming you. But you should at least have consulted with me and listened to my opinion on such an important matter. I've told you that I will not only share your happiness, but your pain as well."

"If I had told you, you'd have asked me to give birth to it. That would ruin both of us. It's no trifling matter to have a kid. We'd have to pay full attention to its upbringing." She looked very serious.

He touched her small hand, "I didn't realize you were so mature.

You've suffered and need more nutrition. I don't know much about this. Since you were a health care worker, buy some tonic for yourself. I'll get some money for you from the bank tomorrow."

"Don't talk to me about money. I'm willing to be with you, hoping that you will be genuinely kind to me. Besides, I have more money than you," she said smiling.

He held her shoulders and felt as if he had just woken up from a dream. "If that's the case, I really wronged you last Saturday night."

"Of course. I didn't want you to spend the weekend here, so I told a lie about a relative. If you had come, my abortion would have been revealed. However, I felt lonely that night and was anxious to meet you, perhaps because I was used to spending weekends with you. It so happened that Arvid invited me to a party. I told you before that he was an ex-councilor, and had stepped down because of a sex scandal. Many people deserted him after his position changed, so he was in low spirits. He was kind to me before and I didn't want to desert him. He attempted to court me, but I gently rejected him. I've kept my relationship with him pure. He has never taken advantage of me and we had at most courtesy kisses and hugs… That night, I was in a hurry and forgot to take my cell phone…"

"Yuanyuan, don't say any more. I'm not manly. Damn it. I was gauging the heart of 'a gentlewoman' with my own mean measure. You can punish me anyway you like."

She smiled slyly, "That's easy. No touching for at least one month."

"Certainly. It's nothing to endure such a penalty. You are a nurse. I'll obey you. But don't cheat me and prolong the time. I come to see you not only for my desire." So saying, his hand stealthily went to her upper body.

"You see, you sound nice but what is your hand doing?" She became flirtatious.

"This iron hand is not obedient. Look, it automatically goes to the magnetic part…" he grinned cheekily.

"You are the number 1 wolf in the world," she said coquettishly.

Chapter Ten

Plan for Meeting Future in-laws in Taiwan

Before the Engagement

47. Childlike Innocence Revealed during a Joyous Trip to the Falls

The sun is shining brightly with waves of clouds rolling.

Lai, Wenxiong comes closer to the porthole of the plane to look down. Every cloud has a silver lining with the sunshine, floating languidly away. He fixes his eyes on them, his train of thoughts being far and wide.

After drinking the white cocktail called "Qiqi", he and Yuanyuan got reconciled. Their feeling for each other was again sublimed. In Lai's opinion, lovers could only accelerate their mutual understanding by constant arguing: some would love each other more profoundly afterwards, while others might say "bye" after quarreling. He and Yuanyuan belong absolutely to the former category.

They got intoxicated in the embrace of spring and laughter, and their carnal and spiritual integration became more harmonious than ever. Lai, Wenxiong came to realize "peak experiences", a theory by American psychologist Maslow. The transporting moments were overwhelming wonder and awe. In their ecstasy, their personality was sublimed. Lai talked to the mirror more than once: Love, you are so mysterious that you can heal old wounds, erase the memory of past misery and inspire lovers to march towards their beautiful future.

Such repeated "peak experiences" not only made Zhang, Yuanyuan more mature as a woman, but also spiritually transformed her into a new person. She turned his sincere concern and love into powerful momentum and studied more diligently. Such exciting "peak experiences" brought her creative inspiration as well. For the first time she wrote, in English, a short poem entitled, "Innermost Feeling of a Maid in Spring" and submitted it to a regional weekly, without telling Lai, Wenxiong. She didn't expect that two weeks after her submission, her poem was published and she received a check of $50. It was not the first royalty she had received. Her poem was published in "Youth Newspaper" while she was studying in junior high and got RMB ¥10. Her essay was published in "Xinmin Evening News" while she was studying in Health School and got ¥20. However, this third time was extraordinary because the poem was written in English and it symbolized the rebirth of a degraded woman.

On the day she received the newspaper and the royalty, Zhang, Yuanyuan called Lai, Wenxiong at once. On hearing the good news, he said "wonderful" several times, as if his graduation thesis had been published. They wanted to celebrate, but she turned down his four or five proposals. Then she suggested a boat trip in Niagara Falls after 9 months' stay here and her simple wish was easily granted.

One Saturday morning, it was a brilliant sunny day without any cloud. They got up early, drank a cup of coffee and a slice of bread with strawberry jam. Zhang, Yuanyuan was in a white Nike sports wear printed with black words while Lai, Wenxiong was in a black sports wear of the same brand printed with white words. Both wore white Nike sneakers. Their matched lovers' dresses made them look neat and vigorous.

Before leaving, Zhang declared proudly, "Today's trip is on me. I'll pay with my royalty."

"Good. It's worth a permanent commemoration. I'll help out if it's not enough." Lai held her close to him.

She talked like a spoiled child, "A boat trip plus lunch is just $50. I made inquiries by phone and it's inexpensive to have lunch on Minolta Tower."

He nodded in gratification and held her hand to depart. Usually they stayed in the car or indoors, so Lai seldom witnessed her personality like a happy bird. At present, it was fully revealed. He just followed her, walking lively toward the docks at Clifton Hill.

While lining up for the cruise "Maid of the Mist", she was humming songs non-stop and Lai was a loyal listener. She didn't stop singing until they boarded the boat after putting on yellow raincoats. She forcefully grabbed his arm, as if she were afraid of dropping into the water.

The cruise was quite stable while passing the crystal curtain of the American Falls, but it was entirely different when it reached the horseshoe of Canadian Falls. All people on board were stunned by the splashing waves. Some of them didn't have time to hide their cameras, so their lenses got wet. Zhang, Yuanyuan was the only one who didn't wear a rain cap, and she just let the water wet her head.

"You little fool, the only one on the boat like this." Lai, Wenxiong hurried to put a rain cap on her.

She stubbornly refused and whispered to him, "I'd like to fully enjoy nature."

He reluctantly gave up by pinching her nose, but held her hands tightly, for fear of her jumping into the water on impulse.

The cruise got closer and closer to the bottom of Niagara Falls, with fallen water sway the boat up and down, and right and left. People on board were screaming in panic, like in the "Titanic" before its tragic sinking. Lai held Zhang's waist tightly, as if they were in real danger.

"How exciting! Gorgeous Falls, I'm willing to be your daughter…" Suddenly Zhang, Yuanyuan shouted at the top of her voice, like a drunken Li, Bai reciting a poem.

Lai, Wenxiong was filled with joy while seeing this. Her behavior showed that firstly she still had childlike innocence and secondly she was gifted with literary talent. The cruise paused briefly in front of the Falls and returned.

"It's a pity: I haven't showered myself fully." She complained.

He touched her wet long hair and said, "If you like it so much, we can come again next week."

She fetched a towel from her leather bag, wiped his face first and then dried her own hair.

Leaving the boat, she said full of emotion, "I have experienced the Falls rather than touring the Falls."

"Yes, the value lies in one's personal experience. You have some qualities of a poet." He took the chance to praise her again.

It was 12 at noon when they stepped into Minolta Tower and found a big crowd of visitors. That building is an observation tower financed by the Japanese camera company and very close to the Falls. The first floor is a gift store, and the 27th floor, a restaurant, the 28th and 29th floors are indoor and outdoor observation towers, while the 30th floor is a display room for Minolta cameras, with a staircase directly to the roof.

Perhaps due to their hunger, or fatigue caused by the intense swaying of the boat, they dashed to the elevator and went straight to the 27th floor. Having been seated, they drank a large cup of Coca Cola and felt better. They ate veggie salad while viewing the Falls, enjoying a distinctive flavor.

Zhang, Yuanyuan talked with feelings, "I'm never tired of viewing the Falls. Different angles show different kinds of beauty. No wonder, it's one of the world wonders!"

"I was afraid you might jump down from the boat without controlling yourself." He said sarcastically.

She retorted crazily, "To tell you the truth: it'd be a rare enjoyment to shut my eyes in the embrace of the Falls."

"You shouldn't violate a taboo. Never talk like that!" Lai, Wenxiong interrupted her at once.

"Sorry, I just talked at random"

"It's not the way to love nature. It should be a sort of personal experience. However, your behavior on board the boat fully revealed your childlike innocence. This is invaluable! A woman without innocence is beyond cure."

Zhang gazed at him with wide eyes, "It's love that recovered my innocence."

He nodded in satisfaction, "We should celebrate just for this. We've got to get drunk tonight."

"I'd join you even at the risk of my life. I'll make some Shanghai dishes for you."

He discovered that her dimples were so charming while laughing that he had already got drunk at the beauty before he drank any wine.

After lunch, they climbed to the rooftop. Without fences or glass, they could enjoy a 360 degrees' panorama of the magnificent Falls. The strong sunshine reflected on the Falls glistened on the water.

Looking at the awe-inspiring scenery, Zhang, Yuanyuan involuntarily recited a poem:

"How is the magnificent Mount Dai?
A boundless mass of green peaks and cliffs
Towering over the states Qi and Lu.
Nature doth summon here Wondrous Beauty;
The Light and Shade could divide and part.
The cumulus doth broaden one's breast;
'T would split one's eyelids to watch homing birds.
Some day I must climb up to the top,
To look down viewing all the peaks small."

(A poem by Du, Fu and translated by Sun, Dayu, p.267, An Anthology of Ancient Chinese Poetry and Prose, Shanghai Foreign Language Education Press -- Translator's note)

Lai, Wenxiong deliberately made things difficult for her, "Great beauty, let me test you: which mountain did Du, Fu climb when he wrote this poem?"

"It's Mount Tai. Dai is another name for it, the highest of the five great mountains in China. Mencius (Master Meng) once pointed out: Ascending Mount Tai, you'll find other peaks small..." Zhang, Yuanyuan talked in ancient Chinese language like a lady of old times.

"Where have you learned all this? You sound so suave." He was a bit shocked.

"From the Internet. I have no other knack but learning by heart at a glance, perhaps because I memorized a lot of songs in childhood. I learned that poem 'Sighting the Great Mount Dai' when I was a kid." She answered calmly.

Lai, Wenxiong put away the camera after several photos were taken with her. In front of the Falls, he said with his hand on her shoulder, "Wait no more. Start your autobiographical novel 'New Camille' by typing on the keyboard. At present, your mood is fit for creative writing."

She responded joyously, "You concentrate on your Ph.D. study. I've got a framework for the novel and half of the outline. I'll play my role soon..."

He nodded constantly in gratification and suddenly desired to kiss her. She attempted to evade, but a hot kiss was landed on her left cheek.

She looked at her wristwatch and it was almost 3pm. She said in a hurry, "It's getting late. I'll have to buy something for cooking Shanghai dishes for you."

"Not necessary. Shanghai babe is sufficient." He said with a cheeky grin.

She was going to strike him when her arm was grabbed with his big hand, so she remained motionless.

48. An Unexpected Birthday Gift

All lovers complain about the passage of time. In the twinkling of an eye, the 29th birthday of Zhang, Yunayuan approached. As it was the first big day worthy of a celebration, Lai, Wenxiong decided to give her a pleasant surprise by doing something unique.

After two classes of "The latest trend in social studies" on the afternoon of June 2nd, Lai drove his dark blue Volvo at flying speed to Zhang's residence at the Lakeshore Building.

Normally a bouquet of red roses is presented on the lover's birthday. Unexpectedly, though, she received a dozen pure white roses.

Seeing her perplexity, he said at once, "White roses epitomize my pure love for you, purer than water and whiter than clouds."

She kissed his cheek lightly to express her full appreciation. He was stupefied to see a bouquet of red roses on the table in the living room. He calmed down quickly, however, and relaxed to avoid committing another "mistake".

"It was sent by a flower shop on behalf of David." She discerned his secret thought and explained on purpose.

He said with natural ease, "Don't forget to thank him by phone. It's not easy for a foreigner to be so concerned."

It was six o'clock and they had been intimate for a while.

Lai said, "Well, hurry and put on some make up. I've made reservations at a British restaurant nearby. I have to wear a tie. It's an exquisite restaurant."

"You should have told me sooner. I've prepared many dishes, all your favorites, since last night." So saying, she picked out some beautiful dresses from her wardrobe.

He picked up his tie and said, "Doesn't matter. We can have the dishes as a late night snack. Seldom do we have such a big day for celebration, so we'll have to get drunk tonight."

The half face of the setting sun got smaller and smaller before it sank below the horizon.

Lai, Wenxiong was driving his Volvo quickly along a street beside the lake while Zhang, Yuanyuan was humming the theme song of the movie "Titanic", a purple sunset in the background.

Zhang had dressed quite simply: a low-cut black dress. Most

striking was the sapphire necklace on her white neck – it had not left her body since Lai gave it to her on Valentine's Day.

Lai's black shirt, matched with a pale gray tie, looked quite stylish. His black trousers blended harmoniously with Zhang's black dress.

Night slowly fell and the nearby city of St. Catharines lit up. The famous "Little London Restaurant" was located in the city center, with an elegant and elitist decor. Even in the hot summer, the two doormen were in evening suits, greeting guests with smiles.

Guided by a waitress, they came to the table at the other end. A candle was lit on each side of the dinner table and a red rose placed in the center. The room, dimly lit, was romantic and fragrant.

After they were seated, two glasses of ice water were served.

Looking around, she commented quietly, "Nice milieu. I never noticed this restaurant nearby. How did you get to know about it?"

"Found on the Internet by chance." He was pleased with himself.

A waiter opened a bottle of English red wine and poured a full glass for each of them before retreating courteously.

They talked joyfully while eating cabbage salad and tomato cream soup in an atmosphere of benevolence and happiness.

Before the main course was served, the waiter came by and asked, "How would you prefer your steak?"

Seeing no response from Lai, Zhang answered immediately, "One medium rare and the other medium."

After the waiter left, Lai smiled, "You responded so quickly. I myself am not sure how I like it."

"I know it's medium rare for sure. Remember? Last time you ordered it medium and found it a bit too tough."

"You've got an amazingly good memory. You should have studied accounting. To tell you the truth, I can't tell the difference between steaks."

She answered after sipping some wine, "I judge by pressing the steak with my finger. I heard a foreign friend describe it like this: if it's soft like a cheek, it's medium rare; if it's like an ear, medium; if it's hard like the tip of the nose, it's fully cooked."

"What a vivid description. Eating is really an art," he said with feeling.

They toasted each other and ate the steak and roasted potatoes.

Then, stewed lamb was served. Frowning, Zhang stared at the lamb blankly.

Realizing what she was thinking, Lai said eagerly, "Don't be afraid. You'll like it once you taste it."

Zhang picked up a piece of lamb with her fork and put it into her mouth.

"It tastes pretty good. No foul smell." She smiled again.

"This is Irish-style stewed lamb with lots of onions, so the foul smell is masked. Come on, eat more while it's hot."

After dinner, two waiters cleared the table in no time and served two cups of coffee.

Just then, the music came to a sudden halt. The waiter entered, holding a cake with little candles on it. A row of people wearing swallowtail suits followed and played "Happy birthday" on violins.

"Happy birthday! Close your eyes and make a wish." Lai, Wenxiong blessed her in a low voice.

She shut her eyes and made wishes. Then she opened her eyes and blew out the candles. All of a sudden, he handed a tiny box to her.

"What's this?" She said smiling while opening the box. She was stunned, her arms held stiff in mid-air, to find a glistening diamond ring.

"Yuanyuan, marry me." He stood up, took out the ring and put it on her third finger.

She murmured while keeping her tears of excitement from rolling down her face, "Am I in a dream? This is like what happens in the movies."

"It's real. Yuanyuan, please say yes."

She could no longer hold back her tears, which rolled down her face like nonthreaded pearls.

"It's too unexpected. I'm not mentally prepared." She sipped coffee.

"It has been half a year, not really a short time, since we fell in love. I noticed your purity in your past indulgent life. Your body charms me and your soul is noble as well. Carnal desire hasn't ruined your soul and an unrestrained life hasn't numbed your emotion. You still retain valuable childlike innocence," he said rhythmically, as if performing in a drama.

"You will not regret this?"

He shook the coffee cup in his hand, "A man of over thirty does not act on impulse. Yuanyuan, I have thought carefully about this. It's God's blessing to be loved by a lady like you."

"I didn't expect that anybody would propose to a woman like me." She lowered her head.

He sipped his coffee, "Yuanyuan, don't say that. I've told you that you should step out of the old shadows and stop being so hard on yourself. What I'm concerned about is our future. I am making plans for us to go to Taipei to meet my parents during the summer vacation at the end of next month. We'll get engaged there and get married at the end of next year after I obtain my doctor's degree."

"What careful consideration. I haven't agreed to marry you yet. Please give me some time to think it over."

"Yunayuan, no more consideration. Say yes. I'll make you happy."

She smiled, "Perhaps you'll change your mind after you read my autobiographical novel."

"Absolutely not. You've told me a lot. Nothing but an incense-burner used by many men. No big deal. I'm fully prepared in my own mind. Otherwise I would not propose to you...By the way, what have you written?"

She put down her cup and answered, "I've finished up my experience in Tokyo and am ready to write about the part in Toronto. The climax is after I move to Niagara, particularly the romantic story after meeting you. I plan to write about my girlhood in Shanghai in the last part; that should be relatively simple."

"It's a good idea to divide it into several parts chronologically. The part in Shanghai, although simple, is equally important, because it involves your family as well as your girlhood dreams to be a star and a writer. Psychological studies show that a person's growth can be traced to trifles during childhood. That's why childhood, hometown and family are eternal subjects that writers dwell on… You write first, in as much detail as you can. After I finish my doctor's thesis in May or June next year, we'll weigh the words in repeated deliberation. Let's eat some cake and go home to read your writing."

"I'm full. How about taking the cake home and eating it later?" Her suggestion was agreed to.

Hand in hand, they walked out of the restaurant to the parking lot. The moon seemed to be dancing in the sky, which sparkled with stars. It was getting cool with dew spreading everywhere.

"What a beautiful and charming summer night!" She said to herself while he started the engine.

"You are even more beautiful. Many happy returns of the day!" Lai, Wenxiong was excellent at expressing his feelings.

She responded in a sweet and charming voice, "You're good at flattering."

"Women enjoy being flattered."

Their laughter and the sound of the wheels combined into a serenade of love, reverberating in the sky over the street beside the lakeshore.

49. Plan to Go to Taipei for Engagement

After Zhang, Yuanyuan consented to marry Lai, Wenxiong, they were like a real couple, as inseparable as body and shadow.

As they missed each other so much, they simply lived together. In the first half of the week, she stayed in his students' dorm at the University of Waterloo. When he went to classes during the day, she stayed at home, doing housework and cooking. In the evening, she took some literary magazines with her while accompanying him to the computer room. On Friday afternoons, they went back to Niagara to spend a leisurely weekend. On Monday mornings, they returned to Waterloo.

The news spread like wildfire. Over two hundred Chinese students soon learned that a Taiwan student in the Social Studies Department had the most beautiful girlfriend. Even Lai, Wenxiong's instructor Prof. Rubina was a bit jealous and commented, in a strange tone, that Lai had found a truly beautiful girlfriend.

When the summer vacation started at the end of July, Wenxiong and Yuanyuan left at once for Taipei. Midway during the flight, she held his hand closely, showing inner uneasiness.

"Why are you so nervous about arriving in Taipei? My family won't swallow you up." He tried to console her.

She said carefully, "You told me that the standard at your home is very high. I'm afraid I'm no match for you."

"Don't be foolish. Your parents are intellectuals while my Dad is only a retired professor. He quit being a vice-principal the year before last. I think our two families are exact matches. Don't worry. They do not know your past."

"If they got to know it, what would happen?" She raised her head, greatly bewildered.

He said adamantly, "That's absolutely impossible."

"I'm not superstitious, but my right eyelid is twitching terribly," she said with her eyes wide open.

He tried to convince her patiently, "That's because you're nervous. Don't worry. If they ask you what you do, just tell them you're studying medical care. Say nothing else. Remember: don't say too much. Anyone who talks too much is prone to error. My Mom, who has spoiled me, is very kind. When he sees how pretty you are, my Dad will certainly like you...Let's stop talking about this. We'd better talk about our future. Frankly speaking, it's only a formality to meet your in-laws. How can we pull back a kite that's already flying in the sky?"

She looked pensive, "I haven't told my family about us. If everything goes smoothly this time, I'll call my Mom after I return to Canada. Before we get married, I'll take you to Shanghai to meet my family."

"That's easy. After I graduate at the end of next year, we can have a wedding banquet in Shanghai first, then go shopping in Hong Kong for what we need for the wedding and hold a formal wedding ceremony in Taipei. We'll have a very decent wedding ceremony, something my Mom is very fastidious about."

She said quietly, "I would prefer a simpler one and a honeymoon in Europe to visit the Eiffel Tower in Paris and Buckingham Palace in England. Don't get angry: I also want to visit Montmartre Cemetery in Paris to visit the character Camille's grave there. She was Dumas' lover, who died at the age of 23…"

"No problem, we'll do whatever you say. I have to tell you, however, that I might not find a job after graduation. We have to be prepared for the worst: we may have to leave Canada for the central United States for two years of post-doctorate studies," he said with his head up.

"As the saying goes: Follow the man you marry, be he fowl or cur. You don't have to worry: I'll follow you wherever you go. The golden Canadian passport is very good. I've got enough money to sustain us for several years."

"Don't worry. Money is not a problem. My family will support me financially until I find a job. How am I supposed to use your hard-earned money? Keep it in the bank for your old age."

"It will be different after you get married. As a married man with a wife, how can you ask for money from your family? If you don't deem my money too dirty, just take it. Don't ask your family for money." She became serious.

Holding her hand he said, "I don't mean that. I'll listen to whatever you say. OK? Shanghai women have the deserved reputation of being rigorous."

She pinched his cheek and smiled, "Good for you. Listen to me strictly and enjoy a man's good luck in love affairs. You'll be taken good care of. If you betray me, I'll kill you."

While the two were laughing and having boisterous fun, the plane was flying quietly. Unconsciously she shut her eyes in his arms. Seeing her sound asleep, he held her more closely and fell into a light sleep.

Suddenly there was hustle and bustle in the plane. Lai, Wenxiong woke up to find that they were in the sky over Taipei.

"Look, Taipei is just below us." He woke up Zhang, Yuanyuan.

She opened her sleepy eyes and saw a sea of lights outside the porthole.

"Lights are the best symbol of big cities, like Shanghai and Tokyo." She blurted out, as if reciting a romantic essay.

"You are simply a poet." He again appreciated her talent joyously.

"After our engagement in Taipei, I'll take you to the renowned Eight Scenic Spots in Taiwan or at least to the Sun-and-Moon Pond and Mount Ali."

"To tell you the truth, sightseeing is secondary. First of all, I have to pass the test of your family. I have butterflies in my stomach."

50. Future in-laws Beam with Happiness

After they left the Chiang Kai-shek International Airport in Taoyuan, Lai, Wenxiong and Zhang, Yuanyuan took a taxi to his parents' home.

The taxi sped along the highway, with car lights and neon billboards glittering on both sides. The closer they got to Taipei, the brighter the lights.

Over an hour later, the taxi arrived at Lai's home, which was a detached two-story house, located in northwest Taipei.

Everybody in the Lai family was waiting eagerly in the living room, including the married eldest daughter who had arrived from

Tainan especially to meet her future sister-in-law. Old Lai, a gray-haired man, was a biochemical expert, who had just retired the year before as the vice-principal of a university—a position he had held for 4 years. He was currently a consultant in a transnational corporation. His eyes through his glasses showed him to be a stern man. Mrs. Lai looked gentle and elegant: she was well educated and sensible and had apparently come from a renowned family. After graduating from the English Department of a normal university, she had taught for two years in a high school and then had stayed at home to take care of her family. The Lai children were strictly disciplined and all four of them had doctor's degrees. Lai, Wenxiong was the third child. The eldest son, with a doctor' degree of computer sciences from the US, was a senior executive in an American corporation in Taipei. The eldest daughter, who had received a doctor of engineering degree in Germany, was a manager in a company in Tainan. Even the youngest daughter Wenhui, who was not diligent, had obtained a doctor's degree in economics from Taiwan University and now taught at a university.

Introduced by Lai, Wenxiong, Zhang, Yuanyuan shook hands with each of the Lai family courteously. Old Lai's face lit up with a smile when he saw Yuanyuan's outstanding features and appropriate manners. Mrs. Lai was beaming with joy, adoring her son's judgment in her heart. His elder brother and sister were all smiles, but his younger sister Wenhui pulled a long face: God knows if it was out of jealousy for Zhang's beauty or for some other reason.

Old Lai, who usually spoke little, opened his mouth, smiling, "Wenxiong, you two must be tired after your trip. Eat something and take a rest to ease the jet lag. We'll go to the Lailai Restaurant to give you a welcome dinner tomorrow evening."

Mrs. Lai invited them into the dining room and said, "Eat some congee. You might not have a good appetite after being on board a plane for so long. The coconut bread is Wenxiong's favorite, newly baked."

Old Lai volunteered to eat congee with them. Other family members, seeing his unusual joy, smiled secretly, but didn't dare to laugh.

After a casual meal, the whole family started chatting in the living room.

Old Lai was quite talkative, "Miss Zhang, Shanghai has changed a lot, hasn't it? I haven't been to mainland China since I came to Taiwan in 1949. Let me think: I went with my father in 1945 when I was very young. My native place is in the south of Fujian. Are your parents still in Shanghai? Where do they work?"

Zhang, Yuanyuan knew that he was probing into her family background in a roundabout way, so she simply told them everything in a gentle voice. "My Dad graduated from Jiaotong University and works as a senior engineer in a steel plant. He was sent to work in Japan for a year and to Germany for half a year."

"That's a famous university. Several of my friends in Taipei graduated from Jiaotong University in Shanghai. Oh, Jiang, Zemin graduated from Jiaotong as well, didn't he?" interrupted Old Lai.

"Since when does Dad pay attention to politics?" Everybody roared with laughter after Lai, Wenxiong's comment.

"Who doesn't know about the No.1 leader in mainland China?"

Zhang, Yunayuan continued, "My Mom is a physician. She graduated from No.2 Shanghai Medical University, the former Zhendan University. I've got a younger brother, who studies at a university in Shanghai."

"From which university did you graduate?" Sister Wenhui inquired all of a sudden.

Seeing an abrupt change in Zhang, Yuanyuan's facial expression and her helplessness, Lai, Wenxiong came to her immediate rescue, "Yuanyuan studied at the medical school attached to a university in Shanghai. At present, she studies health care in Canada."

"At best a college," Wenhui talked in a stiff manner.

Mrs. Lai was quick to respond, "It's good to study health care.

Wenxiong will have a private nurse to look after him for his whole life."

"Right. Girls don't have to study too much. Beauty, virtue and kindheartedness are essential." The eldest brother came to her rescue as well.

"You shouldn't have double standards," Wenhui seemed indignant.

Old Lai said to his youngest daughter, "Different problems should be dealt with differently. You can speak frankly if you have anything against me. It's Miss Zhang's first visit. How can you welcome your future sister-in-law like this?"

Wenhui stood up abruptly and walked upstairs without any facial expression.

"What's up? She seems to have suffered from some shock," asked Lai, Wenxiong.

Frowning, Mrs. Lai answered in a low voice, "Don't laugh at us, Miss Zhang. You're not an outsider anyway. Wenhui has a boyfriend, a businessman from Japan. At one glance, your Dad is firmly against him."

"Even with a doctor's degree, I'm not for him. I suspect he studied very little and he looks like a profiteer, offensive to the eye." Old Lai pulled a long face.

The eldest sister attempted to put in a few good words for her younger sister, "Dad, you're a bit stubborn to reject him after your first meeting. Better ask Wenhui the details."

"The first impression is important. Your Dad has a whole life's experience and does not make mistakes in judging people. I asked and there have been no university graduates in his family for three generations. How can Wenhui have anything in common with him? It's your sister who would suffer. Your Mom is opposed too." Old Lai waved his hand with agitation.

Mrs. Lai tried to smooth things over, "After a period of time, she'll feel better. Wenhui is pretty good but just a bit headstrong. She should go abroad to calm down... All right, let's stop here and take a rest. Your big brother has to go home."

The big sister said to her father tactfully, "I'll talk to Wenhui and bring her around."

Lai, Wenxiong grasped Zhang, Yuanyuan's hand and took her to a bedroom on the second floor. After shutting the door, the two hugged each other madly, as if declaring to the whole world that – the Lai family had accepted Zhang, Yuanyuan!

"I didn't tell a lie when I said my family would like you." Lai said proudly.

Zhang responded timidly, "I was scared to death. Your younger sister looked as if she wanted to devour me."

"She's been spoiled and just gave vent to her anger. Never mind her."

"Your Dad is pretty kind, not as stern as you described."

Lai said with a smile, "He wasn't his usual self. He was glad because you were pleasing to the eye. Our family makes high demands for degrees, but your beauty and wisdom made up for what's lacking. No need to say more. They have accepted you as one of the family, so let's get prepared for our engagement."

Tears of happiness sprang to her eyes when she snuggled up to his chest.

These were tears of joy after several terrifying days and nights. It was her dream come true to be accepted by the Lai Family.

51. The Joyful Lai Family

Like a happy bird, Zhang, Yuanyuan, together with Lai, Wenxiong, flew everywhere in Taipei, attending parties with his high school pals or going to KTV with his university schoolmates, as well as visiting friends and relatives. Her beauty and graceful manners made an excellent impression on everyone. Many flattered Lai for finding such a gorgeous beauty.

Zhang, Yuanyuan, however, didn't find Taipei as nice as she had imagined, perhaps because Canada is a vast land sparsely populated or because she had been born in the metropolitan city of Shanghai and had seen more of the world. The biggest problem in Taipei was transportation: the traffic jams on the highway were unbearable. It took 5 or 6 hours to go from Taipei to Tainan, a distance of around 300 kilometers. This delay would never happen in Canada. Waiting midway, she found it both funny and annoying. The crux of the matter was that there were too few lanes, only two in many places, so vehicles backed up when an accident occurred. This reminded her that she had encountered similar problems on the highways in Shanghai. The designers never predicted that the volume of traffic would be so huge.

Another problem was that there were too many motorcycles in Taipei, a number equal to that of bikes in Shanghai. The minute the light turned green at the intersection, numerous motorcycles, like unbridled wild horses, zigzagged among the cars at amazing speed. The driving speed in the city was flabbergasting; -- the drivers just dashed around madly. For all these reasons, traffic accidents abounded. News of people dying in traffic accidents appeared on TV almost every day, but to no avail: speed demons were not intimidated.

What impressed Zhang, Yuanyuan most favorably was the magnificent Dr. Sun, Yat-sen (Father of the Republic) Memorial Hall and the bookstores, particularly the latter. The beautiful decor of the bookstores made people visit them again and again. There were so many varieties of books that the eye couldn't take them all in. The beautiful cover designs were on a par with those of the original books in the United States, Canada and Japan. On August 8th, she and Lai, Wenxiong stayed in the "Eslite Bookstore" the whole day, buying over 40 Chinese books, including "Sirius", a collection of poems; and "Memory is as Long as the Railway Track", a collection of essays, both by Yu, Guangzhong; "Husband Killing", a collection of novellas by Li, Ang; "Breakthrough" and "Paper Marriage", novels by Chen, Ruoxi; and "Red Ears", a collection of novellas by Mo, Yan, a novelist from mainland China. Yuanyuan also found, by chance, "Camille" in both the English and the Chinese versions.

Leaving the bookstore, Lai, Wenxiong carried the heavy books and seemed puzzled, "You already have the Chinese version of 'Camille': why did you buy this one?"

"Mine was published in mainland China without the English version. I'd like to read the Taiwan translation. It will kill two birds with one stone: I'll read the novel and learn English as well."

"I see. It's a good way to study the language," he nodded happily.

That night when they returned home after attending a feast given by a friend, Old Lai was shocked to see so many books.

Then he said with a smile, "You broke my record. I once bought 33 books at one go. Now the pupil surpasses the master. Good. It's nice for young people to read more books."

"Dad, Yuanyuan published a poem in English recently in Canada. She is good at writing and wanted to be a writer when she was a young girl. She published her first article when she was in junior high school." Lai, Wenxiong took every chance to put in a good word for her.

Old Lai touched his chin and said, "That's good. Practice more and submit regularly to the supplements of the 'China Times' and the 'Unity Daily' in Taiwan. Even publish a book in Taipei when the time is ripe. The publishing industry is developing quite rapidly."

"Wonderful. I'll work harder." She smiled like a sweet peach.

Mrs. Lai came smiling, "Wenxiong, I talked with your Dad and set your engagement date for the 15th. We'll book two tables for the banquet at the Kaiyue Restaurant. Apart from our family, you can invite your pals from university for a lively celebration. You can return to Taipei for the wedding ceremony after graduation next year. You two aren't so young any more. Miss Zhang, you'll have to take good care of Wenxiong, as the last year of writing the thesis is crucial."

"Aunty, please be assured that I'll do my best to look after him."

Lai, Wenxiong thanked his parents and Zhang, Yuanyuan followed suit. He had expected that everything would go smoothly, but it was beyond her expectation.

After that, the whole Lai family was filled with joy. Every word, every expression, every face was inscribed with "happiness". Zhang, Yuanyuan and Lai, Wenxiong were like a lovely couple in the honey jar. Zhang was busy helping Mrs. Lai with household affairs and the old lady showed concern for her. Old Lai praised Zhang, Yuanyuan to everybody he met and even drove the couple in his archaic Benz to go sightseeing in Taipei and to taste delicious food in Ximenting.

While sightseeing in the commercial districts, whenever they found any stores with the word "Shanghai", Old Lai would lead them inside, so that Yuanyuan could say a few words in the Shanghai dialect and feel a growing connection to Taipei. Once, interestingly enough, they entered a fashion store called the "Shanghai Harbor Front", but none of the 5 or 6 assistants could speak the Shanghai dialect. Then the proprietress came out swaggering, but she spoke pure Taiwanese instead of the Shanghai dialect.

Old Lai said in Taiwanese, "My lady, as this is a store by a typical Taiwanese, why is it called the 'Shanghai Harbor Front'?"

"We depend on this name for good business. So this lady is from Shanghai," said the proprietress with a smile.

"Yes. She's my daughter-in-law." He narrowed his eyes into a smile.

The owner took the opportunity to say, "No wonder she's so pretty. Can she do an advertisement for us? Our business will be even better if such a beautiful lady does a commercial for us."

Seeing Old Lai suddenly go silent, she quickly added, "Rest assured I'll pay her well. I'll double the standard pay for an advertisement company, but she must work exclusively for me."

As expected by Lai, Wenxiong, Old Lai grasped his son's hand and said angrily, "Let's go. We don't need the money. Who wants to do an advertisement?"

The proprietress shrugged her shoulders and shook her head. One of the assistants made a face and appeared to be talking to herself. Zhang, Yuanyuan's heart was beating fast. She realized that Old Zhang was a very conservative intellectual. The mere mention of doing an advertisement was taken as baring her all for others. She was lucky to be accepted easily by the Lai family. Lai, Wenxiong held his tongue without betraying his feelings, so as not to reveal any secrets to his father.

Going out of the store, Old Lai couldn't help saying, "What a store, hanging up a sheep's head and selling dog meat."

The three laughed their heads off. Their laughter, with respective ulterior motives, shot to the sky, arousing the whole of Taipei to foolish laughter.

Chapter Eleven

Unexpected Disaster like a Bolt from Heaven

52. Enjoying Flowers and Chasing Butterflies on Mt. Yangming

Boeing 747 of Northwest Airlines is cruising stably in the sky over Detroit Airport in the United States. The closer it gets to the ground, the faster it lands. All of a sudden, Lai, Wenxiong's bitter-sweet memory of the past is interrupted by the rapid deceleration of the plane.

It is 3pm local time on Jan. 14th after he goes through the customs and leaves the airport. The winter sunshine is not really strong, but is still a bit dazzling to the eye. Bathing in the warm sunshine, he can't help but open his mouth to inhale the fresh air of North America. He has planned to take the Greyhound to Niagara Falls, but according to the schedule, he has to wait until 7pm for a bus. He immediately calls a taxi. The drivers shake their heads when they hear that he wants to go to Niagara Falls over 400 kilometers away. A driver of Indian origin asks for $800, which shocks Lai, Wenxiong. The return ticket to Taipei costs just a little over $1,000. These taxi drivers are simply robbers!

Just then, a Chinese man, with a mainland Chinese accent, comes by driving a minivan. Knowing the destination, he asks for $300. Lai bargains him down to $230 and gets into the van.

The snow accumulates into little mountains in every street. Black snow melts into water and slowly flows along the curbs, with black slush littering the road. It goes without saying that a snowstorm has wreaked havoc on this city. Lai, Wenxiong is exhausted after a sleepless trip on the plane, so he wants to make use of the 3 or 4 hours in the van to take a nap. He can at least keep awake tonight to answer the endless questions of the police.

Passing the "Embassy Bridge" on the US-Canada border, the minivan is going at a fast speed on the highway. Leaning back in the wide back seat, Lai, Wenxiong can hardly sleep. He tosses and turns. His train of thoughts surges along with the quick turning of the wheels and centers on a string of questions: if his cousin Lian, Haotien hadn't come to the Lai residence, the family would never have known about Zhang, Yuanyuan's past; if the two of them hadn't gone to Mt. Yangming, Lian, Haotien would have been driven out of the family long ago and Zhang, Yuanyuan's tragedy might not have happened...

Early on the morning of Aug.10th, 2000 Lai, Wenxiong and Zhang, Yuanyuan, both in T-shirts and thin pants, typical casual summer attire, went to the Taipei subway station, hand in hand, then to Sword Pond, and changed to "the Red #5" Bus to the terminus. From there, they walked to the visitors' center at Mt. Yangming National Park.

Zhang had an overview of the park from the Internet and had heard about it on occasion from Lai. She had some vague idea that the park is situated on the verge of the Taipei Basin, with an area of over 10,000 hectares. Besides high mountains and green rivers, unique flowers and flora, there are several hundred animals, as well as waterfalls and hot springs. She also knew that the well-known scenic spot is named in honor of Wang, Yangming, a great philosopher of the Ming Dynasty.

Standing at the entrance and gazing around, Zhang said

emotionally, "Viewing it in person is different. When I saw the pictures on the Internet, I failed to sense its grandeur."

"Of course. I told you that it's really magnificent: three sides encircled by green hills and one gap on the southwest side, facing the Fresh Water River of Taipei, and green grass like a carpet," Lai said proudly as if Mount Yangming were his heirloom.

Zhang cleared her throat and commented, "This is Heaven's greatest gift to the people here. Great nature, you are so gorgeous with graceful hills and rivers, the wind and the moon, and the clear air..."

Lai grabbed her hand and said, "My lady, you are turning poetic again! There is more beautiful scenery ahead. Let's seize the minute; otherwise, we'll miss a lot of scenic spots."

They entered the Park shoulder to shoulder. What met their eyes first was a hidden pond of bone chilling water. Opposite was Honglong Pond, murmuring pleasantly. Walking up the steps and through a forest, they reached the pretty "Cherry Garden". Among the dazzlingly beautiful flowers, Zhang looked around and found fewer varieties than she had expected.

Lai interpreted her expression at once and explained, "It's not the best season to enjoy the flowers. Traditionally, February and March are the blooming seasons, with azalea, cherry and many other flowers blossoming to herald spring. At that time, the visitors push each other instead of walking. The traffic has to be controlled every year, otherwise no people or vehicles can move..."

"I didn't mean that. I couldn't find a camellia. Are there any here?" Zhang was perplexed.

Lai looked around and didn't find her favorite flower. He turned his head and said, "Camellias should be together. Shall we ask the assistants?"

"No. We have to hurry. As a woman, the sight just strikes a chord in my heart. I wonder what has happened to my camellias in Canada. Will they wither without watering? Flowers, like women, require loving care." She was lost in thought.

Lai tried to comfort her, "No problem. Your room is not too dry. If you're so worried, you should have moved those flowers to Old Bailey, the security guard's place. He is pretty nice to you."

"I thought of that, but didn't want to trouble him." She shook her head.

"Forget about it. We can buy some more." He dragged her away.

She was a bit displeased, "Not everything in the world can be measured by money. I have feelings for the white camellia, which is a witness of my life…"

He held her waist closely and said, "My beauty, why do you sound like a philosopher? Women are not supposed to be philosophers."

Talking and laughing, they arrived at the "Joyous Fish Pond". It was uniquely appealing to enjoy the swimming fish while they leaned against the fence. Just at that moment, heaven was not cooperative and a thunderstorm suddenly broke. Lai told her it was not unusual in summer and it would pass shortly. They went to a bar to have a drink and snack and take a rest.

In half an hour or so, the weather was fine again. The hills turned brighter, the trees greener and the air fresher after the rain. The beautiful scenery of "rainbows over the gorges" could be seen everywhere. Zhang snatched the camera from Lai's hand and took many photos of the unique scenery.

Unknowingly, they came to Datun Falls. Yangming Falls, flowing from the opposite mountain, is quite magnificent with a height of 278 meters, although it is not comparable to Niagara Falls. Seeing the falls gushing down, Zhang, Yuanyuan felt as if she had returned to her homeland. She was in such raptures that she sang at the top of her voice.

Hearing this, Lai made fun of her, "I knew you'd get mad at the falls, like a conditioned reflex."

"Well, am I the daughter of waterfalls?" She made strange gestures, looking like a monkey.

Lai squeezed her ear and said, "Waterfalls abound here: we have Cap Falls, Maple Falls, Rocky Falls, Little Guanyin Falls, as well as Xingyi Falls, Xinghua Falls, just to name a few. Each of them has a story of its own…"

"They are absolutely worth the visit!" she almost yelled.

While they were enjoying the waterfalls at Datun, from which they could not tear themselves away, they saw a throng of brightly colorful butterflies, which seemed to be attending a carnival. Zhang couldn't restrain herself from running after them with open arms. For fear of an accident, Lai had to run after her. He turned left or right when she turned left or right, following the butterflies to the left or right; or to the front or back…

After chasing the butterflies for over 20 meters, Lai eventually caught Zhang's hand and forced her to stop. She obeyed and stopped while both of them panted.

"Haven't run like this for so long. I am so tired." She said while puffing.

"You're tired? I was afraid something might happen. When you're like a child, nothing seems too wild for you." He took hold of her hand and walked slowly ahead.

Zhang couldn't control her excitement, "Never saw so many butterflies. They are simply gorgeous!"

"Not too many today. The record shows that there are over 160 varieties of butterflies here, including the phoenix butterfly, the phoenix butterfly with red streaks, the crow phoenix butterfly, and so on. Butterflies with blue streaks are dancing every day." Lai showed a thorough familiarity with the subject.

She looked pensive, "Just now I suddenly thought of the story of Zhuang, Zhou's (or Zhuangzi's) dream of a butterfly."

He nodded, and wagged his head, "*Once Zhuangzi dreamt he was a butterfly, a butterfly flitting and fluttering around, happy with himself and doing as he pleased. He didn't know he was Zhuangzi. Suddenly he woke up and there he was, solid and unmistakable Zhuangzi. But he didn't know if he was Zhuangzi who had dreamt he was a butterfly, or a butterfly dreaming he was Zhuangzi. Between Zhuangzi and a butterfly there must be some distinction! This is called the Transformation of Things."* (2, tr. Burton Watson 1968:49)

She praised him with admiration, "You're marvellous! You can recite the whole paragraph."

He said proudly, "This is the last part of Zhuangzi's well-known 'Discussion on making All Things Equal". I learned it by heart during my high school days."

"The Chinese language study in Taiwan is better than in mainland China," she blurted out.

Lai looked like a teacher, "It's hard to say. My mom is particularly fond of ancient Chinese and forced us children to learn prose by heart. Let me ask you: why did Zhuangzi dream of a butterfly, not of any other things?"

She opened her eyes wide and was unable to answer such a complicated question.

Lai patted her on the shoulder, and replied, "Butterflies are pretty but ephemeral. They are happy even though they have a short life. That's why we assume that Zhuangzi has to dream of a butterfly."

Zhang, Yuanyuan was suddenly enlightened, "You mean Zhuangzi reminds people that life is short yet beautiful. We had better enjoy our short dream of life ..."

53. Unexpected Encounter

It was dusk when they took the bus from Mt. Yangming back to Taipei. Zhang, Yuanyuan, with her rosy cheeks and fair face, looked as charming as the sunset. She was singing nonstop all the way. When Lai, Wenxiong asked her why she was so elated, she replied that it was the happiest day during her trip to Taipei because she had danced with the butterflies and personally experienced Zhuang, Zhou's philosophy of life. Perhaps because she had lived in Canada for so long, she had unknowingly become a daughter of nature.

They entered at the gate hand in hand. No sooner had they come into the living room than they suddenly found Lian, Haotien talking with the older couple. Zhang, Yuanyuan's rosy face immediately turned paper white and she broke into a cold sweat. Lai, Wenxiong stared at Lian, Haotien with gritted teeth.

"Look, speak of the devil, and he will appear. This is Miss Zhang, Wenxiong's girlfriend," Old Lai couldn't help introducing her excitedly.

Lian, Haotien pulled a long face at once. But he still stood up politely, went forward and shook her hand forcefully.

He couldn't refrain from saying, "It's you, Miss Zhang. I haven't seen your graceful dancing for a long time."

"So you know each other," said Mrs. Lai with a smile.

"Not only do I know her, but we are old acquaintances." Lian couldn't control himself.

"Haotien, when did you come back?" Sensing the situation was out of control, Lai, Wenxiong attempted at once to change the subject.

Lian sipped some tea and replied, "The night before last. An old pal asked me to bring some medication from Canada. I took it to a place close by, so I came to visit Uncle and Aunt. I didn't even know that you were back. You keep everything secret from me. You were not so sneaky before. Who taught you that?"

The last words were an obvious challenge to Zhang, Yuanyuan. She was at a loss for words, sitting on the sofa, her face turning from white to grayish yellow. Her hand holding the cup was shaking a bit.

Worldly-wise Mrs. Lai sensed Lian's hidden meaning in his words, so she said to Yuanyuan, "Miss Zhang, you look unwell. Are you tired after climbing Mt. Yangming? Go rest upstairs."

Zhang, Yuanyuan knew that they were trying to get her to leave, so she stood up and left the room immediately.

Entering the bedroom, she collapsed on the bed and couldn't move at all.

"What's the matter, Yuanyuan?" Lai followed her closely and

rushed to feel her forehead.

"What lousy luck. What can you expect from a dog but a bark!" She shook her head nonstop, as if she had contracted a disease.

He grasped her hand firmly and said, "Don't be scared. Keep your cool."

"It'll bode ill rather than well. You'd better go downstairs." She forcefully took her hand from his.

When Lai went downstairs, he found Lian, Haotien was still whispering to the old couple. When he found Wenxiong approaching, he stopped short stealthily.

Old Lai said angrily, "Haotien, don't be afraid. Go on."

Lian, Haotien said to Wenxiong, helplessly, "I'm just telling the truth, nothing false."

"Go on telling the truth." Mrs. Lai urged.

Lian, Haotien talked in a low voice, with one finger pointing to the ceiling, "She was really a stripper. So far as I know, she went to bed with quite a number of men, especially foreigners. It was I who introduced her to Wenxiong."

Old Lai stood up drastically from the sofa and said with controlled fury, "Wenxiong, is this true or false? Don't lie."

"She was engaged in that before." Wenxiong told the truth with lowered head.

"She was engaged before! You have the audacity to bring such a woman home? Go away at once, the farther away, the better!"

Lai, Wenxiong was not convinced, "She has turned over a new leaf. Some people say the grapes are sour because they have no access to them."

Lian, Haotien was swift to refute, "What do you mean? I told Uncle and Aunt for the reputation of the whole family. What's the difference between such a woman and a prostitute? They are to be trifled with, but not to be shown genuine affection…"

"Damn it. What nonsense you talk!" Lai, Wenxiong was so furious that he rose and clenched his fist preparing to hit Lian. Short Lian hid behind the sofa with his hands behind his head and avoided the hit.

"Stop!" Old Lai shouted in such a loud voice that the whole house seemed to shake.

Old Lai grasped Wenxiong's hand. They stood motionless in the middle of the living room.

"You've gone too far and tried to hit him!" Old Lai was still yelling.

Then, Zhang, Yuanyuan dashed downstairs. Seeing the deadlock, she said at once, "Wenxiong, don't do this. It's my fault. I'll leave."

"Where will you go? You'll stay wherever I am…" Wenxiong, with perfect assurance, guided her upstairs.

"Get out of here, you prodigal!" Old Lai went directly to his study after saying the last few words.

"Aunty, Aunty," Suddenly, Lian, Haotien burst out screaming.

When everybody else looked around, they found Mrs. Lai had fainted on the carpet.

"Mom, Mom…" Lai, Wenxiong dashed over to help her up, so did Lian, Haotien.

Zhang, Yunayuan bent over to take her pulse and told him, "Your Mom has had a heart attack. Rush her to the hospital."

"It might be a heart attack. Wenxiong, you drive the car. Hurry!" Old Lai opened the door.

In twenty minutes, they arrived at the Emergency Department of the hospital. Before the doctor saw her, Mrs. Lai had already opened her eyes. Seeing the four of them beside her, she shook her head and shut her eyes again.

"Mom, Mom," Wenxiong called her in a low voice, and she nodded lightly.

A nurse ushered the family members out of the examination room. The four stood tensely in the lobby, without uttering any words.

After a while, the doctor came out and said to Old Lai, "It's another heart attack. She shouldn't get so excited. She'll stay here overnight for observation. If nothing is wrong, she can return home tomorrow morning."

They decided to leave Lai, Wenxiong and Zhang, Yunayuan behind to look after her. Before Lian, Haotien left, Zhang, Yuanyuan glared at him angrily, as if she wanted to swallow him alive. Lian left without any expression.

In the dimly lit ward, Mrs. Lai was resting in bed with her eyes closed. Lai, Wenxiong and Zhang, Yuanyuan sat near her bed to guard her, holding each other's hands for fear that one would fly away if the other loosened the grip.

After 10pm, Mrs. Lai opened her eyes, only to find the two whispering intimately. She could hardly describe her feelings.

"It's pretty late. Go home and rest. Nothing will happen. Come to take me home tomorrow morning."

"Mom, we'll feel ill at ease," Lai, Wenxiong held his mother's hand.

"There are nurses here. What's to fear? Your mom won't go to Heaven this soon."

Lai, Wenxiong patted the comforter and said, "What are you talking about, Mom? OK, we'll leave now and pick you up early tomorrow morning."

54. Mother's Order to Cut the Gordian Knot

The second day after Mrs. Lai was de-hospitalized, she asked her son to have a secret talk in her bedroom.

Without beating about the bush, she said, "I talked to your Dad and he will absolutely reject your marriage. For your happiness, it's better to cut the Gordian knot swiftly. Short-term suffering is better than long-term suffering, Wenxiong."

"Mom, we truly love each other. I don't mind her past, if only she is nice to me now and in the future. Strip-teasing is an occupation in Canada and people marry strip-teasers as well." He was not convinced.

Mother earnestly advised him, "We are Chinese and it's hard for me to accept this occupation. Wenxiong, you know I love you most and comply with all your wishes. You have to listen to me this time, though. I don't want to see you turn into Armand at the end of the twentieth century."

He tried his uttermost to defend Zhang, Yunayuna, "She has long washed her hands of this. She was forced to do it at the beginning. I study social sciences and earth-shaking changes have taken place in modern outlook of value, morality and even chastity. The past is bygones for every one of us."

"But don't forget that today is the continuation of tomorrow. No matter how changed people's outlook is, you shouldn't marry a prostitute. Such a woman has too many contacts with different men and may have got involved in something that might get you killed without knowing what happened."

"Mom, after we return to Canada, she'll move to Waterloo. After I graduate next year, she'll follow me to the United States or Vancouver, far away from Toronto, so nobody knows her past or gets her entangled…"

Mrs. Lai interrupted her son, "Don't be so naïve, Wenxiong. I know you have been a kindhearted person since childhood, but you shouldn't stake your career. We only live once. I'm not cursing her. Can you guarantee that such a woman hasn't contracted AIDS? The incubation period could be very long… In a word, you have to cut contact with her quickly and ask her to return to Canada first. You stay in Taipei for several months to collect material for your thesis. Parting for some time will cool down your emotion… If you find it hard to say, I'll talk to her. If she wants money, we can afford over ten thousand US dollars. No problem."

The son begged, "Mom, never mention money to her. It's miserable enough that her self-respect is hit hard. She is not that kind of person. If she were seeking money, she would have gone with a millionaire. It's out of absolute love that she falls for a poor student like me."

Mrs. Lai said angrily, "Love, love. What a bookworm! Aren't you worried that you wouldn't find a woman? I'd rather you live as a single if you were to marry such a woman. Well, I've told you everything. Don't make your Dad lose his temper and drive you out of the house as well. You know your father's temperament. Nobody could stop him when he flies into a rage. Even I can't come to your rescue then."

Seeing his mother so firm, he had to lower his head reluctantly and got ready to retreat to avoid infuriating her again.

Just then, his mother suddenly handed him a piece of newspaper from the bedside cupboard, "Wenxiong, read this report and get some inspiration. In finding a wife, I don't want you to do something unconventional. It's better to follow the trend and learn from men in Taiwan."

Taking the newspaper from her, he saw the front page headline: "Men indulge in hymen complex, 50,000 fake virgins produced annually in Taiwan".

To prevent Zhang, Yuanyuan from finding it, Wenxiong took the newspaper and tiptoed to the washroom to read the report:

"While there is a growing open trend in the concept of sex, 85% of men in Taiwan still regard 'hymen' as an important condition in choosing a wife. However, in the Taiwan society where tens of thousands of unmarried girls have abortions annually, how can those men with 'hymen complex' discover their 'virgin wives'? The answer is in the hospital of gynecology. Statistics show that over 50,000 Taiwan females go to hospitals or clinics every year for mending their hymens, including girls who have even given birth to babies...

Moreover, the results from the 782 questionnaires to Taiwan men are beyond expectation. 89% of the men feel that 'it's hard to find a virgin' and 76% of them are reasonable to believe that they will not find a wife if they insist on marrying a virgin. Ironically, 85% of the men insist that if they have power and influence, they'll 'certainly marry a virgin'..."

Lai, Wenxiong was outraged after reading this, so he tore the newspapers to pieces, thrust into the toilet and flushed it. He had never expected that the Taiwan men with apparently open mind on sex would hold such a conservative concept. Men in Taiwan! You lack the modern concept or even common sense. A broken hymen does not mean that a girl had sex before. Violent sports activities or inserting cotton wad might break the hymen. Some women have elastic hymens and even having sex would not break them…

However displeased he was or complaining behind the closed door, nothing could change his mother's clear-cut attitude: hoping he'll marry a "decent virgin", rather than a social butterfly like Zhang, Yuanyuan. As a filial son, he would not go against his mother's "decree", especially when she was just de-hospitalized. Even if he held his own view, he had to keep silent. But how was he to explain everything to his beloved Yuanyuan? Clenching his fists and grinding his teeth while opening his eyes wide, he talked to himself in the mirror, "You man, how are you going to pass the hurdle? All mighty God, hurry to save me!"

Like many atheist people, he thought of Jesus Christ only when he was faced with imminent disaster. Will God really show mercy and bestow him with a miraculous cure?

55. Farewell at Chiang Kai-shek International Airport

After supper the next day, Zhang, Yuanyuan suggested that they go out for a walk.

The sky was pitch black, the stars all swallowed up by black clouds. It was a particularly humid and hot night in Taipei and people felt that breathing was difficult.

Holding Lai's arm, Zhang was chasing the black night step by step. It seemed that only the black night knew her true feelings and only the black night could hide her. Neither of them talked. They just wandered along the small trail aimlessly.

Eventually Zhang broke the deadly silence.

"Wenxiong, tell me what you think. Don't seal it in your heart. Your eyes tell me that you are in a dilemma. It's hard to survive between cracks."

He gazed up at the sky without uttering a word, as if he were waiting for God to show His power and present him with a magic cure.

"Ever since Lian, Haotien appeared, your home has been turned upside down. Your parents and your aloof sister have shunned me on purpose as if I suffer from a terrible disease. I've realized that a woman like me will never rid myself of the stigma even after I'm dead. Maybe I'm destined to be unhappy."

He finally opened his mouth, "Yuanyuan, don't be too pessimistic. New trails are blazed by human beings. Please allow me some time and some day I'll convince my family. If not, the worst is to break from the family. Nobody can stop us when we are far away from here in Canada."

"Don't be silly: it's not worth sacrificing everything for me. Your mother couldn't stand such a blow. You have only one mother, but numerous women to choose from. We can be carefree lovers as we were before. Isn't that nice? Be assured, I'll stay the way I am now: I won't go back to being a social butterfly. I'll cut contact with Katyusha and study nursing as soon as possible. I'll try to be self-reliant..."

"Yuanyuan, what do you mean? I can handle even greater difficulties. Time will prove everything," he held her shoulder and pledged vehemently.

"I've promised your Mom that I won't pester you. How pathetic are parents all over the world! If I were your Mom, I'd do the same. Take me to the airport tomorrow morning. I've contacted the airline and I'll take the 10 am flight."

"Are you crazy? You didn't consult with me about such an important matter." He held her even tighter.

She shook her head, "Wenxiong, don't blame me. I had no choice."

"Don't lose your temper at home. Your Mom is very weak and you don't want to lose her. After my departure, return the gold necklace and gold ring to her," she added.

He held her slender waist while they were homeward bound.

"I'll kill that Lian, Haotien. If it weren't for him, we would have gotten engaged tomorrow." He was outraged.

"Man proposes and Heaven disposes. Don't offend such a mean person. He spent a lot of money on me and he did not get what he wanted. Why wouldn't he take this opportunity to get revenge on me? It's the root of trouble that I myself sowed."

Finally Lai, Wenxiong agreed, "You go back to Canada and I'll try to convince my parents gradually. I'll make good use of my time to do research and will return to Canada at the end of this year to spend Christmas with you. I'll call you frequently, but you have to promise me to make good use of your time studying English and writing…"

In darkness, she uttered a light sound of agreement. She felt like crying, but didn't.

That night, only tears and dim moonlight accompanied them. Who says that tears are the tools of women? They are also men's primitive weapons. The two held each other: crying was their only homework that night. They closed their eyes until their tears ran dry. After they woke up, the crying started again…

Early on the morning of August 15th, Zhang, Yuanyuan, with swollen red eyes, pulled herself together and bid farewell to the Lai family. Sister Wenhui was not up yet, so she didn't bother her. They seemed destined not to get along. Zhang, Yuanyuan tiptoed to the sofa in the living room where Old Lai, pretending not to see her, was reading the "China Times" seriously. He looked like an entirely different person from the man he had been a few days ago.

"Uncle Lai, I'll take my leave. Sorry to have caused you trouble." It was hard for her to squeeze out a few words, as if she were a prisoner.

"I wish you good luck," he said perfunctorily, still continuing to read his newspaper.

Mrs. Lai faked a smile and saw her to the door. After saying to her, "Have a safe trip", she shut the door at once, as if fending off some evil spirit.

Lai, Wenxiong drove the age-old Benz towards Chiang Kai-shek International Airport in Taoyuan. Zhang, sitting beside him, looked like a speechless wooden statue. The solemn atmosphere was like that of an execution ground.

"Yuanyuan, I am sorry to have made you go through all this. My Dad is always deadly stubborn. I'll make double compensation to you in the future. Next time you come to Taiwan, I'll drive you all over, including to the eight wonderful scenic spots."

She spoke in a gentle voice, "Don't say that. Taipei is like a dream to me. Never be angry with your family members. The Lai family will return to tranquility after some time. Take care of yourself. Don't drink too much; otherwise you'll ruin your stomach. Don't interfere with your sister's affair. Everybody has his own choice."

"You'd better brace up. I mean what I say. I will marry you and give you happiness." Lai, Wenxiong was still adamant.

"Life is unpredictable and many things are not controlled by us. As the old saying goes: He who gives no thought to future difficulties is sure to be beset by worries closer at hand…"

He knitted his brows and gritted his teeth, "Yuanyuan, I don't like it when you are philosophical."

She pursed her small lips, "One who has seen the ocean thinks nothing of mere lakes or streams. One would naturally become a philosopher."

Driving to the Airport, both of them were crying in the car. Getting out of the car, Zhang, Yuanyuan held a wad of wet tissues.

In the terminal, the two hugged closely and kissed goodbye. Yuanyuan threw herself on Wenxiong's shoulder and couldn't help weeping bitterly.

"Yuanyuan, stop crying, stop…" Before finishing his words, he also burst into tears.

"Sir, we've arrived at the Niagara Police Bureau!" The minivan driver's yelling startles Lai, Wenxiong.

He is a bit dazed when he opens his eyes, feeling the tears in his eyes and still submerged in the heartbreaking parting at Chiang Kai-shek International Airport. He never imagined that the parting there would be their final farewell.

He stretches after paying the driver. Then he marches to the gate of the well-lit Police Bureau.

Chapter Twelve

Eternal Farewell at Chiang Kai-shek International Airport

56. Journalist Fascinated by the Autobiographical Novel

"Toronto Weekly" has published two exclusive reports since Zhang, Yuanyuan's body was discovered on January 1st. These have caused one great sensation after another and the magazine's distribution has risen 30%. Director Wang, all smiles every day, greets Jia, Feng whenever he sees him and rewards his colleagues in the editors' department with an abalone and shark's fin feast at "Scenic Village". After the delicious dinner, Editor-in-chief Guo has pressed Jia, Feng and Wu, Xiaoxian even more to file exclusive reports by tracking the news all day long.

The cover of the issue published on January 6th is particularly sensational, with the photo of a helicopter with a female body hanging from it as the background and the caption in big, bold, black characters: "Death of a Shanghai Beauty in Niagara Falls." In the same issue is a theme photograph of pretty Zhang, Yuanyuan's portrait. The issue published on the 13th explores the theme, "Mysterious death of a Shanghai Prostitute," with two dazzlingly beautiful photos of the dead woman on the cover. These attract readers who pity the beauty for her brief life.

Police Chief Simon reveals that Zhang, Yuanyuan's boyfriend

Lai, Wenxiong arrived in Niagara Falls from Taipei at around 7pm on the 14th. On hearing this, Editor-in-chief Guo suggests that the weekly to be published on the 20th should emphasize the "Revelation of love by the prostitute's boyfriend". If Lai, Wenxiong rejects the interview, Jia, Feng proposes the alternative subject, "Revelation of a girl's heart by her parents". Editor-in-chief Guo agrees reluctantly and asks Jia and Wu to exert themselves to dig up more stuff.

In order not to disappoint Editor-in-chief Guo and to write the most interesting reports for the readers, Jia, Feng is waiting in the reception room of the Niagara Police Bureau at 6pm on the 14th.

Half an hour later, Chief Simon and Policewoman JoAnna bring a man in. There is no need for an introduction: it's Lai, Wenxiong, the man he saw in the photos. Lai looks much older and thinner, but is still handsome, somewhat like the hot star Qin, Han of Taiwan.

Jia, Feng hands him his business card and asks, "Mr. Lai, may I interview you later?"

Seeing his hesitation, Simon immediately pats Jia on the shoulder and comments, "This reporter has contributed greatly to Miss Zhang's case. He translated some of the important documents. He's also from Shanghai and is the same age as Miss Zhang."

"Oh, is that so? No problem, but…," Lai looks at his watch while saying this.

"It doesn't matter. I'll wait for you here, no matter how long it takes." Jia replies.

JoAnna cuts in, "It'll be approximately two hours. You can have supper first."

Simon pats Jia on his shoulder again and says, smiling, "Do you know there is a Chinese restaurant downtown? Eat well and work hard."

Nodding, Jia, Feng is sensible enough to leave the meeting room quickly. As a journalist, he thinks, waiting is not a problem, is it? He once waited for 3 hours for the arrival of a delegation to Toronto as the result of a delayed flight, which caused another group of reporters to wait for a night at the airport. Moreover, he is contemplating writing a novel and may require help from Lai, Wenxiong in the future.

It is 8pm when Jia returns to the Police Bureau. The meeting room is still brightly lit. It's not until 9pm that he sees the three people coming out.

Lai, Wenxiong hurries over to apologize to Jia, "Sorry to have kept you waiting for so long."

"It doesn't matter. It's usual for reporters to wait." Jia's Mandarin is mixed with a strong Shanghai accent.

Lai takes this opportunity to say, "I really appreciate that you translated the two letters for the police."

"You mean the letters Miss Zhang wrote to you on November 15th and December 24th? The police needed the letters urgently and another lady reporter and I are familiar with this case. It was a job easily done." Jia mentions it casually.

Lai, Wenxiong speaks seriously, "There is a lot of significant information in those two letters."

Jia inquires, "Have the police given them to you?"

"Yes, they gave me a copy of the Chinese version. I just glanced over it. How miserable she was!" Lai shakes his head helplessly and swallows down his grief, which has come up to his throat.

Jia asks another question, "The police have told you a lot, haven't they?"

After a brief talk between the two young men, Lai, Wenxiong seems to trust Jia, Feng. As a result, Lai pours out his heart, "Chief Simon briefed me on the progress in solving this case. I carefully reviewed my contacts with Zhang, Yuanyuan for them… That's why it took such a long time. I'd like to ask you a favor: could you drive me to Waterloo and interview me on the way? If there is not enough time during the trip, you can continue the interview at my place. The police haven't found the autobiographical novel, 'New Camille', in the disk left by Yuanyuan. It might be at my place. The police want to uncover important clues to the case."

To tell the truth, Jia, Feng's main aim is to find the manuscript of "New Camille". Ever since he translated Zhang, Yuanyuan's love letters to Lai, Wenxiong three days ago, he has dreamed of obtaining the manuscript. The title is similar to the novel he is thinking about. As the saying goes: great minds think alike. Another title he could use is "A Tale of Two Towers", focusing on Zhang, Yuanyuan's coming from the Oriental Tower (in Shanghai) to the CN Tower (in Toronto). It seems that the title "New Camille" is more captivating. Thinking of this, Jia agrees at once to drive Lai to Waterloo. If he has the pleasure to read the manuscript first, he can discover the major factor which led her astray, and provide new clues for solving the case. He'll write another wonderful exclusive report to satisfy Editor-in-chief Guo's expectations.

As they walk towards the parking lot, Jia raises the subject on purpose. "Zhang, Yuanyuan mentioned her autobiographical novel in her letter to you on Christmas Eve. Is that right?"

Lai replies, "It was I who encouraged her to write it. She was quite talented in writing and had already published something. She entertained the dream of becoming a writer from early childhood. The novel was tentatively entitled 'New Camille', taking the title from Dumas (Jr.)'s renowned novel and adding the word 'New". So far as I know, she only wrote the parts about her experiences in Tokyo and Toronto. I was busy with my studies and read only a small section of it. I promised to revise and polish it in detail after the defense of my thesis at the end of the year. Now everything has come to naught. Alas, life is like a dream!"

"Brother Lai, don't be too pessimistic. The case hasn't been solved yet. Just let me know if you need help, as I am from the same hometown and of the same age as Miss Zhang. Besides, I have been studying the case every day since January 1st, so I know almost as much as the police."

Nodding silently, Lai is grateful in his heart to this "Shanghai man". Since he fell in love with Zhang, Yuanyuan, he has regarded people from Shanghai as smart and capable. He also believes what Zhang, Yuanyuan often said: wherever there are Chinese, there will be Shanghai people, among whom there will be outstanding talents.

Jia, Feng hands the two issues of "Toronto Weekly" to Lai, Wenxiong. When he glances at the covers, his tears roll down like heavy rain. He says uncontrollably, "What a tragic death! My Yuanyuan! Who killed you so ruthlessly? I vow to kill him!"

"The whole thing will come to light eventually. We'll do our best to find more clues for the police," Jia attempts to console him.

Getting into Jia's black Toyota, Lai suddenly asks, "Chief Simon said that Yuanyuan's family is staying at her place."

Nodding, Jia replies, "Yes. They came to Toronto the day before yesterday. I interviewed them. How sad!"

Pondering for a moment, Lai asks in a confidential tone, "Brother Jia, could we stop over there? I'd like to visit them."

Jia nods quickly and contacts Old Zhang by cell phone. The Zhangs are glad to meet Lai.

In the pitch-dark night, Jia, Feng steps on the accelerator and drives towards the building at 100 Lakeshore.

57. Belated Visit to the Zhang Family

After getting Jia, Feng's phone call, the three members of the Zhang family wait silently in the living room. The existing lifeless atmosphere suddenly seems to have picked up a little vigor. Mrs. Zhang goes especially to the washroom to apply some light makeup. Even though her daughter is gone, she shouldn't let herself go: her daughter always paid particular attention to her makeup. This was her nature, but also the cause of her tragedy. Subconsciously, the three of them are curious to see what kind of a person this man is, the man with whom Yuanyuan was madly in love.

"Uncle and Aunt, I'm Lai, Wenxiong, Yuanyuan's boyfriend." Entering the room, Lai introduces himself courteously.

Old Zhang holds his hand tightly as if clutching at a straw. Mrs.

Zhang is dazed, never expecting that he would be more handsome than his photo and a dead ringer for Qin, Han, the famous actor in Taiwan. She can't help admiring her daughter's judgment. Sadly, Yuanyuan didn't have the good fortune to be with him.

As soon as he sees the mourning table in the living room, Lai, Wenxiong steps forward and bows to the portrait of Zhang, Yuanyuan three times. Then he kneels down and whispers to her, "Yuanyuan, sorry for coming late, too late! It's my fault that I left you alone here. If I had been by your side, this would never have happened…I'm the culprit, the Number One culprit. Please punish me."

Kneeling there, he talks to himself foolishly, or talks to his lover, with tears glistening in his eyes. Seeing this, Mrs. Zhang starts sobbing. Zhang, Mingming, Yuanyuan's brother, stands in silence with lowered head. Hearing Mrs. Zhangs's sobs, Lai, Wenxiong can't control himself any more and tears roll down his face.

"Mr. Lai, a dead person can't return to life. Don't blame yourself. We had better try to help the police solve the case so as to catch the murderer soon." Old Zhang attempts to comfort him but it takes a long time to stop Lai's tears.

Together with his father, Zhang, Mingming helps Lai, Wenxiong up and takes him over to sit on the sofa. Then he makes a cup of tea for Lai.

"Chief Simon said that cremation is set for next Monday," he says after sipping some tea.

Old Zhang responds, "Yes, at 4pm on the 22nd. We'll return to Shanghai by air on the 24th, the Lunar New Year."

"Have you considered burial in the ground? Cremation is cruel," Lai says, frowning.

"We want to take her ashes back to bury in the cemetery in the suburbs. It will be easier to visit. There is no family here. Who would care?" Mrs. Zhang interrupts.

"I am here, Aunt. We genuinely loved each other. I was going to marry her. Heaven failed me!"

"We appreciate your kindness, but you are still studying and haven't settled yet… The police told us about you and Yuanyuan. We are really grateful to you."

Lai nods. Fixing his eyes on Mrs. Zhang, he discovers a close resemblance between her and Yuanyuan, especially when she talks. No wonder Yuanyuan used to admire her mother's beauty. If they walked together in the street, people would take them for sisters.

"What about the arrangements for the funeral? Do you need my help?" Lai asks with concern.

Old Zhang pushes up his glasses and replies, "It will be very simple, not really a funeral. We'll pay our respects to the remains before cremation and fetch her ashes on the third day. The police will arrange everything, such as whom to invite. We'll hold a decent funeral in Shanghai, where we have a lot of friends and relatives."

Lai complains, "The police are so inefficient that there is no substantial progress after half a month of investigation. I suggested they invite an American expert to help and a decision on this matter will be made next week. If not, I'll hire a private detective to help. I know of a well-known Chinese detective Mr. Shi, who is honored as the modern Sherlock Holmes. The key for now lies in whom Yuanyuan was with in the five hours before her death. That person is the major suspect."

"The police have done their best. Let's allow them more time. We can't wait till the case is cracked. Please let us know the facts in detail when they become available." Old Zhang is reasonable in his words, showing the nature of a traditional Chinese intellectual.

To Lai, Wenxiong, talking with the Zhang family is like the interesting and enjoyable dialogues he had with Yuanyuan when she was alive. It's a pity that they have met so late. If he and Yuanyuan had been engaged in August last year as they had originally planned, they would have gone to Shanghai to meet the Zhang family. Fate has pulled a prank on them. Time flies in their memories of grief.

58. Important Manuscript Found

It's already 11pm when Lai leaves the building at 100 Lakeshore. The whole city is asleep in the indistinct night with gentle moonlight. Jia, Feng drives his Toyota on the highway to Waterloo.

Jia hands the portable recorder to Lai, Wenxiong and starts the interview in the car.

"Please begin with the first time you met. The more detailed, the better. Rest assured that "Toronto Weekly" will not publish everything and will not publish your real name."

Lai clears his throat, presses the recording button and starts slowly…

When the car finally arrives at the students' dormitory of the University of Waterloo, he is still indulging in memories of the past. He talks while the disk turns continuously.

"Let's go inside and continue the interview. About half an hour should be enough." He turns off the recorder and carries his simple luggage inside.

Aware of a strange odor in the room where nobody has been for such a long time, Lai immediately turns on the ventilator in the kitchen.

"Well, would you like some?" He raises a whisky bottle.

"I wouldn't dare, as I have to drive back soon. My driver's license would be suspended if I got caught by the police," Jia shrugs his shoulder.

"What a law-abiding citizen! I can't survive without liquor these days," Lai admits in a low voice.

Jia comforts him, "A special policy for a stressful period of time. You'll be fine after this hard time."

"I hope so." Nodding, Lai pours himself a drink.

"Where was I? Oh, Yuanyuan went with me to Taipei to meet my family during last summer's vacation…" he presses the record button and returns to his memories of the past.

When he mentions their sorrowful parting at the Airport, Jia eagerly asks, "After you parted on August 15th, did you have any contact with her?"

Sipping his liquor and licking his lips, Lai replies, "Of course there was contact. I called her at least once a week. I remember she mentioned that she had a fever. On the night before Christmas Eve, I phoned her and she seemed to be in a normal mood. By the way, I was sick for over a month after she left Taipei. I had no appetite and languished in bed. My mother forced me to see an old Chinese doctor, who diagnosed me as lovesick. I gradually recovered after taking Chinese medicine for over half a month, but remained in low spirits. Lian, Haotien, the bad egg, phoned me several times and wanted to see me. I rejected all his overtures. I don't want to see him any more. You see, without that guy, August 15th would have been the day of my happy engagement to Yuanyuan. She would have remained in Taipei until we returned to Canada after my sample survey."

"When did you plan to return to Canada?"

"I promised her I'd return so that we could celebrate Christmas together. She longed for the arrival of the New Year in her phone calls. Unfortunately, just as there is unpredictable weather, bad luck befalls people. My mother was diagnosed with second stage stomach cancer at the end of November. By that time, my sample survey was almost completed and I was about to book a plane ticket for Canada. The whole family was at once submerged in misery. After consultation with different doctors, my mother was hospitalized and underwent surgery last week to remove three quarters of her stomach. I certainly could not leave Taipei during this period of time. My older brother even canceled his trip for a conference in the United States. I immediately called Yuanyuan and told her everything in detail. She was very considerate and asked me to take good care of my Mom, emphasizing that one's mother is unique in the world."

Lai continues, "In mid December, my Mom was staying in Taida (Taiwan University) Hospital. As everybody else had to go to work, I took care of Mom day and night. There was no opportunity to call

Yuanyuan. My Mom's surgery was successful and she left the hospital a few days ago. She suggested I return to Canada after the Lunar New Year. My mother seemed more open-minded after her serious illness. She took the initiative to mention Yuanyuan's name while she was in the hospital. I predicted that Mom would soon consent to my engagement with Yuanyuan. I remember that the day Mom was discharged from hospital on Jan. 11th, I phoned Yuanyuan, but nobody answered. I thought she had gone on a trip... Who would have expected that at noon the next day, I would get a call from Chief Simon with the terrible news? My whole family was stunned..."

"What a tragic love story, sufficient for a full-length novel, 'New Camille'!" Jia comments on impulse.

Lai finishes his drink and says, "Yes. I originally promised Yuanyuan to co-write the novel, 'New Camille', but with a happy ending. Who would have thought that it would have a tragic ending? She is gone and I don't know when I'll get over it. I have to finish my thesis, so I'm not interested in writing such a novel. If you intend to do so, I'll provide you with first-hand information, but all characters must have false names to avoid unnecessary trouble."

"It fits in exactly with my wishes. To tell you the truth, I plan to write a novel that will explore the fate of Zhang, Yuanyuan and women like her. Everything in the world is cause and effect. She would not have gone astray without a good reason. You realize this because you are studying social sciences. Well, it's getting late and you haven't slept well for several days. I have to return to Toronto to write my report."

Lai, Wenxiong turns on his computer and inserts a disk. He taps on the keyboard and medical terms in English appear on the screen. When he inserts the second disk, well-known poems and quotations, which Yuanyuan had collected, appear.

"To the best of my memory, the manuscript should be in this box under the file names Camille 1 to Camille 5. The first two of the five chapters are set in Tokyo while the last three chapters center on events in Toronto."

There are ten disks in the box and the eighth disk they try contains the manuscript.

"Well, I'll copy this one for you. I'll be very busy the next two days. I have to translate the manuscript into English for the police. I hope we'll find some clues. I might phone you for some technical terms." Lai says.

Jia is pleased, "Don't stand on ceremony. I'll do my best to help you."

The moon is clear and cold and there is a nip in the chilly air.

At 2am, Jia, Feng exchanges phone numbers with Lai, Wenxiong and leaves, then drives on Highway 401 at high speed to Toronto. As a "night hawk', he is not tired at all. He admires Lai, Wenxiong's courage in courting Zhang, Yuanyuan. How much courage does it take to marry a prostitute! There is a world of difference between Lai and those men who insist on marrying virgins. This difference reflects Lai's open-mindedness and genuine love for Yuanyuan, a love without prejudice. Such true love is exemplary and inspirational for young people in the 21st century.

After drinking a glass of milk at home, Jia falls asleep at once. When he opens his sleepy eyes, it is already 5pm. Good heavens! He has slept for 12 hours, breaking a record of his. Generally speaking, he only sleeps for 6 hours: this time, it is double. It shows how exhausted he must be.

After a pleasant hot bath, he gulps down two bowls of "beef instant noodles" to fill his stomach. Then he quickly turns on his computer to read the autobiographical novel of Zhang, Yuanyuan, perhaps to seek the causes of her tragedy as soon as possible, or perhaps to satisfy his own desire to pry into her affairs.

(Respected readers, chapters 13 to 17 are taken from Zhang, Yuanyuan's manuscript, "New Camille", with captions by this author. The first person, "I," in these chapters is Zhang, Yuanyuan.)

Chapter Thirteen

"Drunken Girl Raped by her Boss at a Nightclub in Ginza"

59. No Gold Found in Tokyo

Memory is a long, long scar. Even when I touch it by chance now, I feel a dull pain. If I touch it intentionally, I experience so much pain that I feel half dead.

When I open the gates of memory, I am filled with a heart-breaking ache. My two-year stay in Tokyo stuffs each of my cells with "resentment". To not a few women from Shanghai, Tokyo is not merely a nightmare, but a sort of shame, a downright grief.

However sorrowful and shameful, it is a significant turning point in my life. However distressed and full of bitter hatred, I have to record it in detail, bearing the sharp pain of opening a wound, with my shivering hand and an open mind.

March 8th 1992 happened to be International Women's Day. With mixed feelings, I said farewell to the Huangpu River, which had nurtured me for 21 years. In an era when male power was getting weaker while the sense of "females propping up half the sky" was expanding, I chose such a day to leave my hometown, perhaps from a kind of subconscious motive and not merely a coincidence.

It was my first trip far away. I had been only to Suzhou and Hangzhou with my classmates and to Nanjing with my family. On March 8, 1992, a lot of people came to the Hongqiao Airport to see me off, including my friends and relatives as well as my classmates at the Health School, such as Song, Lei. In the terminal, my mom's tears were glistening in her eyes. Aged Grandma was crying her heart out. She had brought me up and was dearer to me than my parents. Dad looked helpless but kept silent. He was the only one who opposed to my trip to Japan, but he failed to stop it.

Just before my departure, I couldn't help bursting into tears. Mom grasped my hand tightly and sobbed. My best classmates at the Health School said goodbye to me with envy. Only Song, Lei was against my going abroad. Her theory was: if you stay in Shanghai, you can dally with foreign men, but if you go abroad, foreign men will dally with you. She would never leave Shanghai to dally with foreign men. In her eyes, I must be a super fool.

"Yuanyuan, if you can't stand it, just come home. We don't lack money." Dad was the last to instruct me in a low voice while holding my hand.

At that time, I found his hand particularly warm and forceful. I don't have a strong "Oedipus complex", but he is always an unbending tree in my heart-- tall and firm, never wavering in storms.

The aircraft propellers were turning swiftly with a roaring noise. The plane quickly taxied to the runway and then rose into the sky. This was my first trip by air and I felt curious and a bit terrified. With a sense of weightlessness, I seemed to become an unattached kite, wandering in the sky, cherishing brightly colored dreams of striking gold.

I wondered why I was so determined to go to Japan when I knew full well that life would be hard there and that Dad was strongly opposed. If it had not been for my former boyfriend Chen, Zhiwei, who used me, lied about his wife and deserted me after going to the US, I might not have made this trip. Mom agreed to let me go to Japan in order for me to change my environment, so that I would not attempt suicide again.

I should mention another important reason. During that period of time, all Shanghai people somewhat capable and resourceful were going abroad. Few of my good friends had remained in China. People of the first caliber went to the United States; the second went to Canada and Australia; the third to Japan; and the last of them went to Shenzhen. I was by no means inferior to the others, except that I had failed the entrance examinations for university. Moreover, I have an attractive appearance, the best gift from my parents: since senior high school, most people turn around to look at me. My family had no overseas connections, so I had to rely on myself from the beginning. To demonstrate my capability, I followed the trend to go abroad with great ambition. Shanghai people always aim to go overseas, as if there is gold waiting for the sons and daughters of Shanghai on the other side of the ocean. It is not rare for someone in your family to be an official in Beijing. Only going abroad is rare and unique. Among all the provinces and cities of China, the people of Shanghai, with the proper soil and sunshine, always worship foreign things and respect foreign power the most.

Narita International Airport in Tokyo is vast, bright and imposingly overwhelming, noted for the lovely smiles of the stewardesses. Chen, Changting, my Shanghai neighbor, came to meet me at the airport. He graduated from a science and technology university, was six years my senior, and had studied for a master's degree in computer sciences. He had worked part time in Japan for 3 years. I had entrusted him to advise me about Japan and to help with such tasks as finding a guarantor and applying for a language school.

Driving a second-hand white Honda, he took me to a two-story house in a prosperous district in Shinjuku. I used to think he was a bookworm, but he had become quite smart after being away from home for several years. He asked me numerous questions as if he were an old overseas Chinese man who had been away from Shanghai for hundreds of years.

"This kind of house is called an 'Abbado'. As a new arrival, try not to be picky and choosy like a princess. The kitchen and bathroom are shared with three other people who have come from mainland China as well. When you have money, you can move. It's only twenty minutes' walk from where you'll be working." He talked to me while helping me with my luggage. His greeting speech sounded like a pithy formula: obviously, he had met many people like me.

The tatami room on the second floor was like a tiny pigeon cage. Its monthly rent was 50,000 Japanese Yen. This was highway robbery! However prepared I was mentally, I still felt that the price of housing in Tokyo was shocking.

Putting down the luggage, Chen, Changting said, "Yuanyuan, I have to hurry to get to work. Let's go to the Japanese restaurant to meet your boss first."

Seeing my puzzlement, he added, "Tokyo is different from Shanghai. Here you have to make good use of every minute for work. Every second means money. It's hard to find a job because so many people come to Japan. I called in a favor to get this dish-washing job for you. If you study the Japanese language hard and if you are good at aural and oral comprehension, it will be easier to find another job."

I touched up my makeup, but didn't have time to change clothes before going with him to the "Zen Japanese Restaurant". Aokawa Kakuai, the boss, was a fat, dark, short man about 40 years old. He held my hand closely, his two eyes fixed on my breasts -- he was clearly a wolf. Since I was fully developed, I had got used to such looks, so I was not surprised.

Chen, Changting and the fat boss talked in a strange language, from which I could only understand a few words. After I decided to go to Japan, I had studied Japanese diligently for several months, without much progress, perhaps because of the lack of a language environment. Chen, Changting told me, in the Shanghai dialect, that the boss wanted me to start work tomorrow afternoon. As I did not understand Japanese, I could only wash dishes. The boss praised me for my beauty, however, saying I looked like a movie star. He said I could be a waitress once I mastered some Japanese. I felt as if my head were being crushed. It suddenly dawned on me how important language learning was! When my Dad had stressed the importance of learning a language before going abroad, I didn't quite see his point.

"You have to take care of yourself. Don't let anybody take advantage of you. Japanese men are dirty and mean. Phone me if anything happens. Make good use of your time to learn Japanese," Chen, Changting, more talkative than my Grandma, warned me again and again before parting.

After I returned to my residence, I looked at the mess in the room and suddenly asked myself: Is this the Tokyo that I have dreamed about? Is there gold here?

60. Unbearable Dish-washing Job

Early in the morning of the second day, I go to the language school to register, accompanied by my neighbor Li, Mei. She came here from Hangzhou half a year ago, but she can speak Japanese pretty well. She studies the language part time and works in a coffee shop part time. She tells me that it is hard to find a job unless I have the courage to "go to the sea (engage in the sex trade, --Translator's note)". I have never considered this, although I have read some reports that quite a number of Shanghai women "have gone to the sea". As the saying goes: one does not shed a tear until one sees the coffin. I will not be convinced until I have gained some personal experience.

After registration, I attend a session in a classroom. The teacher is an old Japanese man who speaks idiomatic mandarin Chinese. It is said that he furthered his Chinese study at Beijing University. After an entire morning of classes, my mind is filled with various words, quite a lot of which seem familiar to me because I may have learned them before.

At 4pm, I rush to the "Zen Japanese Restaurant". A girl from Shanghai is washing dishes in the kitchen. Seeing me, she takes the initiative to show me the dish-washing procedure. Today is her last day working here, as she'll start work in a clothing factory tomorrow. Before her departure, she whispers to me in the Shanghai dialect to guard against the men here,-- none of them is good. I thank her for her concern, but haven't paid enough attention. How mean and dirty can they be in the public eyes? The key is I should stand my ground firmly.

It looks simple to wash dishes—you don't need to use your brain. First, I dump the remains of the food into the garbage bin and rinse the dishes under the tap. Then, I put the dishes in good order in the dishwasher, press the button and the machine turns swiftly. Finally I sort out and place the dishes on the shelf. This job is not hard, but the weird smell is unbearable—it is unlike either cat food or human food.

I finish work at midnight and walk alone in the street, panic-stricken. Such loneliness comes from the bottom of my heart naturally and is not feigned. Luckily, Shinjuku is a busy district, with neon lights flashing, cars running continuously and quite a lot of people walking in the street. After getting home, I fall asleep at once on the tatami mat. After all, I have stood washing dishes in the restaurant for 8 solid hours. This is quite unusual for a person from mainland China, who is used to leading an easy life.

On Saturday evening it is unexpectedly busy in the restaurant. I exert myself to wash dishes but still fail to meet the demands of so many customers. Several waiters repeatedly complain about my slow work, and Aokawa Kakuai, the boss, pulls his dark long face and scolds me before leaving. I do not understand what he says, but from his gesture I know he wants me to go faster.

Finally he can bear it no more and asks a waiter who speaks Chinese to tell me, *"Miss, the boss wants you to be faster, otherwise, don't come tomorrow."*

I feign a smile and reply, "Okay, please interpret for me: I'll be quick and give me a chance."

Now I try my best to engage fully in dish washing as if I am in a life-and-death struggle with the dishwasher. I am sweating all over, with my underwear soaked.

While I am working as busy as a bee, a Japanese second chef comes to help me with sorting dishes. He talks in rusty Chinese while touching my buttocks on purpose, "Hey, you are so pretty, why should you do such harsh work? Why not work as a dancer? You can earn a lot of money!"

I have no time to reply and he is insatiable, "I'll introduce a better job to you if you go out with me tonight after the shift -- to be somebody's mistress."

I glare at him, "What are you talking about? Fuck your mother! If you go on, I'll tell the boss."

"Do you think he'll help you? Sooner or later, he'll devour you. He is a big wolf," he says, grimacing.

"Thanks. Thanks for your help. Now you can go." I order him in a loud voice to leave and he returns to his own work, shame-faced. Now I realize that what the Shanghai girl said is good advice.

At 1am early in the morning, I return home with leaden steps. Lying in bed, I toss and turn but can't fall asleep, perhaps due to exhaustion. Looking at my tender hands, which used to play the piano and now have been swollen by constant washing, I taste bitter tears flowing into my mouth. The dishes I washed tonight must be more than all the dishes I have washed in over ten years of my life. In front of me flash the terrible eyes of Aokawa Kakuai and the dishes piling up like a mountain.

Later I feel throes of pain in my lower body. I know it's my horrible "old friend" coming: I was born with menstrual pain. During my periods, I have to stay in bed for two or three days. My mother, a doctor, can do nothing about my pain. She told me that it would improve after marriage. Every month, I vow to be a male in my next life. When creating human beings, God was not fair to make women suffer from such gut wrenching pain. With the unbearable discomfort, I toss and turn in bed while gripping the corner of my quilt with my teeth. Is this the

Tokyo I have yearned for? The house is so old that the whole room trembles when I turn over in bed. I feel sick whenever I go into the kitchen of the restaurant. Even showers cannot wash away the weird smell of the leftover food. Moreover, the icy look of the boss and the dallying of the dirty chef are hard to bear…

Right now I miss my loved ones on the bank of the Huangpu River even more. Why did I come here to suffer instead of working as a nurse in a nice hospital in Shanghai? Pack up and go back home… I recall my father's words at parting. How am I going to face my family and friends in Shanghai? Why do all others from Shanghai persist except you Zhang, Yuanyuan? I do not belong to the weak. I'll bring home a load of money, an astronomical sum of money, if I am to go back. My lady, show your ability as a person from Shanghai and adapt to the circumstances.

In the quiet night, I am filled with confused thoughts. Various ideas come to mind and vanish instantly. Considering the pros and cons and drawing a lesson from a bitter experience, I think that I have no choice but to stay. I have to work for my survival, no matter how lowly the job is. When one is standing under the low eaves, one has to lower his head. If I want to leave the smoky kitchen, I will have to exert myself to master the Japanese language.

61. Painstaking Effort Yields a Sure Reward

Three months later, I have rapidly improved my Japanese language skills: I not only understand about 70 to 80 per cent of what others talk about, but also communicate reasonably well with Japanese people. The teachers and my classmates at the language school are surprised and my co-workers in the restaurant cannot but admire me, "a woman from Shanghai". When the dirty chefs attempt to dally with me, I let loose a torrent of abuse in Japanese and scare them out of their wits.

When I fail to find another job, Aokawa Kakuai, the boss, invites me into his office for a talk. He will transfer me to his new restaurant in the Ginza to be a waitress, with a monthly wage of 250,000 Japanese Yen. Moreover, the company will rent an apartment (what the Japanese call a "Mansion") for me and will pay the monthly rent of 100,000 Yen. My wage for dish-washing is only 150,000 Yen. When I subtract my rent of 50,000, tuition fees of 40,000, and the cost of food, 20,000, I have only 40,000 Yen left. Now that I can make 250,000 Yen every month, minus my tuition and food costs, I shall save 190,000 Yen, almost 5 times as much as I save now. Why not? Feeling elated in my heart, as if I had eaten a jar of honey, I consent at once.

He says smiling, "You are beautiful and resemble somewhat Kurihara Komaki, a former great Japanese star. You can change to the Japanese name Miss Komaki. It's convenient for people to call while you are serving as a waitress."

I agree without reservation. Even when I was in Shanghai, some people told me I resembled her. After I came to Tokyo, several Japanese I met made the same comment. I have seen two movies starring her, "Eternal Love" and "Yearning for the Home Village", which have left an excellent impression on me. It's a pity that she is getting old – the worst fear for women.

Before I leave, Aokawa Kakuai instructs me, "Work hard. You can make a lot of money with your diligence and intelligence. Tomorrow morning, I'll send somebody to help you move. Come in the evening to instruct the new worker about dish-washing. He is a young man from China. Go to the new restaurant to work the day after tomorrow and learn from the manager whose name is Miyazawa Kiichi."

On my way back home that night, I am in high spirits, dancing in the streets. I feel the moon is especially round and the stars particularly bright. I feel as if every road lamp is brighter than before and every pedestrian smiles at me. I am grateful to Aokawa Kakuai from the bottom of my heart. Who says Japanese men are dirty? At least, he doesn't intend to dally with me, not even touch my hand. He only fixes his eyes on my breasts. People have the right to look at others, as long as they don't harass others. Women are born for others to gaze at, especially a beautiful woman like me.

Without even taking off my jacket after returning home, I eagerly convey the good news to my Mom in Shanghai. She laughs for a while at the other end of the phone, and then she starts to cry, "Yuanyuan, my heart aches when I hear that your hands, meant for playing the piano, have washed dishes for three months. I regret letting you go abroad ..."

I try to comfort her, "Mom, it's normal to suffer a little while abroad. I am improving now, right? At least, I won't have to wash dishes. Tomorrow will be *even better."*

"Yes, tomorrow will be better! You have to take good care of yourself. Rest a couple of days during your periods. Don't overwork yourself." Mom shows great concern.

I comfort her again, "Mom, it is different here from China where people can ask for leave at will. Here, every minute and second mean money. Rest assured, I'll look after myself."

Finally, she warns me to be careful while abroad alone and advises me to study Japanese diligently. She reminds me that what my Dad worries about most is my language skills. I proudly ask her to tell Dad that my Japanese has reached a certain level; otherwise, I wouldn't be able to work as a waitress.

While moving, Li, Mei talks to me in the Shanghai dialect with a Hangzhou accent, "You are so capable that you have moved to a 'mansion' in three months. People from Shanghai are smart."

I stretch out my hands and tell her with a smile, "This is the price I paid. How many layers of skin have peeled off?"

Holding my hands, she says, "It's incredible. Such a pretty girl washed dishes! Compared to those Shanghai women who just take off their pants… Excuse me, you are so different…. You know, the coffee shop where I work is not doing well and I might get the sack. Please be on the look out for some opportunities for me."

I hold her hands tightly and thank her for her help, especially her tips in learning Japanese. I promise that I'll let her know if positions become available. I am prettier than she is, but not as capable. She has a promising future, as she is an honor graduate from Zhejiang University. Once she masters Japanese, she can study for an MA degree in chemistry.

The Japanese man who comes to help me move laughs like an idiot with no understanding of what we are talking about. In Japanese society, smart and intelligent men abound. Still, there are also some fools like this man, who have strong limbs and just laugh stupidly all the time.

62. Working as a Waitress, Finally

The newly opened "Zen Japanese Restaurant", located in the prosperous Ginza, is the fifth chain store of Aokawa Kakuai. It is much more gorgeously *ornamented and higher-graded than the previous ones. It takes me just over ten minutes to walk there from my new residence. I stay in a unit on the eighth floor of a 12-storey building. The bedroom is not big and there is a small living room, a kitchen and a washroom. In the morning, I don't have to worry about sharing a washroom or struggling for more space in the refrigerator. It is wonderful to have this small unit, a small world for me alone. Nobody will interfere with me, nor will I trouble others.*

The manager of the restaurant, Miyazawa Kiichi, a tall and slender Japanese man in his thirties, is said to be a good friend of Aokawa Kakuai. I go to work at 6pm for the first time and find the restaurant in an awful mess. Everybody is busy preparing for the grand opening the next day. Out of the 8 waitresses including me, 6 are Japanese girls. The other one is a girl from Nanjing named Sada Keiko. She is said to have married a Japanese man. Apparently, these women have worked as waitresses for quite a long time and know the ins and outs of the business. Miyazawa Kiichi knows that I am a neophyte, so he teaches me every procedure patiently and advises me again and again to familiarize myself with the menu.

Sada Keiko makes time to talk to me in Mandarin, "Your oral Japanese is pretty good, but there is still room for improvement. If you have time, you can watch Japanese TV and learn more idiomatic expressions."

"Thank you. I will study harder." I have also become courteous and bow to her to express my gratitude.

The custom of bowing in Japanese society encourages people to be more courteous. No matter whether they think highly of you or not, they make you feel theirs is a land of ceremony and propriety with their pious appearance. When I first arrived in Japan, I was not used to it. Now this habit has become second nature.

With patience, Sada Keiko tells me, "You'll find out later that some Japanese customers are very picky and choosy. It always pays to master good Japanese language skills. Deep in their hearts, many Japanese look down upon us Chinese. It is even worse if we don't speak good Japanese. Sometimes they don't want to talk to Chinese people."

Of course, I accept this advice from the bottom of her heart, which comes from her own experience. I thank her again and ask for more help from her, as I am a new hire. This conversation turns us into good friends. Nothing can compare with the wondrous "motherland effect".

The next noon is the grand opening of the restaurant. Aokawa Kakuai is dressed in holiday attire, as at a birthday party. His face is glowing with health. He is followed closely by his wife, Kimiko. It is beyond my expectation that an ugly man like him should have such a beautiful wife. Perhaps it is due to his wealth. In this society where money makes the mare go, a rich man can get everything, including a pretty wife.

I heard from my co-workers in the restaurant that the Aokawa Kakuai clan has a huge business, which includes real estate and banking. He has five chain stores plus an advertising agency and owns a monthly health food magazine with a large circulation. Kimiko looks somewhat like the film star Yamaguchi Momoe, with a slender, well-proportioned figure, although she is the mother of two children. Her pampered figure may be the result of her easy life as a rich man's wife. Aokawa Kakuai shakes hands with the celebrities and big businessmen who arrive for the ribbon cutting ceremony. We eight waitresses, in uniform kimonos, stand at either side of the gate to welcome the guests.

After the ribbon cutting ceremony, customers pour into the restaurant for dinner, perhaps because of the grand opening discount of 20% or the effective advertisements. All the waitresses are shuttling to and fro non-stop and the kitchen is a busy mess. Even the manager has to help serving dishes. Business slackens after 3pm, but groups of customers come again before 6pm, with a joyful bustle in and out of the kitchen. After 10 pm, few customers come.

Before closing, Aokawa Kakuai enters the restaurant in a hurry. Talking with the manager for a while, he can't help dancing with joy, perhaps because of the good business at the grand opening.

I am setting the tables for the next day when Aokawa Kakuai swaggers towards me.

"You must be tired after the first day's work. The manager told me you did a good job. I was right to tell him that you are smart and capable," he says with self-confidence.

I bow to him to show courtesy and can't help telling him, "I stayed up last night to learn the menu by heart."

"It's good that you have such Japanese spirit," he says with gritted teeth.

Seeing my perplexity, he adds, "Japanese spirit means down-to-earth and going-all-out in work. If we hadn't had it, Japan would not have developed so rapidly after the War."

I nod without fully understanding what he said.

He suddenly approaches me and whispers into my ear, "Later I'll take you to karaoke in the Ginza as a reward."

I give him a brilliant smile.

63. Getting Drunk at Midnight in the Ginza

After I get into Aokawa Kakuai's black Lexus, he steps on the accelerator and the car races forward.

I never expected that he would drive so fast. Full of fear sitting beside him, I plead with him to slow down, but he seems not to hear me.

"I'm scared to death! Slow down," I can't help yelling.

"Don't panic. I can assure your safety as I have been driving for scores of years. Only at such speed can you earn money in Tokyo," he says smiling.

Amid talk and laughter, we arrive at the "Elegant Karaoke", which is thronged with youngsters, screaming in Japanese at the top of their lungs. They are not really singing but giving vent to their emotions.

Aokawa Kakuai shows disapproval by shaking his head. He goes directly to a reserved room, grasping my hand tightly as if by loosening his grip, I would be snatched away by others.

The sound insulation is so good in this room that I can't hear any noise from outside. The waiter brings a bottle of red wine and closes the door behind him. I never dreamed that there would be a huge pile of MTV's in Mandarin and Cantonese in the room. This makes me very excited.

Aokawa Kakuai pours a full glass of wine for me. Actually, I can't handle it, but I utter no objection to avoid upsetting him. When he proposes a toast, I just sip a little.

"Well, let me hear you sing Chinese songs first."

Singing and dancing have been my forte since childhood and I guest-starred in TV and movies before. As a girl, I always dreamed of becoming an actress. Since my arrival in Tokyo three months ago, I haven't sung a song, let alone danced. It's my first time in a karaoke bar here, while in Shanghai I went crazy at KTV at least once every two weeks and often visited bars.

I pick some MTV's and clear my throat. First I sing "Women's weakness" and "All because of you" by Ye, Qianwen, followed by "Forgetting you is forgetting me", "Obstinacy", "Seduce me" by Wang, Qingwen, and "Dingdang" by Zheng, Xiuwen.

After I've sung six songs at a stretch, I am enjoying myself fully. Aokawa Kakuai, nodding his head, is charmed by my singing and applauds constantly, while saying "encore" loudly. I wonder if he understands the songs. Perhaps he just enjoys the tunes. Unwilling to be outshone, he sings four Japanese songs at one go: these are new and refreshing to me. His voice is just so so, no better than those outside the room; however, he is really dedicated to it. He shouts excitedly, his arm around my shoulder. I don't mind when he takes advantage of me at such a moment.

He proposes a toast and gulps down the whole glass of wine. Even I finish my glass of wine. He pours another half glass for me and I do not refuse it. I feel hot all over and parched with thirst, probably due to the drastic working of the wine in my body. He at once orders a glass of iced orange juice, which I gulp down at one go. He continues to drink wine to his heart's content, looking 10 years younger.

After awhile, he asks me while holding my waist, "Can you sing Deng, Lijun's songs? Many Japanese like her voice."

I grow more excited hearing this name, "Of course, I know many of her songs inside out."

After finding Deng, Lijun's MTV's, I snatch the mike at once. First, I sing "Loving as before", then "If I am without you". When I start singing "Wish for longevity", surprisingly, Aokawa Kakuai sings with me in Chinese:

"When will the moon be bright?

Let me hold a glass and ask Heaven.

I wonder in which year is tonight,

In the imperial palace up in the sky…"

His pronunciation is accurate and he is fully dedicated to the singing. While singing, I feel his big hand roving up and down my back. I haven't stopped him, thinking that he does it subconsciously and will stop when the singing stops.

As expected, once the words "Let's wish for longevity and share the moonlight a thousand miles away" stop, his hand leaves my back. Luckily, I didn't avoid it. It seems as if I proffered a love, which was not reciprocated.

"I am surprised that you sing Chinese songs so well," I am a bit doubtful.

"This is a great poem by Su, Shi, a great poet in the Song Dynasty. It took me several months to learn this song." He feels elated, like a pupil being commended by his teacher.

At his request, I sing five or six songs at a stretch, such as "Affectionate roses", "the Lover", and "Revealing love at moonlit night". I indulge in Deng, Lijun's world wholeheartedly, feeling as if I have returned to my junior high school years when her songs were all the rage in mainland China. Thanks to the Japanese Colonel Inoue who invented karaoke, those who never sing have held microphones. This is a boon for a singing fan like me.

After Aokawa Kakuai proposes the last toast, I feel dizzy and have hallucinations. I must have gotten drunk. Then, I feel that the sky and earth are spinning round. A strong man supports me out of the gate, into a car and up an elevator...

64. Drug-raped by Japanese Boss

At noon the next day, warm sunlight shines on my face through the glass windows. Opening my sleepy eyes, I find myself lying in bed, stark naked, with a light blanket covering my lower body.

Only then do I fully realize that a grave disaster befell me at midnight. Alas! My God! That beastly Aokawa Kakuai has taken advantage of my drunkenness to rape me. Isn't that a breach of law? I will sue him and bring shame and ruin on him...I should also blame myself for losing control and getting drunk in public. My tears of remorse wet the pillow.

I get up to take a shower, soaping my body again and again. I turn on the tap to the maximum and let the rushing water cleanse my body of the filth he left in me. How I wish I could open up my body and bleach every inch of it! However, no matter how strong the water and how much bleach I use, I cannot cleanse my mind of misery and remorse.

Why do I always meet the bad guys? In Shanghai, I was robbed of my virginity by a "bumpkin". Now in Tokyo, I am raped by my Japanese boss within three months of my arrival! Is all this predestined? An outwardly proud princess suffers a tragic fate! I suspect again that I was born under a bad star.

In a daze, I walk to the living room and discover a note, apparently left by him:

"Miss Komaki Zhang, you have a beautiful voice and an even more beautiful body. This is your greatest wealth. If you call the police, there will be disastrous consequences, which would not do anybody any good. I like you from the bottom of my heart. We can negotiate.

Aokawa Kakuai

June 10th"

When I look out of the window, I see crowded vehicles and throngs of pedestrians, which add to my depression. When I look up at the sky, the sun is shining brightly with floating white clouds. Such natural beauty conflicts with my mood. In Tokyo, which boasts of sunshine, blue sky and white clouds, so many evil black hands are wreaking havoc and so many women's dreams have been shattered.

Damn it! It is Karaoke that has caused all the trouble! This is the very first time that I hate Karaoke. After contemplation, I find it is true. Several years ago, only Japanese electrical devices had the Karaoke function, so the Chinese started to purchase Japanese electrical machines like crazy. The naïve Chinese willingly accepted the Japanese economic invasion. They queued up to buy Karaoke machines and sang at home, often involving the whole family. After many years had elapsed, few Chinese can sing well. On the other hand, many other better ways of culture and entertainment have gradually withered away, eclipsed by disgusting Karaoke, cultural junk manifesting Japanese arrogance, craziness and self-glorification. But the Chinese indulge in this cultural junk inadvertently. It is no exaggeration that Karaoke obstructs cultural creativity in China. How many kindhearted girls like me have sunk into this? For the rest of my life, I'll never go to Karaoke again …

Lying languidly on the couch, I read the note of Aokawa Kakuai, the wolf, again and again until I can recite it from memory. Later, I get up reluctantly to make a pot of strong coffee. After drinking two cups, I become more cool-headed.

Isn't Aokawa Kakuai's note giving me pointers? It is not easy to get a monthly pay of 250,000 Japanese Yen plus a free luxury apartment in the Ginza. Since he is willing to negotiate, I can fleece him like hell.

As the old saying goes: Men will die for wealth, as birds for food. Anyway, I got pregnant by a man in Shanghai and had an abortion. Of what the hell use is virginity!

To a modern woman, what is the worth of virginity? Hasn't Huang, Hong, my good friend in high school, become the "concubine" of a Hong Kong businessman? Song, Lei, my classmate in Medical school, warned me that women had to fully appreciate their own value and make the most of it. To a beautiful woman like me, my body and youth are my capital. In an instant, I have come to a full realization of this fact.

At 6pm, I pluck up my courage to go to work at the "Zen Japanese Restaurant" as usual, acting as if nothing has happened. The manager takes good care of me as usual. Business is going very well and a sense of joy prevails there. At closing time, I still don't see Aokawa Kakuai. I don't ask the manager if he will come.

However, I am not scared. He will emerge some day; moreover, I have his note in my hand. I want to see how sly this old fox is and how he is going to negotiate with me.

Chapter Fourteen

"There is no Room for a Gentle Girl in such a Large City as Tokyo"

65. The Price of a Million Japanese Yen

The sun still rises in the east and falls in the west while the moon still waxes and wanes. For many days and nights, I feel I am in a daze, always contemplating how to deal with Aokawa Kakuai, the old fox. The days drag on like years. Eventually, he appears in the restaurant late at night on the weekend. He takes the initiative to talk to me and invites me to the "Picasso Café" at the corner of the street after my shift.

Like its name, the café is decorated basically with Picasso's abstract paintings. He is my favorite Spanish artist.

Posing as a lover of art, I bought several painting albums of European and American artists when I studied at the Medical School. When I open the door of the café, I find the well-known "Three dancers" by Picasso. The three dancers' eyes, breasts and limbs are dislocated and mismatched: eyes are on breasts, front faces and profiles are combined, and two hands stretch out from the breasts, which are amazingly huge.

Seeing me looking around, Aokawa Kakuai waves to me from his seat. I greet him courteously as usual and notice that his facial muscles are quite tense. In an attempt to cover up my own nervousness, I try to comment on Picasso's masterpiece "Peace" on the wall, posing as a connoisseur. "Picasso shows the love of a family in a symbolic way. Look, the child is running after a flying horse, while several naked jugglers are in harmony with nature. All this epitomizes peace."

"I didn't expect that you would know so much about famous paintings. I just enjoy the milieu here, with its touch of European appeal." He takes the opportunity to flatter me.

I continue my comment, "Look at the upper part of the painting: the man carrying a pole with a sparrow in a fish jar on one end and a cage with fish on the other. Everything seems upside down: this indicates that it is no easy job to maintain happiness. People are like acrobats who constantly risk catastrophe."

He shrugs his shoulders and says, "There is some implied meaning in your words. I am a businessman and prefer to talk straight. What do you plan to do? To tell you frankly, I have seen a lot of women, but you are the first Chinese woman that I like. You are not only pretty, but also intelligent. I prefer to deal with people with both high IQs and EQs."

I respond furiously, "You could have told me openly. Why did you take advantage of me while I was drunk? That was rape and sexual violence! Don't you know that?"

"To tell you the truth, I was drunk with the wine and with your songs. Holding your fragrant warm body, I couldn't stop myself from taking you upstairs … When I awoke, it was 3am and the die was cast. I deeply regret what happened. Miss Komaki, tell me how much you want for psychological compensation."

I stretch out a finger and say, "One million, a bargain for you."

"No problem, I'll transfer the amount to your account at the Tokyo Bank."

I didn't expect that he would agree so readily. I regret that I didn't demand two million.

In introspect, several years later, I realize that the million Japanese Yen landed me in a blind alley in a situation that I couldn't get myself out of. If I insist on looking for an excuse, it was Aokawa Kakuai who changed my whole value of life overnight. This incident let me know that women, especially pretty women, can make use of their bodies to earn huge amounts of money.

I have to admit that human beings are the products of their environment. Women, particularly women from Shanghai, possess a strong capacity to adapt to the environment. At present, I identify with the values of Huang, Hong, a classmate in high school, who uses her body in exchange for Hong Kong dollars. I *also understand the dissipation of Song, Lei, my intimate friend in medical school, who makes money by going to bed with men. I am of the same type as they are. Why have I realized it so late? Maybe it is the strict discipline of my family, or the affluence of my parents, or my romantic and humanistic sentiments, which lack financial pragmatism. In retrospect, I allowed Chen, Zhiwei to take advantage of me out of love while I paid the expenses. It was just because of my simple-mindedness and naivety. The ragged verse goes: "The maiden knows not the value of money, and insists on marrying a pauper." Eventually nothing comes of it and only bitter fruits await her. If I had realized it sooner, I would not have been taken in. Like Aokawa Kakuai, men should at least pay money for dallying with girls. Women's looks and youth are their prime capital, aren't they?*

66. Japanese Boss's Concubine

Three months later, Miyazawa Kiichi moves to Osaka for his own business, so I am promoted to manager of the "Zen Japanese Restaurant", and my monthly salary is increased to 500,000 Japanese Yen with two free meals a day. I have also moved to the sixth floor of the same building with a living room double the size of the old one and the rent increased to 140,000 Yen, paid for by the company. Aokawa Kakuai pays for all the luxurious European furniture, such as Italian curtains with gold threads. Why should I save money for him by purchasing cheap stuff? Besides, I also work as a part-time model for "Dragon Advertisements", owned by Aokawa Kakuai and managed by his wife Kimiko. With the pay for modeling jobs done, I earn an extra 200,000 Yen every month.

The only delight for me is that my aural and oral Japanese has reached the level of fluency because I deal with Japanese people all day long. I don't have to go to the language school, but I still pay the monthly tuition of 40,000 Yen to maintain my legal residential status. As a result, I have a net monthly saving of 700,000 Yen in the bank. This is equal to my old salary for more than four years in Shanghai. It is exceptional for a person who came to Japan just half a year ago. It is impossible to earn so much money unless you carry dead bodies or take several hard jobs.

There is no free banquet in the world. Since then, I have become Aokawa Kakuai's mistress, or "concubine", "engaging in the trade" nakedly. The popular saying is: living off others, one has to obey them. I can't resist the temptation of his money or rid myself of his pestering. After the first time, I don't mind the second time. I finally acquiesce after he gets the upper hand of me several times. It won't be too late if I obtain 20 million Yen after a couple of years with him and run away to start a new life. I started with nothing except my capital of youth and good looks. Don't people say: "laugh at poverty not prostitution"? Besides, I serve only one man, in a luxury apartment, like Camille in Dumas' novel. I am not in an erotic salon or street-walking in the red-light district. Human beings should not be penniless. With money, they can accomplish tasks.

I invite Li, Mei, the girl from Hangzhou, to fill a vacancy as a waitress, with a monthly pay of 200,000 Yen. She is moved to tears and praises my competency again and again. She does not know the steep price I have paid, an unspeakable and seedy shame.

Aokawa Kakuai comes to my apartment once every week, mostly at midnight on Thursdays after my shift. He leaves after two or three hours' dallying with me in bed. I guess he may have another mistress, as he is such a wealthy man. Wives turn a blind eye to their husbands' promiscuity, pretending to be happy but feeling bitter in their hearts. No wonder people say that Japanese women hate men to the bone, but they dare not utter their hatred even at the end of their lives.

He looks rough, dark and fat, but he is not really despotic and he is rather gentle with me. After talking to him for a long time, I learn that his clan is not only wealthy, but also scholastic. He graduated from the Business Administration Department of Osaka University. No wonder he is good-tempered. After dealing with him for a long time, I don't feel he is ugly. He is maturely handsome in his middle age. Every time he comes happy and leaves satisfied. The two of us have a sort of tacit coordination. I gradually learn that his wife Kimiko, with an MA degree from Princeton University in the United States, mainly helps him managing the Ad Agency and the Magazine Press. Perhaps because of the influence of their mother, both of their sons study in renowned universities in the US.

Aokawa Kakuai is really adept at doing business, so customers to his restaurant grow in numbers. I learn a lot about management from him. Like many men in Japan, he exerts himself in his work. He tries his utmost to improve the quality of food and service by working each day in one of his five chain stores. Once, a *customer complained about the attitude of a waiter. He reprimanded the waiter to his face in a loud voice. Even when he does not go to the restaurant, he phones every day to inquire about business. He gives instructions to solve trifling problems over the phone and rushes to the scene in an emergency or for big events.*

Several months after my initial contact with Aokawa Kakuai, my savings in the bank rise rapidly. Not that he gives me extra tips besides my monthly salary of 500,000 Yen, but my income from "Dragon Advertisements" has risen unexpectedly fast, exceeding 300,000 Yen every month. It is his intention for me to work part-time in the Ad Agency. It is more interesting than working in the restaurant, mainly because I can indulge my desire for performing, thanks to the accumulated stage experience from my childhood. I work over weekends or on holidays on the ads: one for TV, one for the magazine every month on average, mainly regarding vegetarian food, weight loss or fashion, with no nudity. The most exposed for me is an advertisement on a beach in a bathing suit. I meet over ten workers at the Advertising Agency, and become especially friendly with photographer Ding, Xu, a student from Beijing who studies at a photography school and works at "Dragon Advertisements" part time.

Probably because of the cultural differences between China and Japan, the physiological mystery between Aokawa Kakuai and me eventually disappears and our relationship becomes dull and boring. I am most upset about his coming for only a few hours on Thursday nights, as accurate as a flight schedule. He never has time for me when I feel most lonely at night during the weekends. He either enjoys his nights with his wife or with some other woman. Thinking of this, a nondescript jealousy rises in my heart. Maybe women from Shanghai are the most jealous.

I am really a weird woman. I know full well that my relationship with Aokawa Kakuai is just for the purpose of accumulating funds. Still, along with the time with him, I yearn for more -- more feeling, more care and money, at least in my subconscious. The philosophers put it well: Women's flesh and mind are intermingled. Their carnal desires are controlled by feelings while their minds have a strong touch of carnal desire.

67. Encounter with a Student from Beijing

Probably photographer Ding, Xu, who is adept at catching the expression in one's eyes, has long discerned the perplexity in my mind. It is impossible to deny or escape. No wonder, the eye is the window of one's soul.

One Sunday afternoon, Ding, Xu takes me sightseeing to Harajuku by the Yamanote Line. It is said that Harajuku used to be the residential area of the American troops stationed in Tokyo. After their withdrawal, a lot of stores selling novel goods opened one after another, attracting young men and women who enjoy themselves in the park on Sundays. It has become one of the special places in Tokyo, a Mecca for youngsters to give vent to their enthusiasm and to catch up on the trends.

Droves of tourists pour into Harajuku, one group after another. I have to hold Ding, Xu's hand to squeeze out of the narrow station. I didn't expect that "Takeshita Lane" to the left of the station would be even more crowded.

Seeing my knitted brows, Ding, Xu explains at once, "This might be the most crowded lane in the world. Do you dare squeeze into it? The trip to Harajuku will be in vain if you don't visit 'Takeshita Lane'."

"Why not? The Nanjing Road in Shanghai is also jam-packed with people, jostling each other."

Ding, Xu nods with a smile. Holding his hand tightly, I enter "Takeshita Lane" for a "squeezing baptism". In such a jam-packed place, I can hardly enjoy the many little stores on either side of the lane. We exert our utmost to squeeze out of the lane, with the tip of his nose sweating and my underwear soaked with perspiration.

"I enjoyed myself to the utmost," both of us cry out almost simultaneously at the exit of the lane.

"More interesting things are to follow." Like a big brother, Ding, Xu holds my hand as we go ahead.

The "Yoyogi Park" to the south of the station is a brilliantly colorful world. Standing on the crossover in the park, we find young men and women, with shoulder-length hair and painted faces, singing and dancing wildly. They are accompanied by electric guitars' piercing heavy metal music, and are cheered and applauded by the surrounding crowds of onlookers. There is a world of difference between these young people and the Japanese youths in suits, ties, shiny shoes and immaculate hair we usually see in Tokyo streets.

Actually they are typical PUNKs, the representatives of the new young cultural generation in Japan, with a primitive and blind energy radiating from them freely. They try to give vent to their feelings compressed for a week, so they don't mind alternate forms or orientations, and don't direct animosity against anyone.

"They just live for themselves," Ding, Xu says to himself while taking photos of me nonstop.

He tells me that this used to be the first airport in Japan. It became the Olympic Village in 1964 when Japan sponsored the Olympics in Tokyo. Nobody expected that it would become the world-renowned place for street shows. He says he likes the youthful atmosphere bubbling with enthusiasm, so he loves to seek inspiration here.

It is not easy to squeeze into a wall of people to watch seven or eight handsome young men, hand in hand, singing at the top of their voices. Then, they put on a cool pose, causing a lot of shrieks. Some of them wear tight jackets, some are in long robes; others are covered with shining cloth strips. Their hair and faces are of various colors and they twist their bodies nonstop, as if they would lose their balance if they stop.

During the half-day trip, Ding, Xu uses three rolls of films for my pictures. For me, this is the most enjoyable day I've had in the nine months of my stay in Japan. After eating a Japanese hot pot when we return to the Ginza, we walk and talk happily in the cold streets of December, feeling warm in our hearts. On impulse, we enter a "Hotel for Lovers" with lights twinkling on the roadside.

Under the dim lights, the wild music in Harajuku is still burning in our ears. Who can dampen the fire of youth? Two bodies start a long dialogue, honestly and without restraint. The radiance of Venus shines over two lonely hearts. At this moment, language seems so flat and lifeless. Everything is manifest in the eyes.

After wild lovemaking, Ding, Xu becomes more poetic and recites two love poems by Pushkin. I wonder why he suddenly likes poetry.

He replies, smiling, "I had some poems published in Beijing. I am regarded as half a poet."

So saying, he takes a huge notebook from his backpack. "Look, here are some paper clippings with several obscure poems I wrote years ago."

I read the notebook page by page and find some poems with the name of "Ding, Xu" printed. During my high school years, I also had several poems published, so we instantly share a common language.

While talking and laughing, I discover in the notebook a well-known poem, "To the oak," written by Shu, Ting. Elated, I jump up from the bed, "That's wonderful! I was searching high and low for this poem a few days ago."

Ding, Xu says, "She is my favorite contemporary female poet in China. I always carry this poem with me, attempting to express its meaning and mood with photos. I have conceived several pictures, but I am satisfied with none... Some day I will take a series of pictures to mail to Shu, Ting."

"I love her poems, and Bei, Dao's as well."

"You can take the clipping if you like," Ding, Xu says with a smile.

"I am not supposed to snatch away your favorite. It's simple. I'll make a photocopy and return it to you."

Holding my waist, he suggests in high spirits, "My Shanghai beauty, why not recite the poem to me since you are talented at performing? I haven't heard a sweet voice for a long time."

"No problem. But I haven't done it for such a long time. Don't laugh at me if I make a mistake," I issue the warning first.

Recitation is actually my forte. I get up at once and put on my robe. I read the poem in silence first, then clear my throat and take the role seriously.

"If I love you –
I'll never show off myself
By climbing up your high branches
Like a Chinese trumpet creeper;
If I love you –
I'll never repeat monotonous songs
For the green shade,
Like an infatuated bird;
I'll not send you cool solace only,
Like a spring for a long period;
I'll not increase your height or dignity only,
Like a perilous peak to serve as a foil;

Not even sunlight or spring shower,

No, all those are not sufficient!

I must be a kapok closely beside you,

Standing next to you like a tree.

The roots are deep down in the soil,

The leaves are entwined in the clouds…"

Without my noticing it, Ding, Xu has got up by my side and has started reciting this declaration of love, which reverberates in the night sky of the Ginza.

"…You have your copper boughs and iron stems,

Like knives, swords and halberds,

I have my crimson and full-grown flowers,

Like heavy sighs, and courageous torches.

We share cold waves, lightning and thunder-storms;

We both enjoy mists, flowing haze and rainbows.

We seem to be separated from each other,

But we intertwine with each other forever.

That's great love.

Loyalty lies here:

Love –

Not only your strappy body,

But also the position you persist in,

And the earth under your feet."

68. Willingly Paying instead of Getting Paid

Ding, Xu, ten years my senior, tall, robust and very handsome, is a kind of Prince Charming for girls from Southern China. His demeanor reveals him as a natural and unaffected artist. He has been awarded great prizes both at home and abroad for his photographs, which depict the beautiful scenery of nature. He has told me candidly that his wife is waiting for him in Beijing. The two haven't seen each other for three years, so their future is unpredictable. Although I don't like to compare him to that heartless Chen, Zhiwei, I can't control my subconscious. He is superior to Chen in appearance and disposition. Unfortunately, I lost my naivety long ago: I do not consider the future, but think only about present enjoyment.

Our emotions for each other have become uncontrollable since our first transporting night. I feel exceptionally safe and enriched while lying against his broad and bushy chest, because he resembles a big, tall tree. He often says, "I contemplate life looking at your breasts and I get inspiration by means of your buttocks." Although it sounds a bit vulgar, I like his honesty. Every weekend now, I have places to visit. I wait anxiously for Saturday after each Wednesday. I look forward to meeting him again soon after each parting. He often takes me to Nikko, Izu, and Hakone, carrying a Nikon camera over his shoulder. He presses the shutter constantly while telling me local stories about tourist attractions. He seems to be an "expert on Japan".

What impresses me most is the "Gion Garden" on the east bank of the Kamogawa River. It's said that this was the most famous "Flower Street" back in the 17th century. There were over 700 teahouses and around 3,000 qualified geishas during its peak period. At present, it is still a well-known romantic tourist area, visited by many travelers to Tokyo.

That evening when the garden is bathed in the sunset, I walk leisurely down the "Flowery Trail" in Ding, Xu's arms with many other tourists carrying cameras and backpacks, waiting eagerly for the geishas. Twenty minutes later, I rush to a teahouse with others, only to find three geishas in kimonos coming out with small steps. Even with the scrutiny of so many people and the constant flashes of the cameras, they look poised and at ease while walking to the taxi. Suddenly, I recall the famous poem by Xu, Zhimo in praise of a Japanese girl: "Her gentle and graceful head lowered, looking like a shy lotus flower, unable to cope with the cool breeze…"

"These are geishas on call, to perform in places designated by their patrons. It's said that it costs them over a hundred thousand Japanese Yen." Ding, Xu explains in a low voice.

"They are at least capable of singing and dancing. Not an easy job."

"They say they don't sell their bodies. Who knows? I don't think there is much difference between a "geisha" and a "prostitute". It's easy for women to earn money," he blurts out, disapprovingly.

Hearing his words, I feel my heart throbbing with a guilty conscience. He would perhaps break up with me if he ever found out about my affair with

Aokawa Kakuai. To his mind, a woman like me is worthless. To cover up my uneasiness and fear, I drag him to a riverside traditional eatery without responding to his comment.

With the night falling and the sound of the flowing river, we drink Japanese clear wine, eat raw fish and tempura, enjoying to our hearts' content a night in pure Japanese style. Several years later, I still reminisce about this beautiful night at the riverside and the sincere dialogue with Ding, Xu. Unlike an ordinary student, he aims high and plans to create a series of works entitled "War and Peace", centering on the atomic bomb explosion in Hiroshima. He also cherishes a desire for global travel and dreams of carving his name in the history of world photography.

Since Ding, Xu is a student with a part-time job and does not earn a lot of money, I take the initiative to pay for all the expenses. To make it sound better, it's for the heart, not for money. Otherwise, it's "paying by the female in the love affair", which sounds nasty. I don't mind, however, as long as I am happy. It's not easy to find a bosom friend, especially in a place far from my hometown. More than once, he tells me that he will reimburse me when he has more money. He says that I am not like other women from China, who are stingy with money.

During this period of time, Ding, Xu has created many inspired, excellent works, which surprise many of his colleagues at "Dragon Advertisements". He happens to have graduated from the photographic school, so the company decides to hire him as a regular staff member. He is awarded champion in the Berlin Photography Championship (Youth category) for his photo "Contemplation in Silence" with my half-naked body as model. I have never felt so gratified to be able to use my body to inspire men's creativity. Men use brushes to create art while women use their beautiful bodies to express art.

In comparison to my meetings with Ding, Xu, my few hours' clandestine rendezvous with Aokawa Kakuai every Thursday night seems to take "an age" for me. As usual, I listen to his business stories for over an hour, which occasionally makes me fall asleep. Then, I lie in repose with my eyes shut while he takes a shower. After that, he climbs onto my body eagerly, riding me like a wild bull, biting and gnawing. I experience no feeling at all and just let him give vent to his desire. Sometimes, Ding, Xu's image emerges in my mind. As a shrewd businessman, Aokawa Kakuai might feel dull and bored.

Once, he says to me with dismay while lying on top of me, "Why are you like a piece of wood, without your former vigor and vitality?"

I hurry to find an excuse, keeping in mind all the money I get from him. "I am tired after working from morning till night."

"I've told you not to start working so early. 8 am is ok..."

When I writhe like an eel, he rides me like crazy.

After lying down and holding me for a while, he gets dressed and takes his leave. Seeing him, with his fat body, leaving gratified, I really want to end this seedy relationship. He regards me as a Chinese dish: tired of eating Japanese raw fish seven days a week, he tries to taste something different with me. He has also found a woman to manage his restaurant in a determined way. He has no concern for me, let alone real feelings. Women, on the other hand, need men not only physiologically, but also psychologically.

Unfortunately, I have to submit to reality and maintain this relationship in order to accumulate my goal of 20 million Yen. Thanks to Ding, Xu, the vacancy in my emotional life is filled. I tell him everything like a bosom friend, except for the part about my relationship with Aokawa Kakuai, possibly because I dream of marrying Ding some day. I anxiously await the realization of my financial goals so that I can leave here and start afresh. With a lot of money, would I worry about finding a good man? Even virgin boys will line up.

69. A Vulgar and Barbaric Japanese Man

Things are not running as smoothly and perfectly as I thought. Just as paper can't wrap up fire, truth will come out eventually.

Rumors of my secret affair with Ding, Xu soon spread like wild fire through "Dragon Advertisements". When asked by others, Ding neither admits nor denies. When they ask me, however, I just shake my head. I am afraid of trouble if Aokawa Kakuai learns about it.

On the first anniversary of my arrival in Tokyo, that is, at 10am on March 8th 1993, I hear the doorbell ring after I have finished calling my family in Shanghai. I am scared to find Aokawa Kakuai, who never comes this early without phoning me first. I assume that there may have been a break-in at the restaurant.

After entering the room, he talks to me angrily, "Do you remember this day last year when Mr. Chen brought you to see me? I accepted you, a miserable girl with no understanding of Japanese. Now, you are proud of your position as the manager of a big restaurant, a famous model and a capable woman. Without my help, you would be a stripper ...”

My sixth sense informs me that he has heard of my affair with Ding, Xu. I have to be diplomatic and calm him down, so I hold his hands and ask him to sit down to talk.

He is still excited while sitting on the couch, “So, you want to be Camille? I am not that stupid Count! You get my money, so you are my property. I won’t allow you to fool around with any other men, not even one man! Break it off with Ding immediately! Otherwise I’ll cut off all your income. How can you treat me like this when I provide you with so much?”

At this moment, I must not add oil to the fire of his fury and I try my utmost to calm him down. Men need to be coaxed by women, especially when they are in a rage.

“So that’s it. Don’t get angry. I won’t do the ads any more. Don’t pay attention to the rumors. Mr. Ding and I are both from mainland China. We are just friends. Like a toad, that guy lusts after a swan’s flesh.” I constantly strokes his back with my hand while talking.

“I don’t think it’s so simple. That man is tall and mighty. He has fed you full, right? You are like a dead chick when you are with me. I realized it a while ago. I have dallied with more women than all the men you have ever met. Don’t play tricks on me... As long as you take my money, you are mine to savor. If you don’t like being with me, just tell me. I won’t pester you. Starting tonight, you don’t have to go to work. It’s easy to find a Chinese woman to dally with. I’ve fooled around with women from all kinds of countries...”

“Okay, I promise never to have any contact with him. I’m totally yours.” I lie against his chest while talking coquettishly.

All of a sudden, he kisses me wildly while holding me and tears off my nightgown and bites my breasts. Then, he leads me to the bedroom.

“Not today. I have my period. What about tomorrow?” I beg him while struggling in his arms.

As if he doesn’t hear me, he throws me onto the bed with force and quickly undresses. Using his big hands, he pulls me to the middle of the bed, tears off my underwear and throws himself on my body like a wild wolf.

I feel a sudden, gut wrenching pain in my lower body. Gritting my teeth and with my eyes shut, I just let him ride me wildly.

His hysterical yelling resounds in my ears, "You are mine, you are mine..."

After his beastly behavior, he rushes into the bathroom. My heart shivers violently as I listen to the flow of water.

Bloodstains are all over the sheets. I get a comforter to cover myself, feeling as if my lower body has been amputated. Tears roll down my cheeks nonstop. Today, I have seen clearly the true colors of Aokawa Kakuai. He is despotic and cruel. I dare say that Japanese men are the most vulgar and barbaric in the world. I will never marry a Japanese man, even if I am threatened with death or tempted with a gold hill and a silver house.

After he comes out of the bathroom, he says while dressing, "If you obey me, I'll show you a good life. I can even give you a restaurant as a gift. Well, you take a rest and I'll go to my board meeting."

70. Recalling First Menses and Thinking of Loved Ones

With a loud bang, Aokawa Kakuai shuts the door. Lying in bed, I cry my eyes out. Flowing tears cannot wash away the pain in my heart.

I never expected to be in such misery on the first anniversary of my arrival in Tokyo. My financial lifeline is totally under his control. I am accustomed to managing people and taking charge of accounting for six hours in the evening at the restaurant. I model for ads over the weekend. I live in a high-class building, with luxury furniture and wear dresses by famous designers. I lack the courage and confidence to start from scratch if I leave him. I have no other choice but to part from Ding, Xu. Only in this way can I maintain the status quo. I plan to have a good talk with Ding and to negotiate an amicable separation.

My lower body is still numb. Vulgar and barbarous Aokawa Kakuai, why didn't you leave me alone during my period? I can't help but think of my first period at the age of 13.

That afternoon after school, I was dog-tired with heavy eyelids. Putting down my satchel, I lay down on the bed at once. I felt languid all over and very sleepy,

276

but I couldn't fall asleep. Every cell of my body was filled with annoyance, as if doomsday was approaching. Later, my bladder started to swell and my breasts became extremely itchy. I felt a warm torrent flowing through my body. This failed to find an outlet. It kept burning in my body, making me feel suffocated mentally. Then, my swollen bladder suddenly throbbed violently, impacting all my internal organs, and I started to shiver. All the blood in my body seemed to be boiling like an erupting volcano. Along with my scream, stinking hot blood rushed out of my lower body, soaking my underpants.

Hearing the noise, my Grandma hurried to my room and had a look under the comforter. Seeing the sheet, she said with a helpless smile, "Yuanyuan, don't be afraid. You've grown up." She took a paper package from the wardrobe and handed it to me, "Your Mom has been ready for a year. Follow me to the washroom."

I still felt dizzy after I returned to my room, staring at the bloodstain on the sheet in a daze. It resembled a tiny blooming rose on the sky-blue sheet. This irresistible fiery red symbolized that I had entered puberty and had the ability to reproduce. For nutritional purposes, my grandma quickly made a bowl of boiled eggs and forced me to eat it.

Now, I miss my family members more than at any other time, especially my aged Grandma. Daddy, why didn't I listen to your advice? If you knew what Aokawa Kakuai has done to me, you would hate the Japanese even more. Mommy, my dear Mommy, rescue your daughter who lives in hell. Grandma, the apple of your eye is almost stifled to death…

A week later, unexpectedly, Ding, Xu calls me to bid farewell to me.

After the call is connected, he says nothing. I guess it must be him. I ask him eagerly, "Talk quickly! Why have you become mute?"

Half a minute later, he finally starts to talk, "I'm fired. I'm leaving tomorrow morning."

"Where are you going?"

"An advertising agency in Osaka," he says in a low voice.

It turns out that he was dismissed from "Dragon Advertisements" on the afternoon that Aokawa Kakuai visited me. Probably Ding will never find out the real reason for his dismissal. Luckily, he got another job in advertising quickly in Osaka. I know this is Aokawa Kakuai's evil doing. I can't let Ding know the truth, *however. If he knew, he would bear a grudge against me for his whole life.*

"I'll treat you to dinner tonight," I make the invitation.

"I'm sorry, but I have a lot to attend to. I haven't notified many of my good friends yet." He graciously declines.

"I still have the original of the poem 'To the oak', so I'll return it to you later."

He says, generously, "Not necessary. You can keep it."

I wonder, "Aren't you contemplating taking a series of photos?"

"I have learned it by heart." He bursts out laughing.

Before hanging up, he adds, "Take care of yourself, please. When I have money in the future, I'll come back to Tokyo for you."

I know he is being evasive on purpose so I will not burst into tears. He is cool outwardly but fiery inside. He is capable of withstanding great mental pressure. He always expects me to smile instead of crying.

Ding, Xu is gone, taking with him my love and hopes of the last three months. I have a nondescript sense of guilt. Without me, he would not have been forced to leave Tokyo and his new job. The fond memory of reciting "To the oak" together has turned into a good wish and will be kept in my mind forever.

Since that event, Aokawa Kakuai is a bit harsh with me, watching me carefully. He regards me as an out and out "despicable woman", as if I would commit adultery if he weren't watching. The only difference is that he sometimes takes me to Nikko and Izu for a visit over the weekend.

Every time he has sex with me, I put on the air of enjoying it and pretend to groan or scream to accommodate him. In reality, I have lost any feelings I had for him and my heart is withering. Sometimes, I fantasize about Ding Xu's strong body and derive pleasure from the fantasy.

71. Ulterior Motives in Celebrating my Birthday

I never dreamed that Aokawa Kakuai would invite me to his home on my 22nd birthday.

His home is situated in Akihabara in Tokyo. He lives in a house with a garden surrounded by cherry blossoms. From far away, the cherries in full bloom look like flying snow or flowing falls.

Approaching the house, I see a magnificent yard composed basically of white rocks and green trees. The surging waves of the lotus pond, the twisting bridges, stones and small rocks of various colors resemble beaches, rivers or creeks. The superb craftsmanship exceeds nature and creates tranquility.

Guided by Aokawa Kakuai, I enter a house with black tiles and white walls. Taking off my shoes, I turn right into a huge living room, with a big color TV on the floor. The white couches, white windows and white coat rack look spic and span. I look around, feeling puzzled: why are there no other people? He grasps my hand and sits with me in the couch.

"It's just you and I tonight. You are the mistress. You can go wild here. My wife left for the States to visit our son a few days ago and will return next week. I gave the servants a couple of days off," he explains with a smile.

"No wonder you are so audacious." I point at his nose with my finger.

He takes the chance to hug and kiss me nonstop.

"Well, it's your birthday today. Let me present you with a gift first. I chose it especially for you. I wonder if you'll like it." He pulls a small box from his briefcase, takes out a necklace and fastens it around my neck.

Such a heavy necklace must have cost a lot. I bow to him, "Thanks a lot, Mr. Aokawa Kakuai. It must have cost you a lot."

"It's nothing. I'll give you anything if you obey me. You know why I brought you to this house? To let you see it. If you behave yourself, I can give you this house. I have ten houses like this. At present, real estate is not doing well. I am waiting for business opportunities. Real estate is what I'll engage in. I have managed restaurants for so long that I want to invest in something else." He is talking business again.

"Just like dallying with women. You like to change once in a while?" I sneer at him on purpose.

He grasps my hand and says with a cheeky grin, "Certainly."

"What? Say it loudly. I didn't hear it." I show gritted teeth.

Holding me in his arms and putting me on his knee, he says lewdly while groping my breasts with one hand under my clothes, "I can't tear myself away from these. They are even bigger than a French woman's."

"Don't touch them! Make it clear: do you want to change women and when?" I put on an angry face.

He raises both hands immediately, like a surrendering Japanese soldier, "No, no, I don't dare to."

I burst out laughing and he foolishly follows suit.

I say to myself after thinking, "I would be scared to death living in such a huge house."

"There is nothing to be afraid of. I'll be with you." He holds my waist tightly.

It seems that he cherishes the fond dream of possessing me for a long time. I think to myself: I am not willing to be your concubine for my whole life. I'll say "Goodbye" to you when I have earned enough money.

He proudly adds, "This is not a very big house. You've never been to my parents' house, which is like a ranch. My father is a banker and my uncle is a real estate tycoon. They inherited a lot of wealth. Well, I'll talk about it later. Where would you like to have dinner tonight? I'll have to make a reservation."

"I'd like Chinese food. 'New Shanghai' in the Ginza is pretty good."

"You make the decisions today. Then we'll go to 'Yachiyo Karaoke' after dinner to listen to you sing Deng, Lijun's songs. Okay? Well, I almost forgot to tell you, your pay is going to be increased to 600,000 Yen starting next month. The restaurant is doing well thanks to your efficient management."

A raise in pay is the most practical reward for me. This means I am closer to my savings target of 20 million Yen. If people have perseverance, their dreams will eventually come true. Like me, many women from Shanghai see light after enduring several years' difficulties. They bring home a huge sum of money to honor their ancestors and become self-styled "wealthy ladies" or start new businesses in their hometown.

It is 2 am in the morning when we return to his house after dinner and karaoke. We go wild on the tatami until daybreak when we fall soundly asleep. Anyway, I have somebody to celebrate my birthday with, and he is a rich and dignified man at that. The most miserable time for a woman to be alone is on her birthday. It is simply a shame for a young and pretty woman to be alone on that day.

Since Aokawa Kakuai arranged a unique birthday celebration for me, my relationship with him has returned to what it was before. Over the weekend, he takes me sightseeing and he stays with me at my place once every three or four days. He shows more concern for me and instills some knowledge of real estate in me. It seems that he plans to invest in real estate in Shanghai and needs my help. I just listen to him without fully understanding the business.

I have my own plans, however, and I won't allow anybody to manipulate my future. Aokawa Kakuai, you had better stop daydreaming!

72. Affair Exposed and Forced Departure from Tokyo

Perhaps extreme joy begets sorrow. I am scared out of my wits when Kimiko, Aokawa Kakuai's wife, suddenly charges into my apartment one afternoon at the end of November.

Before I open my mouth, she speaks bluntly, "Miss Komaki, sorry to have bothered you. I know all about your affair with my husband, Aokawa Kakuai. As the old Chinese saying goes, you can't wrap fire in paper. You even had the audacity to spend a night in my home, didn't you? I insist that you leave him as soon as possible. I will never allow him to keep a woman outside our home. I am a Japanese woman who studied in the United States. I am not to be bullied."

Faced with such an overbearing woman, I can only let her give vent to her rage, without uttering a word. It's better to say nothing if it's useless to say anything. Moreover, it is I who should be blamed for meddling in their marriage.

Before leaving, she adds, "Aokawa Kakuai knows that my brother belongs to the violent underworld. I don't want anybody to get killed. Please take care."

Hearing about the "violent underworld", I am terrified and break out in a cold sweat. I often read reports in newspapers and magazines about their murders, bank robberies, arson, theft of expensive cars, etc. Last week, they killed four dancers. I saw a special program on TV about it.

I phone Aokawa Kakuai at once. He had a row with his wife, Kimiko, the previous night, but he didn't expect her to go to my residence in person. He agrees to come immediately.

Aokawa Kakuai hurries to my place with a serious face and bloodshot eyes. It seems that he has told the truth when he says that he didn't sleep the whole night.

I ask anxiously, "How did she find out?"

"I am not clear about it. Probably some servant betrayed me," he replies hesitantly.

"Didn't you give the servants a two-day holiday?" This suddenly occurs to me.

He says scratching his head, "My wife is very shrewd. Small changes in the position of furniture would arouse her immediate suspicion."

"Why did you invite me to your house? It was courting disaster." I fly into a rage.

He also responds in a loud voice, "What's the use of blaming me at this stage? It's better to think of a way to deal with her. My wife is not to be trifled with!"

Terrified, I ask, "Does her brother really belong to a violent society?"

Gritting his teeth, he nods and answers, holding my hand, "Don't be frightened. He won't kill you. My wife is not to be provoked, however. She is not afraid of spreading family scandal, perhaps because of the impact of American culture on her. Her brother must not learn of it. Don't go to work. Let Sada Keiko manage the restaurant. Her husband was a good friend of mine in university. I will feel at ease with her in charge. For your safety, you should temporarily move to a new residence and keep it secret from my wife. Rest assured, I'll still pay you 600,000 Yen every month, but stop working in the ad agency, which is under her administration."

"Do you mean I should leave Tokyo? I haven't done anything illegal."

He nods, "Just temporarily. All these precautions are for your safety."

With Aokawa Kakuai's careful and meticulous arrangement, I move to Nikko, around 150 kilometers north of Tokyo. It is as if some gangsters were chasing me. I meant to go sightseeing in different places in Japan, but now I lack the desire. Moreover, it is meaningless to travel all by myself. I naturally think of Ding, Xu in Osaka. I would willingly throw myself into his arms if I could find him. Unfortunately, I don't have any information about his whereabouts even though I've inquired.

Nikko is a city for tourism, boasting hills, lakes, hot springs and falls. The grave of the formidable Tokugawa Ieyasu is located in the Tosho-gu Temple on Mount Nikko. Ding, Xu and Aokawa Kakuai brought me here several times to see the sights, so I have lost interest. Apart from watching TV, I just sleep. I feel more tired not doing anything, as I am now used to working. A month elapses in my "shelter" and Aokawa Kakuai has never visited me, out of fear.

I can no longer bear the loneliness, so I call Aokawa Kakuai and ask him when I can end this life in retreat. He does not have a definite date. My savings in the bank are close to 20 million. I really want to go back to Shanghai and marry *a man who truly loves me. This amount of money is sufficient for me…*

73. Leaving—the Best Way out for a Vulnerable Girl

A phone call on Christmas Eve with Huang, Hong, my high school classmate, changes my destiny. She is a good friend of mine and we tell each other almost everything. After her graduation from senior high school, she went to Shenzhen with her elder brother for a career. At the end of 1991, we met when she was back with some businessman from Hong Kong, who was ordering goods in Shanghai. She candidly told me that she was her boss's "concubine", whom she stays with once every month. After she made enough money, she immigrated to Canada and now works as a waitress in a Chinese restaurant in Toronto. We have communicated with each other for years. When I tell her that I am eager to leave Japan, she suggests that I apply for immigration to Canada and promises to help me with the formalities.

A week later, Huang, Hong calls from Toronto. The lawyers inform her that the quickest and safest way is for me to get married. It is hard to find a proper man soon, so I should consider a fake marriage that can be arranged if I pay a man 5,000 US dollars. Moreover, she has found such a man for me. His name is Lin, Tianci, a 35-year-old immigrant from Hong Kong and the second chef in her restaurant. Three years ago, his wife eloped with a foreigner, taking their child away as well. He was so furious that he is determined never to marry again.

5,000 US dollars, or around 600,000 Japanese Yen, which is equal to my current salary for one month, poses no problem for me. I promise Huang, Hong at once that I will remit the amount to her for handling the procedures quickly. The sooner I leave this hell, the faster I'll obtain freedom. Staying alone in the apartment in Nikko without any friend or even a visit by Aokawa Kakuai is tantamount to staying in jail, isn't it?

With Huang, Hong's meticulous planning and Aokawa Kakuai's assistance, I obtain a tourist visa to Canada at the end of January 1994. I never expected such efficiency.

On the afternoon of the day before my departure when Aokawa Kakuai comes to Nikko to see me off, he looks downcast and much older than before. This is apparently because of his wife's "torment".

"Will you return to Tokyo?" he asks, while actually knowing the answer.

I sneer at him, "Certainly I would like to, with such a good boss as you. Aokawa Kimiko, however, doesn't welcome me."

He lowers his head, "I am sorry. She has turned more ill-tempered day by day, as if her menopause has come ahead of time. I have fared ill since that event. I still don't know who betrayed me."

"Why are you hen-pecked, not like a typical Japanese man? In Japan, women are just like this." I raise my little finger.

A little embarrassed, he says, "Time is changing and each family has its own problems. I am at the peak of my career and I don't want trouble like this. Moreover, my wife has an American education and believes in women's rights, and her brother…"

"How dare you dally with other women!" I interrupt him with a serious look.

He holds my waist with a cheeky grin, "That's because you are so charming that I can't control myself."

When he tries to take off my dress, I forcefully reject him. At this moment, he still hasn't lost his lust for me.

I stand up and yell, "Get out of here and take off your wife's pants!"

"Shanghai women are fierce. Komaki Zhang, you shouldn't behave like this. I have been nice to you for two years."

I yell like a wild bull, "My name is Zhang, Yuanyuan. I hate the Japanese name just as I hate seeing you."

Brazenly, he attempts to hold me. I raise my hand and box his ears relentlessly.

"How dare you strike me?" He throws himself on me like a stubborn bull.

I dash to the table and pick up the phone swiftly.

"I'll call the police if you don't leave."

Seeing no reaction from him, I shout, "Do you want me to call Kimiko?"

"Okay, I'll go." He leaves, crestfallen.

I feel fully satisfied to watch his fat body disappear from view. It seems that the fury accumulated in my heart for two years has poured out and the humiliation over the two years has been washed away.

On February 2nd 1994, I leave Nikko alone by taxi for Narita International Airport in Tokyo.

The difference is that I leave Tokyo with 170,000 US dollars. This is the money of blood and sweat, and is the result of sacrificing my youth and prime capital for two years. The hardship cannot be described in words and will be concealed in my heart forever as my secret. I hope some day this history of disgrace will be erased from my memory.

The Maple Leaf airplane from Canada for a direct flight to Toronto speeds to the runway. A deafening sound crushes my dream of striking gold in Tokyo-- a huge and beautiful city, which has no place for a vulnerable woman like me. Reality is cruel, sometimes incredibly ruthless.

The plane soars through clouds in the blue sky. Inadvertently, I have a fond dream of North America. Perhaps life is composed of different dreams. A person wakes up from one dream and starts another.

Chapter Fifteen

"Toronto is Very Cold and I Feel Chilly in my Heart"

74. Dreaming under the CN Tower

Although I know nothing about North America, I decided, within a short period of time, to come to this icy cold land. The only reason was to escape from the hell of Tokyo and to inhale the air of freedom. I have to admit that human beings are the products of their environment. They make a living in the environment and the environment, in turn, molds them.

Toronto welcomes me with boundless white snow on the night of February 2nd 1994. Since I grew up in Shanghai, I feel refreshed by the flying snow: for me, the snow is wonderful, not frightening. Because of this, I should be able to make a new path in Canada and live an easy life, or at least live like a human being with dignity.

My classmate Huang, Hong greets me at Pearson International Airport. Since we last met over two years ago, she has put on weight, looking more like a thirty-something woman than a young girl just over twenty. Her face is round and her figure is plump.

"Our campus belle has become sexier now!" Huang, Hong's first words embarrass me a bit.

"You're still sharp-tongued, just like before." I pinch her chubby hand.

She takes over my luggage cart and says, "I'm telling the truth. You see, you are so beautiful that everybody here is looking at you. Oh, you've got so much in your luggage. I told you -- with money, you can buy everything here."

"As a woman, what else do I have except clothing, shoes and cosmetics? A quarter of them are for you."

"Look at me with my fat body. You'd better use them yourself. They might be less expensive here than in Tokyo."

The two of us arrive at the parking lot while chatting. Huang, Hong carries the heavy luggage to the car easily. I am amazed at her great strength, as she was considered spoiled and weak in high school.

Seeing my perplexity, she explains while starting the car, "Are you impressed? My great strength is the result of working as a waitress and carrying dishes. Settling down in a foreign country really changes people."

The roads are flanked with mounds of snow. Tiny flakes of snow are still flying in the sky, like little elves dancing and singing under the shining road lights, heart-warming and lovely. Suddenly the well-known poem "Fast falling white snow" by Yu, Guangzhong comes to my mind:

Gentle snow, you refuse to say anything,

Your whispering and mysterious advice

Goes to my right ear, then to my left,

Such soft hands, gentle snow,

Such tiny lips…"

Seeing me in a daze, Huang, Hong says, "Are you enjoying the snow? You'll find it hard to bear soon. I was like you in my first year here, but now I am scared to death of it."

"Perhaps I was mentally prepared. On the plane, I felt refreshed rather than frightened by the boundless white snow. I have to learn how to drive. In such icy cold weather, it is difficult to go anywhere without a car," I respond quickly.

"It's simple to learn how to drive. Just call a driving school. With your intelligence, you'll learn in no time. It costs a lot to own a car, however. There's a popular saying: Keeping a car is like keeping a wife. That won't be a problem for you since you've got money."

In an attempt to change the subject, I ask her, "You really don't have a boyfriend?"

"How could I lie to you, my old classmate? I told you over the phone that I *work all day long. When would I find time for dating? Well, does that Japanese boss still lust after you?"*

I shake my head. In order to explain why I was so anxious to leave Tokyo, I made up a story that my boss, Aokawa Kakuai, was pestering me. I will certainly conceal my illicit relationship with him even from my best friend. That period of time is a galling shame for me: I want to forget it and never think about it again.

On the way, I ask, puzzled, "Why don't I see the CN Tower? I've read a lot about it in travel guides."

Huang, Hong laughs, "We are going from west to east, and the CN Tower is in the southern downtown area. I've made arrangements: I've asked for the day off tomorrow and I'll show you around downtown Toronto. Of course, we'll climb the Tower..."

Huang, Hong lives in Scarborough, in the northeast of Toronto. This area has a population of over half a million people, 20% of whom are of Chinese origin. One can live in this region without knowing any English, because there are all sorts of Chinese stores, including over a dozen Chinese supermarkets. Huang, Hong lives in a one-bedroom apartment on the 7th floor of the "Kangcui Building." This is only 15 minutes' drive from the "Double Eight Seafood Restaurant" where she works. With her consent, I'll temporarily stay in her apartment until I find my own after I've familiarized myself with the surroundings.

I wake up the next day at noon, -- I feel normal, without any jet lag. Huang, Hong says that I am simply a devil, because it took her a full week to adjust to the time difference when she arrived in Toronto. She drives the car to Highway 401, transfers to the DVP (Don Valley Parkway) and arrives in downtown Toronto in a little over half an hour.

As records have it, the CN Tower is not only the main landmark of Toronto, but also a symbol of Canada, with a height of 553 meters. It is the highest independent building on earth without any pillars, and the American Civil Engineers' Association rated it as one of the seven world wonders. It was built in 1975 and put into formal operation the following year. The top of the tower can withstand strong winds, with the biggest deviation reaching 2 meters. The last section of the tower top was assembled using a helicopter. Its primary function is to send signals for TV, radio stations and microwave apparatuses. An Observation

Tower is located about two-thirds of the way up from the ground.

A ticket for going to the top of the Tower is about 20 Canadian dollars, not cheap. In Huang, Hong's opinion, it is worth the money to go up the highest tower in the world. She has brought several friends here, serving as an "amateur guide". I follow her in the lineup and reach the "Sky Pod" at the height of 346 meters in just one minute-- a really "modern speed".

Huang, Hong becomes excited when she walks to the open-air Observation Tower. She talks while gesturing, "Look, that's Lake Ontario and over there is a panoramic view of the whole city."

It is indeed a majestic view of canyons of buildings in downtown Toronto. Nothing unique is visible in winter, however—all we can see is buildings covered with white snow. It is thrilling to stand on the glass floor to look at the scene underfoot. Huang, Hong does not dare to look down for long for fear of dizziness.

From the "Sky Pod," we come to the "Sky Deck" by elevator. This is the highest Observation Tower worthy of the name, at a height of 447 meters. With the help of a telescope, we can view the scenery within an area of 160 kilometers. If the weather is fine, Huang, Hong explains, we can see Niagara Falls over one hundred kilometers away.

I can hardly tear myself away from the "Sky Deck". Huang, Hong asks me if I have any poem in mind. I tell her that I haven't written poems for a long time. Certainly, none was written during my two years in Japan.

She says with a smile, "Almost every new immigrant in Toronto cherishes a dream."

I hold her hand, pondering, "I was thinking of that just now. Let's have a dream, starting from today."

"It doesn't cost anything to have a dream. I didn't expect our campus belle would still be so romantic..." She laughs loudly while pinching my nose.

75. Kind Mrs. Barbara

I don't see Huang, Hong a lot since she sleeps until 1 or 2 pm after her shift from 4 pm to 2 am. In a week, I become familiar with the area and love the indoor swimming pool and gym, which I have used several times. Moreover, the subway is close by, which is so important for people without cars. Nearby are Chinese *supermarkets and restaurants.*

I intend to rent an apartment in the "Kangcui Building", but Huang, Hong lists many reasons why I should not: the weird smell from so many Indian residents; blackouts and water stoppage due to the building's age; several gun incidents…It is obvious that she doesn't want me to live in her building. I guess she must have some embarrassing secret to hide from me. Although we were like siblings in high school, every woman needs a space of her own. We have been away from each other for several years and we have both grown up after all. I don't want to cause her trouble or jeopardize our friendship over such a small thing.

One afternoon several days later, Huang, Hong introduces me to Lin, Tianci in a café across the street from the building. He is the second chef of the "Double Eight Seafood Restaurant" and my supposed future "husband". Although not handsome, he is not as ugly as Huang, Hong said over the phone. Short and thin, with a typical Cantonese figure, he has narrow eyes, which show some shrewdness.

"Miss Zhang is really beautiful." While saying this, Lin holds my hand and is reluctant to let it go. With a glare from Huang, Hong, he withdraws his hand helplessly.

To lessen his embarrassment, I continue at once, "I should thank you for giving me so much help."

"You are welcome. I have my reward. Huang, Hong has given me the 5,000 US dollars." He speaks Mandarin with a strong Cantonese accent.

After chatting for a while, I broach the main subject, "My tourist visa will expire in three months, so we have to 'register for marriage' soon. It's been over ten days since I arrived in Toronto."

"No problem. You can go to City Hall for the registration after you rent an apartment and settle down, right, Ah Lin?" Huang, Hong first talks to me, then to Lin, Tianci.

"I'll be at your beck and call. I'll never change my mind. You'd better rent a two-bedroom apartment, as I'll have to stay in your place for a while for the inspection by the Immigration Bureau," Lin reminds me.

Huang, Hong says to me with a false smile, "You'll have to install several locks to guard against this wolf."

Lin responds in a hurry, "Please rest assured. As a man, I am fond of women, but I am not a lecher."

I speak seriously, "I believe Mr. Lin is not that type of person. Moreover, I have my bosom friend here. I don't think you have the audacity."

He nods docilely, his face coloring. Huang, Hong can't help laughing when she sees his embarrassment. It seems that this guy is chicken-hearted: this makes me feel more at ease.

On Huang, Hong's recommendation, I rent a two-bedroom apartment on the 12th floor of the "Haoyuan Apartment Building" a week later. This is three blocks away from the "Kangcui Building". The monthly rent is 1,400 Canadian dollars, which is not cheap but poses no problem for me, with a quarter of a million dollars in hand. This is a high-class new building, only two years old, with mostly white residents and some Cantonese-talking Chinese, but with no black people. It boasts a gym, an indoor swimming pool, an outdoor tennis court and a sauna. At its gate is a bus stop, which connects to a subway station. Nearby is a Chinese supermarket, though there is no Chinese restaurant. I am bored to death, as I haven't done anything since I was forced to "rest" in Tokyo at the end of last November. Now that I have settled down and don't have to worry about my livelihood, I intend to study English conscientiously, as well as enjoy the fitness facilities in the building. Actually, I had a pretty good foundation in English during my high school days and learned medical terms at the medical school. I do have to brush up on my English for a year or so after not using it for two years. After that, I'll look for a job.

Because of my desire for a brand new life, I am "absorbed in my study and oblivious of what is going on around me". I feel my life is full of meaning even though I seldom go out. Every day, I have a regular schedule: I get up at 9am and study English for 3 hours. After lunch, I read simple English books for two hours, go to the gym for exercise at 4pm for half an hour and then go swimming for half an hour. In the evening, I mostly watch TV, both in English and Chinese. I watch Fairchild TV patiently although I find Cantonese more difficult to understand than English. Luckily, there are Chinese captions. Huang, Hong advises me repeatedly that it's more important to know Cantonese than English here. I bought a lot of inexpensive English books and tapes in Tokyo and have brought all of them to Toronto. Huang, Hong doesn't have time to see me as she works seven days a week.

Occasionally, she calls in the afternoon for a chat.

I have to mention Mrs. Barbara, an old lady I met in the gym of the "Haoyuan Apartment Building", because she gives me meticulous care in my new life. Over sixty years old, she is a Canadian of Italian origin. Her husband passed away two years ago and her son does business in the United States. Her daughter is married and living in Britain. At present, Barbara lives by herself on the 10th floor of the building. Last year, she retired as a secretary at a computer company. It is apparent that she must have been a beauty when she was young. She still has a slender figure, but there are some wrinkles on her face. She looks like a fifty-year old. I meet her when I visit the gym for the third time. We can communicate with each other, although my English is not good. With body language as well, we feel like old friends. After several meetings, she agrees to tutor me in English for an hour after dinner every day, free of charge. In exchange, I am to go shopping at the supermarket with her once every week and take care of her darling dog, Harley, during her trip to the States to visit her son.

Every evening at 7pm, I go downstairs to Barbara's home for English conversation. Her two-bedroom suite is clean and elegant. One room is a study, with a huge glass-topped desk in the middle, on which are a computer and a printer. The shelves on the four walls are filled with books, many of which were left by her late husband, an electric engineer and amateur poet, with two collections of poems published. At present, she wants to continue her girlhood dream of becoming a writer and is writing a love story with autobiographical elements. Probably because I lack a sense of the warmth of home since I have been overseas for over two years, I feel exceptionally comfortable every time I enter Barbara's apartment. She is always very glad to see me, showing great concern for me.

The snow on either side of the road starts to melt eventually and the sunshine warms everybody. People's faces, tormented by severe winter, bloom with joyful smiles. My oral English is much improved after my own endeavors and with Barbara's tutoring. What puzzles me is that Huang, Hong has not mentioned my "marriage registration" with Lin, Tianci since I moved into the "Haoyuan Apartment Building". Several times, I ask her about it on the phone, but she tells me not to worry. I call several immigration counselors and they all advise me to register for "marriage" before the expiry date of my visa, that is, before May

2nd. If I neglect to do this, I'll have to leave Canada, as a tourist visa cannot be extended.

76. A Loan for a Gambling Debt

Time has been zipping by: it has been almost two months since my arrival in Canada. Like a cat on a hot tin roof, I cannot wait any longer. I phone Huang, Hong and ask her frankly when Lin, Tianci will "register for marriage" with me. Humming and hawing for a while, she can no longer evade my stubborn pursuance and reveals the facts. It turns out that Lin is a gambler and owes 10,000 Canadian dollars to a "loan shark", who is now ruthlessly forcing him to repay the debt. He is worried to death because the debt will increase to $12,000 if it is not paid back within a week. He has no heart for anything other than borrowing money everywhere for the repayment.

Hearing this, I have a big question mark in my mind: is Lin attempting to change his mind about "marrying" me by making up such a story? Surely, Huang, Hong would not have deceived me. Friendships from youth should be trustworthy forever. If she had not helped me, I might still be in Nikko under the evil control of Aokawa Kakuai. I force myself to calm down and request a meeting of the three of us to find out the truth. Perhaps, I can lend a hand.

At noon the next day, we meet at the "Kangcui Building". When I enter Huang, Hong's apartment, I find her red-faced and in a bad temper obviously because of Lin, Tianci, who keeps silent with his head lowered.

"Yuanyuan, look at him. I told him not to gamble and he is still not convinced. He refuses to give up until all hope is gone." Huang, Hong appears to be in a fiery rage.

I try to mediate. "Mr. Lin, whatever happened? Tell me slowly."

He replies in Mandarin with a Cantonese accent, "Miss Zhang, I'm so sorry for the embarrassment. It's my fault that I like gambling. Last month, I went to Casino Windsor to play 'Baccarat' and lost the 5,000 US dollars you had given me. The next week, I borrowed 5,000 Canadian dollars from a 'loan shark' for another gamble, but lost all. Last weekend, with some illusory hope, I borrowed 5,000 Canadian dollars in Toronto and gambled again. At first, I won 3,000 dollars, but then I lost it all again. Two days ago when I finished my shift at work, the loan shark came to pressure me to repay. If I don't pay up, they'll increase 2,000 dollars after a week..."

"You don't dare continue now -- they'll kill you!" Huang, Hong rebuffs him.

"It's meant to scare people," he says in a low voice.

"To scare people only? Did you read in the newspaper that somebody was stabbed to death by a 'loan shark' last month? Do you dare to offend the criminals of the underworld? How many lives have you got? I am afraid of death if you are not. How do you face Miss Zhang, who came from Tokyo depending on you to help her get permanent residence status? She gave you 5,000 US dollars long ago. Now that this has happened, how do I face my old classmate?" Huang, Hong says with tears in her eyes.

In low spirits, Lin, Tianci talks to me, "I'm sorry, Miss Zhang. After I repay the debt, I'll register for 'marriage' with you immediately. Rest assured, I received your money and I'll do what I'm supposed to do."

"What do you have for repayment? Other than your damned life?" Huang, Hong says, panting and dismayed.

Seeing the terrible fight between them, I believe that what they say happened is true and not a trick Lin is playing on me. It is for my sake that Huang, Hong is in such a state. I comfort her and talk to Lin, "Mr. Lin, how much of the 10,000 dollars have you got?"

"Two good friends loaned me 4,000 and Huang, Hong agreed to lend me 2,000 and I'll get 1,000 from my wages in a couple of days. I'm 3,000 dollars short and thinking of other ways to get the rest."

"If it weren't for my old classmate, I wouldn't lend you anything." Huang is still domineering.

I talk to Lin seriously, "Well, don't borrow from Huang, Hong. I'll lend you 6,000 dollars and write you a check. Repay your gambling debt at once to avoid a fatal disaster. You must promise, however, to register for our 'marriage' in a couple of days. Not that I don't trust you, but I can't afford to wait any longer."

"Yuanyuan, how can he have the nerve to borrow from you? Hurry to thank Miss Zhang, Ah Lin." Huang's facial expression eases up.

"Thanks so much! Thank you so much!" He stands up to bow to me.

Huang says immediately, "Ah Lin, go to City Hall to register tomorrow afternoon. Miss Zhang has a lot of immigration formalities to go through. She really can't wait any longer."

Lin nods and agrees at once. Then we discuss the details of the "marriage registration".

Before leaving, I write Lin a check of 6,000 dollars and he gives me a written "IOU" in English immediately. This states that he'll return 500 dollars every month and completely repay the debt within a year. Unexpectedly, his English is pretty good. Perhaps, he learned it in Hong Kong.

77. A Solemn "Wedding"

The next afternoon, the three of us arrive at the Marriage Registrar at City Hall. The formalities are simple: Lin, Tianci shows his certificate of divorce; I show a certificate to prove I am single; we fill in two forms and pay $100. It takes about ten minutes to complete the registration. We schedule a simple "wedding" at City Hall in three days.

In accordance with the immigration Counsel's repeated advice, we should hold a solemn "wedding" because Westerners know that the Chinese are particular about having an extravagant ceremony. We should have a lot of photos taken so that the Immigration Bureau will not suspect that it is a fake marriage. In this way, I can obtain permanent residence as an immigrant. After mutual consultation, Huang, Hong and I decide that Lin, Tianci and I should wear beautiful clothes at the "wedding" and have a banquet of several tables. Besides my neighbor Barbara, Huang, Hong will invite some other guests. I will not accept gifts or money. The sole purpose of all this is to have more witnesses for our "wedding". Barbara is surprised at my sudden marriage. I tell her that Lin and I knew each other in Tokyo. She nods, but seems only half convinced.

The "wedding" is held in a small room at City Hall at 4pm on April 3rd. A priest from Hong Kong presides over the "wedding" while Huang, Hong serves as a witness for the "groom" and Barbara stands up for the "bride". The friends Huang have invited are mostly employees of the "Double Eight Seafood Restaurant". Wearing a white bridal gown and with a heavily made-up face, I feel pretty good as a "bride". I wear a pair of low-heeled shoes to match the height of the "groom". In a brand new black suit and with salon-dyed hair, wearing a pair of stacked heel shoes, Lin looks full of vitality and is about the same height as me. Huang and I spent several afternoons selecting his suit and shoes with meticulous care.

Standing in front of the podium and holding the Bible, the priest speaks in English and Cantonese and asks each of us if we are willing to marry the other. After each of us responds "I do", we present each other with the wedding rings. The guests applaud and the camera flashes nonstop. I have purchased the pair of wedding rings beforehand and put the ring for me in Lin's suit pocket. Then, the guests have pictures taken with the "bride and groom" outside City Hall.

The banquet is held in the "Dragon Dynasty Restaurant", famous for its Cantonese cuisine. Three tables are set up in a room with the golden words "Marriage between Lin and Zhang" on a red background on the wall. Besides Barbara, the other guests are friends of Lin and Huang, mostly couples, dressed in their holiday best. Everyone looks happy. I am a bit embarrassed that almost every guest presents me with a gift or money wrapped in red, although I told them not to.

After the feast starts, two of Lin's pals propose a toast, "Ah Lin, you have good fortune in love to marry such a pretty wife. Why didn't you let the secret out before? To hide the beauty in a golden house?"

"I have to hide this beauty to guard against you wolves," Lin responds swiftly.

Another man raises the glass, "I am surprised at her beauty: she looks like a princess. You should drink more. Ah Lin, bottoms up".

Lin raises the wine glass quickly and drinks the whole thing. It seems he has a real tolerance for wine.

Then, several women come to me, saying, "The bride should drink as well."

Although I have little capacity for wine, it is ungracious to refuse, so I reluctantly drink a full mouthful and feel warm all over. Later, several people press me to finish a whole glass of wine. I am in a predicament.

Lin snatches the glass from my hand, "The bride can't drink. I'll do it instead."

"No, that won't do," they say.

"Why not?" Then, Lin stands up to drink it and the others have to follow suit.

Lin asks me to drink orange juice, so the others won't force me to drink wine. He announces repeatedly that the "bride" can't drink much, so the guests laugh at *him for "loving his wife like his own life". This alone shows that he acts like a husband. Lin drinks at least ten glasses of wine during the evening, thanks to his great capacity for it. Barbara, shaking her head, is frightened by the noise while the others are drinking wine; probably, this is her first Chinese wedding banquet.*

78. Story in the "Bridal Chamber"

After returning to the "Haoyuan Apartment Building" at 10pm, the guests inevitably "tease the newlyweds on their wedding night". This is an old Chinese tradition designed to make everybody happy and to create laughter. When somebody suggests "the groom and bride" kiss each other, Lin, Tianci seems somewhat restrained, but I look natural and at ease, moving closer to him to be kissed, in order to get this "precious photo." Led by Huang, Hong, the guests leave at midnight.

In spite of my exhaustion after a busy day, I am gratified to see 5 or 6 rolls of film have been shot. I have spent several thousand dollars to create the perfect atmosphere for these photos. Lin, Tianci, however, sitting on the couch, looks scary when he stares at me blankly with his narrow eyes.

To divert his attention, I talk to him at once, "Mr. Lin, I'm really grateful to you for drinking so much wine for me."

"Foolish girl, that's what I should do to look like a real husband and to have life-like photos taken. Friends would never suspect that we are a fake couple. Be assured, I will complete the task very well since I did receive your money. Soon, you'll obtain the permanent residence document. Moreover, I don't know how to thank you enough for lending me money to repay my debt."

"If only you would stop gambling. There is no hurry to return my money. I haven't an urgent need for it. You'd better repay your friends their 4,000 dollars first. Well, it's getting late. Go to bed early. Your sheets, blanket and pillow are in the built-in wardrobe in your room."

After a pleasant bath, I go into the bridal chamber and lock the door. I feel comfortable lying alone on the double bed. Normally, I would fall asleep quickly after such a tiring day. However, I can't get to sleep, but toss and turn in bed. I am filled with all sorts of mixed feelings, one after the other. Usually, newlyweds spend the first night in the bridal chamber with red candles burning, but now I am all by myself. Besides, this is a "fake bridal chamber" so I feel a bit desolate.

At the age of 23, I would be willing to marry a Prince Charming, if possible, and enjoy a night in a real bridal chamber. Because of my current circumstances, I have to spend money for an unpredictable fake marriage in order to be free of Aokawa, Kakuai's evil grip and to escape the pain of my life in Tokyo. I don't want any new problems to crop up unexpectedly before I obtain my citizenship. Before leaving Tokyo, I consulted with my Mom over the phone. She was not opposed to my going to Canada for two reasons. First, I have enough money and don't have to do manual labor, which made her feel at ease. Second, my brother might have a chance to study in Canada if I am able to obtain permanent residence as an immigrant. Of course, I didn't tell her about the fake marriage so the family wouldn't worry. I'll be 26 or 27 when I get a Canadian passport in three years – this is not too late to get married. I could return to Shanghai and marry a handsome man who loves me.

It seems that Lin, Tianci is a man with a sense of obligation and looks like a real husband, judging from his behavior tonight. He has moved from his apartment with some of his furniture to my apartment, and stores the rest at Huang, Hong's place. He agrees to pay me $500 for the monthly rent until I obtain citizenship and we "divorce". Hopefully, he will not cause any trouble… While thinking and recalling vaguely the romantic atmosphere, and seeing "the wedding photo" with Lin, I indulge in fantasy and become restless all over.

A young beauty, like a blooming flower, needs a man's loving care for her mind and carnal love for her body. I have neither, only a lonely heart and a body about to explode. At this moment, I miss Ding, Xu in Osaka. I think of his tall figure, his fine-featured face, as well as his tenderness and passion. He is the third man in my life, and perhaps it's the will of God that we had a relationship as brief as a shooting star. Chen, Zhiwei, who broke my hymen, is a despicable man, while Aokawa, Kakuai is an abominable wolf. In comparison, Ding, Xu is a real man, worthy of my love. I love his natural and unconventional grace, his enthusiasm for work and his dedication to his photography …

I fail to fall asleep until 2 am, still thinking nonstop, when I hear a noise in the kitchen. At once, I put on my dressing gown and open the door to see what has happened. It turns out that Lin is boiling some water.

"Miss Zhang, I'm sorry to have bothered you. I'm so thirsty that I have

to make some tea," he explains in a low voice, as if he were a child who had misbehaved.

"It doesn't matter. You must have drunk too much wine and have a hangover."

"Not too much to make me feel like this. It seems that I am really getting old and physically weaker. Would you like to have a cup of tea to freshen up?" He makes a cup of oolong tea and goes into the living room to sit down.

"Drinking tea at midnight will keep me awake. I'd prefer orange juice." No sooner have I said the words than he rushes to get a can of frozen orange juice for me from the kitchen.

I thank him and ask, "Well, you couldn't fall asleep, right?"

Sipping some tea, Lin starts talking slowly, "How could I? Eight years ago, after a jolly night like tonight, I got drunk when my wife married me. I was a business manager in a garment company in Hong Kong while she was a secretary in a lawyer's office. We had a pretty good life, bought a house and had a lovely daughter in the second year of our marriage. My daughter was good-looking like her mother. When my daughter was one year old, my wife insisted on immigrating to Canada. After selling our house, we came to Toronto, a godforsaken, bitterly cold place, and I couldn't find a job. Luckily, my wife got a job as a secretary in a Canadian company. Half a year later, a friend of mine opened a restaurant, the current 'Double Eight Seafood Restaurant', and asked me to help in the kitchen. Isn't it strange? I never worked in a restaurant in Hong Kong, but I learned quickly here. Maybe it's because the environment forces people to change. Gradually, I was promoted to second chef. You know, this occupation requires night work and we are busier on holidays. I didn't have time to enjoy family life. As you know, most people working in a restaurant gamble and I began with mahjong. Then, I bet on more and more until I failed to take my wages home over three years ago. My wife divorced me the day after she found out about my evil habit. She generously told me that I didn't have to provide for my daughter. My kneeling down and begging for forgiveness didn't work, so I had to sign the separation papers... Later, people told me that she had had an affair with a manager of French origin in the company and my gambling was simply a good excuse to get a divorce. That evil woman was vicious. All women have damned easy virtue and are greedy for money... Miss Zhang, I'm sorry. I don't refer to you."

"Where are the mother and daughter now?" I ask eagerly.

"In less than a year, she married that Frenchman. Last year, the whole family moved to Montreal, perhaps for business purposes. I have no connection with them."

"I didn't expect such a tragic story. Everyone has a hard nut to crack."

"To tell you the truth, I don't miss that evil woman. Women are fickle. When I had a decent income, she married me willingly. Then, she despised me for my lowly job as a cook and my misfortune in Canada. What could I do, without any professional skills? I let her go. I'd rather have no wife. My daughter, however, is pretty and lovely and she often appears in my dreams. You are not a mother yet, so you might not understand. Missing my child is engraved on my bones and in my heart. Now seven years old, she might not remember me at all…" He is so sad that his eyes fill with tears.

It is 3 am sharp by the clock in the living room after Lin finishes his story. I do my best to console him, and then return to my bedroom drowsily. Lying in bed, I am still thinking about his tragedy. Maybe as he said, his wife had no desire to have a poor husband with a job as a cook. Still, he should understand that women need love as well as money. He did not have time for her, let alone love her. Modern women are practical. Once they realize that they have to live for themselves, they make wise choices if opportunities arise. The wave of immigration at the end of the 20th century has brought about earth-shaking changes in human beings' values. Some people mix up black and white, confound right and wrong, and turn things upside down. Kind people become more selfish and less human. On reflection, I am no exception – to attain my goal, I have done everything. To obtain money, I became a Japanese man's concubine. To get immigrant status, I spent money for a fake marriage. I have reached this stage of degradation, or to be more exact, the social environment has pushed me to this stage. Or, perhaps the human nature for survival has pushed me to it. I have had no other choice – even if I repent, I would not be saved. I just have to go on.

79. Opening a Restaurant in Partnership with a Former Classmate

The second day after the "wedding", I feel relieved because my lawyer has submitted my immigration application to the Immigration Bureau, with four or five intimate wedding photos enclosed. Based on the lawyer's experience, I can expect immigrant status in six to ten months. I have to wait patiently. While waiting, I plan to study English and do some research on business opportunities. I can't sit idle and use up all my fortune. I have to let my deposit in the bank make more money. It is impossible for me to do manual labor for others or to find an ideal job in this meltdown market since I lack professional skills. Subconsciously, I want to satisfy my craving to be a boss.

Generally, I have a regular lifestyle: I study English hard in my room after getting up and go to the gym in the building at 4 pm and then go swimming. After supper, I practice oral English in Barbara's apartment downstairs. Lin, Tianci works from 3 pm till 1 am and gets up at 1 or 2 pm the next day. We seldom meet each other and he never cooks at home. He has three meals at the restaurant. Living under the same roof, the "husband and wife" don't interfere with each other and are quite harmonious. On his day-off (Monday), he usually goes out after getting up and returns home early the next morning. Occasionally, he shows me how to make a big pot of Cantonese soup, which will last me for a week. It's supposed to reduce my internal heat and improve my appetite. I learn 7 or 8 ways of making Cantonese soup from him and benefit a lot from his instruction. The Cantonese are connoisseurs in making such soup, passing the recipes from generation to generation. All housewives know how to make a pot of soup for the family dinner. There are so many varieties of ingredients in the soup: meat from types of flying poultry and wild animals are among them, plus some Chinese herbs to make it more nutritious and give it a unique taste. Later, if I don't eat such soup every day, I get sick.

On the phone with Huang, Hong, I express my wish to engage in business after I obtain my immigrant status. She encourages me to open a Chinese restaurant, as her boss, Mr. Deng, has earned so much that he is always smiling. I worked in a Japanese restaurant in Tokyo, so I might succeed if I can manage a restaurant in a good location. I reject the idea of opening a Chinese restaurant, though, because I am not familiar with Chinese cooking and the working hours are too long and the environment is too dirty. It's better to do something I am familiar with. Actually, I am interested in opening a beauty parlor, as it is women's nature to love cosmetics and to want to lose weight. This should be a winning business. I worked as a nurse *before, so it won't be too difficult to learn the beauty business. Moreover, my good looks and nice figure will be a living "advertisement".*

I talk about my intention to engage in business with Barbara, who encourages me to study at a university or community college instead of going into business right away. She urges me to make the intellectual investment while I am young and quite well off, as I am quick at learning new things and have a good memory. In the current economic depression, up to nine out of ten businesses lose money. The frequent lay-offs in companies and the closing of businesses run by Chinese people also discourage me. I really appreciate Barbara's instruction and try to follow her directions. I am determined to study medical care again at a university but I need to pass the "TOEFL" test. Barbara helps me borrow "TOEFL" material from the library and promises to find tutors for me among her friends.

Unexpectedly, my calm life is disturbed at the beginning of July. The two brothers who own the "Double Eight Seafood Restaurant" suddenly decide to return to Hong Kong, so they want to sell the restaurant. There are over twenty staff members; faced with the predicament of losing their jobs, they are distressed. As is customary in this business, the new boss brings his own staff, so the old staff can't remain. It is not easy to find new jobs during the recession. Lin, Tianci and Huang, Hong are so agitated that they are like ants on a hot pan. As Lin is the second chef and Huang, the head waitress, they will be unable to find similar jobs with such good pay. Lin is especially worried because it's even harder for him to find a job without a special certificate.

The restaurant, with a capacity of forty tables, has monthly expenses of twenty to thirty thousand dollars, including the rent (over $8,000), wages, hydro and electric bills etc. No small businessman can afford to buy it. The real estate agents have brought around five or six groups of potential buyers, with no result. The Deng brothers decide to lower the price from 350 thousand to 270 thousand dollars, because they are anxious to return to Hong Kong. Still, they fail to find a buyer by the beginning of August.

Hearing the news about the reduction in the selling price, Huang, Hong visits me in my apartment on a hot afternoon.

She and Lin, Tianci intend to buy the restaurant, but Lin has no collateral except his skills and Hong has only 50 thousand dollars in cash. With her credit line, she can get a loan of 100 thousand dollars from the bank, but she is still short 120 thousand dollars. She wonders if I would like to be a partner. Seeing my hesitation, she emphasizes again and again that they will make a profit running the restaurant. Besides, as old classmates, we'll co-operate with one another and will not play dirty tricks on each other.

Lin adds, "Miss Zhang, I have worked in the restaurant for around six years since it opened. Boss Deng makes a profit every month. Don't worry. I'll be responsible for the kitchen work. We'll make money and the capital fund will be repaid soon."

Without clearly expressing my opinion, I make some perfunctory remarks, "I have to think it over as it's a huge investment. To tell you the truth, I won't have any peace of mind until I obtain my immigrant status."

"Miss Zhang, be assured. I'll certainly help you get it. Perhaps you'll get it in a month or two. A friend of mine got it in a little over three months after getting married," Lin says, anxiously.

Huang adds, "Yuanyuan, don't worry. You'll certainly get it sooner or later. If you don't want to invest in the restaurant, could you lend me 80 to 100 thousand dollars?"

Finally I tell them briskly, "Give me three days to think about it. Okay?"

After they leave for work, I cannot concentrate on the difficult "TOEFL" test, but think only about doing business and earning money. The ultimate aim of study is to earn money. If I can avoid 4 or 5 years of study and start earning money right now, why shouldn't I? Probably I'll become a "female millionaire" soon. At this thought, I become ecstatic about earning money and lean towards the idea of doing business with Huang, Hong. Moreover, it was she who rescued me from the sufferings in Tokyo. Isn't it time to repay her for her kindness? Now is the right moment since she is in need. Even if I don't want to be a partner, I can lend her the money. I don't feel comfortable lending her so much money, however. After careful consideration, I decide it is best to be her partner.

In the evening, I tell Barbara everything about the restaurant business. Seeing my eagerness to engage in business, she changes her former opinion and tells me to give it a try.

Still, she seriously reminds me to verify that the "Double Eight Seafood

Restaurant" really does make a profit and how much it earns each month. We should hire a professional accountant to check the figures. Second, while registering for the restaurant, we should make clear the division of shares between Huang and me, and the distribution of dividends, etc. Barbara kindly asks me to consult with her or with her friend, an accountant, regarding legal documents.

I call Huang, Hong after three days' meticulous consideration. I tell her I want to be the bigger and managing shareholder in partnership with her. I also want to meet the boss, Mr. Deng, soon to bargain with him. She agrees over the phone and praises my loyalty as a friend.

At 10 pm the next day, I meet Mr. Deng in the VIP hall of the restaurant. A quick look reveals him to be a shrewd businessman. It seems hard to bargain with him, an "old fox".

He speaks in Mandarin courteously, "Lin's wife is certainly lovely, deserving the reputation of being a great beauty."

"Mr. Deng, you speak with a southerner's accent," I continue at once.

"How smart you are, Miss Zhang! I grew up in Hong Kong, but my mother was from Shanghai like you. I am half a Shanghai-lander. I spoke a little Shanghai dialect while young and speak Cantonese at work." He changes to the Shanghai dialect at once.

"Please excuse me, a young Shanghai-lander, encountering an old Shanghai-lander." I get right to the main subject after the usual greetings.

Mr. Deng answers all my questions and explains the business in great detail, backed by concrete figures from the account books. After two hours' oral wrangling, he has to compromise by lowering his price to my offer: 250 thousand dollars. Later, Huang, Hong joins us sitting beside me in the hall. She is apparently frightened by my quick wit and wisdom and nods nonstop as if suffering from "nodding syndrome".

Finally Mr. Deng jokingly comments, "Times have changed: Old Shanghai-lander has been beaten by a younger one. With you, Miss Zhang, in command, the restaurant will surely flourish."

"Thank you for your commendation. A decision will be made once the account books for the previous two years have been reviewed. There shouldn't be a big problem." I take leave after shaking hands with him.

The next day, Barbara invites a Canadian accountant to check the account books of the "Double Eight Seafood Restaurant" for the last two years. According to the accounts, just as Mr. Deng has said, the net profit is $5,000 every month after deducting expenses and wages. Thus, our investment capital fund will be repaid in over four years. My confidence is redoubled.

80. Double Happiness after Obtaining Immigrant Status

In the last week, Huang, Hong and I have decided that I will contribute 200 thousand dollars and she will contribute 50 thousand dollars in cash towards purchasing the restaurant. In other words, I'll own 80% of the shares and Huang will own 20% and there will be a corresponding distribution of profits. We register immediately as the "Qilin (Chinese Unicorn) Restaurant Company Limited", with Cantonese as the main cuisine and Japanese food as the auxiliary. I employ the original staff of the "Double Eight Seafood Restaurant", with me as the president and Huang, Hong as the general manager. Lin, Tianci is promoted to chief chef, because the original chef, Mr. Deng's brother, has returned to Hong Kong. I also hire a cook for Japanese food, a man who worked previously in Yokohama.

At noon on August 20th, the newly renovated "Qilin Restaurant" has its grand opening. We have spent $10,000 for front-page advertisements in three local Chinese newspapers and have invited Chinese and Canadian politicians and businessmen for a ribbon cutting ceremony. Wearing a violet Mandarin gown with a tiny white floral pattern, I feel a little embarrassed when every distinguished guest stares at me, and Huang, Hong shouts: "How elegant!" To tell the truth, it requires certain conditions to wear a Mandarin gown well. This garment, the "quintessence of Chinese culture", exaggerates the shortcomings of the human body. A fat woman looks like a cylinder in it, while a thin one looks boring and lacks appeal. A woman must have a long neck to appear elegant while wearing a Mandarin gown. I make gestures and pose like a boss. The twenty percent reduction we offer in the first week attracts many customers, especially at the Japanese food counters.

At the peak of dinnertime, over ten waiters find it hard to handle the business, so I have to lend a hand. Huang, Hong never stops smiling, although she is sweating to the tip of her nose. The eight chefs, led by Lin, Tianci, cook in a fervent, but orderly way. I ask somebody to carry a box of beer to the kitchen as a reward, and they work even harder.

I am exhausted when I return home after midnight. I haven't been so busy in the last 8 or 9 months. Still, I am overjoyed because this is my own business. Being a boss, fatigue is nothing: it is worth it if I can earn more money.

After getting home, Lin, Tianci talks to me at once, "Miss Zhang, I never expected that you would be so capable, as well as young and pretty. Where did you learn all this?"

"To tell you the truth, the Japanese restaurant I managed in the Ginza is bigger and more beautifully decorated than ours. We had a total daily business of about ten thousand Canadian dollars. Japanese restaurants, however, are not as complicated as Chinese ones."

"Oh, I see. No wonder you dare to open a restaurant. We chefs all praise you for winning people's hearts. I worked under Mr. Deng for six years, but never got a bottle of beer from him."

"That's nothing. I tried to boost the staff's morale at the Grand Opening. The restaurant depends on you guys. To tell you the truth, I am most worried about the kitchen, because I'm not familiar with Cantonese food. I'll count on you, Ah Lin."

"I've told you not to worry. I learned everything from Mr. Deng, although I haven't been specially trained. Actually, you don't have to go to work so early. It's too much for you to work over ten hours a day."

"In the beginning, I'll go there for several hours at midday before resting at home in the late afternoon, and go at night again. After everything is on track, I'll work at night only."

"Good. I'll be your driver at your beck and call." Lin goes to his room, smiling.

More good news comes and my happiness is doubled. At the end of August, I obtain my immigrant status quite unexpectedly. Even my lawyer is surprised at the efficiency of the Immigration Bureau. After finishing the day's work, I invite Lin, Tianci and Huang, Hong for dim sum at the "Silver Star Eatery" which is open 24 hours. They are surprised when I break the good news to them after we have ordered our dishes.

Lin says patting his chest, "I told you that you would succeed. See, you got it so soon. Good news. Happy tidings. We'll drink to celebrate it."

I at once ask the waiter to bring some bottles of beer, and pour a large glass for myself.

"Now you can concentrate on doing business. You'll soon get back the capital fund based on the current situation. Yuanyuan, wasn't it a good idea to ask you to buy this business?" Huang asks.

Nodding, I reply, "I'm really grateful to you both. Ah Lin, you don't have to return the $6,000 I lent to you, but I really hope you won't gamble again. Nine out of ten people lose, you know."

"Why not thank Miss Zhang?" Huang interrupts.

Lin hurriedly makes a slight bow with hands folded in front to show his gratitude.

It is already 2 am when we leave the eatery. The night air seems particularly refreshing. The moon looks rounder and every twinkling star is smiling at me. This is the happiest I have felt since I arrived in Canada over half a year ago.

As expected, I am unable to sleep that night. I never thought I would obtain immigrant status so soon. So many others have tried all kinds of tricks to get it: some have left wives or children behind; others have resorted to illegal means. It seems that the "fake marriage" that Huang, Hong arranged for me is a feasible short cut. After I become a Canadian citizen in three years' time, I'll "divorce" Lin, Tianci and look for a boyfriend in order to form a real family. Unable to sleep, I phone my Mom in Shanghai to tell her the good news. She is certainly happy for me, but she also advises me to take care. In a mother's eyes, children never grow up. Mothers always give the same advice. As usual, I tell her the result, not the whole procedure I went through for immigration. The actual methods I used would cause anxiety for family members on the other side of the ocean.

"Qilin Restaurant" runs smoothly with a regular clientele as expected. We have a profit of $21,000 in the four months up till the end of the year, which means over $5,000 every month. As we planned, the first year's earnings will be used as the flowing capital of our company, so Huang and I will each receive a monthly salary of $2,000 in the first year. I feel relieved and go to work at the restaurant from 4 pm until midnight, while Huang is responsible for lunch. During the daytime, I go to language school to learn English. After all, I live in

Canada and English proficiency is a necessity. Having passed the driving test, I have bought a brand new black Toyota. This set me back over twenty thousand dollars. Thus, I have spent almost all of the 250 thousand dollars I brought here, with the biggest bet on the restaurant.

81. Home Break-in by Gangsters

Who would have expected that the business at the "Qilin Restaurant" would fall off drastically at the beginning of 1995, with the monthly net profit totaling only $500, about one tenth of the previous months? I immediately look for the cause of this downturn with Huang, Hong and Lin, Tianci. We discover two reasons for it: first, a new restaurant has opened just next door. Their dishes are 20% cheaper than ours, especially for dim sum at noon. Everything costs $1.50 a dish, while we charge $2 for small dishes, $2.50 for medium and $3 for big dishes. As a result, we are not competitive at all. Second, there is a slackening of demand for our Japanese food, with only a couple of customers one evening. Thus, less fresh food is purchased for the restaurant, as the demand is less. A vicious cycle ensues: if the customer tastes something below par, he won't come back.

We reach a decision to maintain the current prices for dim sum, because it's meaningless to attract a lot of customers without making a profit. The customers for dinner are usually different from those who come for dim sum lunch. We offer dinner combos and, in coordination with Chinese super markets, give customers who spend over $100 a bag of scented rice worth $10. Just when I am terribly upset about the state of the restaurant business, my family members in Shanghai suddenly phoned me on February 3rd, telling me that my Grandma, in her seventies, has had a heart attack. Since Grandma brought me up and I have a stronger bond with her than with my parents, I will regret it forever if I don't go home. Moreover, I have been away for three years, so I decide to return to Shanghai at once, leaving the business totally in the care of Huang, Hong and Lin, Tianci.

Miraculously, on the third day after I return home, Grandma fully recovers. Everybody in the family is greatly relieved. Looking at me with tears in her eyes, Grandma tells me that she often sees me in her dreams. She refuses to accept the 500 US dollars I give her, insisting that I must have suffered a lot struggling alone overseas... I can hardly keep from bursting into tears. Perhaps she and I have a special telepathy because she alone brought me up. At a mere glance, she seems to have seen through my changes. Grandma, you are always my good Grandma; but your Yuanyuan is not the old one in your mind. That Yuanyuan has gotten lost and become helpless.

Although I have been away from Shanghai for only three years, the city has undergone enormous changes, particularly in Pudong. Such changes involve great leaps with a solid foundation, not just superficial changes as in Shenzhen. Shanghai is honored once more as the "Paris of the Orient". Many of my former classmates in medical school have got jobs in private enterprises and over half of my high school classmates have gone abroad. It is obvious to me that we have lost our past tacit understanding and congeniality because we are interested in different things now. We have grown up and each of us is going his own way.

Probably because I have obtained immigrant status in Canada, I feel like a visitor returning to Shanghai. I think constantly about the "Qilin Restaurant" in Toronto. I stay for less than three weeks and am anxious to return to Toronto. I am worried about the business.

Before I leave Shanghai, Grandma holds my hand and says to me, "Yuanyuan, don't work too hard at earning money. Enough is as good as a feast. Promise me that you'll celebrate my eightieth birthday with me in a few years. It would be even better for you to return with your sweetheart. You're not too young. You should start a family."

I nod silently, which says everything. Finally, I promise her that I'll come to Shanghai to celebrate her eightieth birthday in June 1999.

Just as I feared, business at the "Qilin Restaurant" is getting worse day by day. Income and expenses balance in February, but there is a deficit of $1,000 in March and $2,000 in April. Huang, Hong and I decide to close the Japanese food section, so the chef is sacked. The number of chefs in the kitchen is reduced from 8 to 6, and the number of waiters from 10 to 8 to cut down on expenses. A part-time worker is hired for weekends.

A horrific event occurs just when business at the restaurant is undergoing this drastic downturn. I am scared almost out of my wits. At dawn one Sunday, the doorbell rings while I am discussing restaurant stock with Lin, Tianci, who is responsible for the purchasing. After Lin opens the door, four huge masked men dash in. *Apparently, they are gangsters. I scream in fear when a man suddenly puts his hand over my mouth. Lin grabs the phone to call the police and two men charge forward to tie up his hands.*

"Behave yourselves, or lose your hand or leg. Give me all your money and jewelry!" The tallest man speaks in Mandarin with a Cantonese accent and brandishes a knife with a horn handle.

"Sir, we don't have much money as we just got married. Please let us go," Lin begs.

"Bullshit. Hurry! We don't have time to wait," the man holding my hands yells.

Getting no response, the tallest man comes to me and says lewdly while stroking my face, "No money? Your wife is not bad, with fine, smooth skin. Let the four of us fuck her, then, we don't demand you a cent from you, ha ha…"

"No, no, please don't! We'll give you money." Lin shouts at the top of his voice.

"You're nervous, aren't you? This guy really loves his wife. Why don't you hurry?" The tall man issues commands rudely.

The other two men follow Lin to his room and take more than $500 in cash.

The tall man, waving the bills in the air, says, "No way! We come all the way here for this little money? Damn it, that's not enough for our trip here. Hey, pals, bind him up and let him see how we fuck this whore…"

The fat man takes a roll of rope from his pocket and two of them get ready to tie Lin up when he kneels down all of a sudden, begging, "Sirs, please don't. I have two credit cards: follow me to the bank and I'll give you 3 to 4 thousand dollars."

"Go to hell. Do you want to send us to death?" The tall man kicks Lin ruthlessly, who yells in pain.

Witnessing this violence, I can no longer hesitate: I don't want anybody to die.

In desperation, I hit on a way out, "Don't beat him. Follow me, I've got money."

Two men follow me to my room. I open the safe in the built-in wardrobe and take out all my cash, around $10,000. These are the total earnings of the restaurant from today and yesterday: I usually deposit the money in the bank on

Monday. A bit dazed at first, the robbers become elated and put the cash in their black bag.

"Big brother, let's go. We've got around $10,000. It's smart of that little whore," the man tells the tall one, smiling.

"Let me warn you: don't call the police. We'll make you suffer if you rat on us!" The tall man waves his knife again.

"It's better to tie them up to avoid trouble." Saying this, the fat man hands another one a rope.

Swiftly, they tie our hands together and leave abruptly while shutting the door lightly. I can't help bursting into tears as soon as they leave.

"Don't cry. Let's try to loosen the ropes first." Lin remains calm.

Lowering his head, he exerts himself to loosen the grip by biting the rope. It has been over an hour since the gangsters left. I burst out crying with my head on his chest.

"Ah Lin, luckily you were home: otherwise, I would be dead."

"Miss Zhang, don't cry. Let's call the police first." Lin strokes my head.

"I'm scared. They'll kill us. Better not call the police," I beg him.

"Then we'll lose $10,000 for nothing when the restaurant is at a critical point. It's my fault for not checking before opening the door. I thought it was Huang, Hong," he says with a guilty conscience.

"I was lucky not to be raped by them. I really appreciate your help, Ah Lin."

"Don't be silly. How could I not help? Am I a man? Moreover, it concerns my safety."

"I'm to blame because I didn't call the home security company when you advised me to. If I had, we could have pressed the hidden button for help."

Lin says as if pondering, "Remember to call tomorrow. Spend scores of dollars to buy peace of mind. Don't tell anybody about this incident. I guess some people who are familiar with us planned the robbery or at least leaked information about us. The gangsters seemed to know that we had a lot of cash here and they were well prepared. We should watch everybody in the restaurant carefully. Well, it's 3 am. Let's rest."

Before entering my room, I tell him, "I have to deposit $10,000 from my private account to the company account. It's the last of my savings."

"*Okay, thanks for your help. When the case is solved, we'll explain to Huang, Hong.*"

Lying in bed, I am panic-stricken and confused. Lin's analysis is reasonable: there might be "internal devils". Who on earth would they be? Could they be the four staff members we just sacked? We explained to them that we were forced to do so because of the drop off in business. The unexpected break in, plus the poor business in the restaurant, is like snow on top of frost, making me shudder. How long will it take to earn the $10,000 we lost? In an instant, I've become penniless, with a dying restaurant and an unpredictable future. I never expected to lose the 250 thousand Canadian dollars I brought from Tokyo within a year or so. Without money, I lack a sense of security… Lin, Tainci, although not handsome, is kindhearted and courageous in the face of danger. I would be willing to do anything for him, even offer him my body. He doesn't take advantage of my misfortune and has never overstepped his bounds in the year we have lived together. He treats me like his sister.

82. Truth Revealed by Means of a Beauty Trap

Since the break in at the beginning of May, business at the "Qilin Restaurant" has not recovered from the setback. We lose money every month and have a deficit of $50,000 by the end of August, the first anniversary of the opening. Our rent has not been paid for three months, there is a pile of bills, and our operating capital is only $300. After some consultation, Huang, Hong and I decide to cut 4 more staff members, leaving 6 in the kitchen and 6 waiters, hiring 2 part-timers over the weekends. We have to get a loan of $100,000 from the bank to pay debts of $50,000, leaving the rest as operating capital to start afresh.

His mind tense with a great sense of urgency, Lin, Tianci invites an old chef from Hong Kong for instruction. After a close study of our menu, we decide to introduce a new series of specials. These include business combos at noon with a 10% discount to attract nearby office staff and dim sum from 9 pm until 3 am at a 20% discount to attract younger customers. For our "first anniversary sale", we spend a lot on advertising.

The ads on the front page of the "Sing Tao Daily" and the "World Journal" have a pretty good result. With the business similar to what it was after the opening a year ago, the restaurant does quite well, especially after midnight when youngsters arrive in groups. Huang, Hong and I ache all over after serving the dishes, but we are happy in our hearts. We want the business to take a turn for the better.

In the four months of our "first anniversary celebration", the business grows steadily and a regular clientele is formed. I am relieved when we have a net profit of $2,000 every month, and hope that this will continue to offset the deficit.

It seems that God likes to pull pranks on people. Just as it did in 1995, after the New Year in 1996, the business at the "Qilin Restaurant" experiences another drastic downturn. It is chiefly because more and more new restaurants are opening nearby and they serve less expensive dishes than we do. From January to May, we have an average deficit of $7,000 and our flowing capital is down to around $10,000. Physically and mentally exhausted, I have lost confidence in my ability to manage the restaurant. After consultation with Huang, Hong, I decide to sell it, at whatever price, as long as we can repay the debt of $100,000 to the bank.

After consultation with the real estate agent, we establish a sale price of $250 thousand for the "Qilin Restaurant". Over a dozen groups of potential buyers come to see it in the two months after the first advertisement, but no transaction takes place. Even after we lower the price to $200 thousand, nobody wants to buy it. We continue to have deficits in June and July, and our flowing capital is down to a mere $200 after the wages and rent are paid. I am like an ant on a hot frying pan, with my heart in my mouth every day. Every night, I have to take sleeping pills and I feel that I am on the verge of a nervous breakdown.

One night, I find some disparities in stock by chance while going through the account book at the restaurant. Why did we buy $20,000 worth of dried seafood when very few customers ordered abalone and shark's fin during the slack season of the recent 6 months? After meticulously checking the 10 invoices, I find that 9 of them were co-signed by Huang, Hong and Lin, Tianci, and only one was co-signed by Lin and me. Pretending to be cool, I quietly slip into the warehouse and find the remaining dried seafood worth only $2,000. I am determined to get to the bottom of this, feeling sure that a fraud has been committed. Being the chief chef, Lin is responsible for restocking, so he must have inside information. I'll find out the truth from him, and then track it down by following the clues.

After careful consideration, I decide to use "the beauty trap". I put on a semi-transparent nightgown that night after work and sit on the couch watching TV with Lin. Pretty soon, he becomes uneasy. I pour a glass of brandy for him. Having drunk half a glass, he fixes his eyes on my breasts, which are half exposed on purpose by me.

Unable to control himself, he throws himself upon me, saying indistinctly, "Miss Zhang, you're so beautiful! I'm sorry, sorry…"

"Ah Lin, there is no hurry. Go to my room. I want to show my appreciation." Hearing this, he follows me docilely.

I didn't expect that he would push me down like a wild bull and force himself on me in bed. Without any strength to resist, I have to let him trample all over me. After his climax, he goes to the living room for his glass of brandy, while I turn on the tape recorder under my bed and start sobbing.

He comes to comfort me, "I'm sorry, Miss Zhang. You're so pretty that I couldn't control myself. Rest assured, it's the first and last time that this will happen. Stop crying. Stop it. I can move out."

I cry in a louder voice and he holds me closely.

"Not for this. You've helped me a lot. Without your help, I would have been gang-raped by those four gangsters. I'm willing to give myself to you every night." I'm still sobbing.

"Then why are you crying?"

"The restaurant is on the verge of closing. I'm so worried that I want to kill myself to end everything."

"Never do that, for God's sake! I'll do everything for you." He pats his chest.

"I'm at my wit's end."

"Don't worry. Business at the restaurant will pick up if we make some adjustments. Don't be silly. Why commit suicide when you're so young? If the worst comes to the worst, we'll start over."

"By the way, Ah Lin, how is it that we bought over $20,000 worth of dried seafood in the last half year and there is so little left in the warehouse?"

After some hesitation, he confesses, while stroking my head, "I knew you'd find out about it sooner or later. It's all the fault of that woman Huang, Hong."

Seeing my frown, he continues, "That woman is too greedy. Many times, I have tried to confess to you, but I'm not bold enough, and I play a part in it as well. She is the culprit. We restock a lot of dried seafood. Then, I steal it from our restaurant and she resells it to other restaurants at a 20% discount. She takes 70% of the profit while I take 30%."

I am dumbstruck but he goes on. *"Miss Zhang, you've given yourself to me, so I'd be a beast if I didn't give you the facts. The break in by 4 gangsters last year was co-conspired by Huang and me. The four are our good friends. After the incident, they got $4,000 and Huang and I shared $6,000. The fat robber is her lover. Before you and I married, it was her idea for me to fabricate the story about a debt to a loan shark. We shared the $6,000 you lent to me. Huang only gave me half of the US$5,000 you mailed from Tokyo… Recently, she has been attempting to get your car. I don't have the heart to cheat you again, as you're so kind and under such heavy pressure with the business. Huang suspects that I cherish a genuine feeling for you… How much cash has been stolen by that damned woman!"*

Before he finishes his words, I experience a total breakdown and collapse on the bed, motionless.

"The only way out at this point is to split with Huang, Hong and don't investigate what happened before. That woman would be ruthless in her revenge. I have $20,000 in cash, which I'll give to you as compensation. I'll manage the restaurant well with you and we'll turn the deficit into a profit in less than half a year…"

I feebly say, *"Ah Lin, thanks for telling me the truth. I want to be left alone for a while."*

Late that night, tears soak my pillow. I never expected that my good friend from high school would resort to such despicable means to harm me. I cry till dawn, till my tears dry out.

83. A Trap by Former Classmate and Sale of the Restaurant

At 3pm the next day, I go to Huang, Hong's residence at the Kangcui Building with a copy of the tape recording. A fat man, sitting on the sofa, seems embarrassed to see me. "Anything urgent, Great Beauty, to come without calling first?"

"Does anybody want to buy our restaurant?" Huang says coquettishly.

On purpose I ask, "Have I met this gentleman before?"

"Oh, he often eats at our restaurant," Huang comes to his rescue quickly.

"Yes, I often go there," the fat man follows suit.

"Well, your voice left a deep impression on me. We talked late that night. There were four of you." I speak in a loud voice on purpose, having confirmed that he is one of the four gangsters at the break in.

"Fatty, you go first. We've got business to talk about." Sensing that something is going amiss, Huang cuts in with a quick wit and the fat man leaves quickly.

"Why are you in such a fury? Has your 'old friend' (period) come? I forgot to ask you if you still suffer from pain during your periods." She attempts to change the subject on purpose.

"Huang, Hong, we were good friends in our girlhood. Why do you treat me like this? Don't pretend any more. You know full well in your heart that you have behaved badly." So saying, I take the tape recording from my bag and throw it on her tea table.

"So, Ah Lin reveals everything after he takes advantage of you in bed. He has a share in everything, that bad guy!" She suddenly changes into a vicious woman that I have never seen before.

"We were good friends and I regarded you as my kin."

Lowering her head, she says, "Human beings will die for wealth, as birds for food. I am not as pretty as you are and not capable of earning money. I've used up all the money I earned in Shenzhen, earned with my blood and sweat..."

I yell in a hoarse voice, "You were not like this before."

"Miss, humans change. Have you heard that human beings are the products of their environment? You are supposed to have read a lot." She is using lame arguments.

"Just talk to me if you need money. I will give it to you. Why did you resort to such means? You know, I can sue you with this tape recording. This is Canada, with its sound legal system," I fly into a rage.

"My dear, don't forget that you are not a Canadian citizen. I can sue you for the fake marriage at any time! I have evidence and the Immigration Bureau will deport you." Shaking her folded legs, she becomes arrogant.

"You, you...I was blind to your premeditated plot. Do you know how difficult

it was for me to earn the money in Tokyo?" I am fuming with anger.

Gloating over my misfortune, she answers, "How hard? Just took off your pants. You think I don't know? What else can Shanghai women do? Either work as a dancer or be a mistress. Even the newspapers say so. How could you earn so much money in two years with a regular job?"

I burst into tears, "Why did you trap me if you knew?"

She lowers her head again, "My lady, I'm not the old Huang, Hong."

"Do you want to push me to my death?" I seem to say to myself.

"Zhang, Yuanyuan, you can't intimidate me with death. I've seen a lot of women like you. What are you afraid of? You have a huge capital: your sexy figure and your outstanding looks. You can have money all over, from top to bottom, from inside out..."

"Huang, Hong, you've really changed."

"As the popular saying goes: it's not my fault. It's the fault of society." She looks perfectly assured, as if justice were on her side.

She laughs lewdly, "I haven't finished. You can go on taking off your pants in Toronto."

"Why don't you do that then?" I ask with gritted teeth.

"My body is fat and, nobody wants to see it." She touches her chest and strokes her waist.

"How despicable you are!" I blurt out.

"Are you any better, my camp beau? Go to work at the massage parlor. Don't waste any time!" She has stood up and is ready to drive me out.

"I've been really blind!" I turn and run away.

She warns me again, "Don't forget about your fake marriage, which is illegal."

For several nights after I return home from the "Qilin Restaurant", I can't fall asleep. I can't understand why my sisterly classmate would harm me brutally like that. Who says that friends of childhood are the most reliable? To hell with them! Nobody can be trusted in this world except my parents who gave me life. If Aokawa Kakuai has ruined my body, Huang, Hong has thoroughly ruined my mental world. The damage done by the latter is greater and fiercer.

One morning at 3 am after tossing and turning, unable to sleep, I quietly get up and slip into my car for a ride. Aimlessly, I drive to downtown Toronto and *arrive at the well-known Bloor viaduct. This huge elevated bridge, with a history of over eighty years, is an outstanding engineering work, connecting two main streets from east to west – Bloor and Danforth. It was once one of the landmarks of Toronto.*

As record has it, construction on this bridge began in 1915. Using the most advanced technology at the time, 250 people worked simultaneously every day. With two bridge approaches on both banks, four piers connect in the middle. Because the upper riverbanks are sandy, the foundations of the piers were built on rocks. The laborers dug very deep underwater to erect those piers and filled them with thousands of tons of steel and concrete. It took three years to complete this double-deck bridge. The designers of the bridge were so far-sighted that they had railways built under the bridge for the future development of the city. Although built during the hard times of the First World War, the bridge has facilitated transportation in Toronto for many years. Fifty years later, it was much easier to build the Bloor - Danforth subway line.

I park my car in the parking lot of the bridge approach and stroll on the bridge alone, hoping the autumn wind will awaken me from my confused state of mind. Passing a telephone booth, I stand in the middle of the bridge, overlooking the DVP, with the magnificent sight of an incessant stream of cars and twinkling lights. During the daytime, there is a beautiful view of green trees on the hills and blue sky and white clouds. No wonder, this bridge has become attractive to those who want to commit suicide. In the past ten years, around a hundred people have jumped to end their lives. Twenty tragedies occurred last year. Hence, this bridge is customarily called a "suicide magnet". As more and more people killed themselves here in recent years, the government put up four telephones on the bridge to provide psychological counseling for potential suicides. The local residents strongly recommend installing devises to prevent suicide so no more tragedies will occur; unfortunately, this initiative will take a long time to accomplish.

If I jumped over, I'd end my life of 25 years and all my misery. Instantly, the viper Huang, Hong; the disgusting "Qilin Restaurant"; the pestering debts would all vanish… I feel as if I've gone back in time to the bank of Huangpu River five years ago: after strolling back and forth on the riverbank, I almost jumped into the river because of that heartless lover …

Just then a man suddenly grabs me from behind. I scream in panic.

"Miss Zhang, don't be scared. It's me, Ah Lin," says the man while still holding me, as if I'd jump down if he were to loosen his grip.

Looking aside, I find it really is Lin, Tianci.

"I was scared to death: I thought you were a wolf." I signal for him to loosen his hand.

He was still holding me tightly. I ask, "Why won't you loosen your grip?"

"Miss Zhang, don't do it! You're still young," says he in a loud voice.

Hearing this, I finally understand his intention. Unable to control myself, I throw myself into his arms and my tears wet his clothes.

Patting me on the shoulder, he says, "When I watched from afar, I thought you really intended to jump."

I pretend to be calm, "I'm not that silly!"

"Good, good! Even when faced with the greatest difficulties, never think of suicide," he talks to himself.

It turns out that he was watching my every move after I walked on to the bridge. He had followed me in his car until he almost ran out of gas in front of the viaduct. He sped to the gas station and then drove to the viaduct, looking high and low for me until he found my car in the parking lot. He drove onto the bridge at once.

Feeling him loosening his grip, I say subconsciously, "Ah Lin, you are not bad by nature."

"Miss Zhang, don't mention that! I owe you too much. Get in my car and we'll go to get yours in the parking lot. It's getting late." He helps me into his car.

When I look up, I see a gentle lilac light in the east, getting brighter and brighter. I look at my wristwatch and see that it is past 5 am already.

"Miss Zhang, you see the first glimmer of dawn will come in no time!" He uses this metaphor as he starts the engine.

Without responding, I fix my eyes on the glorious morning sun with all its shimmering rays. Will it be a fine day today?

Eventually the "Qilin Restaurant" is sold for the low price of $150,000 to a man from Taiwan in mid-September. Only $3,000 is left after the loan of $100,000 is repaid to the bank and all the arrears of rent are paid. According to our contract, I write a check of $600 to Huang, Hong, which comprises 20% of the remaining amount. Then, I separate from that woman forever. It's better to be far away from such a heartless woman, a woman whose conscience has been eaten by a dog!

I have to rent a less expensive apartment as I have only around $2,000 left. I reach an agreement with Lin, Tianci. I don't want him to repay me a cent and he promises to "divorce" me a year or so after I become a citizen. I'll obtain my freedom then. I have rejected his request to co-manage the "Qilin Restaurant" and his assurance to earn money. The mere mention of the word "restaurant" makes me sick. I don't intend to waste my youth in such an environment.

On the night before leaving the "Haoyuan Apartment Building", I go downstairs to say goodbye to Barbara. It has been three or four months since I saw her last. She finds me thinner and haggard. I have a good cry on her shoulder. After listening to my story, she calls me a foolish but lovely girl.

Before my departure, she advises, holding my hands closely, "My child, get up wherever you fall down. That's the Canadian spirit. Youth is your capital. It's not too late to start over. My door is wide open to welcome you. Call me and I'll do my best to help you."

Nights are cool at the end of September in Toronto. Lin moved out yesterday. I feel extremely lonely all by myself in the apartment. At midnight, I am scared when there is heavy rain with thunder and lightning. With the autumn rain, it will get colder gradually. I feel chilly in my heart when I realize that the terrible winter is coming soon.

Chapter Sixteen

"The Desperate Struggles of a Stripper"

84. Difficult Job-hunting

"Mean tricks are the passport for a mean person while nobility is the epitaph for a noble person."

The well-known poem by the obscure poet Bei, Dao, extremely popular in China in the Nineteen Eighties, is still fresh in my memory.

Although I am not very noble in my soul, I am still nobler than those people who are despicable. At least, I am faithful to my friends and I never intend to harm others. When I arrived in Toronto two and half years ago, I was a "little wealthy lady" possessing 250,000 Canadian dollars. Now I am penniless, ruined by my former classmate Huang, Hong. I have to thank that lady for teaching me a "vivid lesson" – always take precautions against others.

At the beginning of October 1996, I move from the Haoyuan Apartment Building to downtown Toronto, where the rents are very high. A shabby basement apartment costs me $600 a month. The $2,000 that I have will only cover the rent for two to three months. The black Toyota I have driven for over two years is my only property. The mere thought of my age, 25, sends cold shivers down my spine – how can I survive if I don't earn money at the end of my youth? Only by putting all my worries and pain behind me can I face the future.

I hunt high and low for a job. I won't look for one in a restaurant for fear of reminders of my painful past. It's impossible to obtain an office job with my current level of English. Companies run by people from Hong Kong won't hire me because I don't speak Cantonese. Thus, I have very little choice: I can work in a supermarket as a laborer or in a massage parlor. I have read reports that the latter is work in the sex trade and not professional massage. I am unwilling to get involved in this.

Two months have passed and I still haven't got a job. I feel helpless and hopeless, living alone in a dark basement. I feel as if I am in a living hell. If I pay the rent for the third month, I'll have only $50 left. Faced with the crisis of survival, I'll have to sell my car. Luckily, I paid the annual insurance premium at the beginning of the year. If I had to pay $200 every month, I'd have been penniless a long time ago.

Just then, I read an enticing ad in the English Newspaper, the "Toronto Sun": "The striptease training center will help you earn $300 a day". Striptease art is not new to me. Huang, Hong and I went to watch it once. It is a performing art that "allows only watching, not touching". Strip bars are one of Canadian men's places for entertainment. Some people joke: You've made the trip in vain if you didn't visit the CN Tower or a strip club in Toronto. The former resembles a penis, standing aloft in the city center and adding boundless vitality to the city. The latter involves sexy female breasts and buttocks, the hallmark of feminine beauty. Yin and yang are in a rare balance in the city. No wonder Toronto is one of the most livable cities in the world, an ideal place, with good feng shui, for settlement by people from China, Hong Kong and Taiwan.

With some curiosity, I call the striptease training center and get an immediate interview. Miss Mary, the general manager of the center, interviews me. A forty-something green-eyed blond, tall and slender, she would be a beauty if she didn't have wrinkles on her face. She tells me that she has been a stripper for over twenty years and likes the occupation very much. She opened the training center recently after she started to get older. She praises me for my ideal figure for dancing: she says that it will attract western men. She finds my oral English not fluent enough, but quite sufficient for a stripper. I follow her to the training hall and dance a few steps. Smiling, she promises me that I can get a license and find a job, guaranteed, after two weeks in the advanced training class. I am fully confident in this occupation, as I have been fond of singing and dancing since childhood. Moreover, it's really *enticing to be able to earn two to three hundred dollars a day! I decide to register at once, but I am scared by the tuition of $3,000. Seeing the changing color of my face, she says, smiling, that she'll give me a 20% discount. If I pay $2,400 in cash, there will be no tax. I agree to give it to her within three days.*

I intend to borrow the money from my "husband," Lin, Tianci. When we parted, he promised me that he would give me help at any time. Finally, I decide not to deal with him to avoid future trouble. I find it embarrassing to borrow from Barbara in order to learn how to strip. Besides, foreigners aren't in the habit of making personal loans. Without any other friends in Toronto, I'll have to sell my beloved Toyota.

I get several quotes from second hand car dealers. The highest bid for my car is only $12,000. I spent $20,000 for it two years ago and it has a mileage of only 30,000 kilometers. Unfortunately, I have no choice in this transaction. As I am used to driving and the striptease training center is twenty kilometers away, I can't manage without a car. I go to the same car dealer the next day and buy a second-hand Nissan for $6,000. After paying the tuition, I'll have a little over $3,000 left. My monthly rent plus car insurance and gasoline, without food, will cost me over $800. This money will keep me going for about three months.

I can only "fight with my back to the river" – to win or to die. I lay all my hopes on earning money for survival by stripping. I can't afford to fail; I must succeed.

It seems that Mary at the training center is a bit partial to me, often giving me extra individual instruction. She finds that I have a good sense of music and am adept at learning new things. It takes me only a week to master all the courses, including dancing skills, etiquette, makeup, dressing, etc. In the second week, in addition to the consolidation of the previous courses, she mainly brushes up on rock 'n' roll. When she asks me if I have an English name, the name "Camille" slips out of my mouth. She approves. I like the name because I love the camellia as I love my life. I also admire the novel of the same title by the great French novelist Dumas (Jr.).

On the last day of the training, Mary takes me to the MW Striptease Club on Yonge Street. The boss, George, a fat bald man with a moustache, looks exactly like the leader of an underworld society in the movies. Obviously, Mary and George are old acquaintances. They look a bit disgusting while they kiss and hug.

Holding my hand, George says, "What an oriental angel! Anyone Mary recommends is nice."

"Of course, otherwise you'd kill me." Mary responds flirtatiously while she holds his hand.

"Well, Camille, change your clothes and wait in Box 3 for a few trial photos." So saying, George leaves.

Mary takes me to Box 3 and asks me to change my clothes while warning me, "Don't be nervous. No matter how many people come to see you, you must smile and undress with coquettish skills. You will succeed."

Later, George brings in a man with messy long hair. He is said to be Thomas, the first DJ. Mary smiles to them and takes her leave.

Thomas nods to me and the music starts. Wearing a bra and briefs, I dance merrily to the rhythm of the music while smiling a little. When the second melody begins in four or five minutes, I dance while slowly taking off my bra and twisting my upper body. My two breasts seem to be flying. When the third melody sounds, I shyly and slowly take off my briefs, shooting out coquettish glances while twisting my waist and buttocks.

"Okay. Not bad," Thomas blurts out as soon as music ends.

Covering myself with a blanket, I wait for their comments, my heart beating fast. The feeling is similar to the anxious wait for the results after the entrance exam to university. I have the premonition that this is a turning point in my life.

Rolling his big eyes, George says to me, "Camille, when can you start to work?"

"Any time." My whole body is singing and dancing with joy, like a happy bird.

Thomas says, "Let me see. Start tomorrow. Try to succeed at the very beginning. You have to watch the organic coordination of dance and music."

Before leaving, Thomas adds, "You are the first Chinese woman we've employed. Perhaps, the business will be even better."

Mary, who is waiting outside, rushes to embrace me tightly, making it hard for me to breathe. I am overexcited and there are tears in my eyes. It is so difficult to find a job and I don't have to worry about my rent for a few months. I treat her to a Bloody Mary to show my appreciation. I order a glass of Singapore wine to soothe myself.

Before parting outside the bar, Mary says, smiling, "Dance well, my sweetheart. They are going to promote you and make you famous. They say you are an Oriental sex devil. Don't forget that it was I who discovered you when you earn the big bucks."

"There is an old saying in China: He who is a teacher for one day is like a father for his whole life. I'll visit you, Mary." I respond with a smile.

85. A Stripper's Struggle

December 20th 1996 is the first day I work at the "MW Striptease Bar" on Yonge Street. This is an important turning point in my life, because from now on, naked, I'll have to face men of different races, colors and ages. George, the boss, makes it clear that the company pays no wages. I have to survive on patrons' tips. It is hard to predict whether the future will be good or bad.

When I arrive at the bar, Thomas asks me to the box to tutor me individually on the organic coordination of music and dance. Finally, he and I decide on three familiar melodies to use tonight. This man, who seems not caring much about his appearance, looks cool and detached. His eyes behind his glasses are extremely sharp and profound. He doesn't talk much, but he always talks precisely and works with passion. As soon as the music starts, he assumes his role and dances to the musical symbols, so to speak. He advises me not to be too eager to go up on stage to dance, but to watch the senior dancers' steps and learn from them.

Finally, Thomas talks to me seriously, "You have a foundation for dancing. It would be good if you could pay more attention to the harmonious coordination of action and music. At 8 pm sharp, the prime time, I'll let you do your first dance. Before 8 pm, don't perform on the stage: just dance casually for patrons and familiarize yourself with the environment. Take time to watch the dancers on stage."

The business is a bit slack in the afternoon. An aged white stripper is dancing on stage wildly under the dim lights. The neon lights of beer ads are sparkling on the wall, while neon ads of naked ladies twinkle indistinctly. About ten strippers are wandering around at the base of the stage in the dark, soliciting patrons. I also walk around several times to see how business is going. Boxes excluded, the hall is quite big, with a capacity of 150. Although the boss clearly states that the patrons are not allowed to touch the dancers, several of them, to my surprise, permit the customers to stroke their upper bodies. Some in the boxes even allow patrons to touch their lower bodies. Lewd laughter is heard.

Purposefully, I sit in front of the quiet bar and order a "screwdriver" cocktail. I want to talk to Allan, the bartender, to find out the reason for this activity. Mary has advised me repeatedly to build a good relationship with the bartender, because strippers have to pay for their drinks unless they are treated by patrons. Around forty and terribly emaciated, Allan looks like a drug addict, but his curly hair makes him look natural and unaffected.

"Congratulations on your new start. This is my treat." Allan is all smiles when he sees me sit down, perhaps glad to have someone to chat with.

I merely mention the strippers being touched by customers when Allan starts talking, "As you are green, you'll learn gradually. If you dance routinely, you'll earn less than $60 a day and exhaust yourself with the dancing. If you permit the patrons to touch your upper body, you'll get $200 a day, guaranteed. If you allow them to touch your lower body, you'll get $300 a day. Moreover, if you follow them after the shift, you'll earn even more. You have to take precautions, however: some men are diabolical. Do not get into their cars casually. There are 2,500 licensed strippers in Toronto alone, so the competition is fierce. How can you earn money if you don't use your brains?"

Now I come to realize what it means by "earning $300 a day" in the newspaper ads. I've taken the first step, however, so I haven't much choice. I have to wait and see while preserving my purity.

Seeing my perplexity, Allan reminds me, "Be aware that dancing on patron's legs is prohibited here. Police will conduct surprise searches and some of them are in plain clothes. Of course, it's another matter to let patrons touch you. The key is your sense of propriety."

"Allan, thank you very much for your guidance. Your kindness is greatly appreciated. I'll treat you to a glass of wine now and a Chinese dinner later. Do you like Chinese cuisine?" I secretly give him $10 and he stretches out his hand to get it, while saying "no".

"Certainly I do, but wait until you earn more money. It will be your show tonight. Today is Friday, the best day for business. Besides, you should build a good relationship with Thomas, who is a famous DJ. He graduated from the Royal Conservatory of Music and works part time here. He is a good friend of George, the boss, who consults with him about everything. Thomas is more powerful than a full-time manager." Putting the money in his pocket, Allan talks excitedly.

I am grateful to Allan from the bottom of my heart. I believe that "one talk with him benefits me more than reading books for ten years".

After 5 pm, customers come into the bar in groups, some in suits and leather shoes, and others in heavy down-filled jackets. Seven or eight waitresses in mini-skirts start to get busy. Several of them are said to have been strippers who became waitresses as they got older.

While I wander around at the base of the stage, a fat man waves to me, so I go and sit in front of him on a small stool.

"How come I never saw you before? Is this your first day?" The fat man shakes hands with me courteously.

I reply with a story Mary has made up, "I came from Windsor yesterday."

"Oh, I see. It's good to have you here. I am Victor. I come here almost every day. I'll try somebody new today."

When the music starts, I take off my jacket and twist my body in my pink bra and panties. The fat man looks at me while drinking his beer. In three minutes when the music ends, I slowly take off my bra. The fat man fixes his eyes on my upper body, without stirring. When the second melody starts, I continue to dance. After the third melody begins, I am stark naked. The fat man glares at me as if he would devour me. This is frightening.

"Beautiful, so beautiful! You are an Oriental Venus!" As soon as I stop dancing to the music, the fat man applauds eagerly.

"Take a break, then continue, please." He gives me $50 and orders an iced orange juice for me from the waitress.

Usually, a group of three dances lasting three minutes costs a customer $10. That means I'll have to dance four more groups for the fat man. Unexpectedly, after I dance two more groups, he gives me another $50 and orders a glass of "Singapore commander" wine for me. What has he got up his sleeve? After going to the washroom, I go over to Allan the bartender to inquire about Victor. Allan says that I've met my savior. The fat man is a computer engineer, upright and generous, and a good friend of George's for many years. Living close by, he comes here almost every day. Reassured, I return to the fat man and dance two more groups. He asks me to take a rest and says he will see me later. He really is a gentleman and hasn't touched me at all during the half hour that I've danced for him.

Later, a white man waves his hand at me. He asks me to dance five groups of dances and pays me $50. When I dance the fourth group, he attempts to touch my upper body, but I politely refuse. He hasn't done anything improper since then. It seems that the patrons are pretty civilized. Within two hours, I've earned $150: easy money.

At 8 pm, the hall is almost packed. I wait beside Thomas backstage in the sound room, getting ready to go on stage. Along with the thrilling rock 'n' roll music, Thomas introduces me in a cadenced and rhythmic voice, "Dear friends, the first dancer on stage will be Camille, the Oriental goddess. At 25, coming to Toronto from Windsor, she is an experienced stripper with a strong sense of rhythm, so she is very popular in the USA and Canada!"

With a smile on my face, I go on stage leisurely, wearing an almost transparent white gauzy cape and white high-heeled shoes. Walking to and fro on stage for a little while, I let the gauzy cape drop naturally onto the floor, revealing my black bra and black panties. This arouses stormy applause throughout the hall. I twist my body rhythmically, closely following the music.

When the second gentle and crisp melody starts, I slowly take off my bra and show off my firm breasts, which cause quite a stir in the audience. Then, I hold my bra and swirl it in the air several times before throwing it in the direction of where Victor sits. This causes a commotion. I exert myself, twisting my body to the rhythm of the music.

When the third sentimental melody begins, the lights on stage suddenly dim. By now, I have taken off my panties and shoes and am lying on a carpet, stark naked. To the rhythm of the music, I raise my two legs, forming an angle of 90 degrees with my back. Then I open my two legs and close them quickly, revealing my private parts indistinctly. There is a hubbub under the stage with some people whistling nonstop. Then I hold my legs tightly with my two hands. Twirling my body 360 degrees by using the strength of my back, I suddenly stand up, show my body naturally and dance at a fast pace. Another stormy applause explodes, mixed with blowing kisses and screams. Some patrons simply throw cash onto the stage.

"Dear Spectators, seeing is believing. Now you've enjoyed the exquisite dancing skills of Camille, the Oriental goddess. She'll be performing on stage again at 11 pm. Please don't miss it." Thomas praises me again.

The strenuous performance of over ten minutes has me perspiring all over. Covering myself in a large blanket, I rush to the shower in spite of the customers' disturbance. After a shower and an application of fresh makeup, I sit resting in front of the counter. Several strippers immediately leave, as if I were the plague. I'll have to guard against them: they may be suffering from the "jealousy disease".

Allan, the bartender, treats me like a princess, hands me a glass of iced orange juice and says, smiling, "I predict that you'll be successful right now at the very beginning. Right? To tell you the truth, we haven't had such a sensation for several months. The patrons prefer the new to the old faces. What else can we do? You should be grateful to Thomas who is really doing his best to promote you."

Before responding to his comments, I am invited to dance again. The whole night sees me dancing for one group after another and my purse is soon filled with money. My second performance at 11 pm causes another commotion in the audience. It is only after midnight that I have time to go back to Victor, the fat man, who is talking with three friends.

He gladly puts his arm around my waist, and says to me, "Sit down. George has got sharp eyes to invite you here, Oriental Venus."

I reply unaffectedly, "I am a newcomer, and it's very kind of you to patronize me. I'll treat you to a drink since business is good today."

"Are you kidding? How can I let you treat us?" The fat man pulls a long face. "You've treated me a lot. Give me a chance."

The waitress serves five bottles of Molson beer. Everybody warmly congratulates me on my successful first show. People at other tables all look at us. It is nothing to treat him to a few bottles of beer. I want to win the fat man's favor, so he can be my temporary support at least. The relationships in this sort of environment are very complicated and those strippers, who seem hostile to me, are difficult to deal with. Being alone, I need to find someone rich and powerful *to rely on. When I was naïve and immature before, I was swindled and suffered great losses. From now on, I, Zhang, Yuanyuan, must think carefully before I act.*

At 2 am I finish work and politely refuse two patrons' invitations to dim sum. It takes a little over twenty minutes to drive home, an ideal distance. Lying in bed exhausted, I am unable to fall asleep. I never expected that I'd earn over $800 on my first day. Perhaps, I am lucky and have met an eminent person who will help me. Perhaps fortune comes in cycles. I have been down on my luck for so long, it's my turn to have a lucky break.

86. Chance Encounter with a Student from Taiwan

During the Christmas and New Year season, business at the MW Strip Bar flourishes. I work six days a week and have a day off on Sunday. My daily average income is around $300. Other dancers are doing pretty well, except some of the older ones who only earn about $100. They wish the customers would touch them.

Victor, the fat man, treats me quite well, often asking me to perform for him. In the first month, I earn over $7,000, a sum which is hard to earn doing any other high-ranking job. Moreover, my breasts and lower body have never been touched by anybody and I have not had any illicit relationships with customers. Thus, I look at stripping in a new light: strippers have no inevitable link with the selling of their bodies. The occupation is not degrading if one preserves one's purity.

As Allan the bartender predicted, February and March are slack months for the business, perhaps because people have to tighten their belts after the New Year. Thanks to my old patrons, I can still earn about $3,000 a month. But it is harder to make money during these two months. In the slack season, customers pick and choose strippers, especially those who are totally "open" to them. If I reject the customers the first time, they won't choose me the second time and will pick others instead.

After much consideration, I decide not to be aloof while I am engaged in this trade. If I can earn money, what do I care if they touch my upper body? It's not sexual intercourse, anyway. Finally, I decide to be "open" about my upper body, but keep my lower body off limits, unless there is a particularly good bid.

It really broadens my horizons to engage in this trade, and to meet all sorts of men. It is understandable for single men to request sex. For those who have wives, they want something exotic or perhaps they lack sexual communication with their wives. They would rather bring their sexual fantasies and requests to us. I want to remind women that once they marry, they should satisfy their husbands' desires and fulfill their duties as wives. Who can the wives blame if they fail to satisfy their husbands, who then go elsewhere for pleasure? Maybe that's perfectly justified. A successful woman controls a man's wallet and makes him desire her every night.

Some customers attempt to become intimate with me as soon as we meet. I find this detestable and ludicrous. In their eyes, strippers are lowly beings and are just tools to be used to satisfy their sexual urges. I meet a student from Taiwan, named Lian, Haotien in February. A self-professed Ph.D. student at the University of Toronto, he wants me to go to bed with him the first time we meet. I refuse, but he keeps pestering me. He comes every week, sometimes twice a week, for me alone. I pity him, so I allow him to touch my upper body. He pays me generously for this favor.

In April and May, Lian brings his cousin Lai, Wenxiong to the bar. Said to be a Ph.D. student at Waterloo University, Lai has a cool appearance. We seem to be connected by fate and talk cordially with each other from the very beginning.

I still remember faintly the first question I ask him, "What's your relationship with Qin, Han (a famous actor in Taiwan –translator's note)?"

"You must have seen a lot of movies by Qiong, Yao," he says, smiling.

"You're not answering my question, though." I look in his eyes and speak a bit naughtily.

He moves closer to my ear and answers, "Not comrades, nor brothers, let alone a father and son. We are both from Taiwan. That's all."

I can't help but laugh at his peculiar manner. We go on talking about movies: he is thoroughly familiar with the film stars in mainland China, such as Chen, Chong and Liu, Xiaoqing. Later, he treats me to a drink and we talk so excitedly that we almost forget Lian, Haotien sitting beside us.

I hint to Lai to go to the box and he follows me immediately. This kills two birds with one stone: to leave that disgusting Lian and to "open" my upper body to Lai. Usually, I don't allow customers to touch me on the first meeting, even at a high bid. Who knows what kind of a person the customer is? Perhaps, he is a policeman in plain clothes, and then I'll get into trouble.

In the dim lights, Lai stealthily strokes my breasts while telling some humorous erotic jokes. He seems a bit worried that the police might charge in. I find him foolish, but sweet. He seems to be interested in my feet and starts stroking one foot.

"You are unique. What's intriguing about my foot? Is it better than my breasts?" I am puzzled.

He answers seriously, as if he has discovered a new continent, "You might not realize that your feet are very sexy and are not inferior to other parts of your body."

I am curious, "That's something new. It's the first time people have praised my feet. I read in the 'Water Margin' that Ximen, Qing strokes the bound feet of Pan, Jinlian and arouses her sexuality…"

He speaks pedantically, "Study of the feet is a branch of learning for which you could write a Ph.D. thesis… Speaking of feet, I wonder if you have seen the shoe museum? Just near by. I went there this morning. It's worth your while to visit it."

"Engaged in this occupation, where would I find the leisure time to go sightseeing? Our days and nights are reversed, you know. Besides, I'm not really interested." I speak directly into his ear because of the loud music.

He says with minute care, "You should take a walk in the streets during the day time to get some sunshine. That would be beneficial to your health."

Never has anybody shown such care for me in the strip bar. I am touched to the bottom of my heart. My gratitude to him, hidden in my memory, makes our reunion a few years later an experience I will treasure forever. This Lai, Wenxiong will play a significant part in my later life, which I'd like to keep secret for now.

Perhaps the coming of Lai, Wenxiong has brought me good luck. My business picks up in June and I earn over $6,000, almost the total of my earnings during the two previous months. Things are looking up for me. My mood is completely controlled by my earnings: I am elated if I get over $5,000 a month, but become downcast if I earn less than $3,000. At present, I have savings of more than $20,000. I hope that the positive trend will continue in June.

With my purse full, and in higher spirits, I finally have the desire to go sightseeing in the streets. My favorite place is Yorkville, a fashion street, not only good for shopping and walking for ordinary people, but also a magnet for YUPPIES. Actually, it is a commercial district, which extends along Yorkville,

Cumberland and Bloor with a tiny park, exquisite clothing stores, art galleries, furniture stores, pet stores, restaurants and cafes. A lot of people work in the Yorkville area. Quite often, people can catch a glimpse of American and Canadian movie stars there.

Bloor Street, famous for its expensive boutiques, boasts such famous brands as Chanel, Hermes, Emporio Armani, and Versace. I buy many of my dresses in these stores. I enjoy visiting them even when I'm not shopping. Walking for three hours, buying just a couple of pairs of underwear—these activities do not tire me. Apparently, this energy is owing to my good mood. Women are, after all, moody beings.

On my way home, I pass the Bata Shoe Museum and find a crowd of people waiting there. It turns out that there is a ticket sale and this attracts a huge audience. I have not visited the museum since it opened over a year ago. Recalling Lai, Wenxiong's strong recommendation last time I saw him and thinking that I have lots of time, I join the queue.

I have read in the newspaper that this is the only shoe museum in the west. It boasts the largest collection of shoes in the world. With five stories, the magnificent museum was built by private funds: no government money was spent. The name of the museum comes from Bata Shoes, one of the biggest shoe companies in the world. Around 10,000 shoes are on display, spanning a period of 4,500 years.

The museum is a world of shoes. Even the signs in the cloakroom and on the walls are made of leather, the material for making shoes. Badges with pictures of the various kinds of shoes are displayed on the railings of the stairs. The goal of this design scheme is to reflect the theme of the museum in every corner of the building.

The eccentric shoes are really charming. The wooden shoes of the moon shiners of Belgium; the clogs of Japan; the high-heeled shoes of Sirikit, Queen of Thailand; the soft-wood high-heeled shoes of the courtesans of 17th century Venice and the slippers worn in the Burmese court are all displayed here.

I can hardly tear myself away from the shoes of Winston Churchill, Picasso, Elvis Presley and Elton John…I think I have discovered Lai, Wenxiong's intention in recommending this museum to me. Not only does he like my sexy feet, but he also hopes that I will follow a bright path with my feet. I can clearly recall *the words he said, smiling, before he left. He said that he would visit me again for my sexy feet. On my way back home, a proverb suddenly comes to mind: "A journey, no matter how long, is started by taking the first step". How do I start on the uncertain road ahead?*

87. The Bartender, a Beast in Human Form

At the end of July, something sensational happens to Allan the bartender and me. It almost results in death. The memory of this incident still makes my hair stand on end. He is a sinister and despicable man! It's not that I want to curse him: he deserves damnation and will come to no good end.

One late night after our shift, he invites me to Chinatown for dim sum. As usual, I sit on the back of his high-speed motorcycle, holding onto his waist and feeling thrilled. In his mid-thirties and unmarried, he declares that he has lost interest in women because he has seen so many naked women at the bar. He lives in Toronto alone, while his parents reside in Quebec. Since the very first day I started work at the MW Strip Bar, he has given me a lot of help, advising me on relations with other people. We talk about everything and are like brother and sister. Under my influence, he has become interested in Chinese culture and is fond of Chinese cuisine. Every two or three weeks, we go to Chinatown for dim sum. I long ago discovered that he takes drugs and advised him to quit, to no avail.

In the middle of our dim sum dinner that night, he attempts to borrow $3,000 from me. He says he wants to buy heroin at a cheaper price and has only $5,000 on hand. I have lost so much money in the past because of my blind trust in others that I "turn pale" at the thought of anyone borrowing money from me. Furthermore, Allan hasn't returned the $300 he borrowed from me three months ago.

I give him a flat rebuff, "I really have no money. As you know business is slack these days."

"Nobody in our bar has any money if you don't. You are the No.1 star in our MW Bar," he says with a false smile.

"You're kidding. I don't allow customers to touch my lower body. How could I earn more than the others? I really have no money. Plus, I have to mail money to Shanghai as my Grandma is seriously ill."

"Well, don't pretend to be poor. You'll get several hundred dollars when you go to bed with Victor, the fat man."

"You believe these rumors, don't you? To tell you the truth, he has never touched me at all. I swear to God." I raise my hand.

"Okay, I'll think of some other way if you say no."

"Allan, as a friend, I would like to advise you: drug trafficking is not a legal business. The police will be after you."

"To tell you the truth, I want to earn more money. If I were a woman, especially a pretty woman like you, I would be sure to earn a lot. All I would have to do is take off my pants. It's so simple."

I remain silent. In his eyes, women like us are just machines for sex. He thinks that I have been such an object for a long time. I am so wronged that I couldn't cleanse myself even if I jumped into Lake Ontario! Perhaps in many people's eyes, there is no difference between a stripper and a whore.

After dim sum, I ride on Allan's motorcycle, still laughing on the way. After some time, however, I become aware that something is wrong. Normally, he takes me back to the bar and I drive my own car home. But now he is riding fast along Lakeshore Boulevard. Fewer people and less traffic can be seen on either side. My instinct makes me panic, so I turn and shout, "Allan, where are you going? I want to go home. Let me get off."

"Shut up! Otherwise I'll push you off," he responds rudely.

The motorcycle is heading east along a road with wild grass on both sides. My sixth sense indicates that a disaster may befall me soon. Frightened to tears, I feel like a lamb on the way to the slaughterhouse.

The motorcycle stops in front of a dumpsite. Taking off his helmet, Allan grabs my hand and pulls me forward.

"What are you up to, Allan? I can lend you $3,000. Don't act foolishly."

"$3,000? It's not that easy. What I want is $30,000, or $300,000."

Passing the dumpsite, we come to a shabby big house, probably an old barn scheduled for demolition. He pulls me into a room and turns on his flashlight. The room is almost vacant with only a tattered bed and a lot of beer bottles. There is a horrible smell.

"Sorry to have put you to such inconvenience, Oriental Venus. Tonight I'll

teach you how to make money." Rolling his green eyes, he opens his mouth lewdly.

Seeing me standing there dumbly, he pushes me onto bed, tears my dress and rapes me like a wild beast.

There is no use yelling in such a desolate place. I just shut my eyes and let him have his way with me.

Around twenty minutes later, he sits up, fully satisfied, and says while smoking, "You are really worthy of your name. You're great, in fact. You should make loads of money."

"Why did you treat me like that? I thought of you as my brother…" I burst out crying.

"Don't cry or your head will be chopped off! Don't you know that I'm a member of the 'Thunder Motorcyclists'"? He draws a knife with a long handle from under the bed.

I am scared out of my wits when I hear the name "Thunder Motorcyclists". I have read about their crimes in the newspapers. They are good-for-nothing youths, mostly unemployed. They like to live in abandoned houses, scribbling anti-government or racial stuff on the walls, stealing, robbing, raping etc. Last month they killed three prostitutes and burned down a strip club. The police are looking for them. I never suspected that the outwardly kind Allan would be one of them.

"Scared to death? I won't kill you if you obey me. I depend on you to earn money. I chose you a long time ago. If you listen to me, I guarantee that you'll earn $1,000 a day."

Allan tells me his "great scheme". He wants me to quit my job at the MW Strip Bar and reserve a room at the downtown Hilton Hotel. I will be a high-ranking prostitute with a fee of at least $300 per person. He will still work as a bartender in the bar and procure patrons for me, ten a day. By these means, he'll be my pimp and get 50% of my income.

My God! Overnight, have I become a prostitute under the control of the gangsters?! I shiver with fear and am in a cold sweat. Allan, you beast in human form, this "wonderful plan" of yours will make me your ready source of cash so you can take drugs and rape me at will. What a great idea: kill two birds with one stone!

"Do you agree or not? If you call the police, I'll throw you into Lake Ontario!"

He rudely pinches my upper body.

I'd be looking for trouble if I rejected him flatly. I'd rather evade the current trouble with some diplomacy.

"Allan, it's not a bad idea. However, we have to think more carefully. To tell you honestly, George the boss and Thomas are pretty nice to me. I can't just leave them. I want to have patrons during the day at the hotel and dance in the bar at night." I am begging him.

"That's OK for the time being. You can quit the bar job when we have more patrons." He slams me down again, holds me tightly and pushes into me roughly, as if he hasn't been with a woman for decades.

It is almost daybreak when I stagger back to my own little nest. The golden rays of the sun look like a black curtain to me. My tears have run dry. I never expected that I would escape the abyss of suffering in Tokyo to fall into a living hell in Toronto. Who says human beings can control their fate? My destiny is always under the control of others. God, please open your eyes and rescue me, a lonely and vulnerable woman.

88. Forced Prostitution under Gangster's Control

In the afternoon, I have to pluck up my courage to go to work at the MW Strip Bar. Allan, the bartender, greets me with a smile, as if nothing has happened. I intended to pour out my grievances to the boss, George, or to fat Victor, or to phone my friend Barbara, but I am terror-stricken at what Allan said before parting: "Don't tell anyone or you'll be dead in three days."

I have to bear all this pressure alone, weighed down with anxieties every day. I use delaying tactics to deal with Allan: I avoid private meetings with him and rush home after work. Like a badly frightened bird, I am so scared that I am afraid I might go crazy.

One night a week later, when I start the engine of my car after my shift, a man suddenly stands up in the back seat. I scream in fear.

"Shut up! I'll kill you if you scream again. Oriental Venus, why haven't you replied after a week? Drive your car to the Hilton Hotel and go straight to Room 708, where a friend of yours is waiting." I hear a young masked foreigner's voice.

'Who are you? Don't act recklessly," I beg him.

The man with the mask answers, "Do you have to ask? You're lovely, but foolish. Be assured, I don't kill innocent people. But, you have to co-operate with us."

This man must be Allan's cohort. I don't dare say anything. I drive according to his instructions and park my car at the Hilton Hotel. The man jumps out of the car and vanishes.

I go straight to Room 708 and find the door unlocked. The vacant room horrifies me. I collapse on the couch, my heart beating wildly. In ten minutes, Allan charges into the room, alone.

"Do you like it here, my Oriental Venus? It's a bit small, but it costs a hundred bucks a day." He pushes me roughly on to the bed.

"Keep me company for a while first. In an hour, a distinguished guest, an old American man, will come. An hour with him will earn you US$600. Good enough for you?" Before I say anything, he is all over my body.

In an hour, an aged foreigner comes knocking at the door. He says he is 70 years old, but he looks 60. After having sex with me for an hour, he pays US$700 and leaves, satisfied. Immediately, Allan rushes in and snatches away US$300.

"No more talking. You stay here from now on. Two customers will come tomorrow before noon and three in the afternoon. Every customer pays $400 for an hour. I'll let you know about tonight's customers later."

After Allan leaves, I cry my eyes out while taking a shower in the bathroom. No matter how much I wash, I can't cleanse myself of this shame. No matter how I cry, I can't rid myself of my misery. I'll always remember this date: August 8th 1997. This is the first day I work as a prostitute and get increasingly involved in prostitution. I don't know how on earth I got on this path of no return. Is it my fault or society's fault?

Having thought about it seriously for several days and nights, I decide to "divorce" Lin, Tianci after I take my citizenship oath at the end of August. Then, I'll quietly leave the MW Strip Bar and extricate myself from Allan's control. Since I have "gone to the sea" as a prostitute, I want to rid myself of others' control so I can keep my hard-earned money. Involvement with the "Thunder Motorcyclists" will surely end in disaster or violent death.

At the citizenship oath, I almost burst out crying while singing Canada's *national anthem. Under the beautiful and poetic maple leaf, how many dirty black hands are stirring? I shouldn't blame Canada, though. It was my own choice to embark on the treacherous road of immigration. Nobody beat me or forced me. I have only myself to blame for my stupidity and ignorance. I can blame neither heaven nor earth. My own destiny led me to this place.*

The "divorce" with Lin, Tianci is simple and easy. He hasn't changed much after a year, but he stares at me as if I were a rare animal.

Realizing the meaning of his stare, I say to him self-consciously, "Ah Lin, have I aged a lot?"

Without answering, he just nods. Then he speaks pensively, "Miss Zhang, don't work too hard. The road ahead is still long."

"Canada implies hardship. Everybody has to struggle for survival." I pretend to be nonchalant.

At present, he works as the second chef at the "Chongqing Restaurant" in Scarborough, living an average life, still single. Huang, Hong is said to have returned to Shanghai and is managing a restaurant.

Before parting, he says repeatedly, "Miss Zhang, I'm really sorry. I was heartless to you before…"

I hold his hand, "It's not important to me any more. Ah Lin, I wish you good luck."

On the night I leave the MW Strip Bar, I tell George that I have something urgent to do in the USA and will return in a few days. He is not pleased, but he can't refuse. Nobody can control me in Canada now. It's my freedom.

Chapter Seventeen

"I am Trapped so Deeply that I Can't Get out"

89. Meeting a Professor while Soliciting Patrons at the Airport

Having quietly left the MW Strip Bar, I eventually rid myself of Allan's pestering and get far away from the evil control of the "Thunder Motorcyclists". I feel at the bottom of my heart that I am genuinely free. I can do whatever I please now.

To avoid further trouble, I move to the west end, close to Pearson International Airport, far away from downtown Toronto. The waiting rooms in the airport are my main place for procuring patrons, especially those "whore-mongers" from all corners of the world who seek carnal pleasure in Toronto. I get the inspiration of choosing the airport after I read an item in the newspaper about an Asian prostitute who does a lot of business at the Vancouver airport.

During the traveling season, the airport is full of people. I always pick those businessmen from the United States who look wealthy. One day, I meet a businessman who comes to Toronto from New York for a business meeting. That night, I service him in an airport hotel and he gives me US$1,000 instead of the original $500, because he finds my service "first rate". Of course, only occasionally do I have such "generous patrons". Sometimes I don't find any patrons for two or three days. Perhaps my price is too high: at least $300 a night. Occasionally, I'm willing to accept half the price.

At the airport, I meet all sorts of men, some of whom embarrass me. One night, I haven't managed to get a client after wandering in the waiting rooms for three hours. When I am about to leave, a very beautiful woman with an American accent walks towards me. After a while, I realize that she is bisexual and wonders if I would like to spend the night with her.

On hearing of homosexuality, I am filled with fear, because there is a great possibility that gay people might be HIV positive. I gently refuse her, but she tries to convince me while holding my hand tightly, "My bedroom skills would amaze you and stimulate you."

To tell the truth, I am tired of seeing women's bodies after working in the strip bar. It sickens me to go to bed with a woman. I might never be able to accept homosexuality mentally in my life.

The most interesting experience is my encounter with Professor Green. One night, I see a peculiar man in an airport café. He came to Toronto from Boston for a meeting and had an appointment with a friend in the café before returning to Boston. His friend suddenly called, however, saying that his wife had been in a traffic accident. The result was that the professor's appointment was canceled. Two hours before departure, he meets me. I start a conversation with him when I see him at a loss what to do.

After an exchange of words, he postpones his flight to the next day and calls a taxi at once and takes me to the nearby "Holiday Inn". He doesn't look like a wealthy businessman and claims to be a history professor at a university in Boston. He speaks a little Chinese and says that he lived in Shanghai for a year. I am interested in him because Chen, Zhiwei, my first love, also studied in Boston. I intend to learn something about the customs and habits in Boston. I agree to accompany him for the night for US$200.

It is the first time I have met such a "virtuous gentleman". Usually, whore-mongers are anxious to go to bed, but this professor seems to have no intention to touch me. When I try to entice him, he tells me seriously that he just wants to pay money to talk to a prostitute. He is writing a book on "the development of prostitution".

When I realize his intention, I ask him not to use my stage name, "Camille," or mention that I'm in Toronto: he consents to my terms. Having treated me to a

Japanese dinner in the hotel restaurant, he asks me to lie on the bed in the hotel room while he sits on a nearby sofa to talk with me and take notes. He asks a broad range of questions, such as why I pursued this occupation. I tell him that I have been forced to do so. He asks me if I feel comfortable sleeping with a different man every night. I tell him that having intercourse with strangers has nothing to do with happiness or emotion. It's just for money.

Questioning me for three or four hours, he never touches me. He is a rare eccentric person: sitting with a sexy woman at his disposal, he never gets restless. I wonder if he is normal in his sexual function.

He is very familiar with Chinese history, and is able to tell the brief history of "the Tang, Song, Yuan, Ming and Qing Dynasties" in standard Mandarin. He knows the names of the emperors of all those dynasties. He mentions that the Song patterned poetry, written to music, was inspired by prostitutes, who made great contributions to Chinese music.

When he suddenly comes towards me, I expect that he will throw himself on me, but he just sits beside me and asks, "Excuse me, are you from Shanghai?"

"It's not necessary to ask this, Prof. Green, is it?" I respond naughtily.

Returning to the sofa to sit down, he continues, "Camille, to tell you the truth, I stayed in Shanghai for a year, teaching English language and American history. I know something about Shanghai girls. When I first met you at the airport, I got the impression that you were one of them."

Nodding, I agree with what he has said. With his encouragement, I tell him briefly how I was cheated by my first love, raped in Tokyo, fell victim to my former classmate's scheme in Toronto and forced to go astray.

"It's wonderful material for a movie. I'll recommend it to my friends in the film circle when I return to Boston."

Once again, I urge him not to reveal my identity and he promises to just use the phrase, "a Chinese girl", or some other name. He says names are just symbols; the key point is to describe a kind of living situation.

At 10 pm, he suggests we have coffee in the café downstairs. I agree readily, like a daughter traveling with her Daddy.

While drinking coffee, he says sympathetically, "Prostitution is an age-old problem. It will not vanish as long as mankind exists. The history of Chinese prostitutes can be traced to a long time ago. There is a lot of material in this regard in the US, both in English and Chinese. The best known prostitute is Ah Cai."

"Could you tell me her story?"

Nodding, he begins slowly, "During the gold rush in California from 1848 to 1854, about 450 thousand Chinese people, mostly men, came to San Francisco. The proportion of men and women from 1901 to 1910 was 94.4 to 5.6 in San Francisco. What a great disparity! The consequences can be easily imagined. Prostitution was as flourishing an activity as opium smoking in Chinatown at that time."

He continues with some indignation, "In the Chinese world at that time, men dug gold in mines while the women dug gold in the men. Ah Cai, a Chinese woman, was the most famous among the prostitutes. At twenty, she was pretty like a flower, with big black eyes, a slender figure and uniquely Chinese lotus feet. What was rare in her was her noble temperament. She spoke both English and Chinese, so patrons of all nationalities poured into her residence."

He goes on, as if giving a lecture in class, "Using slick and sly methods, Ah Cai got her legal resident status after going to court several times. She sued those whore-mongers who gave her copper sand instead of gold sand in payment for their visits. She went through a lot of hardship and enjoyed fleeting fame. Her brothel was doing such good business that her neighbors took her to court. She got one tael of gold sand for each of her services and did very good business. After awhile, she accumulated a lot of money. When she got older, she bought young girls as prostitutes and became a madam, running a brothel. She was said to marry a foreigner and later cohabited with a white man who lived off the avails of her business. She enjoyed a calm and steady life in her later years and died at 100. What a legendary life!"

Now, I really do believe that he is a professor. Only professors are this learned. Glancing at his watch, he says, "Go to sleep. It's getting late. We'll go to the airport early tomorrow morning. Your car is till there, right?"

At this moment, I would do anything he wants me to do. I respect and admire him, and we are bound by money as well. Unexpectedly, he never touches me and prefers to sleep in a single bed, while I sleep in the other bed in the room.

Before going to sleep, he sighs with emotion, "As early as in the 1930s, a writer in the States wrote a novel entitled, 'Immigrants', which was later made into a movie, creating quite a sensation at the time. The beginning of the novel goes roughly like this: Immigrants have neither profound understanding of the role they play, nor do they cherish any dreams about history. They never think that they are part of history and they share the mystery of their landing places, but they don't know anything about these places. Grief absorbs them, so they feel sick and the sufferings in their bodies wear them down."

Pretending to be profound, I respond, "Immigration exacts a price and requires spiritual rebirth."

"That's pretty good. You're also a philosopher." So saying, he falls fast asleep. Later, I hear him snoring.

Early next morning, Prof. Green pays me US$200 and gives me his business card. He is a history professor with a Ph.D.

"Call me if you need help. It's possible my friends in Hollywood would invite you to perform!" He takes his leave with humor.

I can't help but throw myself into his arms. He lowers his head and kisses me lightly on my forehead, like an old uncle.

It is a pity that after moving several times, I don't remember where I put his card. If I had it, I would certainly call him.

90. Disaster after Stripping at Patron's Place

My business at the airport drops off sharply in the winter, perhaps because the heavy snow in Toronto discourages travelers. It is understandable: who wants to suffer the scathing wind here? People would rather fly to Florida to escape the winter.

The slack business makes me shiver at the end of 1997 and the beginning of 1998. Few patrons come and my earnings barely cover my rent. I lower my price to $100 a night, but still fail to solicit customers. All my savings from the MW Strip-tease Bar will be gone in the near future.

Just when I am worried about money, I come across an advertisement in a local English language newspaper, "High pay for strippers performing at patrons' homes". I promptly call the XY Performing Company. The receptionist says that "the pay is based on quality," with the highest pay being $200 per performance for *half an hour and the lowest $75. In spite of my abhorrence of stripping and my rebellious mentality, this price is so alluring that I have to take a chance.*

The next afternoon, I go to the XY Performing Company for an interview, meticulously made-up. Bill, the director for public relations, receives me and asks a few casual questions before inviting me to perform in another room. After viewing two dances, he and the deputy general manager nod and decide to employ me. After a brief consultation, the deputy general manager leaves.

Bill says to me, "Camille, you've had professional training. Still, there is some difference between our performances and those in a strip club. For example, we'll dress you as people in all walks of life in accordance with our customers' requests. That's why you still need some training."

I ask candidly, "How much do I get for a performance?"

A bit surprised, he glances at me through his glasses and replies, "$120 for a stark-naked performance of around half an hour, and the patron will give a tip of 15%."

I've seen a lot of those foreigners in the MW Strip bar, so I demand impolitely, "You know my professional skills. I won't do it for less than $150."

"Okay, $150. It will increase to $200 in three months. The ceiling is $250. Do a good job." He is quite straightforward.

I return to my old profession of stripping. It's hard to say if I am happy or sad. Life is a cycle and always returns to the starting point. Everything is destined and nobody, however capable, can escape destiny.

One Saturday night, I am called to the home of a newlywed couple. The house is noisy with mostly female guests. The bride and groom seem perplexed when they see me.

A fat woman greets me with a smile at once, and says to the newlyweds, while holding my hand, "We sisters have invited her for a strip-tease demo."

"You know, the bride is too shy in the office. This stripper will give you two an unforgettable experience," says a genteel lady, who must be a secretary.

Another spectacled lady makes a face while holding the bride's hand, "She'll make you enjoy your wedding night even more!"

The bride lowers her head shyly, her face flushed. No wonder! Bill told me over the phone that the bride studied in a British religious school and was brought up in a traditional English conservative family.

After the bride and groom clearly understand why I am here, I take out a CD and the groom places it in the CD player. Along with the melodious music, I first take off my jacket, and twist my body in my black bra. When the second melody starts, I dance while taking off my bra and skirt slowly. I twist my body with force, showing my sexy breasts with only my black silk panties on. When the third melody starts, I take off my panties and throw them onto the groom's head. He is startled and scared, as if he had seen a ghost. I don't blame him, as he is an IT worker, dealing only with computers. The whole house resounds with applause after my performance.

After things get quiet, I pick up my clothes and change in the washroom. Altogether, it lasts half an hour and the fat woman gives me $250 before I leave. Easy money.

Another memorable event happens in a high-class law office on Bay Street one Friday afternoon. Bay St. is the well-known financial and business center in downtown Toronto, filled with people in fine suits who look sanctimonious. A group of employees is holding a 50th birthday party for their boss. They want to have a unique party in the office and the boss is said to enjoy patronizing strip bars. Many of his big transactions have been done in bars.

Entering the high-class office building, I feel different, as if I've become noble. Originally, I was supposed to perform wearing panties with my upper body bare. When the boss sees me, he stealthily touches my buttocks, and suggests immediately that I perform naked. His words create a big laugh in the office. Professionals are really different. They watch me perform quietly, abiding by the rules. Two lawyers are embarrassed to say that it is their first time to watch strip tease.

The boss ridicules them, "You have the face to say that. You should be fired for this."

His words make people split their sides with laughter, pushing the atmosphere to a peak. After three songs, the boss wants me to dance another round, and promises to cover the cost. He is as good as his word: he generously writes a check for $500 before I leave.

During the last half year, I have been requested to pose as a nurse, a cowgirl, a student, a teacher, a maid, a policewoman, a widow, etc. I usually go to places to *strip over weekends. Sometimes I do three performances a night. Thus, I live pretty well, earning $4,000 to $5,000 a month. I kill time by watching TV, taking walks in the streets or going to the libraries. Occasionally, I solicit patrons at public places as a "side occupation".*

As always, the good times do not last long. On Christmas Eve 1998, I am called to dance for a Vietnamese family. They are celebrating the 40th birthday of "Second Brother Long" that Saturday night. They are actually overseas Chinese of Vietnamese origin. Almost everybody speaks Mandarin.

When I dance the first melody wearing a bra, some younger people start to get restless. After I take off my bra and reveal two breasts, one of the men cries out in wonder and tries to stroke me. I am so frightened that I retreat at once. Luckily, an older person prevents him from advancing. When the third melody sounds, and while I carefully take off my panties, an older person suddenly grabs my buttocks, scares me and I scream...

"Stop! What a shame. I've asked you to be well behaved..." Second Brother Long stands up at once to stop the man.

He then apologizes to me, "Miss, we're so sorry..."

Just then, the doorbell rings. Four or five fully armed policemen charge into the room with a search warrant. Second Brother Long and the others are at a loss as to what to do. Among the officers is one policeman of Chinese origin, who speaks Cantonese, Mandarin and Vietnamese. After searching, the police discover some marijuana grown in water in the sun- room. The police estimate that this has a market value of one hundred and fifty thousand Canadian dollars.

That night, I am taken to the police station for questioning. The next day, Bill, the director for public relations of XY Performance Company bails me out. It seems that performing in patrons' homes is not easy and is even risky in many instances. While I am in the midst of my dilemma, the police charge the XY Performance Company, because they manage an underground brothel and provide sex to customers under the name of strip tease.

Fortunately, I have never "sold my body" in the half year I have worked there, although I am investigated by the police as well.

Finally, four strippers at the company are charged with prostitution. Bill and the others are accused of operating a brothel and the XY Performance Company has to be closed down. Once again, I become a vagrant girl without an "organization". It is hard for my countrymen to imagine the suffering of "alternative women" overseas. It is difficult to be a prostitute anywhere in the world.

91. Involvement in Drug Trafficking

Snow is flying madly when the XY Strip Tease Performance Center is forced to close. After so many years in Canada, this is the first time that I am terrified by snow. Actually, I am more afraid of "losing my job" and of the loneliness in my heart than I am frightened by the severe cold weather.

After giving it a lot of thought, I decide to move back to downtown Toronto where many five-star hotels are located and I can catch the "big fish". Now, I have no other choice. Taking off one's pants is the easiest way to earn money. Once my womb is open, cash will flow into it. If I am prepared for the worst now, I'll return to Shanghai for a good life after I earn two hundred thousand Canadian dollars. Perhaps I'll find a handsome young man and enjoy the second half of my life.

Is it fate or God's will? Shortly after I return to Toronto at the beginning of 1999, I almost suffer a sexual assault by a wolf while I am procuring in front of the "Four Seasons Hotel". Luckily Katyusha, a Russian girl, helps me and punches the man's face, while Old Hawk, her boyfriend, rushes out to subdue him and rescue me. From then on, I share a unit with Katyusha in an apartment building on Church Street in downtown Toronto.

It might be a coincidence or destiny. Close to where I live on Church Street, there was an old brothel, according to some older overseas Chinese people. They jokingly called it the "chicks' coop", because Cantonese people call prostitutes "chicks". Its origins are not known. When the Chinese came to the USA and Canada during the Gold Rush, they didn't bring their wives. They went to brothels for their physiological urges. Moreover, foreign prostitutes with their tall figures, golden hair and green eyes were really alluring. The Chinese men were willing to squander their money to satisfy their sexual needs. Having sex with the foreign prostitutes, the men experienced a sense of novelty and gratification. The Chinese whore-mongers were never stingy on tipping after sex. Thus, more and more brothels were set up near Chinatown and the hard-earned money of sturdy Chinese men quietly flowed into foreign prostitutes' pockets.

When I retell this gossip to Katyusha, she seems quite happy, saying proudly that we are bringing into full play the traditional Chinese culture. I find her words both funny and annoying. This woman, beautiful both in her facial features and her body, is a sexy flirt, who attracts every man. Her breasts are so large and sexy that they almost appear to be fake. One night before going to bed, she sees my eyes fixed on her breasts, so she takes off her camisole and grabs my hand to stroke them.

She says with pride, "These are the greatest gift bestowed on me by my parents. Ever since high school, these have caused trouble. Once, a gymnastic instructor stroked them. He was fired the next week after I reported his conduct to the principal."

I tell her with embarrassment, "I thought they were fake, but they are real. They are even bigger than those of that Canadian star, Pamela Anderson. You should go into the film business."

"Yes, to shoot those sex movies especially…" It is no surprise that her lewd laughter and magnetic voice have enticed so many wealthy patrons.

With her guidance, I quickly catch some "big fish", particularly the Northern European men she introduces to me. She also sends the short Asian patrons to me, because, in her words, she doesn't want to see them die in her bed after her torture.

I never expected, however, that Old Hawk, her loyal boyfriend, would be a drug trafficker. By accompanying Katyusha when she transported 20 kilograms of heroin to Windsor, I unwittingly get involved in drug smuggling. If the gangsters had not killed Old Hawk to keep the smuggling secret, I would have ended up in prison.

Katyusha almost loses her courage to survive after the death of Old Hawk. She stays at home for several months, like a walking corpse. Eventually, she moves to the north of the city and is said to be stripping there. In my professional eye, however, she is not a first-rate stripper, as she is too tall and her bottom is not very sexy. But her breasts offset her shortcomings. After she leaves, I move to a smaller one-bedroom unit on Queen Street.

I still try to procure patrons near some of the luxury hotels, mainly those for tourists. I can catch one or two "big fish" every week. What I fear most is the Toronto Police Bureau's frequent crackdowns on prostitution. They send a lot of policemen out almost every night for a blitz on the established "red-light districts": the infamous Carlton and Church streets downtown; Regent Park in the east; Parkdale in the west; the Kingston area in Scarborough; the Jane-Finch corridor in North York; and Bay and Yonge Streets downtown. The headquarters of the Police Bureau is situated close to Church Street where I often solicit patrons. This area is naturally the hardest hit.

One late night after I finish my job and leave the Hilton Hotel, a speeding police motorcade scares me out of my wits. I see in the newspaper the next day that they arrested prostitutes -- 5 illegal immigrants of Thai origin, under the control of a criminal group.

Another night I am lucky to escape a detective in plain clothes. A little after 11 pm while I am soliciting at the Eaton Center at the intersection of Yonge and Dundas, a tall Asian Man tries to engage me in conversation. I find him somewhat familiar, thinking that he might be a patron of the MW Strip Bar where I worked. He talks to me in English first, but changes to Mandarin with a Cantonese accent after realizing that I don't speak English fluently. When he starts to speak Chinese, I remember that he is none other than the Chinese policeman who discovered marijuana in the Vietnamese home where I stripped. He can also speak Vietnamese.

I change the subject quickly, "Sorry, I'm waiting for a friend. I didn't quite understand what you said before."

"Waiting for a friend this late?" He seems displeased.

"It's my freedom. Is it illegal?" I retort impolitely.

He has to say with a smile, "Be safe, then."

I say "Thanks" and slip away. When I arrive at the next street, I find a police car waiting on the street corner, with a policeman sitting inside. Patting myself on the forehead involuntarily, I congratulate myself for being so lucky.

It is even more difficult to escape the entanglement of the underworld society than the policemen. One night at the end of August, I am procuring patrons in a café at the Holiday Inn. A short man of probable Asian origin starts talking to me in Mandarin. He professes that he is a Chinese of Malaysian origin and he agrees to pay me $150. Following him upstairs to Room 303, I discover another person sitting on a sofa.

Noticing my surprise, the middle-aged man stands up, saying, "Miss Camille, don't be nervous. I won't devour you. Please sit down."

"How do you know my name?" I ask hesitantly.

"To tell you the truth, we've been watching you for a long time. Don't be afraid. You'll be fine if you co-operate with us."

"What on earth do you want me to do? You have to line up if you want to go to bed," I am furious.

The middle-aged man replies, "Miss, you've misunderstood me. You must know about the big case last month in Toronto, when four prostitutes were stabbed to death on the same night."

"Haven't the police solved the case? I understand that the Thunder Motorcyclists did it," I say, a bit perplexed.

"The police only revealed half the truth. The four prostitutes were working for us," he continues.

"So you are the Black Bats from New York?"

"Yes, Miss. You are smart." The middle-aged man finally smiles a little.

I've read in an English language newspaper report that the Thunder Motorcyclists based in Quebec and the Black Bats from New York are vying for territory in Toronto. The latter gang is a criminal clique composed mainly of Asians who are engaged in prostitution and drug trafficking.

The middle-aged man speaks slowly, "I don't need to elaborate as you are obviously a smart woman."

I am unaware of what he has up his sleeve, so I ask him, "What on earth do you want me to do?"

"Don't play the fool. You are on pretty good terms with Allan, the bartender at the MW Strip Tease Bar. Allan is a key member of the Thunder Motorcyclists…" He talks with gusto.

I respond straightforwardly, "Do you want me to obtain information by infiltrating their group?"

"Yes! You are so smart that you are worthy of being a woman from Shanghai. Be assured, we'll protect you secretly," he says, smiling.

Since they know so much about me, it is hard for me to escape their evil control. As the saying goes: only a fool goes looking for trouble.

I don't agree immediately: "This is so sudden. Let me think about it."

"Okay, you can think about it for three days."

So saying, he hands me his card with a simple name and phone number: "Jiang Shan 416-888-3333"

When I get home, I collapse on the floor, motionless, as if my bones have been crushed. I feel like a ball of soot or a pool of water. Coming and going, going and coming, I always return to the starting point. I have to deal with Allan, that devil, again. Ruthless gangsters, why don't you leave an innocent woman alone? Why? Good heavens, what am I going to do? …

Recalling my painful experience, I have no choice but "to escape". Three days later, instead of calling Jiang Shan, I secretly move out of my apartment and stay in a small hotel, getting ready for my "escape".

The next evening, a hair-raising incident occurs. When I come out of a café near the small hotel, a man feigning madness assaults me. After some entanglement, I quickly leave. At this point, a woman from across the street charges towards me all of a sudden and sprays something onto my face. Thinking quickly in a desperate situation, I turn suddenly and kick her groin before I escape… I discover after returning to the hotel that the ends of my hair have been scorched. I assume that this must be a plot to ruin my face, a realization that makes me shudder and break into a cold sweat. Who did it, the Thunder Motorcyclists or the Black Bats? Probably the latter. This accelerates my "escape plan".

At noon on August 22nd 1999, I secretly leave Toronto, driving a secondhand Nissan with simple luggage and savings of a little over $50,000 in the bank. I drive to Niagara Falls, one of the Ten Wonders of the World.

Am I leaving to escape from the tiger's den, or jump out of a firetrap, or bait bigger fish? To be exact, I, a degraded woman, am going to seek some room for survival, liberty and freedom. Besides, Casino Niagara has been doing a good business since its opening, attracting 20 million tourists annually. I want to earn money from the gamblers and tourists. I will be bound to catch the "big fish" if I go fishing. The casino is separated from the United States by a river. It would be easy for me to escape to the other bank if I want to.

Driving on the highway, I see the CN Tower, from the rear mirror in the car. The tower still resembles an erect penis, standing magnificently against the Toronto skyline. My present mood is entirely different from that of 5 years ago when I climbed the tower with Huang, Hong. At that time, I was proud and cherished a fond dream. At present, the situation is completely different and my dream has been crushed.

Chapter Eighteen

Truth Revealed by a Belated Posthumous Letter

92. A convenient Punching Bag

It is already past 9 pm on the 15th when Jia, Feng finishes, at one go, Zhang, Yuanyuan's autobiographical novel, "New Camille". Although only half-finished, the novel is shocking and tragic enough to move him to tears. Apart from Zhang's literary skills, the content and plot are equal to or better than most other immigration literature. The author's candidness and honesty are worthy of admiration. What literature requires is passion and sincerity. Zhang, Yuanyuan has apparently achieved this. Even after turning off the computer, Jia fails to calm down.

Different characters in the novel appear in his mind, and a series of questions arises. Poor Zhang, Yuanyuan: is it true that beautiful women always suffer an unhappy fate? Evil Japanese Aokawa Kakuai! Why did you violate the naïve Shanghai girl? Insatiable Huang, Hong! Why did you drive your former classmate to a dead end? Disgusting Allan, the bartender! Why did you force an innocent girl into prostitution? Russian girl, Katyusha! Why did you involve her in drug trafficking? Mysterious Black Bats! Why did you tail her and pursue her so closely? The fake husband Lin, Tianci; the lover in Tokyo, Ding, Xu; the boss in the strip bar; her foreign neighbor

Barbara and others appear and reappear, swirling through his mind.

For over an hour, Jia, Feng remains immersed in the sad story of Zhang, Yuanyuan. He decides to turn on his computer and select the best parts of her manuscript to create a feature story, "Secret story of a prostitute from Shanghai" for Toronto Weekly on Saturday. Such an exclusive inside story will create a sensation. It may even attract foreign media attention.

Just then, Lai, Wenxiong calls from Waterloo with a husky voice. He tells Jia, Feng that he hadn't read Zhang, Yuanyuan's manuscripts carefully before because he was busy with his studies. He just listened to Yuanyuan's oral retelling of the story off and on. Now, he reads and translates the main parts of the manuscript, with tears in his eyes. He is so grieved that he pauses often while reading. He hopes that the police will find some important clues and solve the case.

Finally, Lai, Wenxiong speaks in a begging tone, "Yuanyuan lived such a miserable life that I want to give her a decent funeral. However, her family members intend to have a cremation. I want her remains to stay in Canada, buried close to Niagara Falls. She loved Niagara Falls so much that she joked several times that she'd like to be buried here as 'a daughter of Niagara Falls'. I wonder if her family would agree. You are from the same city and her family trusts you. Could you help me persuade them? Thanks a lot!"

Jia, Feng answers without much thought, "I don't think there's a problem. You'll have to hurry, as a grave has to be purchased beforehand."

"That's OK. I'll pay for everything." Lai, Wenxiong says, generously.

As soon as Lai, Wenxiong puts down the phone, there is a knock at the door. It turns out to be Lian, Haotien: this is disturbing to Lai. He goes back into the room without asking Lian in.

"What the hell are you here for? You bastard!" Lai, Wenxiong lets out a torrent of abuse.

Lian responds with a long face, "Wenxiong, you can abuse me or even beat me. I won't strike back. I'm damned. I'm really damned!"

"Why the hell are you here? Go jump into Niagara Falls! Why are you here? You wanted to go to bed with Miss Zhang? Have you got a magic potion? I should have killed you for this!" Lai shouts at the top of his voice, totally irrational.

Lian shrinks down on the couch in the living room, motionless, like a beaten dog.

Lai charges forward, grabs his collar and lifts Lian up. Lian trembles all over, his face turning purple.

"Don't go wild. Wenxiong, pardon me this time. Remember we were like brothers when we were children…"

Seeing him in such a sorry plight, Lai suddenly loosens his grip on Lian, who collapses on the couch again, like a pool of soft soil.

"What's the use of scolding or beating you, now that she's gone? Nothing can compensate me for my loss. Who will return my Yuanyuan to me? Who? Tell me!" Wenxiong asks in utter exasperation.

"I know. It's totally my fault. Without my gossip in Taipei, such a thing would not have happened to Miss Zhang," Lian says hesitantly.

"It's not merely a fault. It's a crime! The police haven't confirmed your innocence," Wenxiong speaks with gritted teeth.

"I'd rather be imprisoned to redeem my sin. The most important task now, however, is to help the police catch the murderer as soon as possible. It has been over half a month since Miss Zhang died, but there is no substantial development in the police investigation." Lian attempts to change the subject on purpose.

Quick-witted, Lai responds, "Don't forget that you're still one of the suspects. The police can summon you at any time."

Lian, Haotien suddenly kneels down, "Wenxiong, trust me. I am absolutely not the murderer. As you know, I am timid and afraid of death. I do not have the courage to kill people."

"You don't have to tell me this. Talk to the police." Lai purposely attempts to vex him.

"What I said is true. Otherwise, I will come to no good end. I'll be struck down by a car in the street," Lian says incoherently.

"Don't play tricks. You became abnormal as you thought of Miss Zhang so constantly. What would you not resort to?"

Lian says, his head lowered, "I admit that I thought of her all day long. I really didn't know that you two had fallen so deeply in love. I guess for you it was like a modern fairy tale. If I had known, I would not have behaved the way I did. As the popular saying goes: a friend's wife should never be humiliated. Moreover, we are blood related."

Lai ridicules him, "So, you still remember that! How absurd! You're totally abnormal. There are many, many good women in the world. Why did you pester Zhang, Yuanyuan?"

"I'm abnormal. I am! I should have consulted a psychiatrist sooner. She was so beautiful, with her charming skin, figure…" Like a mad man, Lian talks to himself, Zhang, Yuanyuan's body flashing in his mind.

"So? Is it a crime to be beautiful? How can those stars in Hollywood survive, pursued all day long by wolves like you? It is ridiculous that you can't control yourself! Are you a boy of 10?" His hot temper diminished a little, Lai becomes increasingly contemptuous of his cousin.

Lian talks to himself again, "I just don't understand what happened in the five hours after I parted from Miss Zhang early on the morning of December 29th."

Lai interrupts at once, "Haotien, did you go to the casino?"

"How can I lie to you? I swear on my ancestors' graves that I did go to the casino." Lian raises his right arm, looking serious.

Lian continues, "I know that the police haven't found any suspects for this five-hour vacuum period, so I'm the scapegoat. Actually, I am more anxious than anyone else. If the real murderer is not found, I will be the chief suspect. I won't be able to clear my name even if I jump into the Yellow River. I'll be sent to jail for my sins…"

"Well, this is not the police bureau. You'd better report honestly to Police Chief Simon," Lai tries to convince him.

Lai doesn't want to talk to Lian any more. He just gives vent to his anger and Lian is a convenient punching bag. Now Lian seems to be babbling interminably.

It turns out that Lai's Mom had called Lian tearfully after Lai boarded the plane. She urged him to visit Wenxiong, for fear of his doing some harm to himself. Of course, Lian didn't reveal his own "crimes" to them, but he promised to "take care of" Wenxiong. Lian had phoned Lai throughout the day, but nobody answered at Lai's home. Lian worried that some accident might have happened, so he drove for over an hour from Toronto to Waterloo. In fact, Lai was at home the whole day, but he had unplugged his phone to concentrate on translating Zhang, Yuanyuan's manuscript.

Subconsciously, Lai glances at the clock and finds it is almost midnight. Lian says he has to work the next day, so he should return to Toronto. He used to stay overnight while visiting Lai in Waterloo, but now Lai doesn't show any inclination to invite him to stay. Lian stands up to take his leave.

Before leaving, Lian says repeatedly, "I really didn't know that you two had such profound feelings for each other…"

"Did you think there's no genuine feeling in this world? You'll understand what love is after you finish reading Zhang, Yuanyuan's autobiographical novel. You'll understand her, sympathize with her and love her spiritually," Lai speaks eloquently.

"Is that true? When will it be published?" Lian asks with some doubt.

Lai answers resolutely, "Soon. A reporter-turned writer is penning it quickly. It might become a best-seller in Chinese literary circles."

"Can you tell me the title of the book?" Lian asks as he puts on his overcoat.

"It's 'New Camille' for the time being. But everything should be kept secret for now. It will be on the market after the case is solved. At present, this case involves so many people and is so wide ranging that the police are a bit confused."

"I'll read it carefully after it's published. Don't forget to let me know when you've set the date for her funeral. Please allow me to attend. Don't tell her family members, of course," Lian requests again.

"In view of your mean behavior, how am I ever going to forgive you?" Lai shakes his head.

Lien begs shamelessly, "Wenxiong, give me a chance for redemption."

"For that, you'd be better ask Zhang, Yuanyuan!" Lai slams the door forcefully.

93. Request for her Burial

Lai, Wenxiong has made an appointment with Police Chief Simon for a meeting on the afternoon of the 16th at the Police Bureau. The purpose is to report to the chief about important clues found in Zhang, Yuanyuan's autobiographical novel. Getting up early, Lai also calls the police director for a meeting at 4 pm.

After lunch, Lai drives from Waterloo to Niagara Falls with the translation and the original Chinese scripts he has sorted out. He has taken this road many times and it took only the twinkling of an eye to get there, with beautiful Zhang, Yuanyuan sitting beside him, talking and laughing. Today, the road seems longer and longer, and her face and smile are always in his mind. He wonders how many more times he'll drive this road. If the Zhang family agrees to her burial in the Niagara Region, he'll come often, at least once a month. If the Zhang family insists on cremation, then half of her ashes will remain in Canada. He plans to place the cinerary casket in his residence in Waterloo. He'll find a burial ground after his graduation at the end of the year.

Lai arrives at the Niagara Police Bureau right on the dot of 2 pm. Chief Simon and Policewoman JoAnna are waiting for him in the meeting room.

"This is the English version of the main content of Miss Zhang's autobiographical novel. All the materials related to the case have been translated into English. Hope my translation is not too much below par." Lai, Wenxiong hands Simon a thick stack of pages in English.

Simon scans a few pages and immediately asks his secretary to make two photocopies. A few minutes later, all three of them have copies. Lai explains items of note to them while referring to the translation. Chief Simon highlights the scripts with a red marker from time to time.

After reading a few pages, JoAnna comments at once, "Mr. Lai, your English is so good that the meaning of the translation is perfectly clear."

Chief Simon glares at her, "A Ph.D. student's English is naturally up to the standard."

"Not really. Some Ph.D. students can't express themselves very well. We've met quite a lot of them." JoAnna purses her lips.

Simon grows a little impatient, "Mr. Lai is a Ph.D. in sociology. How could his English not be good?"

Lai says, with some embarrassment, "I was in a rush and couldn't afford to pay attention to language rhetoric. I just translated the main ideas accurately."

After the three of them talk for nearly two hours, the police have a general picture of what happened before and after Zhang's writing of the novel "New Camille". They are most interested in those people who were involved with Zhang, including Aokawa Kakuai and Ding, Xu in Japan, Huang, Hong and Lin, Tianci, in Toronto, Allan the bartender at the MW Strip Bar, Jiang Shan of the Black Bats and the Russian stripper Katyusha.

Speaking of Katyusha, Lai adds a further comment, "This woman is complicated and infinitely resourceful. You'd better find her. She tried to involve Zhang, Yuanyuan in drug trafficking."

Chief Simon says, "When you first told us about Katyusha, we contacted the Toronto Police that very night. They confirm that she is not in Toronto, and perhaps has left the country."

Lai describes in detail the features of Katyusha, hoping for a nation-wide "wanted" poster. Simon doesn't agree to it, saying that he is contacting the Royal Canadian Mounted Police in Vancouver.

Finally Lai requests, "It has been over half a month since Miss Zhang's body was found. I know you've done a lot, but there are no new developments. Her parents suggest that you ask the American FBI to get involved in the case."

The word "America" seems to touch a nerve in Simon. He argues, "There is no guarantee that the FBI will do any better. They'll spend a lot of time studying the background material with which they are not familiar."

Seeing his sensitivity, Lai says more explicitly, "At least the FBI's methods of detection are more brilliant, and their machines more sensitive. Besides, there is a well known detective of Chinese origin."

"I understand what you think, Mr. Lai. But I can assure you that the machines we use are exactly the same as FBI's. As for the quality of policemen, opinions differ." Chief Simon stares at him.

Lai explains repeatedly, "Don't get me wrong. I didn't mean to criticize you. I just want you to consider this option as soon as possible."

Sensing some smell of gunpowder in their talk, JoAnna, smiling, attempts to be the peacemaker, "We understand what the family members think and we've tried our best. Simon hasn't slept well since you returned to Canada. Luckily, he can stand to lose weight. If it were me, I'd be reduced to bones and skins."

Simon pats his belly, "Weight loss, thanks to Miss Zhang."

The three of them burst out laughing together, easing the tense atmosphere. It would appear that women are indispensable to the police bureau. Without their calming influence, men would certainly fight each other. Women are born to be mediators.

Accompanied by JoAnna, Lai, Wenxiong goes to the Bureau Director's office. The director looks younger than he expected, about the age of Simon, between 40 and 50. After a few greetings, JoAnna takes her leave.

The director knows that the family members are not satisfied with the development of the case, so he immediately asks Lai if he has any constructive suggestions. Lai repeats what he said before: consult the FBI and begin a joint investigation. The director agrees to consider this option, but says that he has to consult with Simon.

Seeing that he is "playing Taiji (to postpone a decision – Translator's note)", Lai asks helplessly, "When will you ask the FBI to get involved?"

"Rest assured, Mr. Lai. I'm going to an urgent meeting on this case. I'll exert pressure on them." The director answers readily and briskly.

Lai doesn't want to say any more. The only reason for this meeting with the director is to exert pressure on "the Special investigation group for No. 1 female corpse".

At 7 pm sharp, Jia, Feng, correspondent for "Toronto Weekly", comes to the 100 Lakeshore Building in Niagara Region as promised, where Lai, Wenxiong is already waiting for him in the lobby. Before going upstairs Jia exchanges greetings with Bailey, the security guard, as they have become friends.

The three members of the Zhang family are glad to see them. The atmosphere in the apartment becomes enlivened at once. Actually, the family members think of Lai as kin after the meetings of the last few days'. His relationship with Zhang, Yuanyuan was so special that it even surpassed that of a couple. Jia is from Shanghai, which "endears" him to the family. Moreover, he has devoted himself to the case from the very beginning. The Zhang family appreciates such a nice news reporter.

Old Zhang says to Jia, Feng, "I am sorry that you had to make a special trip from Toronto."

Jia hands a big package of delicatessen goodies to Mrs. Zhang. "Some Shanghai-style chicken and BBQ pork, as well as jellyfish for you."

Mrs. Zhang responds, "I'm a bit embarrassed. You come from afar and bring these to us."

"Just for a change of taste. Of course, the food is not as delicious as the yellow chicken in Shanghai. Since this is a tourist region, it's hard to get it."

Lai adds, "The downtown Chinese restaurant might have it, but it is not as tasty as Toronto's."

Zhang, Mingming makes two cups of Dragon Well tea for Lai and Jia. At their first meeting the night before, Mingming decided that he likes this "brother-in-law". Only it's such a pity that my Sister is gone so soon. God was not fair when he separated this lovely couple.

With everyone seated, Old Zhang anxiously asks, "What did the Director say, Mr. Lai?"

"He agrees to attend tonight's urgent meeting and to exert pressure on the special investigation group. At the appropriate time, they will invite the FBI to get involved. However, Chief Simon is a bit tough and somewhat hostile to the FBI."

Sipping tea, Jia comments, "The policemen here don't think highly of the American police."

Old Zhang gives Jia a cigarette and lights one for himself, "Please don't mind, Mr. Lai. I'm addicted to smoking while talking."

Mrs. Zhang takes the opportunity to persuade him, "If you go on smoking like this, Mr. Lai will not dare to visit us."

Lai continues at once, "Never mind. I used to smoke, but I quit after coming to Canada. My instructor, you see, is allergic to smoking."

Having inhaled hard, Old Zhang advises, "To speak from the bottom of my heart, the policemen have done their best. We shouldn't rush them too much. Some cases are not easily cracked, so we have to wait patiently…"

Lai regards what Old Zhang says as quite reasonable. He is an old man who has braved the storm and seen the world. Compared with him, Lai himself is a bit rash. Perhaps it's because he is so eager to know the truth.

After they finish smoking a cigarette, Mrs. Zhang reminds Lai, "Didn't you say over the phone that you've got something to talk to us about?"

Seeing that Lai is hesitant, Jia broaches the subject, "Oh, well, after reading Zhang, Yuanyuan's autobiographical novel, Mr. Lai is all the more anxious for her burial ..."

"Well, Yuanyuan's story is so touching that I haven't the heart for a cremation. Moreover, she was very fond of Niagara Falls. She joked to me that she would like to be buried here, to enjoy the thundering of the great falls. She called herself the 'daughter of Niagara Falls.' I would recommend burial," Lai continues.

The three Zhang members are not surprised as Lai brought this up the night of his arrival. They have talked about this and have anticipated that Lai would mention it again.

Old Zhang speaks first, "Mr. Lai, we know your kindness. It's Yuanyuan's luck to have met a kind man like you. However, there is a practical problem: if she is buried here, how are we to visit her? It is, after all, not as convenient as traveling form Shanghai to Suzhou."

Mrs. Zhang talks, while sobbing, "Yes! Leaving her alone in Canada is pitiable. For so many years, she wandered overseas all by herself. Now I can't bear to let her stay here alone. I regret having allowed her to go abroad..."

Sipping tea and clearing his voice, Lai says, "Aunt, don't grieve too much. Yuanyuan will not be lonely here, because I'll accompany her for good. If she is buried here, I'll move to Niagara Region."

"Suppose you can't find work here after graduation? Then what would you do?" Mingming cuts in.

Without much thought, Lai answers, "That's simple. I'll look for a job within a few hundred kilometers of here. This area includes Buffalo in the United States, where a lot of universities are located. It is not a problem."

Old Zhang lights another cigarette and continues, "What her Mom means is that she would be alone in Canada, and it would be hard for us to visit her. We'd rather have a cremation and take her ashes to Shanghai."

Jia interrupts in time, "Mr. Lai means what he says. He will move here. He is a trustworthy, learned man and he loves Yuanyuan more than himself. You'll understand after you read Zhang, Yuanyuan's autobiographical novel. The two letters she wrote to Mr. Lai explain everything."

Mrs. Zhang says, "We absolutely believe in Mr. Lai's true love for Yuanyuan. Few people are like him these days."

Lai says pensively, "Even if I give in and Yuanyuan's remains are transported to Shanghai for cremation, it's still too cruel. Please let her stay here. I'll try to make it easier for you to visit her. The simplest way is to let Mingming study in Canada, and then you can apply to visit him."

Jia continues at once, "That is a good way out. Mr. Lai can help him contact some universities. It will be easier to get a student's visa."

Zhang, Mingming responds while pouring tea for them, "I don't have to study in Canada as there are lots of opportunities in Shanghai. Still, I can consider this option if it would be easier for my parents to visit my sister."

Hearing that their son has suddenly changed his mind, the old couple is a bit surprised. Then, they calm down and exchange a look.

Mrs. Zhang explains, "After what happened to Yuanyuan, Mingming didn't care about studying abroad: he was even averse to it. Originally, he planned to study in the United States."

"I talked to my sister, who wanted me to study in Canada." Mingming cuts in.

Lai says, "It's the same if you go to the United States. It's also easy to study in Canada."

Finally Old Zhang concludes after some discussion, "Since Mingming is determined and he is a third-year student in university, it won't be long before he can study in North America."

This is tantamount to agreeing to a burial in the ground. Lai stands up hurriedly to thank him, grasping his hands tightly. He is as elated as if Zhang, Yuanyuan had agreed to marry him.

Mrs. Zhang shows a smile of consolation, which Lai had not seen before.

"Yuanyuan was lucky to have such a nice boyfriend," repeats Mrs. Zhang.

Jia takes the opportunity to comment, "It happens only once in a blue moon that a person is so madly loved even after death."

Then, they discuss the burial in detail. Jia suggests that the burial should be held before the 23rd, with the help of the police. The three members of Zhang family will return to Shanghai on the 24th.

Time slips by quickly and it is 9 pm. Jia reminds Lai of their other plan.

"Uncle, Aunt, as the police have been slow to crack the case, I plan to hire a private detective to help solve it. What do you think?"

Old Zhang replies after a few simple questions, "It's a good idea, but you have to watch your relationship with the police. Pay attention to the 'extent' of everything. We Chinese are good at propriety."

Lai responds with joy, "Please don't worry. I'll go to Toronto soon to look for Shi, Lei, the magic detective of Chinese origin."

94. Bureau Director's Attendance at Urgent Meeting

At 8 pm sharp on January 16th, the urgent meeting of "the Special investigation group" is held in the brightly lit meeting room of the Niagara Police Bureau. Besides the six members of the group, the Director and several policemen in military uniform attend the meeting for the first time. People in this circle know at a glance that it is a significant meeting with the attendance of the Director in person. It is also obvious that the group will be expanded. All this contributes a serious atmosphere to the meeting.

Chief Simon makes a report to everybody present, "Based on the material provided by Lai, Wenxiong, the boyfriend of the deceased woman, Lai saw the Russian girl, Katyusha, with his own eyes. There is a detailed record of this in the autobiographical novel, "New Camille". Our investigation during the past two days reveals that Katyusha was involved in the drug-trafficking case of twenty-kilos of heroin, which took place at the beginning of the year before last. Old Hawk, who died, was her boyfriend. Based on the information provided by the Toronto Police Bureau, Katyusha left Toronto for Russia in October of last year. Unfortunately, there is no record of her exit with the Airport Exit and Entrance Administration Bureau. In addition, the RCMP in Vancouver reports that a group of Russian prostitutes is quite active in Burnaby Area of Vancouver. Among them are two named Katyusha…"

Lighting a cigar, the Director says, "Please ask the police in Vancouver to get all the Katyushas' photos and email them to us as soon as possible. Lai, Wenxiong can make a positive identification."

Simon continues, "At the beginning of last year, Katyusha attempted to persuade Miss Zhang to engage in drug trafficking in Asia. Thanks to Mr. Lai's scheme, Zhang, Yuanyuan succeeded in parting from her. However, grass-roots people underestimate the strength of organized criminal groups. Even though Miss Zhang changed her telephone number, they could still find her. In this high-tech era, criminal ways are more and more advanced."

Policewoman JoAnna asks, "Chief Simon, do you suspect that after finding that she had been deceived by Mr. Lai and Miss Zhang, Katyusha took advantage of Mr. Lai's absence and made trouble for the latter? The tragedy occurred right there. Possibly Katyusha attempted to coerce Miss Zhang into drug trafficking in Asia while Miss Zhang strongly resisted. In a hot argument, Katyusha, who was tall and strong, could have killed her unintentionally and caused the tragedy."

Chief Simon lights another cigarette, "In Miss Zhang's novel, she mentioned her relationship with the Black Bats from New York. To be more accurate, she came to Niagara Region on August 28th 1999 to escape their pestering. The Thunder Motorcyclists, the sworn enemy of the Black Bats, once controlled Miss Zhang in prostitution. This case is snowballing. My driveway is filled with snow."

A thin policeman asks, "The two gangster cliques were both looking for Miss Zhang. Is it true that she was very popular?"

Chief Simon pursues the subject, "The aims of the two groups are different. Allan, the junior chief of the Thunder Motorcyclists, intended to make money out of Zhang's prostitution and enjoy sex with her. Jiang Shan of the Black Bats, however, wanted to obtain information from her in order to annex his opponents. By these means, he could control prostitution and drug trafficking in Toronto, in coordination with New York."

The Director clears his voice, "Right. The Greater Toronto Area is an important communications line: many criminal cliques land in Vancouver, and hide in New York, via Toronto. As a springboard and for transit, Toronto is a place many gangsters are interested in. The Canadian and American governments have paid attention to this and have established a transnational group, especially responsible for it."

Policewoman JoAnna cuts in, "We are contacting the New York Police Bureau for background information on the Black Bats. What kind of a person is Jiang Shan, the Malaysian man?"

A policeman who once worked in New York says, "The Black Bats occupy quite a large territory in New York, with many members of Vietnamese origin. They dare to fight with the Black people in Harlem. I suppose Jiang Shan is a small potato, or not very experienced; otherwise, Miss Zhang would not have been able to escape to Niagara under his very eyes."

JoAnna is not convinced, "I don't think so. Jiang Shan seemed to have underestimated Miss Zhang's capability; however, if he was qualified to set up a base in Toronto, he must be an intermediate figure. The Black Bats must have known that there are other cliques besides the Thunder Motorcyclists in Toronto, such as the 18

Arhats of Asian origin, the Green-eyed Party of Italian origin, etc. They've come well prepared. There are quite a number of people of Vietnamese and Fujianese origins in Toronto, who have historically had close relationships with the gangsters of New York."

A fat policeman, trying to change the subject, says, "We'd better put Allan, the bartender of the MW Bar, on an arrest list."

Simon shakes his head, "Why order his arrest? Do you have any evidence?"

"Hasn't Miss Zhang's novel described it in detail? Her love letter also reveals that she was first followed by that gang at the end of November," blurts out the fat man.

The Director interrupts at once, "It's a novel, with a strong literary nature, not her diary. It can serve only as a reference for solving the case. Its authenticity has to be explored. It is not time to order the arrest of Allan, the bartender. Still, Simon, you should ask the Toronto Police Bureau to keep an eye on him. Don't let him slip away. You should also take time to investigate the Black Bats in New York. At this point, I'll reveal a little secret: the two gangster rings made peace in Montreal recently. There is some indication that they are trying to collaborate against the "Wild Wolf Motorcyclists" in Quebec. Miss Zhang's novel reminds us that she escaped from the Black Bats and that her face was almost ruined by them."

JoAnna agrees with the Director's opinion, "We should accelerate our investigation of Jiang Shan. The Black Bats have got a firm hold in Toronto and are expanding into Quebec Province in the east."

Chief Simon, lighting another cigarette, changes the subject, "According to Miss Zhang's novel, Aokawa Kakuai, her partner in Japan, is not a decent guy. The brother of his wife, Kimiko, is a member of the 'Violence Corps', which is the largest gangster ring in Japan and a transnational criminal group. We have notified our embassy in Japan about this case and have requested detailed information on the 'Violence Corps', especially background information on Kimiko's brother. We'll also check to see if Aokawa Kakuai came to Canada at the end of last year."

JoAnna has a different opinion, "It's not necessary for Aokawa Kakuai or his wife, Kimiko, to commit a crime in Canada. It has been several years since Miss Zhang left Tokyo and she didn't mention any involvement with Aokawa Kakuai here. The mere mention of his name made her want to kill him."

The fat policeman interrupts, "Do you mean we should not take the time to check Aokawa Kakuai right now? I think that's reasonable."

The Director cuts in, "It will not take a lot of time. Just make a few calls and send a couple of emails. With enough hands, we should try solving the case from different angles."

Chief Simon, nodding, agrees with the Director. Several other policemen deem it necessary to investigate Aokawa Kakuai, as he was a key figure in leading Miss Zhang astray.

The Director advises Chief Simon again, "We must also watch our relations with the media. Never allow the media to reveal the details of the case: this might alert the criminals."

Both Chief Simon and JoAnna understand what the Director means. Citing an anonymous source, an English TV station reported last night that Miss Zhang had been involved with the largest gangster ring in Tokyo. After repeated checking, they found that one policeman from this investigation group had let slip this information. Furthermore, the Director doesn't approve of the active involvement of "Toronto Weekly" in the case.

Simon immediately reminds everybody, "What the Director says is right. Ask all media to talk to me alone for interviews to avoid putting out conflicting views."

Then Simon turns to the Director, as if he is talking to him on purpose, "The Chinese weekly has given us a lot of help. Some letters were translated by two of their correspondents. Normally, we wouldn't have let them know so much, but we needed to read the English translation and couldn't find anyone else to do the work. We were a bit embarrassed that they didn't accept payment."

"Luckily, the two correspondents have kept their promise and have never published anything that was beyond our restrictions," JoAnna adds.

As if sensing something, the Director says, "Yes, you talked to me about this Chinese weekly that should be commended. We still need to pay them for their translation. Write a check to their editor-in-chief and praise the two reporters. The police and the people should cooperate with each other."

Chief Simon nods: this problem seems to be solved. In fact, they know that the Weekly has published exclusive reports, which would inevitably involve this case. Luckily, the reports are in Chinese, which the mainstream media might not pay much attention to.

Before the end of the meeting, the Director declares, "To solve the case more quickly, we'll add three members to the Special investigation group. One is from New York and he knows a lot about the Black Bats and is familiar with that city. Another has been engaged in many cases in Tokyo and speaks Japanese. This will make it easier to communicate with the Japanese police."

Pointing to a policewoman sitting beside JoAnna, the Director continues, "This policewoman just graduated from the police school. She can learn on the job."

Simon is a bit displeased with this unexpected deployment. The Director, having sensed his displeasure, continues to say, "The addition of members does not mean that you are not capable of doing the job. We just want to speed up the case."

Actually, everybody knows that Lai, Wenxiong had a special meeting with the Director and exerted pressure on him. Lai clearly wants the Director to get the FBI involved, and has informed the police that he will hire a private detective to help solve the case. The Director asked Simon before if he wanted the FBI to get involved, and Simon flatly refused. At present, Simon had better keep his mouth shut, to avoid being reprimanded by the Director in front of the new members.

Finally, the Director demands a quick solution to the case, as if he were issuing an ultimatum, "I hope everybody, led by Chief Simon, will crack this case as soon as possible. I'll give you another week. Without substantial progress in a week, this case will be upgraded, or we'll have to invite the FBI to help!"

What the Director said puts pressure on everybody. The whole meeting room is permeated with a tense atmosphere, which seems to follow all of them home.

95. Magic Detective's Search for Clues

Just as Lai, Wenxiong has expected, the emergency meeting at the Police Bureau has not had any substantial result when he calls Chief Simon early on the morning of the 17th. Lai is fearful that the police might put this case aside. Many murder cases have been delayed for several years or even decades until they become unsolved cold cases.

Edgy, Lai decides at once to consult the chief detective Shi, Lei of the "Flying Eagle Detectives" in Toronto. Lai had phoned Shi the day before: Jia, Feng, the correspondent of "Toronto Weekly" highly recommended him.

It is around 11 am when Lai gets to Toronto. Detective Shi is studying the faxed material in his office.

In his fifties, Detective Shi is not tall, but is sturdily built. He is said to have extraordinary martial skills and to be able to deal with 4 foreign attackers. A renowned detective, he is honored as the "Chinese Holmes". He served for several years in the RCMP while young, furthered his studies in the United States and has a good relationship with both the Canadian and the American police forces. Even the FBI often consults him for help. Besides Chinese and English, he speaks French and Japanese fluently.

Having exchanged greetings, Detective Shi says to Lai, "I just called the Director of the Niagara Police Bureau, who will fully support me. We have cooperated before.'

After getting a deposit of $5,000 from Lai, Detective Shi starts work immediately and promises to give him a progress report within three days. First, he inquires about the details of the relationship between Lai, Wenxiong and Zhang, Yuanyuan. Then, he studies Zhang's autobiographical novel, "New Camille". Jia, Feng, the correspondent for "Toronto Weekly", an old acquaintance of his, especially phoned him to give him information about the case. Detective Shi promises to devote all his time and energy to this case, putting aside his other assignments.

Detective Shi fails to fall asleep after reading Zhang, Yuanyuan's manuscript late at night. Smoking a cigar, he searches for minute clues in each chapter and paragraph. All signs indicate that suicide can't be ruled out, but homicide seems more likely. If it is homicide, there are two chief suspects. Lin, Tianci, the chef of the "Chongqing Restaurant", was insatiably avaricious and cheated Zhang, Yuanyuan out of money in collaboration with Huang, Hong. It is possible that he went to Zhang's home to extort money from her. When Zhang refused, he might have killed her unintentionally after an argument and thrown her into Niagara Falls to cover up the murder.

Allan, the bartender at the MW Strip Bar, is another major suspect. From her tone in the novel, Zhang hated him so bitterly that she could have killed him herself with a knife. It is possible that Allan and Zhang had a chance meeting at Casino Niagara. Pestering her, robbing her of money and raping her, he might have attempted to force her into prostitution again to earn money for him. She might have refused him and they could have fought beside Niagara Falls. Furious, he might have pushed her in the water or forced her to jump down.

Deeply inhaling on his cigar and exhaling rings of heavy smoke, Detective Shi deliberates: he can't rule out the possibility that Aokawa Kakuai of Tokyo might have done this in Canada. Or perhaps Zhang, Yuanyuan, denied the approval of Lai's family, gave herself up as hopeless and called Aokawa Kakuai, attempting to return to

Tokyo. Detective Shi, keen-witted and capable, decides to start with the two suspects in Toronto and follow the clues. If no result is scored in Toronto, he'll consider the Japanese angle.

At noon the next day, Detective Shi and Brother Chuan, a man who is familiar to both the police and the underworld, go to the "Chongqing Restaurant" in Scarborough. Brother Chuan and Brother Guang, the boss of the restaurant, were friends in Hong Kong for many years. Everybody is overjoyed to hear that the Magic Detective Shi, Lei is here. Brother Guang invites them to a special room for dinner. After discovering the reason for their visit, Kuang orders Lin, Tianci to come to the room immediately.

Brother Guang talks to Lin as if reprimanding a kid, "Ah Lin, this is the magic detective. You have to speak the truth. We are all good friends."

Detective Shi asks directly, "Do you know that Miss Zhang is dead?"

"What? Has someone killed her? A beauty really suffers an unhappy fate." Shocked, Lin seems to be unaware of the news.

"We don't know yet. That's why we are here to talk to you."

"What's the point of talking to me? I am sorry that I cheated her out of her money."

Detective Shi gets right to the point, "Did you contact her recently?"

Scratching his head, Lin replies, "We haven't seen each other for a long time. I don't even know where she was. Such a beautiful woman didn't want to contact me. But she was really a nice person."

Having asked a few questions, the experienced Detective Shi can judge whether someone is telling the truth or not. He gestures to Lin to return to work. Brother Guang can guarantee that Lin worked until 4 am on December 29th. There is further evidence in the staff attendance record of the restaurant. According to the forensic pathologists, Zhang, Yuanyuan was certified to have died at 5 am on Dec. 29th. Lin is crossed off the murder suspect list because he could not have driven from Toronto to Niagara in an hour.

96. Feigning Insanity to Obtain Blood Sample

On the night of the 18th, Detective Shi arrives at the MW Strip Bar on Yonge Street with Bob, a tall and fierce-looking foreign partner. Based on Zhang, Yuanyuan's description, they identify Allan the bartender at first glance: thin and tall, with the look of a drug addict.

Bob greets him affectionately, "How are you, Allan? Don't you remember me? I'm Bob. It has been several years since I moved to California to do business. Hey, you look just the same, still so thin, still taking that stuff. This is my friend Glen, from Quebec. You two can talk in French."

Both of them sit at the bar, each ordering a Manhattan. Detective Shi greets Allan in French, and talks with Bob about the new American President, George W. Bush. Then, they each order another Manhattan and give Allan a $10 tip. Allan takes the time to converse with them.

When Shi, Lei leaves for the washroom, Bob suddenly lowers his voice and asks Allan quietly, "Buddy, is that Chinese woman, Camille, off today? Last time I was here, you recommended her to me and I still have fond memories of spending the night with her at the Hilton."

"She made a lot of money at Casino Niagara…Well, I only heard others talking about her. I haven't seen her," Allan stops short.

"Okay, forget it. I'm tired of western women and want some variety. Are there any Asian women on hand?"

"How about a Korean woman? She's top-notch in bed. Tomorrow night, she'll be dancing here. You can take her away after her shift."

"Good. Thanks a lot! Do not mention this to Glen when he comes back. He is a friend of my wife."

When Detective Shi returns to the bar, Bob nods to him knowingly. They order another Manhattan each and give Allan another $10 tip while they continue talking. Then Detective Shi talks in a louder voice and seems to talk to himself in French.

"Allan, what did he say in French? I don't understand."

"Oh, he said that his wife goes to bed with him just once a month. He is thinking of divorcing her." Allan translates it into English for him.

Bob says, "He must be drunk. He can't hold a lot."

"Who says I can't hold my liquor? Come on, a whiskey with ice, please," Detective Shi feigns insanity in a loud voice.

"Give him a glass of ice water," Bob replies in a hurry.

"No, no, I want whiskey…" Detective Shi yells while breaking the glass of ice water Allan hands him.

The glass is broken and Allan's hand is bleeding. Sharp-eyed Bob stands up at once and quickly grabs Allan's bleeding hand, dries the blood with a paper tissue and thrusts the paper into his pocket in no time.

Bob apologizes, "Sorry, Allan, he is drunk. I'll compensate you for the loss."

"Whiskey, whiskey with ice…" Detective Shi continues talking to himself.

"I'll go to the washroom to wash my hands. I'll be back in a minute. Don't let him drink any more."

Bob rushes to the washroom and swiftly places the bloodstained paper into the vacuum bag he has brought with him. Then he rushes back to the counter, gives Allan $20 and says, "I'm extremely sorry. This is just a token of my apology. I have to take him home at once."

"It doesn't matter. We bartenders often get our hands cut." Allan refuses in words, but stretches out his hand for the money.

Bob grabs Detective Shi's arm and walks out of the bar. They rush to the parking lot to head to a nearby hospital.

"Big Brother, such a small case could have been handled by us, your subordinates. As a famous detective, why did you have to fake madness?" Bob is puzzled.

Detective Shi, sitting beside him, explains, "A friend in the media entrusted me to solve the case. Three months ago, they published a special edition on me. This publicity was more effective than advertisements. Besides, the dead woman was miserable. She will rest in peace if we catch the murderer soon."

The results of the blood test are ready quickly: the AB blood type matches that under Zhang, Yuanyuan's nail. This is the very result they expected after working so tenaciously the whole night. They clap each other's hand to congratulate. Allan, how can you escape from the net of justice?

The next day, Detective Shi faxes the result of the blood test to the Police Bureau of Niagara Region, requesting the immediate arrest of Allan. The police contact the manager of the MW Strip Bar and confirm that Allan did not work the night of December 28th. The manager says that Allan phoned in at 4 or 5 pm that day, saying that he was sick with a high fever. The police decide to order the immediate arrest of Allan.

At questioning in the afternoon, Allan insists aggressively that he was in Toronto on the night of December 28th, but fails to produce any witness. The police put him in custody and order a DNA test by a new machine purchased from the United States, with a same day result.

Late that night, the DNA report indicates that Allan's result does not match that of the semen in Zhang, Yuanyuan's womb. That means he didn't rape Zhang, Yuanyuan. Simon plans to question him again the next evening. If there are no discrepancies in Allan's story, they'll have to release him.

Detective Shi feels uneasy after getting Chief Simon's phone call. His heart sinks again into darkness. He never expected that the baited big fish would slip away into the water. Lighting a cigar, he is lost in thought.

He exhales a puff of smoke in the dark night, shifts in his chair and calls Lai, Wenxiong at once, asking him to rush to Toronto the next morning for further analysis of the case.

97. Mystery Solved by a Belated Posthumous Letter

Seemingly in the twinkling of an eye, twenty days have passed since the discovery of Zhang, Yuanyuan's remains. Heavy snow still falls off and on, and Niagara Falls still flows nonstop. However, to the three members of the Zhang family and Lai, Wenxiong, the twenty days seem like thousands of years, during which life becomes more unbearable day by day.

Early in the morning on Saturday, Lai drives to Toronto for his appointment with Detective Shi. At noon, as they rack their brains to piece together what happened in the four months before Zhang's death, Lai gets a phone call from Chief Simon. The chief informs him of a letter found this morning by Bailey, the security guard at the Lakeshore Building. The letter was received yesterday, mailed by Zhang, Yuanyuan and returned from Taipei. Zhang wrote the letter in Chinese from Niagara Falls to Lai, Wenxiong on December 29th. Just as the old saying goes: A storm may arise from a clear sky. Things change instantly in the universe.

"A posthumous letter! It must have been written by Zhang, Yuanyuan. Why not rush to Niagara Falls now? The police are waiting for you to translate it into English," Detective Shi replies quickly.

"Really?" Lai is still a bit doubtful.

Detective Shi waves the keys in his hand, "I'd better go with you, as you are so distracted."

Getting into Detective Shi's Mercedes Benz 320, Lai is on tenterhooks. Is this ominous or auspicious? In about an hour, the mystery could be solved.

Chief Simon and Policewoman JoAnna are waiting quietly in the meeting room when Lai and Shi arrive at the Niagara Police Bureau. It is the first time that Detective Shi has met them, so business cards and introductions are exchanged.

"Mr. Lai, this is the letter." JoAnna hands it to him.

On the envelope is stamped "Returned--wrong address". The date for the return of the letter is marked in hand-written numbers: "2001.1.12."

After reading the envelope carefully, Lai discovers that Zhang had written the wrong address. The Lai family's address is "#172, third block, XX Rd. (North)", but she wrote: "#271, Eighth block, XX Rd. (South). He opens the letter and confirms that it was written by Zhang, Yuanyuan, although a bit hastily.

The full letter reads as follows,

"Wenxiong,

When you receive this letter, I will be buried in the Atlantic Ocean, or the St. Lawrence River, or possibly in Lake Ontario. Please excuse me for my helplessness and respect my choice. Death is not terrible. It is horrible to lose the courage to live.

It would take so much courage to jump from such high Falls. But I do have the courage, as a result of the pressures from life, from society and from myself.

Let me first tell you my recent horrendous experience. Last night, your disgusting cousin Lian, Haotien pestered me all evening. He attempted to drug-rape me, but failed. I got rid of him at midnight and regained my freedom.

The moment I entered my unit at the Lakeshore Building, I was kidnapped by two masked men. From their talk, I recognized that they were members of the "Thunder motorcyclists": one was Allan, the bartender at the MW Strip Bar, and the other was the masked young man who forced me into prostitution at the Hilton.

I had a chance meeting with Allan when I went to a Chinese restaurant for take-out on Christmas Day. I couldn't get away from him and he forced me to go to a nearby hotel. Three men gang-raped me and forced me to return to Toronto for prostitution within a week. If I refused to earn money for them, they said they would kill me. I had meant to wait until you come back for a discussion about whether we should move to Vancouver to be far away from these gangsters. I never expected that they would find my address so quickly.

The two knew I had recognized them, so they simply took off their masks and loosened the nylon string on my neck. They ordered me to follow them to Toronto at once, but I rebuffed them resolutely and attempted to call the police. They threw themselves on me like two mad dogs, and hit and kicked me. I resisted them, scratching them with my nails and biting them. Allan drew out a knife with a long handle to stab me. I warded it off with my arm. Scared out of my wits, I had to agree to go to Toronto with them in a few days.

When Allan went to the washroom, the other young man threw himself on me to rape me. Seeing me collapsed on the ground, motionless, they robbed me of $5,000 in cash and stalked off.

Wenxiong, I am aching all over right now, unable to hold the pen steadily, but I'll go on writing, because you are the only one in the world who understands me and because we love each other truly. I will never regret our love; however, Heaven doesn't help me. We have an affinity for each other, but not the luck to get together. I pledged to you that I wouldn't allow any other man to touch me after I fell in love with you. I would be faithful to you in the second half of my life. Unexpectedly, I could not keep this simple promise. How am I worthy of your absolute sincerity? I am so sorry for my incapability. I never thought that our parting at Chiang Kai-shek International Airport would be our last meeting. I have never doubted your feelings for me. How I wish I could be your bride, wearing a wedding gown, walking the red carpet and spending the second half of my life with you… However, it is a mistake for you to love a woman like me.

I still insist on the words: a mother is unique while other women are plenty in this world.

Another reason for my suicide is that I contracted AIDS. This diagnosis was made in October. I'll go to God sooner or later with this fatal disease. I'd rather go sooner to avoid the coming ordeal. You had better go for a medical check. If you have contracted AIDS, it is my unpardonable sin. Once someone contracts AIDS, he suffers for the rest of his life.

If possible, please continue writing 'New Camille' after you get your Ph.D. I just want to warn people like me, beautiful, vain, simple-minded, but eager to do things well, to think before acting. If you like, you could donate part of the royalties to the Canadian AIDS Foundation. In the last few months, they have given me unimaginable courage for survival.

Well, Wenxiong, take good care of yourself. I'll go first and wait for you. If we can't be a couple on earth, let's keep each other company in hell.

Last words from Yuanyuan, forever loving you!
At 2:45 am, December 29th, 2000."

"Why, why? …" Lai yells nonstop, his face bathed in tears.

All of a sudden, Lai can no longer support himself and collapses. Luckily, the police are well-prepared and medical personnel rush to help him to the couch.

Chief Simon says calmly, "It's her posthumous letter, is it? Mr. Shi, could you please translate it?"

"Yes, it was the last letter of Miss Zhang." Detective Shi conveys a general summary of the letter to the police as quickly as possible.

Hearing the contents of the letter, Simon shakes his head with teary eyes while JoAnna turns her head and weeps…

98. Gangsters Caught by Fully Armed Policemen

Calming down in no time, Chief Simon asks Detective Shi, Lei to transcribe Zhang, Yuanyuan's posthumous letter immediately. Then, he discusses the details with Policewoman JoAnna.

That evening, Chief Simon goes to the interrogation room in person. When he sees the aggressive Allan, he becomes high-strung and furious.

Sitting down, Allan yells to Simon ferociously, "Set me free at once! I haven't committed any crime. Have you got any evidence? I'll hire a lawyer."

Forcefully suppressing his anger, Chief Simon asks again, "Allan, on the early morning of December 29th, where were you?"

"I told you before. I was in Toronto!" Standing up, Allan yells, as if he were interrogating Simon.

"Thwack!" Simon boxes Allan's ear with the back of his hand.

"You are still lying!" Simon adds in a loud voice.

Allan goes crazy while covering his face with his hand. "The police are beating people up. I'll sue you! I'll sue you!"

Two policemen, armed to the teeth, charge into the room and

grab his hands. He is forced to sit down, but continues to insist that he has been wrongly accused.

"Just sue me. I'd rather be disciplined: I won't let you go! Absolutely not!" So saying, Simon drops the English translation of Zhang, Yuanyuan's posthumous letter in front of Allan, with a copy of its original Chinese version.

With justice on his side, Simon asks him, "Look, what's this?"

Scanning the letter with his head lowered, Allan responds hesitantly, "I'm not the murderer! I'm not..."

Chief Simon finally calms down, "Hurry up and tell us who the other person is? Where is he?"

Scratching his head, Allan answers, "He's hard to find."

"No matter where he goes, we'll arrest him and bring him to justice, even if he has been burned to ashes. If he is not found, you'll bear the whole blame for him, okay?" Simon stares at him, his eyes as big as bulbs.

Allan has to behave properly and confess, "Ok, I'll confess. He is Paul and he should be at his home: the City of Hull in Quebec."

"Just opposite Ottawa?" asks Simon.

Allan nods. Chief Simon knows that Hull is just opposite Ottawa, separated from it by a river. The laws of Quebec and Ontario are entirely different, however, creating loopholes for criminals. Hull is also an important stronghold of "the Thunder Motorcyclists". Two months ago, they had a bloody fight with another gang. The death toll was more than ten people. Simon thinks, "Hull is not a small place. Where exactly can we find Paul?"

"Do you know his exact address?" asks Simon.

Shaking his head, Allan says, "I only remember that his parents manage a bar, probably named the 'Leon Bar'. The family lives upstairs. He stays with his parents when he goes home and stays with me when he comes to Toronto."

Before leaving, Simon asks him again, "How did you find Miss Zhang's whereabouts?"

This time Allan has to behave himself and does not dare tell a lie. Based on past experience, he figures that the police have ample evidence. It turns out that, based on some information, the gangsters were able to confirm that Miss Zhang lived in Niagara Region and engaged in the sex trade in the casino for a while. Allan sent his gang to look for her at the end of November last year. One of them found her in the casino, but she managed to escape. On Christmas day, Allan and his gang went to Casino Niagara for fun and happened to meet her in front of a Chinese restaurant when they went for dinner. They forced her to a hotel and gang-raped her...

Simon finds that what Allan said matches the information he has got. Pointing at Allan's head, he asks, "Where did you get the information that Miss Zhang was in Niagara? Speak the truth!"

"I heard it from Paul. You can ask him," answers Allan.

Returning to the office, Chief Simon calls the Police Bureau in Hull, asking them to provide information on the "Leon Bar" at once. Then he calls the Director, but nobody answers. The Director might have gone out, as it is Saturday. Simon doesn't like to bother him, but he fears that Paul might escape, so he calls the Director's emergency cell phone number.

The Director is just leaving a cinema when he gets the call. He says, "Pal, you're so capable of finding people. I just turned on my cell. I took the whole family to the movie 'Crouching Tiger, Hidden Dragon'. It was pretty good. It might get an Oscar. I suggest that everybody in the Bureau go see it...Let's get to business. What's so urgent?"

The Director becomes excited when he hears that they have got Zhang, Yuanyuan's posthumous letter, Allan has confessed about his cohort and the case is almost solved. He feels the same as when he was awarded the title, "Excellent policeman," years ago. He announces immediately that all members of "the Special investigation group" should report to the Police Bureau at 8 pm and enter the first class alert for war.

Before 8 pm, all nine members of the investigation group arrive at the meeting room of the Police Bureau. The Director arrived an hour ago and is now whispering to Chief Simon.

In simple words, Simon allocates tasks to everybody and the Director says, "Because the Thunder Motorcyclists are fierce, we have to be carefully prepared in combat readiness. Each of you notify your contacts separately and we'll meet here again in an hour."

Instantly, the whole bureau gets busy and all ten telephone-lines are in use simultaneously. According to their assignment, they contact the Ontario Police, the Quebec Police, the Hull Police Bureau, the Royal Canadian Mounted Police, etc. The Director summons Policewoman JoAnna alone to his office, asking her to console Zhang, Yuanyuan's family on behalf of the police and inform them of the police plan to arrest all suspects.

As Hull is 550 kilometers away from Niagara Region, they have to take a helicopter. But the patrol copter can hold only 5 persons, so they need a second. Chief Simon remembers his former classmate at the police school, who is now Deputy Bureau Director in Toronto. Over the phone, his classmate promises to provide him with a patrol copter for the second half of the night.

In an hour, the Hull Police Bureau faxes a detailed map of the "Leon Bar". Later, the Hull Police Director calls Chief Simon, advising him to take action at 3 am, after the bar is closed, to avoid unnecessary casualties. He has sent police in plain clothes to check out the situation. They found that the owner's son is Paul, who is helping at the bar. Two policemen have been sent to watch Paul.

At 1 am on the 21st, Chief Simon and 7 policemen, armed to the teeth, take two helicopters from Niagara Region. The Director drives with them in person to the airport and returns to the Police Bureau to await their news.

Very soon, the two helicopters arrive at the military airport of Hull, 550 kilometers away. A big bus from the Hull Police Bureau is already waiting at the airport. The Niagara police arrive at the bureau and before they finish their coffee, over ten RCMP members arrive as well. Over 30 fully armed people of the three parties form a team for coordinated action to discuss a scheme for solving the case. Finally, two plans are made to start the operation at 4 am. If the Thunder Motorcyclists do not get involved, they will follow the simple Plan One. Otherwise, Plan Two will be employed to meet and fight the gang head on.

When the clock hands point to 4, Simon and seven policemen, led by scores of Hull policemen, surround the "Leon Bar." Over ten RCMP wait in ambush a dozen meters away to provide reinforcement at any time.

When they ring the doorbell, nobody answers. A Hull policeman in plain clothes knocks on the door forcefully and shouts in French, "Boss, I want a drink. I want liquor. I'll pay double…"

After a while, some noise is eventually heard. An elderly man comes to open the door while complaining, "Who wants a drink? It's past time. I will be in trouble with the police if I sell liquor…"

No sooner has he opened the door a crack than several armed policemen charge into the bar and rush to the second floor.

"What's the matter? We haven't committed any crime… Are you genuine or fake police?"

Chief Simon shows the search warrant at once and says to the old man in not so fluent French, "Sorry to bother you at such a late hour. I suspect that your son is involved in a murder case."

So saying, Chief Simon charges upstairs. Paul, in his bathrobe, is yelling at one of the policemen outside the bedroom, "Why arrest me? I'm sleeping…"

"Just for this!" Simon shows him the warrant for arrest. "We are from Niagara Region. I don't need to say any more."

"I haven't done anything against the law." He pretends to be innocent.

Simon yells, "Do you know Allan?"

"That guy's a spineless coward!" Paul says to himself.

Simon shouts again, "Do you know Miss Zhang – Camille? Follow us, won't you?"

"I didn't kill her! It's the truth." Paul seems panicky.

Hearing some noise from inside the room, another policeman shouts, "Watch out! Somebody is inside."

Quick-witted, he kicks open the door and four policemen with rifles charge into the room. In bed, a naked woman is punching in numbers on her cell phone, apparently calling other gang members for help. Two policemen leap forward, snatch away her cell phone and restrain her in bed while she struggles to cover herself with the comforter. Several policemen enter the room and find a pistol under the pillow and two rifles in the built-in wardrobe.

At this time, cuffed Paul follows Simon docilely into the bedroom. Seeing the young woman, Simon recalls Lai, Wenxiong's description at once.

He blurts out while walking towards her, "You're Katyusha, a Russian, aren't you!"

"How did you know?" She raises her head in astonishment.

"We've been looking for you for a long time! Put on your clothes and let's go visit Niagara Falls!"

99. Daughter of Niagara Falls

"Yuanyuan, Yuanyuan, come back, come back at once…I want to marry you…" Lai, Wenxiong talks in his sleep and wakes up the three members of the Zhang family. Mrs. Zhang can't help bursting into tears.

It is 8 pm on January 20th. Lai is lying in bed at Zhang, Yuanyuan's residence in the Lakeshore Building. This is the bed in which he and Yuanyuan spent so many beautiful nights.

"Why am I here? Am I in a dream?" Opening his eyes, he asks Zhang, Mingming beside him.

It turns out that Lai fainted at the Police Bureau that day and the police sent for the Zhang family. When they heard about the posthumous letter, Mrs. Zhang fell into a swoon at once. The doctor gave her an injection of sedative immediately. He told them that Lai needed rest badly because he had not slept well and had suffered a heavy mental blow. He'd be okay after a good, sound sleep. That's why Mr. Zhang asked the police to bring Lai to Zhang's residence to sleep…

Lai is sobbing while listening to Mingming, "Oh, why was Yuanyuan so silly? Why? I would never have blamed her if she had just waited for me to return. It's my fault, my…"

Old Zhang pats the comforter and says meaningfully, "Mr. Lai, don't blame yourself. Your love for each other was genuine."

Mrs. Zhang recalls with tears in her eyes, "My child was born sentimental. I didn't expect her to be so fragile in her heart."

Lai sits up in bed, "She was strong enough to bear a lot of pressure. It was Allan and his gang who were so brutal and cold-blooded! I could kill them!"

Mr. Zhang lights a cigarette, "This news adds another disaster to our misfortune. At least, we have got the truth before we leave. Once gone, no matter what happens, she won't come back."

Lai speaks, tears rolling down his face, "Her death has made me feel very guilty and has filled me with regret. If I had come back sooner, this would not have happened. But my mother was undergoing an operation …"

Mrs. Zhang stops sobbing, "Mr. Lai, that's fate. You and Yuanyuan were predestined for one another, but you didn't have the luck to be together. It was due to her unhappy fate. I wonder if our ancestors did something wrong and Yuanyuan had to bear all the blame."

Old Zhang continues with the subject, "Why was this child always headed towards a dead end? After the failure of her first love, she attempted to jump into the Huangpu River. After being cheated by her high school classmate in Toronto, she thought of jumping over the bridge. Finally, she jumped into Niagara Falls…"

"Uncle, she was the daughter of Niagara Falls as well as the daughter of nature. Her psychological character was pretty strong. You see, Niagara Falls is so high and awesome that people are terrified to watch it, let alone jump into it. In addition to suffering from AIDS, Yuanyuan was in total despair. I could only trust fate. If she could wait for me to return, we might be in Vancouver now and nothing like this would have happened," Lai says helplessly.

Old Zhang comments gently, "I have thought about this again and again: in my family or my wife's family, no one other than Yuanyuan has committed suicide. I can't find any hereditary gene."

"She suffered a lot while struggling overseas for so many years. I've told you about a small part of her life. When Jia, Feng finishes his novel, you'll see that she was under great pressure during her short life…" Lai replies candidly.

Just then, the doorbell rings: it is Policewoman JoAnna. Lai gets up from bed to greet her in the living room.

Walking towards him, JoAnna asks with concern, "Mr. Lai, are you feeling better? On behalf of the Director and Chief Simon, I've come to visit you."

Nodding, Lai thanks her for the police concern. He never expected that the police would be this humane and caring.

JoAnna says, her head lowered, "To tell you the truth, I almost fainted this afternoon. Working on this case, I have become imperceptibly attached to Camille. I really didn't expect such an ending… Anyway, she was an outstanding woman."

Mr. Zhang tries to change the subject, "JoAnna, we are sorry that you haven't had a good rest. We are grateful for the work of everybody in the investigation group."

JoAnna declares with a smile, "I've brought you good news. The police are keeping a close watch on Allan's cohort, the man who contributed to Yuanyuan's ruin as well. He will be caught in a day or two."

Zhang, Mingming cuts in, "Will they be charged if my sister committed suicide?"

"Of course they will, in varying degrees. If they hadn't forced your sister, would she have ended up in a blind alley? They will hire lawyers for their defense, of course," JoAnna replies.

After she leaves, Lai wants to take leave as well, but the Zhang family invites him to stay for fear of an accident while driving. The funeral is on the 22nd. He had better stay there and sleep on the floor.

Before going to bed, Mrs. Zhang suddenly asks Lai, "Did Yuanyuan ever have a dog? When I was sorting through her things, I found two beautiful suits of dogs' clothing, seemingly worn before."

Lai replies slowly, "Yes, she once cried about this. Shortly after we got acquainted at Niagara Falls, she had a gray dog, Huanhuan. Yuanyuan spoiled it as she would her own child. Once, Huanhuan damaged her lovely dress and she hit it in anger. Huanhuan disappeared the next day! We looked for it high and low, but couldn't find it. She grieved the loss for quite a long time. She would be sad whenever its name was mentioned. She never got another pet."

Mrs. Zhang suggests, "These two suits can be buried with her in the grave."

Nodding, Lai thinks that women are always considerate. A mother understands her daughter best.

"She had a cat, also named Huanhuan, when she was young. I persuaded her not to keep it, because I didn't like the mess," Mrs. Zhang murmurs to herself.

At 3 pm the next day, the Niagara Police Bureau holds a press conference. Jia, Feng and Wu, Xiaoxian come from Toronto. Actually, they had heard about it the previous night from Detective Shi, Lei. Chief Simon presides over the press conference. He doesn't seem too tired, although he was in Hull catching the gangster all the previous night. He feels relaxed, perhaps because the case has finally been solved.

He has no alternative but to declare that Zhang, Yuanyuan killed herself. Several hours before her suicide, however, two gangsters violated her. Now these men have been arrested. The police unexpectedly caught the Russian woman Katyusha, who had abetted Zhang, Yuanyuan in drug trafficking. Finally, he stresses that the police had never ruled out suicide during the course of their investigation.

After the press conference, Jia and Wu go to visit the Zhang family and Lai, Wenxiong. Having exchanged greetings, Lai drags Jia to an inner room for a quiet conversation.

"Have you read Yuanyuan's posthumous letter? I've made a copy, especially for you." Lai says, with a touch of mystery.

"Marvelous! Detective Shi, Lei told me about it over the phone, but I haven't read the written version. Thank you so much!" Jia is elated.

"After much thought, I've decided to hold a closed-door wedding before the funeral tomorrow to fulfill Yuanyuan's unrealized wish." Lai says, grasping Jia's hand.

Jia replies frankly, "I dreamed of you two walking on the red carpet last night!"

Lai holds his hands closely for a long time.

"What time would you like me to help you tomorrow?"

"At 12 noon. Please come with Miss Wu and the photographer."

100. A Wedding before the Funeral

On the morning of January 22nd, 2001, the blue sky is crystal clear, without any blemishes and the golden sun shines over the vast land, warming up everything on earth. With such rare nice weather in winter, people might think that the Maiden of Spring has arrived were it not for the bare trees and the glistening snow accumulation.

Torrential Niagara Falls, majestic under the sunshine, attracts more tourists to and fro. In Suite 414 of the Lakeshore Building, though, a somber atmosphere reigns, because in a few hours the white-haired will bury the black-haired. No one in the Zhang family speaks and Lai, Wenxiong, sitting in a daze on the sofa in the living room, utters not a sound. No one wants the sad moment to come a second sooner.

At 10 am, somebody delivers 99 red roses, a pack of CD's and some colored paper. When the Zhang family appears puzzled, Lai admits that he ordered them over the phone. The Zhang family is even more perplexed: why are roses being delivered for the funeral? What on earth is this man from Taiwan doing?

With curiosity, Zhang, Mingming asks Lai, "Is this for the funeral today?"

"Uncle, Aunt, and Brother, I am sorry that I made this decision on my own. At noon, we'll hold a closed-door wedding. I would like to fulfill Yuanyuan's unrealized wish and let her be my bride!" So saying, Lai kneels down to make the request.

"Mr. Lai, please stand up! We'll consent to any of your wishes..." Mrs. Zhang comes to help him up.

Old Zhang speaks with emotion, "Nowadays, few men are this infatuated. Yuanyuan was very lucky!"

With the Zhang family's immediate consent, everybody starts to decorate the place. An hour later, the solemn mourning hall has been turned into a joyous wedding hall. Golden paper replaces the black frame on the portrait of the deceased. On the wall is a piece of huge red paper with the words "Marriage between Lai and Zhang" in Wei style, written surely by Old Zhang. 99 red roses are stacked in front of the portrait, creating the atmosphere of a lady smiling among flowers.

At noon, the "wedding" begins. Besides the four of them, "Toronto Weekly" correspondents Jia, Feng, Wu, Xiaoxian and Photographer Li, Zhihao also attend. Li is responsible for taking photos.

Lai, Wenxiong, standing beside Zhang, Yuanyuan's portrait, speaks distinctly, "You are all witnesses to my marriage to Miss Zhang, Yuanyuan today. My special thanks to you three for coming from Toronto."

At this moment, the pleasing song, "Melody of absolute love," comes from the CD player: "Absolute love surpasses human thinking.

Faithful followers, kneel before God in praise. May God bless this couple, who'll love each other forever…"

Jia, Feng walks forward with the Bible in his hands: "My Lord, please allow me to preside over this special wedding, which is woven with great love and no dust or prejudice. Just as you have taught us: we should love one another, because love comes from God. Those with loving hearts are born of God and know God…"

After a long prayer and words of encouragement, Jia asks in all seriousness, "Mr. Lai, Wenxiong, do you consent to marry Miss Zhang, Yuanyuan?"

Lai replies respectfully, "Yes, I do. I'll never regret it. Yuanyuan, I've done this not only to fulfill your wish. I swear to you that I'll never marry any other woman. You are the only woman I will ever love."

Everybody's eyes are moist with tears when they hear this. Nobody expected that Lai, Wenxiong would make such an important choice in life. This is not only a declaration of love, but also a pledge. For genuine lovers, love can take any form; love is freedom; love is engraved on one's bones and heart; and love surpasses everything else.

With tears in her eyes, Mrs. Zhang blurts out, "On behalf of Yuanyuan, I heartily accept Mr. Lai, Wenxiong's love. My daughter, it's your honor to have such a nice husband, and we are so proud of you…"

Old Zhang smiles, his eyes wide open, "We are proud of such a kind son-in-law!"

Lai goes forward and nods, holding Mr. And Mrs. Zhang's hands, "Father-in-law and Mother-in-law, thank you very much!"

Zhang, Mingming, patting Lai on the shoulder, speaks tenderly, "Brother Wenxiong, there is no need to thank us as we are one family."

Jia, Feng speaks quietly, "Miss Zhang can rest in peace in Heaven."

Others nod in tacit agreement with Jia. Lai walks towards Jia, and looks at him for a while before they embrace each other impulsively. This is a unique wedding, an unprecedented ceremony. It is not a fairy tale or a legend, but a reality in life.

As pre-arranged, at 2 pm, the hearse carrying Zhang, Yuanyuan's casket heads out from the postmortem center and drives to the Lakeshore Building, moving slowly along the lakeshore, so that Yuanyuan can visit Niagara Falls again and listen to its sound.

In black overcoats, the three members of the Zhang family sit in Lai, Wenxiong's Volvo, following closely and slowly the black hearse along the Niagara River. Strangely, the warm sun at noon seems to have hidden itself to shed tears. The joyous "wedding" has somewhat reduced people's grief. Still, at present everybody has a heavy heart, like the low-lying dark clouds.

Viewing the torrential falls outside the car window, Lai, Wenxiong reminisces about the times when the two of them enjoyed the beautiful scenery of the falls together. Regretfully, Yuanyuan is now gone and everything turns into past memory. The only consolation is that she eventually came back into the embrace of the falls. The Zhang family has no heart to view the falls. They just fix their eyes on the hearse ahead, in the vain hope that Yuanyuan, revived, might get out of the hearse and enjoy the sight of the falls once more... Mrs. Zhang cries constantly, dries her eyes and cries again, her sobs mingling with the roaring of the falls to form a melancholy soul-calming melody for the beautiful woman.

Just when the hearse is heading for the graveyard, the weather suddenly changes drastically. Instantly, black clouds cover the sun, and the north wind whistles. With the gray sky and the sulky ground, heavy snow seems imminent and it almost feels as if the end of the world is approaching...

"Evergreen Cemetery", one kilometer away from Niagara Falls, looks desolate and gloomy. The tombstones of different sizes and heights, standing on the vast ice and snow, look particularly chilly and deserted.

The only exception is a grave on the left side, surrounded by over thirty people, both Chinese and western, in black overcoats.

Among them is Chief Simon in a black leather coat. Policewoman JoAnna stands beside him. A tall and thin western priest, standing before the grave, presides over the burial. Around the grave are stacked white camellias. On the granite tombstone is a small photo of Zhang, Yuanyuan. Besides her English name and dates of birth and death, there are also several big Chinese characters: "Rest in peace, Yuanyuan, my beloved wife--   Wenxiong"

Apart from the three members of the Zhang family, Lai, Wenxiong, Jia, Feng, Wu, Xiaoxian and Li, Zhihao from "Toronto Weekly", the rest of the mourners are all westerners. They include her ex-boyfriend David, ex-councilor Arvid, Old Bailey, the security guard at the Lakeshore Building, lawyers, doctors and all kinds of businessmen. Lian, Haotien, the wolf, intended to come, but was rebuffed by Lai, Wenxiong. Lai stands close to the Zhang family and Li is busy taking pictures.

After the priest, Bible in hand, says a few words, several tall men carry the casket to the grave and are ready to spread the soil when Lai, Wenxiong suddenly jumps into the grave. He seizes the casket lid like a mad man and shouts, "Yuanyuan, you can't go, you can't, Yuanyuan…"

Two heavily-built men charge forward to help him up, but he is still yelling nonstop, "Yuanyuan, don't leave me behind! Don't go…"

He shouts himself hoarse as if attempting to wake up the dead. He doesn't stop yelling until two people hold his arms so he can't move. Then, he calms down. All the onlookers sigh and shake their heads. Some of them burst into tears.

Chief Simon walks towards Wenxiong and pats him on the shoulder, "Mr. Lai, don't be so grieved. Take care of yourself."

Seeing that her "son-in-law" is so faithful and sincere, Mrs. Zhang can't stop crying loudly, adding to the sorrow. Many people can't refrain from crying.

The priest, glancing at Lai, speaks distinctly, "Miss Zhang was fortunate and will wait for you in Heaven with your deep love. Please restrain your grief, Mr. Lai."

Following his words, people spread the soil with shovels. Soon the grave is filled. Then, all the people at the grave bow to the tombstone to pay their respects. The north wind whistles and heavy snow falls as if Heaven itself is complaining about the unfairness of such a young death. Calling her daughter's name, Mrs. Zhang cries her heart out. Zhang, Mingming, supporting his mother, can't keep from crying. Old Zhang, with gritted teeth, forces himself not to cry. Lai, Wenxiong murmurs while crying, as if talking to Zhang, Yuanyuan alone. Sad David holds Lai's hand closely after paying his respects and shakes hands with Old Zhang before leaving.

Ex-councilor Arvid holds Old Zhang's hand tightly for a long time before speaking hesitantly, "Your daughter was outstanding…"

The mourners leave gradually, so the graveyard becomes deserted. Jia, Feng comes to hold Lai's hand, and Old Zhang holds their hands, while Chief Simon comes forward to wrap their hands in his own. The four men's eight big hands are holding closely together – the untold meaning of this moment is doubtlessly caught in Li, Zhihao's lens.

Before they leave the cemetery, it is snowing heavily and the vast land is all white. Lai walks between two old people, with one hand holding Old Zhang's arm and the other holding Mrs. Zhang's. Zhang, Mingming, Jia, Feng and Wu, Xiaoxian follow them closely.

Staring at the tombstone, Lai says to himself, "Yuanyuan, I'll move to Niagara next week to be near you."

"Wenxiong, it's really very kind of you to do so," says Old Zhang.

Mrs. Zhang talks to Lai in a low voice, "Take care of yourself. You have to finish your graduation thesis."

A few meters away in the parking lot at the gate, Lai suddenly catches sight of a dog, running quickly from afar, leaving a string of footprints in the snow.

"Dad, Mom, this is Huanhuan! Really. I know it. The gray dog." Lai can't help shouting while pointing to the leaping dog.

With the snow falling more heavily, the gray dog runs along a circle in front of them and then slips away. Subconsciously, they turn their heads back, only to find that the gray dog runs directly to Zhang, Yuanyuan's grave and stays there. From the chilly and desolate land come Huanhuan's nonstop howls…

On the Creation of *Tears for Camellia*

Bo Sun

I was pondering how to write my next novel after my first novel "Men at 30" was published as a trial balloon in the literary circle: How could I portray human nature most vividly and incisively? How could I achieve a breakthrough among the myriads of immigration novels? ... Around that time, a number of tragedies occurred among the immigrants around me, some of which I found in the newspapers or on TV while others I just overheard. As a writer with a strong sense of responsibility, who wants to face the reality head-on, I have lost interest in playing with the pain of the new immigrants. After cool deliberation, I planned to touch the seamy side of the immigrant's life. I wanted to depict women instead of men, especially those who live on the fringes of society. I intended to explore the physiological, psychological, cultural and social factors that land "alternative women" in a blind alley. I hope that this will encourage the readers to think about human nature, to show concern for women and to reflect on the trend of immigration.

When I touched on the sensitive topic of prostitution, I naturally thought of "Camille" by Dumas (Jr.), so I re-read the classic novel. Finally, I decided to stand on the great man's shoulders, so to speak, to describe, with reference to the original theme of "Camille", how

Zhang, Yuanyuan, a self-styled Camille, turns from a pure and naïve girl into a prostitute. Like the great master, I deeply sympathize with prostitutes and harbor a bitter hatred for the society that causes such abnormal phenomena.

As a news editor of a Chinese Daily for a long time, I have obtained indirectly a great deal of valuable material. As a special correspondent for a large weekly, I have interviewed people from various walks of life and this has greatly helped my literary writing. To make the description of details more true to life in "Tears for Camellia", I paid streetwalkers to get first-hand material by just talking with them. I also visited massage parlors to contact "alternative women". I had several conversations with strippers to dig deep into their psyche. It is safe to say that Zhang, Yuanyuan, the protagonist, is the composite of five or six unfortunate girls. Zhang, Yuanyuan at almost every stage can be traced back to her prototype. That is why Zhang, Yuanyuan is representative of "alternative women".

To make the novel more tantalizing while conceiving its plot, I experimented with the skills of integrating detective inference and exotic love in a foreign land, instead of a pure love story. Paying more attention to the story line, I started with the discovery of an anonymous female body on the Niagara River by tourists. The police try to solve the case with several possibilities in mind, such as murder for money, murder to silence somebody, manslaughter or murder for love. The lead character's misery is revealed naturally by several suspects. Only at the end of the novel is the mystery of her death disclosed. Obviously, I employed the artistic skills of western mystery and detective novels in its structure. The miserable life of the "new Camille" and the cracking of the case comprise two parallel yet intertwining plots. The result is that it is not just a popular detective novel while the old theme of prostitution is extended into the new century. The gist of the novel, however, lies not in the building of suspense or the investigation of the case, but rather in the discovery and analysis of Zhang, Yuanyuan's spiritual journey and the psychological track that lead her to her ruin. The trend of immigration has not abated yet and "Tears for Camellia", like a mirror of the era, reflects the dirt and soil in the great waves, and the streaks of blood and tears behind the sunshine of immigration.

Translator's Note: "Alternative women" is a euphemistic term for disreputable women.

Reflections on Spirit and Flesh

—A Review on Tears for Camellia

Tianguo Hong

(Literary Critic, Ex-president of Chinese PEN Society of Canada)

A woman goes overseas, engages in prostitution, contracts the fatal disease of the century and dies at Niagara Falls: this can be regarded as the most miserable and brutal story in the trend to immigration. Zhang, Yuanyuan, a girl from Shanghai, takes this road. Sun, Bo, a young writer from Canada, unfolds the treacherous road Yuanyuan follows with a literary touch, showing the character's frustration, with a mixture of tears and blood.

Reflection on immigration literature usually takes the form of reflecting spirit using a spiritual approach. "Tears for Camellia – A Social Butterfly's Spiritual Journey Overseas", on the other hand, reflects spirit with flesh. To be more exact, it reflects the human soul of a woman selling her body. This reflection gives the reader a more thorough, transparent and incisive insight, but it is a very complicated insight, mixed with love, hatred, deep regret, pity, and all five flavors (sweet, sour, bitter, pungent and salty).

In Sun, Bo's mixed feelings towards Zhang, Yuanyuan, his sympathy for her takes the lead. The author sympathizes with the fragile girl who struggles helplessly in a complex and evil society. In this sense, the first reflection on "Tears for Camellia" is on the social level. It is not Yuanyuan's own nature but rather the social environment, which forces her to engage in prostitution. There are stages in her decline. First, the university lecturer Chen, Zhiwei, her first love, cheats her emotionally. Second, Japanese boss Aokawa Kakuai violates her. Then, her high school classmate Huang, Hong swindles her out of her money. Later, Allan, the bartender, forces her into prostitution. The Thunder Motorcyclists and the Black Bats blackmail and entice her. All this is backed up by a protective social shield. It is the hidden evil and swindling in a prosperous western society that basically causes thousands of less competitive people to embark on a tragic path. The novel, "Tears for Camellia," reminds all immigrants that they face an advanced society, which holds a lot of potential but is also filled with evil and deception. Only through disciplined mental preparation can people discover room for survival in immigration.

The second reflection on "Tears for Camellia" is on the cultural level. Zhang, Yuanyuan struggles before she goes astray. These are cultural struggles. Zhang knows that prostitution is contrary to her moral upbringing and is a betrayal to a woman's dignity. Still, she fails to resist social intimidation and financial enticement. Finally, she yields to the concept that "my body and youth are my capital". In the struggle between two entirely different cultural concepts, this novel explores the fundamental reason for Zhang, Yuanyuan's failure in that struggle. As a beautiful girl, she doesn't study hard and has no special skills, but she admires luxury and affluence. Thus, she becomes a slave to her financial goals.

Can a prostitute reform herself? The clash of the cultural concepts occurs between the Taiwan student, Lai, Wenxiong, and his parents. The emotionally touching love between Lai and Zhang is a little bit of sunshine in this otherwise bleak novel. Unfortunately, that sunshine is devoured by the traditional Chinese cultural concept that "prostitutes can't be wives". Lai could have been a savior for Zhang, but the savior's sparkle dies out too soon.

The third reflection is on the level of human nature. Chen,

Zhiwei, a peasant's son, tries to take revenge on urban women. Japanese businessman Aokawa Kakuai shamelessly dallies with women using money as bait. Aware that Zhang is enticed by money, Huang, Hong cheats her again and again. Allan, the bartender, seeks money and sex brutally. These examples demonstrate the darkest side of human nature. "Tears for Camellia" exposes the evil in human nature in clear-cut fashion. This evil forms a contrast to the sympathy for the unfortunate Zhang, Yuanyuan and an admiration for the true love that Lai and Zhang experience. Sun, Bo is a young writer full of emotions who understands what to love and what to hate. In his reflections on human nature, he reveals his own human nature.

(Originally published in *Xinmin Evening News*, Oct 14th, 2001)

Tears for Camellia as a Warning to the World

Da Lu

(Senior news correspondent)

Recently Bo Sun, a young writer residing in Canada, published a novel entitled "Tears for Camellia – A Social Butterfly's Spiritual Journey Overseas". This work depicts a tragic female character up against social reality and serves as a warning to the world. Zhang, Yuanyuan, born into a senior intellectual's family, worked as a hospital nurse, and goes to Japan, following the trend of studying abroad in the 1990s. First, she becomes the mistress of a restaurant boss and then she goes to Toronto, Canada, by means of a fake marriage. After her failure in business because of a fraud, she is reduced to stripping and prostitution. Although she enjoys genuine love in between, the relationship is crushed by the chilly reality. Finally, she ends her young life at Niagara Falls.

I believe that many of the new immigrants or students who live or work overseas, especially in the Chinese communities in Japan and North America, might have met and are familiar with such a tragic character as Zhang, Yuanyuan. There are certainly stories of students succeeding in their struggle for survival, but more of them have undergone torment and suffering. Of course, few are like Zhang, Yuanyuan who endures extreme tragedy.

It is human nature to seek personal development by going to

economically developed countries and regions. In the coastal areas of China, there is a long tradition of people going abroad to survive by legal or semi-legal ways. From the end of the 1980s to the beginning of 1990s, the trend of going abroad reached a peak, progressing from young people studying abroad with relatives' help to almost everyone trying to go abroad. I remember hearing people asking such questions in Shanghai: "When are you leaving?" or "You haven't left, have you?" There seemed to be an irresistible trend. North America, Europe, Japan and Australia became first choices at different stages. Even tiny countries in the Mediterranean were visited. It is under such circumstances that Zhang, Yuanyuan follows the trend and goes to Japan for spite after her failure in her first love. Thus begins her wandering life in foreign lands.

In previous literary works of a similar genre, women became prostitutes because of family poverty or lack of education. Sun, Bo, on the other hand, explores a different type of woman. His character Zhang, Yuanyuan is a new urban woman from a well-to-do family; has received a good education and boasts a pretty nice temperament. Eventually, though, she collapses on the road to survival overseas. It is evident that the author has a fairly unique view in exposing the general weakness in human nature and in describing the female protagonist's hopelessness and helplessness in her struggle to survive in foreign countries.

The tragedy of Zhang, Yuanyuan reminds us of Chen, Bailu in Cao, Yu's play. Although Chen, Bailu is a social butterfly, she aims to get rid of the feudalistic shackles and to seek women's liberation. It goes without saying that the play was progressive in that society. Chen suffers setbacks in seeking personal liberation and is reduced to prostitution for survival. It is society that forces her into that situation. People mostly sympathize with and understand her. Her yearning for a bright future leaves a profound impression on the reader.

Zhang, Yuanyuan, however, is different. She lives in the modern society, where liberated women prop up half the sky and enjoy certain rights. Before and after she goes abroad, Zhang has many chances to make choices. She loses these opportunities because of her vanity, her arrogance and her pitiable self-respect. She has no face to return to her homeland as she is. Eventually she heads to the abyss with no redemption. Based on this view, Zhang, Yuanyuan lags far behind Chen, Bailu. Zhang retrogresses scores of years from the road of liberation and gives up the ideals, which were sought diligently by intellectual women in Chen's age.

Zhang retreats willingly to the status of women who are subordinate and dependent on men. After reading the book, people will undoubtedly feel sorry for Zhang, Yuanyuan's choices.

(Originally published in *Xinmin Evening News*, May 13th, 2001)

Author's Appreciation
Bo Sun

It took Ms Baimei Sun, a translator I respect, about a year to finish translating my novel—*Tears for Camellia*—into English. Ms Elizabeth Warrener (a retired librarian from the Toronto Public Library with a BA degree in French and Italian literature and a Masters degree in library science) kindly read the entire English version and made revisions section by section. The manuscript was polished several times before it was finalized.

Out of their mutual love for literature, they have exerted themselves in spreading Chinese literature to the world. I am greatly touched by their meticulous work, especially their revising job during the heat waves. Not all Chinese writers are as lucky as I am. I will always remember their wholehearted help and therefore express my sincere appreciation!

Bo Sun
July 15, 2017

www.ingramcontent.com/pod-product-compliance
Lightning Source LLC
Chambersburg PA
CBHW021957050726
47498CB00001BB/192